MICHELLE GAGNON

KIDNAP & RANSOM

MIRA®

If you purchased this book without a cover you should be aware
that this book is stolen property. It was reported as "unsold and
destroyed" to the publisher, and neither the author nor the
publisher has received any payment for this "stripped book."

Recycling programs
for this product may
not exist in your area.

ISBN-13: 978-0-7783-2826-1

KIDNAP & RANSOM

Copyright © 2010 by Michelle Fritz-Cope

All rights reserved. Except for use in any review, the reproduction or
utilization of this work in whole or in part in any form by any electronic,
mechanical or other means, now known or hereafter invented, including
xerography, photocopying and recording, or in any information storage or
retrieval system, is forbidden without the written permission of the publisher,
MIRA Books, 225 Duncan Mill Road, Don Mills, Ontario M3B 3K9, Canada.

This is a work of fiction. Names, characters, places and incidents are
either the product of the author's imagination or are used fictitiously, and
any resemblance to actual persons, living or dead, business establishments,
events or locales is entirely coincidental.

MIRA and the Star Colophon are trademarks used under license and registered
in Australia, New Zealand, Philippines, United States Patent and Trademark
Office and in other countries.

www.MIRABooks.com

Printed in U.S.A.

For Taegan

DECEMBER 15

One

Cesar Calderon stepped outside to light a cigarette. It was a gorgeous night, unseasonably warm for December, even in Mexico. He took a deep drag and tilted his head back, aiming the smoke toward a waning moon.

"Quieres?" he asked, turning to his bodyguard. Moreno had stationed himself a few feet back, just outside the restaurant door. For this trip Cesar had selected one of his less imposing employees, determined to maintain a low profile despite the circumstances.

"No, gracias," Moreno said.

Calderon nodded, then inhaled. Thalia would be apoplectic if she knew he'd taken up smoking again—even if it was only socially, on business trips like this one. Before returning home he'd have to make sure his clothes were laundered or he'd catch hell for it. Out of habit, he kept a close monitor on the surrounding area. The dinner was being held around the corner from their hotel in the Zona Rosa. It was one of the most exclusive sections of Mexico City, although in his opinion these past few years it had slid into tackiness, upscale antique stores ceding to kitschy tourist traps. Shame that they had booked the St. Regis instead of the Four Seasons.

A couple strolled arm in arm, the woman tilting her head back to release a giggle as her companion guided her into a bar down the street. A few storefronts away, a pair of feet jutted out of a doorway. Cesar's eyes narrowed at the sight of them. He turned back to Moreno and raised an eyebrow. Taking the cue, Moreno went to investigate. Grumbles from the doorway, a tirade delivered with the slurred speech of an addict.

"It's nothing, sir," Moreno said in a low voice before falling back into position.

Heroin, Calderon thought, shaking his head. It used to be that the drug only passed through Mexico, but in recent years addiction levels had spiked. The latest law decriminalizing small amounts of heroin and cocaine hadn't helped matters, in his opinion. An already poor country was now being ravaged by the same disease as its wealthier neighbor to the north. A decade ago, the sight of a stoned man collapsed in a Mexico City doorway would have been an oddity. Today it was rapidly becoming the norm.

Back inside the restaurant, someone laughed loudly— probably Leonard. Bastard always got drunk and inappropriate at these conferences. The other night he'd actually asked Cesar to share a hooker; he shuddered at the memory. The sad truth was that his field attracted people from a wide range of backgrounds, some shadier than others. After recent events, Calderon had decided this was the last time he'd appear as the public face of the company. These business trips were draining, dangerous and put too much of a strain on his already fragile marriage. From here on out he'd leave the heavy lifting to Linus.

Calderon turned at the sound of screeching tires. A white van careened toward him. He frowned and automatically panned right, to the opposite end of the street…where he discovered a garbage truck blocking the intersection. Calderon's eyes widened as he realized what was about to happen. He spun on his heels, braced to dash into the restaurant. Saw Moreno's head tilted back at an odd angle, hands clutching his throat as blood jetted from between his fingers. The addict stood behind him, brandishing a knife.

Clearly no escape that way. Calderon tossed his cigarette, scattering a trail of embers as he swiveled and bolted across the street, hoping the sudden move would throw them off.

Too late. Hands gripped him from behind, dragging him toward the van's open door. His calves smacked the metal frame as they pulled him inside. The last thing he saw was the shocked expression on the maître d's face, frozen behind the host stand. Then a hood was yanked over his head, the van door slammed shut and a voice barked in Spanish, "Wall one, wall one, we have him! Wall two, move in behind us."

Calderon let out a yelp at the sudden, sharp pain in his thigh. *Mierda,* he thought, *they're drugging me…*

Then everything went black.

JANUARY 25

Two

Riley adjusted his grip on the MP-5. It was almost dawn. Aside from the sound of an occasional car, the streets below were silent. Almost eerily so, considering Mexico City had more than eight million residents. Riley looked down the line of men in the hall. Four of them pressed against the wall in tight formation, wearing urban camouflage and night-vision goggles. Outside he had Decker manning the wheel of their getaway van, and a sniper and observer in the building opposite. Eight total: more than enough to overwhelm the team holding Cesar Calderon. Still, despite the weeks of planning to set this operation in motion, it was hard for Riley to shake the sense that something was off.

Just nerves, Riley told himself. He had good intel that they were only dealing with three kidnappers. Monroe and Kaplan, his sniper/observer team, would create a distraction, taking out at least one of the bad guys at the window. The rest of his unit would swarm the apartment using a five-man cross-button entry strategy, eliminating the other two kidnappers and egressing with their hostage. All told, the operation should be over in less than five minutes. An airfield ten miles away had a plane waiting, and they'd be stateside by noon. Easy, just like Smiley had promised.

Riley's earpiece buzzed. "Target confirmed. Are we green?" Kaplan asked in a low voice.

"Confirm green, we are in position," Riley replied.

"Roger that. Sighting in."

Riley glanced at his watch. Despite the early hour, he worried that one of the other apartment doors might open, ruining the element of surprise. They were in a run-down tenement building in Iztapalapa, one of the worst slums in Mexico City, which was saying something. The walls were riddled with holes, they'd sent rats scurrying in the stairwell as they ascended, and the whole place stank of piss and rotten meat. All things considered, there were sections of Baghdad he'd feel safer in.

Plus, the kidnappers they were about to engage were no ordinary hacks. Los Zetas was an elite paramilitary organization, former Mexican army soldiers who defected to work for a drug cartel. The men he was about to confront had been through the same training as his unit. They had attended the Western Hemisphere Institute for Security Cooperation in Fort Benning, Georgia, learning firsthand from the best in the business the very techniques he was about to employ. All of which made this one of the most dangerous rescue attempts he'd ever participated in. And, officially at least, it was the first he was solely in charge of.

The hostage was something of a unique case, too. Cesar Calderon was the CEO of the Tyr Group, the world's premier Kidnap and Ransom organization. Calderon had personally negotiated the release of hundreds of people over the course of his career. Then, five weeks ago, he'd been snatched from a security symposium where he was the keynote speaker. He walked out of a restaurant, disappeared into the back of a white van and hadn't been heard from since. The rescuer became the victim—ironic, Riley thought. He'd never met Calderon personally, but in addition to being his boss, the man was a legend in K&R circles.

From inside the apartment, *Narcocorridos* music blared at top volume. Riley guessed that the neighbors were either Zetas sympathizers or too frightened to complain. The music provided good cover for the kidnappers, and had the additional benefit of disorienting and demoralizing their hostage. On the plus side for Riley, it meant his team didn't have to worry about a stealthy approach. Hell, they could be escorted by a ten-piece band and still not be heard over the racket emanating from the apartment. Amazing that anyone could sleep through that, but after a while they probably tuned it out.

His earpiece buzzed: "Request permission to engage," Kaplan asked. The spotter was probably itching to get this over with. He and Monroe, the sniper, had to keep their focus on the apartment from across the street, without any backup, putting them in the most vulnerable position. Especially in this barrio, where each building was more dangerous than the next.

"Permission granted. Fire, fire." Riley turned and gave the rest of his team the Go signal. Two of them moved forward to flank the door, a compact battering ram between them. He'd act as point man—first through the door and ready to take out whatever lay on the other side. The clearing man would follow, covering his back. The rest of the team would split up to sweep each room, securing the hostage and eliminating any hostiles with extreme prejudice.

Over the din inside the apartment, he heard the distinct sound of shattering glass. Monroe must have shot out the window, hopefully eliminating one of the hostiles at the same time. Riley nodded. The ram swung back, and the door burst inward with a splintering of wood.

"What the fuck was that?" asked Monroe.

Kaplan refocused the Elcan scope on his M-16 rifle, most spotters' weapon of choice because it provided the best night vision. He was spotting for Monroe, arguably one of the world's best snipers. Monroe had come up through the ranks of the Army's elite Olympic sharpshooting team, racking up medals until he got tired of firing at bull's-eyes and joined the private sector. The two of them were ensconced in an apartment across the street from their target. They'd built their nest a few feet back in the room so the gun muzzle wouldn't be spotted, and covered most of the window with strips of burlap. The figure they'd zeroed in on had vanished, the window he'd been standing in front of now completely shattered.

"You got him."

"Bullshit, I didn't get anyone," Monroe said. "I haven't fired yet."

"What?"

"I was about to, when the window blew."

"So what the—"

The door behind them suddenly exploded. Kaplan's hands jerked instinctively to cover his head, before he regained himself and swung the M-16 around.

A sharp pain in his shoulder, followed by one in his chest. Something wet smacked into his face, and he jerked sideways away from it. Men swarmed the room, faces covered by masks attached to black helmets, giving them a wasplike appearance. They all carried machine guns. Kaplan slowly raised his hands in the air, gasping slightly from the pain in his chest where the second bullet had hit.

It didn't seem to have penetrated his vest, but a stream of blood flowed from his shoulder.

They rolled Kaplan onto his back. He winced: Monroe hadn't been as lucky. There was a big hole where the back of his head used to be. Kaplan recognized the damage: hollow point bullets. And they were brandishing military-issue LMT modular weapons—almost impossible for civilians to get their hands on, even in Mexico.

They zip tied Kaplan's hands together behind his back and yanked him roughly to his feet. As they jerked a hood down over his head, Kaplan wondered why they hadn't killed him yet.

Riley swept into the apartment. The hallway was empty, which was surprising: breaking down a door usually brought someone running. The music was loud, but not enough to cover that.

He waved the rest of the men down the hall to search the bedroom on the right. Jordan stayed on his heels as he paused outside the door on their left, which according to their intel led to a living room. Once they entered the room he'd break right while Jordan moved left, hopefully throwing off any hostiles waiting inside.

Riley took a deep breath, then lunged quickly around the door frame and into the room, automatically panning from side to side with his gun. It was also empty, and if the blueprints were accurate the apartment wasn't that big. Jordan lifted his eyebrows, and Riley shrugged. He motioned for them to approach the door at the far end of the room silently. Jordan nodded.

Riley heard the rest of the team heading away from them toward the kitchen. No gunfire yet, so they hadn't encountered anyone, either. According to plan, they'd check the kitchen and adjoining bathroom, while he and

Jordan entered the bedroom where they expected to find Calderon.

Riley moved as silently as possible, rolling through his feet. Music blared from the back room, underlaid by a sitcom laugh track. At this proximity the noise made his ears smart, and that was through a helmet. The door leading to the bedroom was closed, a simple padlock securing it from the outside. Jordan stepped forward with his shotgun. Riley raised his gloved hand, counting down: three…two…one…

The lock blew away, taking a good chunk of the cheap door with it. Riley swept into the room. Aside from a bed, there was no other furniture. The windows were boarded up. On the right, another door led to the bathroom. Jordan moved to clear that while Riley held his MP-5 steady on the room's sole occupant.

The hostage was lying on a bed, hands and feet trussed. The black hood covering his head was knotted loosely around his neck. His clothes were filthy, an undershirt mottled brown with stains and a pair of suit pants that were nearly reduced to shreds. The head jerked toward him, and he heard muffled pleas.

Jordan stepped out of the bathroom and nodded: all clear. Despite this, he wore an expression of concern. Riley felt the same way: they should never have been able to enter the apartment without encountering resistance. The abduction of Calderon had been done with precision by a skilled team. No way they would leave Calderon alone and unattended. And still no gunfire from the other side of the house, yet the rest of his team hadn't reappeared. Riley glanced at his watch: ninety seconds since they'd entered the apartment. The little voice in his head was screaming at him to grab this guy and get the hell out.

Riley nodded for Jordan to cover him. He shouldered his MP-5 and unholstered his sidearm. Crossing the room in two steps, he aimed the gun with one hand while untying the hood with the other. He yanked it off and stepped back, keeping his weapon leveled at the man on the bed. The guy was bruised almost beyond recognition, cheeks sunken and gaunt. His eyes were wild, hair matted with blood, mouth duct-taped. He didn't look much like the hale, robust man in the company photos, but it was hard to tell. Six weeks as a hostage would ruin anyone's good looks.

Riley barked, "Don't move!" He edged in again, ripped off the duct tape. "Where are the hostiles?"

A slow smile crept across the guy's face. At the sight of it, Riley went cold. "Behind you, *amigo*," the man said.

Riley spun. On the other side of the entryway, five men had assault rifles fixed on him and Jordan.

"Fuck," Jordan muttered.

Riley debated for a second, tightening his grip on his weapon. One handgun against enough firepower to take out a village—he didn't like his odds. Still, he'd faced worse.

"Don't be a fool, *señor*," the man continued. "We have your other men. Surrender and they all survive."

Slowly Riley lowered his weapon. The guy's wrist bonds must have been faked, for he was suddenly at Riley's side, yanking the handgun from his grasp. Gritting his teeth, Riley linked his hands behind his head. Gunshots, right by his ear. He whirled around in time to see Jordan's body collapsing to the floor. The bastard was standing over him, grinning.

"Lo siento," he said casually. "You brought too many."

"Fuck you," Riley spat, unable to contain his rage.

The guy ignored him, barking orders to his men. The hood he'd just pulled off was tugged over Riley's face. It was difficult to breathe through the thick fabric. His hands were zip tied behind him. They pushed and prodded him down the hall. Riley considered yelling, but knew they were in Zetas-friendly territory; there was little chance any locals would come to the rescue. In this town, it was hard enough to gauge whose side the police were on.

He stumbled a few times on the stairs. Hit a landing and heard a door clank against the wall. They must be leaving through the same service exit his team had used to enter the building. The sound of an engine running, and Riley was suddenly sent flying forward. He smacked his head against something hard. Hands shoved him against the far wall into a sitting position. Other people crashed into him, muttering curses. An engine roared, and the vehicle they'd been loaded into peeled away from the curb.

Riley swayed, bracing his feet hard against the floor to stay upright. It felt like a van—probably the one they'd requisitioned for their own getaway. He wondered how many of his men had survived, and what was going to happen to them. Most of all he wondered why the hell any of them were still alive. Clearly they'd walked into a trap—someone knew they were coming. Riley resolved right then and there to find out who. And if he managed to come through this in one piece, he fully intended to hunt them down and kill them.

JANUARY 29

Three

Kelly Jones relaxed. The water surrounding her was warm, womblike. She let herself drift as images flashed across her mind's eye. Agent Leonard barking a command as he ran alongside her, before vanishing in a flash of light and heat. Her former partner, Rodriguez, laughing at his own jokes. Her family, all together again, making pancakes. And finally Jake Riley, the man she had promised to marry. She was focusing on his easy grin, the way his eyes crinkled when he smiled, when a voice jolted her back to the present.

"That's not bad. Now raise and lower it *one* more time."

Kelly opened her eyes. She was floating on her back. The ceiling above the pool danced with the shadows of ripples. From this distance it almost appeared alive, like some great writhing beast. She gritted her teeth and tried to do what she was told, focusing on her right leg, forcing it to resist the hand pressing against her quad. A bead of sweat rolled down her forehead and into the water.

"Not bad. But try to raise it *all* the way up."

"It'd be a hell of a lot easier if you stopped pushing it down," Kelly muttered, teeth clenched.

"Sure would, but *that's* not my job. Remember our goal?"

Kelly had disliked the physical therapist on sight, and her chirpy voice with the irritating habit of emphasizing every other word had only become more grating over time. Still, she was supposed to be the best in her field. And to get back on active duty, Kelly would tolerate almost anything. Even a she-devil named Brandi.

"*One* more time and we're *done*."

"That's what you said before the last one," Kelly protested.

Brandi shrugged. "I lied. C'mon, *you* can *do* it!"

Kelly closed her eyes again. She strained hard, clenching her leg muscles and gluts. There was a splash: her stump had broken the surface of the water. She let her head drop back down, still unaccustomed to the sight of it.

"*That's* what I'm *talking* about!" Brandi exclaimed, clapping her hands together. "All right, now you're done. See you on Thursday."

"I thought we could meet tomorrow instead," Kelly said. She hated the pleading tone in her voice, but she needed this. The more PT she did, the faster she'd be able to get back to work. Seven months off and she was climbing the walls. At this point it felt like another few weeks would kill her. And the only person who could clear her for active duty was standing in front of her, ponytail pointing straight up like an exclamation point, glossy pink lips pressed firmly together.

"Now, Kelly." Brandi shook her head disapprovingly. "*Remember* our chat about *recovery* time?"

"I'm never sore the next day anymore," Kelly protested.

Brandi's expression didn't soften. "No *way,* missy. I

will see you on *Thursday*." She leaned in. "But if you like, I'll sneak in an extra half hour."

"Gee, thanks." Kelly resisted the urge to roll her eyes. She watched Brandi swim fluidly over to the ladder. The pool wasn't kept locked, she reasoned. There was nothing to keep her from sneaking in tomorrow to do the exercises herself.

As if reading her thoughts, Brandi called back over her shoulder, "And don't even *think* about coming in here alone. I'll have Ray at the front desk buzz me if you do."

"Wouldn't dream of it," Kelly sighed.

"*Sure* you wouldn't. See ya!"

Kelly watched Brandi bounce toward the locker room. What she'd give for her sidearm at a time like this. Not that she'd actually shoot the girl, but the thought of scaring the smug grin off her face was tempting. Of course, then Kelly could definitely kiss her job goodbye.

With a deep sigh Kelly dived, kicking hard with her good leg and digging her right arm in deep with each stroke to keep moving in a straight line. Reaching the side of the pool she gripped the ledge hard, using her triceps to haul herself out of the water. Her upper body was strong, more defined than it had been before the accident, thanks to months in a wheelchair. She flipped herself around so that she was sitting, then drew her left leg out of the water and used it to push herself back. Kelly kept her eyes averted as she reached for a towel.

Thanks to a grenade explosion, her right leg now ended just below the knee. It happened on her last case, back in July. Kelly had been chasing a skinhead who was determined to blow up a dirty bomb at the U.S./Mexico border. They'd managed to stop him, but at the last minute he pulled the trigger on a grenade. Four FBI agents had been killed instantly, including Agent Leonard. Another agent had suffered serious injuries, but pulled through. He was back on active duty already. Sometimes it was hard for Kelly not to resent him.

She'd been running away from the truck when the explosion occurred, which probably saved her life. Unfortunately a chunk of metal landed on her leg, crushing it, and she'd sustained internal injuries. The doctor claimed she was lucky to have come out of the coma, plus they'd been able to save most of her leg. Kelly dried herself off, then snapped on her prosthetic. Without the skin-toned polyurethane foam cover, the carbon fiber pylon that substituted for her lower leg made her look like a cyborg. *Lucky* was not the first word that came to mind.

As Kelly made her way to the locker room, fighting the limp that took over when her muscles were tired, she focused on the floor, avoiding the eyes of everyone she passed. Everywhere but here she was able to keep the damage out of sight. She'd thrown away every skirt, dress, and pair of shorts she owned. She even wore sweatpants to bed now, removing the prosthetic under the covers when the lights were off.

She flashed back on Jake. He'd been the portrait of compassion, staying by her bedside during the entire healing process, then having his apartment reconfigured to suit her new needs. He'd even offered to support her financially if the FBI refused to put her back in the field. The problem was, he'd become such a good nursemaid that sometimes it seemed like that was all they were anymore, and she hated feeling like a patient. Occasionally Kelly caught him looking at her with pity, but when she confronted him, he always protested that his feelings for her hadn't changed.

And yet, he'd barely touched her since the accident.

Not that she blamed him. If she couldn't stand looking at herself, how could she expect anyone else to feel
differently?

In the locker room Kelly dressed quickly. The show-
ers here were public, so she always waited to wash off at
home. She tugged a scarf around her neck as she pushed
through the door to the street, instantly swept up by the
mass of people swarming Fifth Avenue. The physical
therapy center was located on a tiny block in Midtown,
across from St. Patrick's Cathedral. Christmas had come
and gone, holiday cheer vanishing along with the fancy
window displays. After a week of steady sleet the streets
were a mess, puddles of filthy, freezing brown water
pooled along the curbs. Everyone pushing past Kelly
looked as miserable as she felt, shoulders hunched against
the cold, bundled up so that only their eyes were visible.
Because of that, it took a minute to recognize the woman
grabbing her elbow.

"Kelly? God, I can't believe it's you!"

"Monica?" For a second Kelly experienced one of
those surreal moments where she thought she might be
dreaming. She'd worked a case with Monica Lauer the
summer before last, a nasty one where dueling serial kill-
ers squared off in the Berkshires. She hadn't seen her
since. "What are you doing here?"

"I should ask you the same thing. Wait, don't tell me.
You married that gorgeous man of yours and live here
now."

"Kind of. Well, no, not married, but…we're living together. And engaged."

"Well, good for you." Monica pulled off a glove and
waved her left hand at Kelly. "Just took the plunge myself.
Howie and me meet up here, since it's about halfway between Bennington and D.C."

"You married Howie?" Kelly said. The brash lieutenant and the forensic anthropologist were the definition of an odd couple. But then, maybe that's why it worked.

"Yep. He was so great all through Zach's recovery." A flash of pain crossed Monica's face. She waved it away. "Anyway, a guy like that you gotta lock down, know what I mean?"

"Sure. How is Zach?" While they were working together Monica's son had sustained serious injuries, almost becoming the final victim in the case. Kelly suddenly felt badly about falling out of touch. The last time she'd contacted Monica was over a year ago, by email. Of course, at least for the last seven months she had a decent excuse.

"Better. Not a hundred percent yet, but he's taking classes at the community college. His short-term memory is still a little ragged, but…" Monica shrugged. "He's alive. That's all that matters."

"Right." Kelly cleared her throat, thinking that was an easy sentiment to express when you hadn't faced the alternative. "Anyway, I should—"

"Oh my gosh, I must be keeping you from something. But listen, I'd love to grab coffee sometime. I leave tomorrow, and Howie and I have dinner plans tonight, but maybe the next time I'm in town? I come down every few weeks."

"Yeah, sure. That sounds great," Kelly responded mechanically. She dutifully entered Monica's mobile number in her phone, knowing full well that she'd never call it, and that any messages Monica left would go unanswered.

"All righty, then. Great seeing you, Kelly. Can't wait to sit down and have a real chat!"

Kelly watched Monica vanish back into the throng. It was nearly dusk and rush hour was about to start in earnest. She'd have to hurry if she didn't want to end up standing in the subway car the entire ride home.

Before tucking her cell phone back in her purse, she reflexively checked the call log. Nothing today. Jake was out of town on business, but he usually called by now. She considered dialing, but a hard shove from behind almost sent her flying. Kelly gritted her teeth and put the phone away. All she wanted was a hot bath, a glass of wine and a Vicodin. Everything else could wait.

Jake Riley kept his eyes closed, listening to the bustle outside the door. If he concentrated he could distinguish voices, individual conversations. Someone at the water cooler was complaining about stalled negotiations in Colombia. Another voice was speaking Russian, a one-sided conversation over the phone. From down the hall, the distinctive sound of coffee brewing, accompanied by loud laughter. Above all that he registered stiletto heels clicking toward him. That gait he'd recognize anywhere.

He opened his eyes just as the door to his office was thrown open.

"Where are we on the Stanislav case?" Syd asked.

"Hello, Syd. Nice to see you, too."

Syd Clement shut the door behind her, crossed the room and plopped down in the chair facing him. She eased her feet out of her heels and propped them up on the desk, inches from his own. At this distance, he could almost feel the heat coming off her stocking feet. He caught himself examining her perfect toes.

"The Stanislav case?" she prodded.

"Dubkova is handling it. He thinks one more week, max."

"Yeah? Dubkova's an idiot." Syd's toes tapped the air impatiently.

"Syd, he's been a rock star for us so far. Three successful negotiations, no casualties."

"Those were in Russia. The Ukraine is a whole other beast. I know the Ukraine."

Jake repressed a sigh. This pattern had become all too familiar. A month or so stateside and Syd got antsy. He'd already had to stop her from intervening in two other active cases that, in her opinion, were taking too long to resolve. What she failed to grasp was that in the private sector, patience and diplomacy usually produced better outcomes than strong-arm tactics. Syd was always a fan of the more forceful approach. Jake weighed his words before speaking. "I think Dubkova deserves another week. The kidnappers are starting to cave. He's already talked them down another million. One more and we're in the range that Centaur is willing to pay."

"Fine. But if they don't come down in a week, we send in a team."

"Sure," Jake agreed, knowing full well that by the end of the day Dubkova intended to have the ransom terms decided, which rendered the entire debate moot. And the prospect of an operation was guaranteed to preoccupy Syd until then.

The company they had co-founded a little more than a year earlier, The Longhorn Group, had taken off in leaps and bounds. They specialized in Kidnap and Ransom cases. Insurance companies that issued K&R insurance kept them on retainer.

Last July they had been the only two in the office. Now there were more than thirty full-time employees on payroll. When one of their clients was kidnapped they mobilized a team to respond, including specialists who coached the families on the negotiation process, and bodyguards to provide protection in case the kidnappers tried to snatch more victims. And if the negotiations fell apart, or the kidnappers became too volatile, The Longhorn Group sent in a recovery team comprised former Special Forces operatives. Their success rate thus far had been impressive: more than forty cases handled in less than a year. Most of the hostages were ransomed out at a price the insurance company was willing to pay. In ten cases they'd been forced to send in units to recover the hostage. Only one case had gone south, thanks to a trigger-happy kidnapper. That one still haunted Jake, but in the grand scheme of things, The Longhorn Group's record couldn't be better.

Of course, part of the boom could be attributed to the explosion in kidnappings worldwide. From the waters off the coast of Somalia to beach resorts in the Philippines to the sleepy streets of Silicon Valley, nowhere was completely safe anymore. In the past year they'd handled cases in Colombia, Guatemala, Italy, Spain, the United States and, increasingly, Russia, where kidnappings were becoming as ubiquitous as those nesting dolls hawked as souvenirs. There were rumors that in the recent elections, one party's entire campaign was financed by ransom money.

Most people were unaware of what a successful ransom negotiation required, especially when an insurance company was involved. The kidnappers invariably made exorbitant demands, either financial or otherwise, in the first stages of negotiation. A frantic family, desperate to see their loved one released, would try to meet those demands. The problem was that paying the full ransom almost guaranteed that the same victim or another family member would be targeted in the future. In the mid-90s, a Hong Kong billionaire was snatched. His family paid the $10 million dollar ransom without any negotiation.

A few years later, he was taken again, and this time the kidnappers wanted double the amount. Even though that ransom was also paid, the businessman was killed.

A seasoned hostage negotiator described it to Jake as roughly equivalent to buying a rug in a Moroccan bazaar. The kidnappers initially wanted something outrageous. A negotiator's job was to bargain them down, convincing them that the family didn't have that kind of money available, the insurance company refused to pay that much or that what they were asking for was simply impossible if it involved something like the release of political prisoners. A great negotiator wore the kidnappers down, until both parties agreed on an acceptable ransom. And with luck, the time and trouble involved meant that the hostage would be safe from future targeting.

Of course, the fact that human lives were at stake made the game more challenging. Walking away was simply not an option, although going in for a snatch and grab was. Which was why The Longhorn Group employed both highly trained negotiators and commandos. Always good to cover your bases.

"So. What else is on the docket?" Syd said.

Jake glanced at the papers on his desk, although he could cite their current cases off the top of his head. "Fribush just left Colombia, the tourists are all safe and sound. We've got Manchester handling that thing in Sardinia, and Jacobs is still in Croatia. Sumner called in from Pakistan, things aren't going well over there."

"Really?" Syd perked up. "I love Pakistan this time of year."

"It's January, no one loves Pakistan now. Besides, I thought we agreed you were on desk duty for a while."

"It's been a while. If I stay much longer, I'll lose my

mind. Look, I'm even starting to get fat." Syd pinched a fold of cashmere sweater over her taut stomach.

Jake grinned. "You could use a little flesh on those bones."

She tossed a paper clip at him. "Go to hell, partner."

Jake's phone buzzed, interrupting his retort. He pushed the speaker button. "Riley."

"Your brother is here to see you."

Jake raised an eyebrow. "Which one?"

"Oh, I didn't know you had more than one." His new secretary sounded flustered. "I'll ask."

"No, that's okay. Send him in."

Syd let out a low whistle. "One of the infamous Riley brothers, huh? This is exciting."

Jake didn't answer. His younger brother opened the door, a wrinkled overcoat draped over his arm. He was a younger, heavier version of Jake: same salt-and-pepper hair, same blue eyes. His face was flaming red, either from the cold or nerves. Jake walked around his desk to greet him. "Chris!" He embraced him. "What are you doing in town?"

"I, uh…" Jake followed his eyes and sighed. Syd tended to have that effect on men.

"Syd Clement." She dropped her feet to the floor and extended a hand in one fluid motion. "I bet you've got some good Jake stories for me."

"I guess." Chris looked completely bewildered.

"Let me take that." Jake peeled the jacket off his brother's arm and hung it on the back of the door. "Have a seat."

Chris nervously perched on the chair beside Syd, sticking to the edge farthest away from her. As Jake sat back down, he took inventory. He'd missed the family Christmas celebration since Kelly wasn't up for it, so it had been over a year since he and his brother had seen each other. About that long since they'd spoken, too. Chris was an accountant, married his high school sweetheart, still lived in the town they grew up in. Other than their blood, they had nothing in common.

"So, Chris. What brings you to New York?" Syd asked, breaking the silence.

"Well, it's kind of…private."

"Really?" Syd arched an eyebrow and leaned forward in her chair. Chris shied away. "The plot thickens. I can't wait to hear it."

"Syd, take a hike," Jake said. "We'll finish up later."

"I always miss the good stuff," Syd huffed dramatically. She slipped on her heels one at a time, then pointed at Jake. "Remember, one more week and I'm on a plane to the Ukraine. You promised."

"Bye, Syd."

"Lovely meeting you, Chris." She winked at him, then turned and left the room.

"So that's your, uh…"

"Partner."

"Right." Chris looked around the office appreciatively, taking in the floor-to-ceiling windows with a view of Central Park, plush carpeting, oil paintings on the walls. Jake could almost see the calculator in his head tallying it up. "Looks like you're doing okay."

"It's been going well. Better than I hoped, actually. How about you? Susie and the kids okay?"

"Oh, they're good." Chris examined his hands, chapped and ruddy from the weather. "Sure is cold here this time of year."

"Sure is." Jake fought the urge to grit his teeth. Chris always took forever to get to the point. He'd start with the weather, then move on to something equally innocuous, like sports. "So what's this private thing?"

He hoped Chris wasn't going to announce that he'd left his family and needed a place to stay. He had one of the most stable marriages Jake had ever seen, and besides, Kelly wasn't really prepared to handle company yet.

"It's Mark."

Jake went cold. His older brother had joined the military straight out of high school. He was a lifer, ended up a Navy SEAL. And with wars going on in multiple countries, this wasn't the best time to be an enlisted man. "What happened?"

"I'm not sure." Chris plucked at the pleats in his corduroy pants.

Jake's heart clenched. "Did you get notification?"

Chris shook his head. "Oh, no, nothing like that. He's out of the service, anyway."

Relief swept over Jake. He'd been braced to hear that Mark had been killed by a suicide bomber or an IED. "When did he get discharged?"

"About six months ago. He's been working for this company."

Jake couldn't picture his rugged older brother in a suit and tie. "What company?"

"I have it here." Chris dug around in his pocket and pulled out a piece of paper.

Jake had to squint to read it. "A tire company?"

"No, it's Tyr Global."

"You're kidding," Jake said. Tyr Global was the world leader in K&R work. They'd been in business for almost four decades, and pretty much wrote the book on hostage negotiation. "Doing what?"

"He didn't say. But he showed up at our door a week ago, told me he was going out on an operation. If I didn't hear back from him by the twenty-seventh, something went wrong. That was two days ago, Jake." Worry furrowed his brow. "So I figured I'd better come see you. I didn't know what else to do."

Jake leaned back in his chair, frowning. "So he left the service and went to work for one of my competitors. Typical."

Chris shrugged. "Probably reckoned you were still ticked off at him."

"He would have reckoned right."

"Would you have hired him?"

Jake's face flushed. "I don't know. Probably not."

"Well, there you go, then."

"So what do you expect me from me?"

Chris leaned forward in his chair and jabbed the desk with his index finger. "He's our brother, Jake. And this is what your company does, right? You go in and save people."

"You could have just called to tell me what happened."

"I could've. But I wanted you to say no to my face. And if you won't help, I leave for Mexico City tonight. End of story." Chris crossed his arms and glared at him.

Jake drummed his fingers on his desk. "Even after what happened, you're willing to risk your life for him?"

"Yup."

"You don't even speak Spanish."

"Neither do you," Chris retorted. "You know it's what Mom would have wanted."

The words hung in the air between them. Jake deliberated. The thought of Chris navigating the underbelly of Mexico City, one of the most dangerous metropolitan areas in the world, was laughable. He'd wind up getting himself killed. Jake sighed. "Tell me everything he told you. Where he was going, what was supposed to happen."

"Yessir." Chris looked relieved, and Jake felt a wave of pity. This had been a big burden for Chris to carry. He of all people knew that Mark would never want help from Jake. But whatever Mark had gotten himself into, it would take more than an accountant to get him back out.

Ten minutes later Jake eased closed the door to his office. After relaying everything he could remember, Chris had passed out cold on his couch—chances were he hadn't slept much the past few days, sitting there waiting for his phone to ring. Jake walked down the hall to Syd's office, waving off a few employees who tried to approach him. He rapped twice on the door before letting himself in.

Syd was lying on her couch, flipping through a magazine. "How's the reunion going?" she asked without looking up.

"Not good. Look's like my older brother has been kidnapped."

"What?" She sat up. "Where?"

"He was running a snatch and grab for Tyr south of the border. Mexico City, Chris thinks, but he's not a hundred percent sure. Something must have gone wrong. He was supposed to check in two days ago."

"Maybe he's holed up in some Tijuana bar celebrating," Syd said skeptically.

"Not Mark." Jake shook his head emphatically. "If he could call, he would have. You hear any chatter from Tyr?"

"No, but I can put out some feelers. I've got a guy over there." Syd crossed to her desk, all business now. "Wasn't Calderon snatched in Mexico City?"

"I was thinking the same thing," Jake said. Although it wasn't public knowledge, the head of Tyr Global had been kidnapped six weeks earlier. Tyr had gone to great lengths to keep word from getting out—after all, having their frontman snatched wasn't good for business.

"They'd send their best to get him back," Syd said thoughtfully as she tapped through screens on her computer. "Your brother that good?"

"Maybe. He spent more than two decades as a SEAL, tours in Somalia, Afghanistan, Iraq."

"Sounds like my kind of guy," Syd said approvingly.

"I'm sure he'd love you," Jake said.

"Well, then, we'll have to arrange a meeting. Give me ten minutes."

Jake let himself out. He fought the urge to pace the halls while he waited. A few people looked up from their desks quizzically. Switching direction suddenly, he headed to the front desk, grabbing his jacket from the closet on the way out.

"Mr. Riley, are you—" his secretary called after him.

He ignored her, marching into the outer hall. He hooked right by the elevators and threw open the door to the roof. It wasn't supposed to be accessible, but one thing he and Syd learned early on was that this line of work attracted smokers, and providing a place to indulge went a long way toward keeping them happy. With that in mind they'd struck a deal with the building's management company to construct a small, sheltered space on the roof. Ducking in, he was pleased to find it unoccupied. He eschewed the chairs, preferring to pace the few feet back and forth.

Even in this weather, the view was striking. Central Park sprawled out below him, all stark branches and grass blanched gray. In the distance off to his left, he could see whitecaps on the reservoir, while to his right the Midtown skyline marched toward the glare of Times Square. Farther on, the tip of Manhattan merged with the horizon. Jake gnawed his lip, checking his watch. *Jesus, Mark,* he thought to himself. *What the hell did you sign up for?*

The creak of a door behind him and Syd appeared. She held the collar of an enormous fur coat up to shield her ears.

"Seriously, Jake, the roof? Make it a little harder on me, why don't you."

"What is it?" He could tell by her eyes the news wasn't good.

Syd shook her head. "Tyr lost a team four days ago. They had good intel on where Calderon was being held and decided to move in quickly. Lost the whole team. Three found dead on site, the other five are missing."

"Mark?"

"Not one of the DOAs. He was the team leader, so chances are they'd keep him alive."

"What are they asking for him?" Jake's chest had gone tight. In spite of himself, he pictured Mark swinging from a rope above the river they used to swim in, letting go at the top, arms pinwheeling as he vaulted through the air.

"That I couldn't get—Tyr is going to great lengths to keep this quiet. You don't want to know what I had to promise my guy for this intel."

"Do they know where they were taken?"

Syd said, "Rumor has it they were all snatched by a Los Zetas offshoot. They pretty much own the eastern *delegaciones,* so Tyr is sending a team there."

"Crap. This just keeps getting better," Jake said.

Los Zetas were mercenaries who did the dirty work for Mexican drug cartels. They had kidnapping perfected to a science, executing the initial grab flawlessly, constantly

moving their prisoners to thwart attempts to track them…
They were the world's best at what they did. None of
which boded well for Mark and his unit.

"What do you want to do?" Syd asked, studying
him.

Jake shook his head. "I don't know. Maybe we call Tyr,
offer to do a joint operation?"

"They won't go for that." Syd shook her head. "They're
still pissed off about the Lodi case. I doubt they'll even
take our call."

"Well, shit, Syd, Mark's my brother." Jake ran a hand
through his hair. "I can't just leave him down there to
rot."

"So let's go get him."

"That's nuts. Tyr will go ballistic."

"If we run into them, we make it clear that if they want
trouble, we're more than willing to give it to them—one
press release about what happened down there, and they
can kiss all their major contracts goodbye. And that's
if we even run into them." Syd snorted. "Doesn't sound
like they're the best of the best anymore. No offense," she
added.

Jake thought it over. The steady sleet tapered off, replaced by chunky white snowflakes. "All right," he said
finally. "But we're not taking anyone off an active case.
Who does that leave?"

"Fribush is already in the air en route to Texas, we can
have him dropped off in Mexico City instead. So we've
got him, you, me—"

"I need you to stay here and hold down the fort," Jake
protested. "We can't both go."

"The hell we can't."

"I mean it, Syd. One of us has to stay." Jake didn't add

what they both knew he meant—if things went south, someone had to survive to keep running the firm.

"This is your brother, Jake. You need the best we've got on it." Syd stared him down. "That's me, and you know it."

Jake started to argue, then thought better of it. Of all the trained operatives they had, Syd was the best by far. And she managed to inspire a blind loyalty in the men that no one else could duplicate. "Fine," he finally agreed. "But I want Jagerson and Kane backing you up."

"Perfect, I was going to suggest them," she said. "And Maltz."

"No way." Jake shook his head. Michael Maltz had nearly been killed on their first case the previous July. Ever since he'd been undergoing extensive physical therapy. As far as Jake knew he hadn't been cleared to go for a long walk, never mind conduct special operations.

"He's fine, I checked him out myself," Syd insisted.

"Checked him out how?"

"Ran him through the course at Langley, plus a few others. Trust me, he's ready to come back. And aside from him, everyone else is committed to other cases."

Jake mentally ran through their roster in his head: she was right, short of hiring a freelancer, all their other field operatives were assigned elsewhere. And freelancers were notoriously iffy. "That makes a team of six," he said dubiously.

"Lean and mean, just how I like it." Syd grinned.

Jake wished he shared her conviction. One thing about Tyr, they attracted top talent. If Mark had been ambushed, anyone could be. Considering the adversary they faced, he'd prefer going in with a small army.

"It'll be fine, Jake. Trust me." Syd glanced at her watch. "Nearly six o'clock. I'll handle the travel logistics, you contact the rest of the team and reroute Fribush's plane."

"Okay."

"Great. We'll be out of here by midnight."

Jake watched her head toward the stairwell. Unless he was mistaken, there was a distinct bounce in her step. Nothing cheered Syd up like the prospect of an armed confrontation.

His cell phone buzzed and he glanced at the caller ID: Kelly. Jake groaned inwardly. He'd arrived home late last night from a business trip to California and had opted to sleep at the office instead of going home. Jake told himself he didn't want to wake her, but deep down he knew it was more than that. He gazed blankly out at the skyline. Kelly wasn't going to like this. Since the accident it was almost overwhelming how needy she'd become. It was understandable, considering what she'd been through, but still. He barely recognized her anymore. Sometimes it felt like the Kelly he'd fallen in love with died in that explosion, and now he was living with her shadow.

Jake ran a hand across his face, wiping away stray drops of water. Dodging the issue wasn't going to make it go away, but he couldn't deal with it now. He had to save Mark. When he came back, they could have that talk.

He shook his head and went back inside.

Four

Mark Riley came to with a jolt, reflexively reaching for his weapon. His fingers fumbled, finding nothing. It always took him a few seconds to remember.

He rolled his head from side to side as he took inventory. The surviving members of his team were in the same positions as when he'd fallen asleep. Kaplan, the spotter, lay on his back by the door, wheezing slightly thanks to his broken ribs. A bullet had grazed his shoulder, too, but so far there were no signs of infection. Flores and Wysocki were on their sides, foot to foot along adjoining walls. Decker, their driver, was the lucky bastard enjoying a turn on the cot. Aside from that, the room was bare: four walls and a filthy mat that might have been white once. The door to the bathroom had been removed, the only window was painted black. A radio in the corner blasted music nonstop. Hard to believe, but it barely registered. His hearing would probably never be the same again.

Mark shook his hands, trying to increase circulation. So far they'd only removed the zip ties binding their hands to allow them to eat, and then only one at a time. The Zetas were nothing if not cautious. Tough to scarf down food with the barrel of an LMT aimed at your chest, but he'd gotten used to that pretty fast, too. The food wasn't bad, surprisingly. He'd even swear the tortillas were homemade.

This was the third dump they'd been stashed in. By the street noise he surmised they were still somewhere in Mexico City. Soon after being tossed in the first van they'd been drugged. He'd come to in a room much like this one, all of them stacked against the wall like cordwood. A few hours later they were moved again. No drugs that time, but the Zetas drove in circles for hours, obviously intent on disorienting them. They could have ended up in an apartment next door to the first and Mark wouldn't have been able to tell.

Something must have happened to convince their guards that the last place wasn't secure, because they were hustled out in broad daylight. Mark caught a glimpse of ugly tenement buildings through the weave in his hood before being stuffed back into the van. Another few hours of jostling against each other through turn after turn, the driver muttering under his breath until someone barked for him to shut up. Then this place.

Wherever they were, the Zetas seemed to feel they were safe from discovery for the time being. Three straight days they'd been trapped in this eight-by-eight-foot cell. They'd been forced to strip on the first day, so instead of black commando gear they now sported a motley assortment of clothing that suggested their captors had a sense of humor. Kaplan was given a T-shirt two sizes too small with Britney Spears grinning from the front. Decker wore a UNC Tar Heels sweatshirt with the sleeves cut off and a pair of red sweatpants. Flores had a white dress shirt, missing the buttons, and Wysocki was stuck with jean shorts. All in all, they looked like refugees from a zombie film.

Mark lumbered to his feet and shuffled to the bathroom,

trying not to wake the others. In order to kill time, they spent much of their captivity napping. Judging by the dim light filtering around the edges of the window, dusk was falling outside. In another half hour or so the Zetas would serve dinner, then leave them alone for the night.

Mark took a piss, never an easy feat with bound hands, and splashed some water on his face. There was a curtainless stall in the far corner that spit out a thin stream of tepid water. Despite hailing from different military branches, they'd all been conditioned to appreciate the comfort of routine. On day one Mark had set the schedule for showering, exercise and shitting. So far no one had questioned his authority to do so.

That morning had been Decker's turn, followed by Kaplan, Flores, Wysocki and him, staggered three hours apart so that the towel they shared had time to dry. Tomorrow Kaplan got the dry towel, and they went back through the rotation.

Hopefully by the time his turn rolled around again, they'd be headed home. Mark heard a muffled grunt followed by an oath.

"Stop kicking me, asshole," Flores growled.

"I was sleeping, asshole, it was an accident," Wysocki mumbled back.

"Both of you shut the fuck up," Decker called from the cot.

Mark stepped into the door frame. "Your turn to shit, Sock. Use it or lose it."

"Aye aye, cap'n." Wysocki, or "Sock," was already clambering to his feet. He was a huge bear of a man, six-five, with a nose that had seen one bar fight too many. He'd come up through the SEALs like Mark, although they'd never served together. Rumor had it that Sock had received an involuntary discharge, but there was no mention of it in Tyr's file. Not that it would surprise him. Sock wasn't the type of guy who handled authority well. Mark had him in his crosshairs as a possible troublemaker.

He moved to the opposite door, putting some distance between himself and whatever Sock was about to deposit. That might have been the worst part of the ordeal so far, five men on a steady diet of beans sharing a bathroom with no door. Thank God none of them had developed dysentery, otherwise it would have been truly unbearable.

"So, Riley—" Flores said. He was the smallest of the group, just shy of six feet with a thick mop of black hair.

Mark waved him quiet, picking up a noise on the other side of the door. They all waited, ears cocked. After a minute, he nodded for him to continue.

Flores kept his voice low. "Like I said earlier, I got people here. We storm the door when they unlock it for mealtime, secure a vehicle and once I figure out where the hell they are—"

"You know the city?" Mark asked.

"Not well. Lived here for a while when I was a kid, though."

Mark shook his head. "I've counted five guys so far. We've got to assume they're all here, all the time, even if they might be working shifts. These aren't some *campesinas* who couldn't handle a .22, they know their shit and they'll be expecting something like that. We can take one of them, but that leaves four to deal with and one weapon between us. Plus for all we know this whole sector is a Zeta nest. According to company intel they own entire barrios. So say we overwhelm them here, then we've got to get out of the building and into friendly territory. Bad odds."

Decker was nodding in agreement. Sock reappeared in the doorway and leaned against the jamb. "So what, we sit here with our thumbs up our ass waiting for the cavalry? 'Cause I gotta tell you, I've been with this organization a long time. And they're not coming for us unless someone's willing to pay."

"For all they know Calderon is with us," Mark argued.

"Bullshit. They probably already sent in another team and got him stateside. And we're written off as a loss." Sock snorted.

Mark shook his head. "We'd already be dead."

Sock looked away, but didn't say anything.

"What's the plan?" Decker asked.

Mark examined him. The former Marine had barely spoken a dozen words the entire time they'd been here, so he hadn't gotten a read on him yet. According to his file he served two tours each in Iraq and Afghanistan, mid-forties, no family. A lifer, like him. "They're going to have to move us at some point—that's the weak link. Fewer guards in a contained space, transportation is covered. It's our best shot."

He looked at each in turn. Decker and Flores nodded.

"Sounds good," Kaplan said. "I'd rather die in a van than this shithole, anyway."

After a few beats, Sock shrugged. "Yeah, why not."

Mark figured it was as close to an endorsement as he was going to get. "No more chatter until after dinner," he said. "Then we'll map it out."

"Absolutely not," Jake said.

"Why not?"

Kelly glared at him, jaw set. He avoided her eyes as he

said, "The doctors haven't even cleared you for desk duty yet. And we don't know what we're in for down there."

"You don't think I can do it." Kelly crossed her arms over her chest.

"I didn't say that—"

"No, but you were thinking it."

Jake ran a hand across his face. This wasn't going well. It seemed like lately, all they did was fight. "I'm thinking that I almost lost you seven months ago. And the last thing I'm going to do is pit you against a bunch of paramilitary goons in Mexico."

"So you're leaving me behind for selfish reasons, then."

"Yeah, I guess so." Jake moved past her and dropped onto the couch, exhausted. He'd been prepared for the fact that Kelly wasn't going to take the news of his trip well. But the last thing he'd expected was that she'd ask to come along. "I mean, Jesus, Kelly. My brother is missing, and now I've got to fight with you?"

Her eyes softened. He held out his arms and she went to him, obviously trying to mask her limp. Kelly dropped into his lap and rested her head against his shoulder. "I feel so useless," she said.

"You're not useless."

"I am. At least, everyone treats me like I am. I'm so sick of people feeling sorry for me, giving me that look."

"Putting yourself in danger isn't going to change that," Jake said.

She stiffened. "You used to say that if you could have anyone watching your back, it would be me."

"Yeah, I know." Jake shifted. "But…"

"But what?" Kelly said. "Now that I'm a cripple, you don't feel that way anymore?"

"You're not a cripple."

"As long as everyone else insists on treating me like one, that's exactly what I am."

She took his hands in hers and rubbed them, even though hers were the ones that felt cold. "I need this, Jake. Let me prove I can still do this."

There was an intensity to her gaze that Jake hadn't seen in a long time. He thought it over. If he said no, the way things were going it would be the death knell for their relationship. Plus if Kelly was this determined, she might follow them anyway. At least he'd be able to keep tabs on her if she was part of the unit.

"We leave in twenty minutes," he said. "Pack light."

Kelly's face split in a grin. He hadn't seen her this happy since before the bombing, Jake realized with a pang.

"You mean it?"

"Nineteen minutes and counting."

Kelly popped off his lap and loped toward their bedroom. Jake winced internally at the thought of how Syd would react to this development. "Damn it, Mark," he muttered under his breath. "Still nothing but trouble."

"Anything?"

"Not yet, Mr. Smiley. But they cleared another sector."

Linus Smiley snorted derisively and waved the assistant out. It had been four days since his team was snatched. He was having a hell of a time keeping the latest fiasco from the board of directors. The loss of an entire unit in addition to Calderon would send them into crisis mode, and that was the last thing he needed. Especially now. He had to hold them off for a few more days, long enough for the new team to clean up this mess…not that they'd made any progress so far. He'd sent in a double unit of men, the best of who he had left, and all they'd managed to do was figure out where the captives weren't.

As it was, there had been too many delays. The board had insisted on waiting nearly six weeks before sending a team after Cesar, convinced that at some point the kidnappers would contact them with a ransom demand. But so far, nothing—and by the time he'd managed to mobilize a team, the trail had gone cold. They'd been fortunate to get that tip about the Zeta apartment—or at least, that's what he'd thought at the time. Clearly someone had been setting them up. The question was, why? Cesar Calderon was worth a substantial amount, and not just in monetary terms. Smiley had lain awake the past few nights trying to figure out the end game here.

He sighed and dropped down in the chair behind his desk, tapping his fingers in a steady cadence. After a moment, he pressed a button on his phone. "Emerson, get back here."

Emerson scuttled in, looking harried. "Yes, Mr. Smiley?"

"Who do we know high up in Mexican military command?"

Emerson shrugged. "I'm not sure, sir. Mr. Calderon always dealt with those contacts directly."

"But you've worked with him for years, right?" Smiley emphasized each syllable.

"Yes, sir." Emerson was visibly uncomfortable.

"So unless you're completely incompetent, you should be able to find those names in his files."

"That depends, sir."

"On what?"

"On how high up you want to go. Mr. Calderon kept most of the top tier names somewhere else."

"Where?"

Emerson shrugged in reply. Smiley fought the urge to hurl a paperweight at him. With Calderon gone, he'd had to step in and fill the vacuum. What he'd consequently discovered was that the layers of separation instituted by Cesar had prevented anyone from realizing how scatter-shot and disorganized the company really was. While each individual quadrant performed well, if one manager was removed the whole house of cards collapsed. Which was happening now, unless Smiley could figure out a way to shore the damn thing up. Typical of Cesar to keep his top contacts in his pocket. He always wanted to play hero.

"Get me whoever you can," Smiley snarled. "Someone has to be running those Zeta assholes. I want to find out who."

JANUARY 30

Five

"This is bullshit. You should have cleared it with me."

"The way you clear everything with me first?" Jake grabbed his duffel bag off the carousel. He'd managed to avoid her until now, but with Kelly in the bathroom and their men staggered around the room waiting for luggage, Syd had cornered him for a dressing down.

"This isn't a goddamn holiday, Riley, it's a mission."

"It's my brother we're going after," Jake retorted. "And I thought we could use another set of arms."

"Another set of legs would help, too," Syd said under her breath.

"What?" Jake said sharply.

"She's just going to slow us down," Syd said. "And if she does, I don't have any problem leaving her."

"For the record, I didn't want you coming along, either," Jake said.

"Now I'm sorry I did."

Kelly reappeared over Syd's shoulder, and Jake forced a smile. She looked past him. "Oh, there's my bag."

Her limp was more pronounced after the long overnight flight, and she moved clumsily toward her duffel. Jake went to help her, but she stopped him with a sharp look.

"So, Kelly." Syd watched her struggle. "All better?"

Kelly set her jaw. "Absolutely."

"Jake probably told you what we're in for."

"I've been briefed," Kelly said.

She tried to push past, but Syd blocked her. "Just so you know, things are different down here. We won't be following any rulebook."

"Happy to hear it," Kelly said.

"Yeah?" Syd raised an eyebrow. "I doubt you'll feel that way when we've got a hostile tied to a chair."

"Quit it, Syd," Jake said, stepping forward.

She opened her mouth to respond, but was interrupted by the approach of Michael Maltz, flanked by Jagerson, Fribush and Kane.

"We ready?" Maltz asked, eyeing the three of them.

"Yes," Jake said. "Let's pull out."

Kelly brooded in the rear of the rental car. She had known going into this that Syd would be less than thrilled to have her along. The two women had managed to avoid being in the same room for more than five minutes ever since The Longhorn Group was formed. Kelly hadn't trusted her from the beginning. Syd Clement embodied the complete lack of moral standards that Kelly associated with CIA agents. Success at any cost. The end justified the means. Never in a million years would Kelly have started a company with someone whose world view was defined by "us versus them." She'd told Jake as much, but he'd gone ahead and established the partnership anyway.

Syd would go out of her way to make her life difficult on this mission. On top of everything else, she still had an ax to grind with Kelly for forcing her off a case. Not that she'd actually managed to—Syd had gone ahead and done what she wanted anyway, consequences be damned.

And because of her actions, a lot of people in Phoenix had lost their lives. More than once in the past few months, Kelly had toyed with the idea of turning her in for that. She'd only kept her mouth shut for Jake's sake.

They'd opted for two cars, ostensibly to have more options if something happened to one. Kelly suspected it was also meant to keep her and Syd separated as much as possible. Jagerson was driving. He was small for a former Delta guy, but sported the same sheared head, thickly muscled arms and boxy jaw as his compatriots. Jake sat in the passenger seat beside him. As if sensing her gaze, he turned and gave her a thin smile.

Kelly shifted her eyes away and pretended to fiddle with her phone. Under her lashes she took in Michael Maltz. Funny that Syd had been so opposed to her joining the team, yet had insisted on Maltz. He'd nearly been killed in the Phoenix incident, and still looked much the worse for wear. A mottled mass of burnt flesh ran across the left side of his face into his scalp. He'd lost the hearing in the ear on that side, and was missing a finger off his right hand. According to Jake, the rest of his body was largely held together by titanium pins. Kelly couldn't believe that after all that, he was still willing to work with Syd. Hell, she couldn't believe he wanted to keep doing this sort of work at all. Of course, under the circumstances she was hardly one to talk.

Kane, Fribush and Syd were in the other car. They'd offered to gather the equipment and meet them back at the motel. Kelly wondered for a moment what kind of equipment they were getting, and where it was coming from—then decided that if she ever wanted to go back to the Bureau, she was better off not knowing.

When Jake showed up yesterday he'd nearly caught her digging through a stack of case files her former partner had swiped for her. Just being in possession of those without formal permission could cost her job, but Kelly was going nuts sitting at home without anything to do. She figured if she could spot something that had been missed, she'd be forgiven for not filing the proper paperwork. And with any luck, that might help get her cleared for active duty again.

So far the search had been unproductive. All she'd ended up with was a mass of paper cuts and the conviction that sometimes the follow-up from her people had been less than thorough. For instance, a case she'd been involved with a few years earlier had been marked as Closed, even though the killer's body never turned up. She'd argued for more resources, but her boss at the time was more interested in filing one in the "win" column. Stefan Gundarsson had last been seen falling into a river, bleeding from a gunshot wound, and that was good enough for him. Kelly remained skeptical. Sometimes people who had been shot in the head continued walking around as if nothing had happened. She'd have felt better about it if a body had turned up.

One victim's family apparently agreed. They'd hired a P.I. to investigate further. Last year while Kelly was in a coma, the investigator had contacted the FBI. He claimed to have stumbled across irrefutable evidence that Gundarsson was alive and well in Mexico. But the FBI refused to reopen the case without more proof. Reading through the file last night, Kelly couldn't help but think that if she'd been on active duty when the tip came in, the results might have been different. And then Jake walked in and announced that he was headed to Mexico on the next flight. It had seemed like fate.

A horn blared, jerking her back to the present. Despite the predawn hour, they were trapped in a bleating, smoggy mass of cars in various stages of dilapidation. Vendors edged through the gridlock selling candy bars, key chains, cigarettes and a host of other random items, from gum to razors. A guy in a ratty T-shirt materialized and rubbed filthy rags across their windshield, ignoring blasts from the car horn to get him to stop. As Jagerson guided them forward in fits and starts, Kelly was suddenly overwhelmed by the noise and strangeness of her surroundings. A vise clamped around her chest, and she struggled to breathe.

Not now, she thought, gritting her teeth. She pulled her backpack onto her lap and dug through it for her pills. When she couldn't find them Kelly experienced a moment of panic so intense she nearly passed out, terrified that she'd forgotten them in the mad rush to get ready. Then her fingers closed on the smoothness of the bottle and she exhaled hard. She palmed a pill and slipped it in her mouth. Glancing up, she discovered Maltz watching her. Wordlessly he handed her an unopened water bottle. She nodded her thanks and took a swig. Kelly tried to hand it back, but he waved it away.

"Keep it," he said in a raspy voice.

"You okay?" Jake shifted in his seat again, voice laden with concern. He knew that she had these attacks, although she'd never let on how frequently.

"I'm fine," Kelly replied. "How much farther?"

"Next block," Jagerson answered.

"Good thing," Maltz said without looking at her. "This traffic is killing me."

It happened sooner than Mark expected. He awoke to the door being thrown open by a Zeta brandishing an LMT. Had to be close to dawn; despite the fact it was still dark outside he felt well rested. And after years of early-morning drills, Mark's internal clock always jarred him awake at 0500 hours.

The guard jabbered at them in Spanish.

"What now?" Sock grumbled from the cot.

"He wants us to get dressed. They're moving us again," Flores translated, casting a sidelong glance at Mark.

Mark nodded, his pulse quickening. It was time.

In two minutes they were all awake and seated side by side on the cot.

Another Zeta came in with the hoods and pulled them over their heads while his partner covered them. Mark waited his turn, staring down at the floor as directed, praying they would leave their hands zip tied in front rather than changing them to the back.

Time must have been pressing, because as soon as Mark's head was covered, hands pushed him out the door. He and the others were jostled along a hall and down a flight of stairs. A temperature shift, cool air raising the hair on his arms as they were propelled into the night. Same drill as before, they were shoved into a waiting van. The door slid closed, then a screech as they pulled away from the curb.

Mark strained his ears. It was critical to determine how many Zetas were in the van with them. The last time he was pretty sure there had been three. He hadn't heard anyone else fall in line with them, but there hadn't been a delay so a driver was probably already at the wheel. They'd planned for three, including sack boy and the gunman. Any more and their plan would probably fail.

Kaplan wheezed beside him. Mark drew his knees up to his chest, then lengthened them as if stretching. He didn't hit anything, there was a clear path in front of him. *So far, so good,* he thought.

A mutter from the front seat: the driver, sounded like

the same one as before. They'd dubbed him "Crybaby" since he constantly complained.

Someone snarled for him to shut up. That would be "Scarface," the guy who liked to wave his gun around. He'd been in the room when they were first grabbed, and accompanied them on every move so far. Mark figured he'd be the toughest to deal with—guys like that were always itching to pull the trigger.

Mark waited, but the van lapsed into silence. Blood roared in his ears. They had decided to wait at least ten minutes before making their move, allowing time for their captors to settle into complacency. It was a gamble, though. This time, they might only be taken a few blocks. There was no way to tell if they'd be in the van for hours or minutes.

The street noise outside was muted. Mexico City was comprised of sixteen boroughs sprawled across almost six hundred square miles. Add in the surrounding area, and you were facing another ten million people in three thousand square miles, an area larger than the state of Delaware. It was a hell of a haystack for anyone to find them in, which reinforced the realization they were more or less on their own.

The van picked up speed. Mark recognized the familiar sound of tires bumping over reflectors, and his heart leaped. They were on a highway, almost too much to hope for. Even if another car was following them, their ability to interfere would be limited. It was now or never.

He doubled over suddenly and groaned. There was no response. Mark clutched his gut and moaned louder.

"Cállate!" Scarface growled.

"Jesus, my stomach!" Mark gasped.

A murmured exchange in the front seat—he'd guessed right, there was someone else up there. The muzzle of a gun nudged his leg. Scarface barked something in Spanish.

"He wants you to be quiet." Flores sounded panicked. "If you don't shut up, he'll shoot you."

"Tell him to put me out of my misery," Mark said through clenched teeth, rocking back and forth as if convulsed by spasms. "I swear I'm going to shit myself."

Flores repeated what he'd said. Scarface talked over him as he translated, sounding increasingly irritated.

"He said, go ahead, Yankee swine, you deserve to wallow in your own shit."

"Tell him to go fuck himself," Mark spat.

Apparently Scarface knew enough English to understand that. The muzzle of the gun returned, this time pressed against his chest. Mark held his breath as the van rocked them back and forth, praying the safety was still on. Scarface's leg brushed his as he called out to the front seat. The Zeta on the passenger side was clearly in charge, a low voice ordered Scarface to stand down.

Too late, Mark thought, taking advantage of the distraction. While Scarface argued with his boss, Mark grabbed the muzzle of the gun with both hands and thrust up sharply. At the same time, he swept sideways with his legs, knocking Scarface off his feet.

A grunt as Scarface landed, air squeezed out of his lungs. The sound of the rest of the Tyr team scrambling. Mark struggled for a second with the hood covering his head. The van swerved sideways as his fingers finally found a purchase and yanked it off.

Chaos reigned in the rear of the van. Sock and Flores were struggling to hold down Scarface, who bucked against them, nose broken and bleeding. Sock punched him, three swift blows to the head. Scarface's eyes rolled back and he went limp.

Decker and Kaplan were engaged in a battle with the driver and passenger. The LMT had come to rest beside Mark. He flipped it around in one smooth motion.

A gun went off in the front seat, the explosion so loud his ears rang. Kaplan collapsed backward. Mark shoved past him and drove the muzzle of the LMT against the passenger's head. "Drop it!" he yelled. "Flores, tell this motherfucker to drop the gun!"

The driver had slowed. "And he needs to keep driving at the same speed," Mark snapped.

The Zeta in the passenger seat had dropped his Glock, but still wore a shit-eating grin.

"What are you smiling at, asshole?" Mark shoved the muzzle farther into the guy's chest.

The guy gave him another bemused look, then said something to Flores. Both he and the driver blanched. The driver began muttering something that sounded suspiciously like a prayer.

"What did he say?" Mark demanded.

"He said the van is wired to blow. All he has to do is push a button," Flores said.

"Bullshit," Mark said.

The guy held up his other hand. A transmitter was nestled in his palm. Mark wasn't a demolitions expert, but he'd been around enough to recognize the real deal when he saw it. He swore under his breath.

"What the fuck do we do now?" Sock asked.

"Tell him to give me the transmitter." Mark kept his gaze locked on the guy. "He doesn't want to die any more than we do. He hands it over, we'll drop them off at the side of the road. He can tell his boss we overpowered them."

"They'll kill me anyway," the man said in thickly accented English before Flores could respond.

"Then run. Get the hell out of here," Mark said.

The man just shook his head. Mark recognized the look in his eye. He'd seen that same expression on a kid's face at a roadblock outside Baghdad, right before the blast that took out half his unit.

Mark dived forward a second too late. There wasn't even time to shout a warning before the guy pressed the button.

Six

They'd been at the motel for over an hour when Syd knocked on the door. Jake opened it to find her, Kane and Fribush loaded down with two duffel bags apiece.

"A little help?" she grunted.

Jake took one of the bags from her, staggering slightly under the weight. She hauled the other into the room, Fribush and Kane at her heels. Jake slammed the door behind them and double-bolted it.

"That was quick," he said.

"Ya gotta love Mexico," Syd said. "They were even having a sale on C4. We cleaned them out. Figured we were doing the country a favor, getting this stuff off the streets."

"I feel like a patriot." Fribush pulled an Uzi out of one of the bags and looked it over appreciatively.

Kelly sat on a threadbare comforter mottled with stains. Her jaw had tightened, but she didn't say anything. Jake wondered again what the hell he'd been thinking, allowing her to come along.

"So what's the plan?" Maltz asked. He was sitting on a chair in the corner, methodically cleaning his nails with a knife.

"I heard from my contact at Tyr. They narrowed the search down to two boroughs." Syd unfurled a map of the city on the bed. Kelly shifted to make room for it.

Syd pointed at two boroughs on the Eastern side of the map. "Iztapalapa and Iztacalco. Think of them as the South Bronx of Mexico City. Both Zeta-friendly, lots of safe houses there. The initial raid took place in Iztapalapa, and Tyr thinks they hung around."

"Where's the Tyr team?" Jake asked.

"They've spent the past week combing through Iztapalapa block by block. They came under fire a few times, thought they might be close."

"What about the AFI?" Kelly asked.

"Who?" Maltz said.

"The Agencia Federal de Investigación. They're kind of our—" Kelly caught herself. "The FBI's counterpart in Mexico City. Is Tyr coordinating the search with them?"

"I doubt it, since a quarter of their agents work for the Sinaloa Cartel," Syd snorted.

"But I thought—"

"This isn't the United States, Jones. The police don't help you here. In fact, they're usually the first to put a bullet in your head."

Kelly started to say something, then abruptly shut her mouth. Jake considered interceding, but unfortunately Syd was right. With every K&R job they had done in Mexico, their main goal was to avoid the authorities as much as possible, paying the right ones to look the other way. Tyr probably functioned on the same model. The neighborhoods they were talking about were basically war zones. If a Mexican cop wanted to last more than a week on the job, he avoided them at all costs. The Zetas were an occupying army in those territories. And considering that, some C4 might actually come in handy.

He could see Kelly trying to reconcile that, and felt for her. This was way past anything she had ever been involved with. With any luck she was already considering booking a flight home.

She surprised him by saying, "So we're avoiding the Tyr team, too."

"Naturally," Syd said.

"Where do we start?" Maltz asked.

Syd pointed to a spot in the upper right section of the map. "Tyr is here now, and moving north. I say we start above them and move south. There's a rumor that some Americans are being held in a building in the northeast quadrant. Zetas are known for moving captives around, but we might get lucky. We'll ask around, see what stones we can overturn."

"Where did you hear the rumor?" Kelly asked dubiously.

"Sorry, hon. That's classified," Syd said smugly.

"Syd has a lot of friends who owe her favors," Jake explained. He didn't add that he referred to them as her "shadow network." He'd long ago learned better than to doubt her information. In his experience, those rumors were always right on the money.

"Why do you think anyone will talk to us, if the Zetas control everything?" Kelly pressed.

Syd dug into one of the duffels and withdrew a handful of cash. "Because we'll be paying them. And if cash doesn't work, we'll try something else."

Kelly abruptly stood and went to the bathroom. Jake followed her. She stood in front of the mirror staring down at the floor. He could hear the rest of the team suiting up in the bedroom.

"You don't have to stay," Jake said gently. "We both know this isn't your kind of thing."

"Is it yours?" she asked, raising her head to meet his eyes.

"My brother is out there," he said, although that rang hollow even to his own ears. The truth was, aside from The Longhorn Group's first case, Jake hadn't done much work in the field. He usually left this sort of thing to Syd and her cohorts. He never questioned how any specific job had been accomplished, probably because in the end he didn't want to know. As long as the hostage ended up safe and sound, he figured they'd done their job. But now that he was here, facing the reality of paying off criminals—or worse—the reality of what they were about to do struck home. Maybe he should book them both on a flight, and leave the rescuing to Syd.

Jake shook his head, dismissing the thought. He couldn't expect others to risk their lives for his brother if he wasn't willing to do the same. But getting Kelly to understand that… "I don't like it any more than you do," he said. "But—"

A loud rap on the door interrupted him.

"We're moving out," Syd said, voice tinged with impatience. "You kids coming along?"

Kelly replied, "We'll be right there."

Mark opened his eyes. The van was filled with dense, acrid smoke. He coughed to clear his lungs, struggling to see.

He was lying on his back with a body sprawled across his legs. The van had come to rest on the passenger side. The driver's head split the windshield, glass shards fragmenting the night sky into a dark constellation. It didn't look like he'd be coming around anytime soon. Or probably ever again.

A muffled groan as the figure by his feet shifted: Decker.

Mark turned his head. No sign of the guy who had triggered the explosion. He looked for the LMT, couldn't find it. *Shit.*

Mark struggled up to sitting and nudged Decker's shoulder. "You okay?"

"Yeah, think so." Decker said blearily.

"We gotta go," Mark said.

"Right." Decker awkwardly pushed off his legs and climbed stiffly into the rear of the van. Mark followed him.

There was an enormous hole in the middle of what had been the van's floor. *So the bomb hadn't been wired to kill everyone, just them,* Mark thought. Flores and Kaplan were crumpled on top of one another. Scarface, or what was left of him, was scattered across the interior. He must have been directly above the bomb when it blew, absorbing most of the blast. Thank God for small favors.

"Where's Sock?" Decker asked. There was no sign of him. The rear door was open; through it Mark could see dirt and scrub brush. He heard a car passing by, not too far away. The van had rolled a few times, but they were probably still close to the highway. Mark went to check Flores and Kaplan.

They were both covered in blood, though it was impossible to tell how much of it had come from Scarface. He eased Flores off Kaplan. Flores started in response.

"Wha—"

"You okay, man?" Mark asked.

Flores raised a hand to his face. It came away bloody. "This mine?" he asked.

"I don't know. Anything hurt?"

"Shit, everything hurts." Flores slowly moved his arms and legs. "But I don't think I'm bleeding."

Decker was bent over Kaplan. "He's hurt," he said. "Pretty bad."

Mark joined him. Kaplan was still unconscious, his face so pale it glowed in the dark interior. Carefully they turned him over. A bloodstain the size of a quarter marked the exit wound.

"At least it passed through," Decker said.

"You have EMT training, right?" Mark asked.

Decker nodded.

"All right." Mark checked the interior again, hoping to find some sort of weapon, but there was nothing useful. "We've got to move out. Chances are hostiles will be here soon. Do what you can to stop the bleeding. We'll take shifts carrying him."

"What about Sock?"

"What about him?" A voice boomed from outside. Sock suddenly appeared in the doorway.

"What happened to you?" Decker asked.

"Came to and that asshole was heading out. Thought I'd try to stop him."

"So where is he?" Mark asked. Sock looked largely unharmed, which was almost miraculous considering how close he'd been to the blast.

Sock looked away. "Bastard was too fast. But we gotta get moving. I think he had a phone on him. Got this, though." He held up the LMT.

"I didn't hear any shots fired," Mark said.

"Couldn't get a clear line of sight," Sock retorted. "Figured I'd save the ammo."

"Kaplan got hit," Flores said.

"Yeah?" Sock glanced over. "We leaving him?"

"Never leave a man behind," Mark said, surprised. "We'll take shifts carrying him."

"Carrying him where?" Sock asked dubiously.

Mark didn't answer. He climbed out of the van, easing past Kaplan, Flores and Decker. The air felt cool on his face. Dawn was breaking over the mountains. To the west, city lights shimmered through a smoggy bubble, casting a yellow glow toward the brightening sky. Still Mexico City, he noted with relief—he'd been right, they hadn't been moved far. That should make it easier for Tyr to arrange air transport out.

The van had come to rest in a dusty field fifty feet from the highway. Not good—anyone driving by could see it, especially now that day was breaking. A hundred yards away stood a shabby adobe building that appeared abandoned. Another stretch of field and trees, then the city reared up again. He had no idea where they were. Hell, he didn't even know what time it was.

"Which way?" Sock pressed.

"Back toward the city," Mark said with more conviction than he felt. "We'll be able to contact Tyr and get medical supplies for Kaplan."

"I vote we head east," Sock argued. "Zetas own that town, we head back there they'll grab us again."

"We won't have to lay low for long," Mark said. "Once we make contact, they can have us out in under three hours. There might be another unit here already."

"Yeah? You sure the first door we knock on won't be opened by el Jefe?" Sock turned to the others. "Outside, we got a shot. We can hunker down at a farm somewhere, get Tyr to send in a chopper. The city, we gotta deal with cops and other assholes who're gonna wonder why our buddy has a hole in him."

Decker and Flores looked uncertain. Mark considered

for a minute. Sock was right—they might have a better shot surviving in the rural areas surrounding the city. Urban warfare was a bitch; he'd be the first to admit that. But if he ceded his authority now, he knew from experience there was no getting it back. And he didn't like the thought of Sock as their de facto leader. Something about him was off, Mark could smell it. He wasn't about to follow someone he didn't trust with his life.

"We head west, back to the city," he said firmly. "Move out."

Sock appeared ready to argue, but Flores and Decker were already moving, Kaplan cradled between them. Sock eyed Mark for a second as if sizing him up for a fight. Mark watched his hand, saw the index finger move toward the trigger of the LMT by his side. After a beat, it relaxed back down.

"You're the boss," Sock said. "But if we get pinched again, I'm saying I told you so."

"We get pinched again, we won't live long enough to talk about it." Mark reached for the LMT. Another pause, then Sock handed it over. Mark slung it over his shoulder and they headed across the field.

"All due respect, sir, I'm not buying it." Linus Smiley listened to the voice on the other end of the receiver, mouth tightening. "If Cesar Calderon was such a friend to the Mexican people, I don't understand why you're refusing to assist in his release."

Linus had spent the morning being rerouted to different people in the hierarchy of the Mexican government, each of whom eagerly pawned him off on someone else. He had no idea at this point if he'd managed to ascend the ladder to someone who could actually accomplish something, or if he was still dealing with a low-level bureaucrat annoyed by the interruption of his breakfast. "I understand that initially we refused outside assistance. But clearly that situation has changed. Now we have three dead employees, and another five who are presumed hostages. At what point do you folks actually get off your asses and do something about it?"

There was a long pause. Finally the man on the other end said in heavily accented English, "Mr. Smiley, in the past year more than two hundred of our citizens were kidnapped in Mexico City, and another eight hundred nationwide. And those were only the ones reported, the real number is likely two or three times that. We have had five hundred homicides, more than a hundred in Mexico City alone. Are you implying that the loss of Americans is more important?"

"That's exactly what I'm saying," Linus said. "We're not talking about some guy running a taco stand, Mr.—" he glanced at his sheet of handwritten notes "—Ortiz. Cesar Calderon is a major player on the global scene. If anything happens to him—"

"I don't believe I can assist you, Mr. Smiley," Ortiz interrupted. "Allow me to transfer you to someone who can."

Linus fumed as mariachi Muzak once again poured from the receiver. He slammed it down. Jesus, he hated Mexico. Bunch of incompetent bastards whose third world status was more than deserved. Russia and the former Soviet bloc nations had problems, but at least money talked over there. Pay off the right person, you could get nearly anything done. Had Calderon been snatched in Kiev, Linus would have had him home in less than a week.

He pressed the intercom button. "Get the team on the line."

Linus paced while he waited for the connection to come through. He'd sent sixteen men down there, led by Ellis Brown. Cesar had personally lured Brown from his career as a Navy SEAL into K&R work, and Brown was his go-to guy for snatch-and-grab operations. He would have led the first team, had even called to volunteer, but Smiley wanted him to finish up another operation in Colombia. A mistake, maybe. One he was now able to rectify.

"Brown here."

"Secured line?"

"Yessir." Brown's tone implied that the question itself was offensive.

"Progress?"

"Still no sign of the whale," Brown said.

"Whale" was the code name for Calderon. "What about the rest of them?"

"We think we found a safe house where they were kept, but there's no movement. Probably gone already." There was a pause. "One of our contacts said we're not the only ones looking for them. You send in another unit?"

"You're the only ones down there." Linus's brow furrowed.

"That's what I thought, sir."

"Americans?"

"Definitely. Asking a lot of questions about the minnows."

The minnows were the missing unit. That was odd. Linus slumped back into his chair. What the hell was going on down there?

It was already beyond strange that someone had snatched a hostage of Calderon's caliber without providing proof of life, or contacting either Tyr or his family with a ransom demand. What could they be after? Had they simply killed him as a warning to K&R companies working in the region? If so, his body should have turned up by now. When a local police chief crossed Los Zetas, his head was found in a cooler outside his precinct. Los Zetas weren't shy about sending messages. And why seize the rest of the unit alive, then not attempt to ransom them out, too? *Fucking Mexico,* Linus thought. He'd never understand it.

"New orders, sir?"

"No, stay the course. The whale is your primary objective, minnows are a bonus."

"What about the other team?"

"You run across them, find out what the hell they're doing down there."

"Any limits?" Brown asked.

Linus pondered for a moment. "None," he finally said. "They've got no business interfering. Do what you have to."

He hung up the phone and glanced at the clock. It was an hour earlier in Mexico City, just before 10:00 a.m. Linus wasn't accomplishing anything by phone. The board meeting was less than a week away. By then, he'd have to have Calderon back, dead or alive, and news on the missing unit. He buzzed the intercom again. "Book me a flight to Mexico City."

Kelly tensed on the edge of the backseat as Syd and Kane approached the bodega. Syd's contact claimed the owner was Zeta-friendly. Apparently he and his wife stowed hostages in the apartment above the store. He was responsible for making sure they didn't escape, she kept them fed.

Nothing about this was sitting well with Kelly. They only had the word of one of Syd's shadowy connections to go on, and God only knew what his motivation was for ratting out the bodega. "What if they've got nothing to do with Los Zetas?" Kelly had asked back at the motel.

"Then we go on our merry way," Syd claimed.

Kelly very much doubted that was true. The bodega door closed behind them. Almost subconsciously she began to count, trying to keep herself from imagining what was going on inside.

What the hell am I doing here? Kelly wondered. She'd been so gung ho to feel useful again, she hadn't thought through what kind of moral compromises working with Syd would present. Already she felt dirty, and they hadn't even done anything yet. She was no Pollyanna; she knew there was a seamy side to Jake's new line of work. She just hadn't realized how seamy.

Kelly had hoped that coming down here would restore her sense of purpose, and that after they found Mark she'd have a chance to look into the allegation that Stefan Gundarsson was still alive. But the reality of that suddenly seemed absurd. Jake would flip if she told him she intended to track down a fugitive alone. And the truth was, she didn't even know where to start looking. She hadn't been able to get in touch with the P.I. who provided the earlier lead. She didn't speak Spanish, and based on what everyone was telling her, the Mexican authorities wouldn't be helpful. On top of which she didn't have the authority or clearance to be doing any of this. She'd wanted to dig up enough concrete evidence to convince her boss to reopen the case and put her in charge of it. But that possibility seemed increasingly remote.

Out of the corner of eye she examined Jake. His face was inscrutable. For a second, it seemed as if he were a total stranger, and she was seeing him for the first time. She flashed back on the day they'd met, in the command-center trailer during her campus case. He seemed colder now, harder. It had been a long three years for both of them. Had he really changed so much since then? Or was her mind messing with her again?

Kelly shifted in her seat. Her leg was sore. The pressurization on the plane had caused it to swell and the socket of her prosthetic felt unusually tight. The lack of sleep wasn't helping, either. The Xanax had worn off and she could sense the panic lurking, waiting for an opportunity to rush in. It felt like there was a spotlight on their cars, as if everyone passing by had pegged them as intruders. Kelly knew she was being paranoid, but she couldn't help herself. Half of her was afraid that at any moment someone might open fire, drilling their cars with automatic weapon fire. The other half was worried that the people inside the store were involved in the kidnapping of Mark's team. And she could imagine what Syd would do to them if that turned out to be the case.

Syd emerged from the store with Kane at her heels. She pulled on a baseball cap, their signal to meet her at a prearranged location a block away.

"Must have gone well," Jake commented from the front seat.

"How do you know?" Kelly asked.

"No shots fired," Maltz said from beside her. They were in the same seating arrangement as before, with Jagerson driving. She had yet to hear him say a word, and was starting to wonder if he even spoke English.

Kelly gazed out the window at the passing storefronts. They were in the northeast quadrant of Iztapalapa. To her eyes it was indistinguishable from the rest of Mexico City: row after row of run-down buildings, streets riddled with potholes, choking smog and horns and blaring music. Her only other trip to Mexico had been a vacation in Puerto

Vallarta years before. *This is a far cry from that,* she thought wryly.

Jagerson eased the car over to the curb.

Syd approached Jake's window. She leaned over as she spoke. Kelly's eyes narrowed at the peek of bra revealed by that maneuver.

"Shopkeeper is dirty all right. He didn't have them there, but he probably has others."

"How do you know they weren't there?" Kelly interrupted.

Syd barely glanced at her. "Because he heard a rumor that the guys we're after were in a van crash on the Mexico-Puebla highway early this morning. They were being moved out of the city. He thinks the hostages got away."

"He's sure?" Jake asked.

"Sure enough," Syd said. "I made a call, we should have a copy of the accident report within the hour."

"Are they all okay?"

"Apparently."

"How'd you get him to tell you all that?" Kelly asked. "How do we know he's not lying?"

Syd grinned at her. "I asked nicely." She turned back to Jake. "I've got the general location of the crash. I say we head out there, see what we can find. It's only a few clicks east."

"What about the other people?" Kelly asked.

"What other people?"

"You said he was keeping other hostages above the store."

"Yeah?" Syd gazed at her levelly.

Kelly turned to Jake. "There has to be someone you can call."

He paused a beat before saying, "Kelly, no one's supposed to—"

"Someone must be looking for them. Maybe one of the other K&R companies."

"Not if they're local," Syd snorted. "Hell, you don't even have to have money to get kidnapped down here. Some of the gangs offer a layaway plan."

Kelly stared Jake down. Finally he said, "I'll have Demetri drop the AFI an anonymous tip." Syd started to protest, but he cut her off. "Meanwhile, we go check out that crash site."

"What if the cops are still there?" Maltz asked.

"They won't be," Syd said. "Happened early this morning, everything'll be cleared up by now."

"And if some of the Zetas are there?" Kelly asked.

"Then we consider ourselves lucky," Syd said. "I'm dying to talk to one face-to-face."

Seven

Mark Riley hunched in the shadows beside the pharmacy. One of the great things about Mexico was that you could get almost anything in their drugstores, from Botox to antibiotics. Until recently, most were poorly guarded. But lately addiction levels had spiked, and there had been a corresponding rise in pharmacy robberies. Many, like the one he was currently facing, had taken security precautions: an armed rent-a-cop was perched on a stool inside the doorway. He was clearly bored, eyes glued to the television set behind the counter. Still, he had a gun, which complicated things. Mark would prefer getting what they needed without hurting anyone. Hopefully this guy wouldn't want to play cowboy.

"What do you think?" Decker asked in a low voice.

Mark had nicked a baseball cap from a sidewalk cart, and he pulled it low over his eyes. "We could try another one. Not a fan of dealing with a guard."

"We could. But Kaplan doesn't have a lot of time," Decker pointed out.

He was right. It had taken longer than expected to find a safe place to hunker down. They'd left Kaplan, Flores and Sock in an abandoned building a few blocks away.

Kaplan was losing blood too fast for them to stick together. And Mark wasn't willing to leave him alone with Sock. So he and Decker set off to raid a pharmacy for meds and a cell phone. According to the locals, this was the only one open for blocks in any direction.

"How's your Spanish?" Mark asked.

Decker shrugged. "I can get by."

"All right, you do the talking. Make sure they know we don't want anyone to get hurt, we'll just take what we need and be gone."

"Got it."

Mark took a deep breath. It was a little after 1000 hours. Despite the fact that it was late January, the sun beat down, baking the scene in a shimmery cast. A river of sweat ran down the center of his back. He was light-headed from hunger, tired and shaky in the aftermath of the crash. He'd never stolen so much as a candy bar in his life, and here he was about to knock over a drugstore. He shook his head.

Mark slid the LMT up from the ground beside him, holding it close by his side as he stood. He lined it up with his leg as he approached the door, Decker at his heels. Of the remaining team members, Decker struck him as the most capable and trustworthy. Hopefully he wouldn't be proven wrong.

The guard glanced their way as the door opened with a tinkling of bells. Small guy, early twenties with a scraggly moustache. His gaze started to slide away, but then he frowned: something about them had registered. As he shifted back toward them, Mark slammed the butt of the gun hard against his temple. He crumpled off the stool, landing on the floor with a thump.

Decker locked the door behind them. The store was empty. Mark frowned. There had been someone behind the register when they cased it five minutes earlier. Bathroom break, maybe?

A chunk of plaster blew off the wall behind his head. Instinctively he dived, hitting the floor. Decker landed beside him.

"You okay?" Mark asked.

"Holy shit!" Decker said, checking out the hole punched through the wall above where the guard had been sitting. "What was that, a missile launcher?"

"Double barrel loaded with triple-ought buck, I'm guessing," Mark said.

Another chunk of plaster exploded, a few feet lower than the last. Mark slid the LMT to Decker and signaled for him to move to the far side of the store, near the bandages. From there he'd have a better angle to cover him.

Mark commando-crawled toward the cheap plywood counter, praying it wouldn't occur to the shooter to fire through it. After a few feet he entered a long aisle of cold and cough supplies. The good thing about a double-barrel was that after two shots it had to be reloaded, and reloading was a pain in the ass, especially if you were an amateur all hopped up on adrenaline. Mark scooped a bottle of cough syrup off the shelf by his head and hurled it toward the door.

Another explosion, the shot wild. The window shattered, glass peppering the floor by the door. Movement across the room—and another shot. A puff of packaging exploded a few feet above him.

Mark jumped to his feet and lunged for the counter. He slid across it and landed in a crouch. Turned and found himself facing a girl in her twenties. Shorts peeked out the bottom of her white coat. Her hair was pulled back in a ponytail, glasses askew on the bridge of her nose.

She fumbled frantically with a shotgun shell, trying to chamber it.

He grabbed the gun by the muzzle and pulled, yanking her off balance. She splayed out on all fours, glasses falling to the floor. One more tug and the shotgun was his. He palmed a few shells, tucking them in his pocket before chambering two.

"Por favor, señor," she said, scrambling away from him. *"No me moleste."*

"Tranquila," he said, before calling out, "All clear!"

Decker's head popped up above the counter. "Jesus. Annie Oakley, huh?"

"Yeah." Mark glanced at her. Both hands covered her head, as if she were attempting to ward them off. "Tell her to relax. We gotta scramble, cops'll probably be here soon."

"Sure." Decker rattled off something in Spanish. Whatever he said didn't make the girl noticeably calmer. On the other side of the counter, the guard moaned.

"I'll handle him." Decker vanished. Mark grabbed a plastic bag from a stack below the register. He kept one eye on the girl as he scanned the locked, refrigerated cabinets. *"Antibióticos?"* he finally asked.

She didn't answer. He came closer, kneeling beside her. She avoided his eyes.

"Lady, the faster we get this stuff, the faster we leave," he said.

"You'll kill us anyway," she replied in surprisingly good English. "Fucking junkies."

"We just want to help our friend," Mark said. "Morphine, coagulants, antibiotics and we'll be out of your hair."

"Your friend was shot?"

He nodded. "We were kidnapped."

"So go to the police."

"I don't trust the police."

"Got the bandages and the phone," Decker called. "We ready?"

"Almost." Mark turned back to the cabinet. Toward the end of the row he spotted a bottle marked *Morfina*. He used the butt of the shotgun to shatter the case, causing the girl to suck in her breath sharply. Mark carefully stuck his hand in, avoiding the broken glass, and drew out two bottles.

Kaplan could live without anticoagulants, but antibiotics were crucial. If they could get him through the next few hours, Tyr would be able to reach them and he had a shot at surviving. But once infection started, it was tough to beat.

"Antibiotics?" he asked again. The girl refused to look at him. He reached back into the cabinet, swept an armful of bottles out and sent them crashing to the floor. They shattered in quick succession like bottle caps.

"Ay!" she cried. "They're over there!"

He followed her pointing finger and spotted the antibiotics in the opposite cabinet. Punched a hole in the glass again, then drew out two bottles. "Syringes?"

She motioned toward the drawers below the cabinet.

Mark tried one: locked. "You got a key, or should I shoot the lock?"

The girl fumbled in the pocket of her jacket. She drew out a key ring and tossed it to him.

He caught it, unlocked the drawer and slid it open. Grabbed a box of syringes and tossed them in the bag with the other stuff. Turning to leave, something caught his eye. He bent again, shifting the other boxes aside. The girl stiffened as he drew out a package: white powder wrapped in layers of plastic.

"Dude, we gotta bolt." Decker reappeared on the other side of the counter. "What's that?"

"The cops aren't coming, are they?" Mark asked.

The girl slowly shook her head.

"Los Zetas?"

Her expression shifted at the name, but she didn't reply.

"Shit," Decker said.

Mark's next words were interrupted by a spray of automatic weapon fire. He dived to the ground, landing hard. The counter in front of him bucked and splintered as dozens of rounds pumped through it. Over the barrage, he heard the girl screaming.

"They've been gone too long," Sock said. "Something went wrong."

"It's only been an hour," Flores replied. "Maybe there wasn't a pharmacy nearby."

"Yeah, or maybe they got smart and decided to ditch us. It'd be a hell of a lot easier to get out of this shithole if we weren't dragging around a guy with a gunshot wound."

"They'll be back." Flores turned his attention to Kaplan. The T-shirt he'd been using to apply pressure to the wound had soaked through. He replaced it with another from the stack Sock had stolen on his foray outside. Kaplan wasn't looking good. He was getting paler by the minute, more waxy-looking. He'd probably lost a few pints of blood by now. It was giving Flores a bad sense of déjà vu. A year ago he was in the mountains on the border of Pakistan and Afghanistan, running interference between the local warlords while trying to determine which of them was still Taliban. When their convoy was coming back from the nearest village, one of his buddies got hit by a sniper. They waited more than three hours for a Medevac chopper. As it was landing, his friend bled out. Kaplan had that same look now. If Riley and Decker didn't get back soon, he was done for.

Sock wasn't making the situation any easier. He'd returned ten minutes earlier with the T-shirts and some tacos he'd scrounged up, and hadn't stopped pacing since. This was Flores's second mission with Tyr, and the first time he'd worked with Sock. The guy struck him as a typical SEAL asshole, convinced he was better than everyone else because he could wear a scuba tank. He'd run into the type a lot since entering the service: didn't like them then, and couldn't stand working with them now.

The irony was that Flores had taken this job because it was supposed to be safer. He was sick of getting shot at in some sand-blasted country where everyone hated Americans. Now here he was, in his hometown, facing the same situation. You had to laugh.

He thought for a minute of Maryanne, six months pregnant and waiting for him. Wondered if Tyr had even told her that something went wrong. They promised to take care of relatives if anything happened to him; he'd felt pretty good filling out a whole stack of paperwork attesting to that. But you had to wonder. If the company could screw up an operation this badly, how good was their word?

Kaplan groaned. Flores lifted his head, forced the mouth of a water bottle between his lips and got a few drops down his throat.

"We should leave him," Sock said. "Riley and Decker might have gotten picked up again—we're probably still in Zetas territory. We get our hands on a phone, we can call in, get help."

"Why didn't you come back with a phone?" Flores asked.

"Didn't see any," Sock said defensively.

Flores didn't answer. It seemed off, that Sock could find T-shirts and tacos but hadn't managed to get his hands on the cell phone they really needed. But then, this whole operation had been screwy. None of them had discussed it yet, but clearly someone had set them up. That raid had gone too wrong too fast, like the Zetas knew they were coming. The question was, who told them? A member of the team, or someone higher up in the organization?

Flores furtively eyed Sock. Riley and Decker seemed okay, and Kaplan was just plain unlucky, first the broken ribs, now this. But Sock had been exhibiting odd behavior from day one.

Sock went to the doorway again and eased it open an inch to peer out.

"Shit." He yanked his head back.

"What?" Flores asked.

"We got company," Sock said grimly, pulling a handgun out of the waistband of his jeans shorts.

Before Flores could ask where the hell he'd gotten another gun, the door blew inward. Something hit the floor, then rolled toward them. He instinctively threw himself over Kaplan as the grenade came to a stop a few feet away.

"See? Nobody here," Syd said as they pulled on to the shoulder at the side of the highway.

Kelly didn't respond. Jake was driving, Maltz was beside her in the backseat. This time Syd had insisted on riding with them. "I know where we're going," she'd tossed over her shoulder, jumping in the front seat beside Jake.

It galled the hell out of Kelly, but she didn't say anything.

A steady stream of cars whipped past. Kelly realized she had yet to see a single police car, despite all their driving around the city.

"How do you know this is the spot?" Jake asked.

"GPS," Syd said. "Plus those." She pointed at a set of skid marks that started in the middle of the road and zoomed off the shoulder past them into the desert.

It was a desolate stretch of road, dusty scrub brush and trash running a few hundred yards to a line of dying trees. The building on the far end looked abandoned. Past the trees, Kelly discerned the bleats and rumbles of the city. To her left the terrain climbed sharply, barren foothills hunching out of the gritty soil.

They got out of the car. Kane had pulled up behind them in the second vehicle. He, Jagerson, Fribush and Maltz followed Syd as she marched off into the brush. They spread out, examining the ground in formation. Kelly picked her way behind them, avoiding a soiled diaper and empty fast-food containers. The van's tracks in the dirt were marred by the wheels of other vehicles and footprints: probably from emergency units that had responded to the crash.

"You okay?" Jake asked, coming up beside her.

"I'm fine," she lied. The constant sitting around in cars was wreaking havoc on her leg. It had stiffened up to the point that every step was torture, but she wasn't about to admit that to anyone.

"You're awfully quiet."

"There hasn't been much to say," Kelly retorted. "What with torturing storekeepers and leaving kidnap victims with their captors."

Jake grabbed her elbow, stopping her. "Why did you want to come?"

"You know why."

"I don't," he said, shaking his head. "I know you want to prove you can still do your job. But this isn't your job. This is my job. And clearly you hate it."

"It's not what I expected," she finally said.

"Outside U.S. borders things go down a little differently. Whether you like it or not, that's just how it is. If I want to save my brother and whoever else is with him, I've got to respect that."

"I know," Kelly said. "It's just—"

"Got something over here!" Syd was waving her arms a dozen yards from the tree line.

Jake took off at a trot. Kelly struggled to keep up, running a few steps alongside him before falling back. When she finally reached them, her face was flushed from the effort.

"Blood trail," Syd said. "They did a pretty good job covering it in the immediate vicinity of the crash, but it was probably still dark, they missed some spots."

"Where does it go?" Jake asked.

"More over here!" Fribush yelled from the tree line.

"So they went back to the city. Interesting choice," Syd said.

"They probably thought it would be easier to hide there until they got in touch with Tyr," Jake mused.

"Maybe they've already been picked up," Kelly said. "Is there any way to find out?"

"I would have gotten a call," Syd said. "Let's split up. You and Maltz each take a car and wait for us on the other side of these trees." Syd bent down and gazed through them. "Looks like there's a road a few hundred feet away, it should show up on the GPS."

"I'll go with you," Kelly said. "Have Kane take the car."

"Kelly—" Jake said.

"Your leg is bothering you," Syd said flatly. "Unless you rest it, you'll be useless."

"I'm fine," Kelly insisted.

"You're not. And part of the deal here is that I'm in charge of the unit's health. You injure yourself more, it makes everyone's life harder."

"But—"

"It's not a request, it's an order," Syd said.

The rest of the team stopped and looked up at her raised voice. Kelly's cheeks burned. She glanced at Jake, who shrugged.

"She's right, Kel. It's not personal, it's just—"

"Give me the keys." Kelly held out her hand.

He started to say something else, then shut his mouth and handed them over.

Kelly turned on her heel and marched back to the car. Despite her best efforts, she couldn't hide the limp. She fought back tears as she slid into the driver's seat. The worst part was that they were right: she wasn't capable enough to be here. From the look of things, she might never be able to do her job properly again. If their positions were reversed, she'd feel the same way: what was the point of having a partner who couldn't keep up? And if she was this useless, what the hell was she going to do with the rest of her life?

There was a rap at her window. Kelly turned to find Maltz peering down at her. She wiped away the tears with the back of her hand. *Great,* she thought. Not only was she crying, but she was doing it in front of the only person more messed up than she was. She rolled down the window.

"Syd can be a pain in the ass." Maltz bent over and crossed his arms on the window frame.

"She's right," Kelly said. "I'd hold them up."

"Maybe." He looked past her to where the others had vanished into the tree line. "It's tough, huh?"

"Yes," Kelly said. "It is."

"Hang in there." Maltz cuffed her lightly on the shoulder. "It'll get better." He turned and walked back toward the second car.

"Are you sorry?" Kelly blurted out.

He stopped and turned. "Sorry that I made it?"

She instantly regretted the question, but nodded.

"Every day. But what the hell, right?" He grinned at her. In spite of herself, Kelly grinned back. He tossed her a salute, then kept walking. Kelly watched as he got into the driver's seat. In spite of everything, she felt better.

Eight

The automatic gunfire went on and on, but as far as Mark could tell no one had entered the store. They seemed dead set on making sure there were no survivors before risking it. The counter in front of him had been punctured by dozens of bullets; it was a small miracle he hadn't been hit yet. He hoped Decker had been as lucky.

Mark had landed a few feet from the girl. She was facing him, hands over her ears, face twisted in a rictus of fear. She hadn't stopped screaming since the shooting started. The plastic bag full of meds had landed near him. He grabbed it, tucking it in the back pocket of his jeans. Hopefully some of the bottles had survived the fall. Mark checked to make sure he still had the spare shells for the shotgun, then reached out and grabbed her arm. She started at the contact.

"Is there another way out?" he yelled over the noise.

The girl didn't appear to have heard him. He dragged himself closer, shouting directly into her ear. "We have to get out. Is there a back door?"

"They'll kill me!" she yelled back.

"They'll kill you anyway," he shouted. He could see her thinking it over, realizing he was right.

Decker scuttled around what remained of the counter.

"You hurt?" Mark yelled.

Decker shook his head. "The guard bought it, though."

The girl scrambled forward on her belly. Mark motioned for Decker to follow. Wherever she was going, it couldn't be worse than here.

There was a sudden lull in the fire. Mark peeked through one of the holes in the counter and saw boots crossing the threshold into the store. He hustled after Decker.

The girl had crawled into a back room the size of a closet. Once inside, she scrambled to her feet and started tugging at a pile of boxes on the floor. "Help me!" she cried, exasperated. Decker helped push them aside. Underneath lay a trapdoor. The girl hauled it up and descended a steep flight of metal stairs. Decker followed. Mark went last, pulling the door closed behind them and turning the bolt. It wouldn't hold their attackers off for long, but might buy them a few minutes.

The stairs ran through a concrete shaft. The air was cold, dank. The girl hit a switch and low-level bulbs flickered on.

"What is this?" he asked.

"The pharmacy used to be a bar. This was where they stored the liquor," she said.

"Which way out?" Decker asked.

She pointed, and Mark pushed past her. Up ahead, a short flight of stairs led to a set of double doors, bolted from the inside. A smooth ramp ran parallel to them.

"For kegs," she explained.

The sound of thumping metal behind them: someone was trying the door. Voices shouted orders in Spanish. Then the steady pound of bullets against metal.

"Where does this come out?" Mark asked.

"Follow me." She unbolted the lock and pushed the doors open.

It took a second for Mark's eyes to adjust to daylight. He focused on Decker, running ahead of him down the long alley behind the store. A line of metal service doors abutted overflowing Dumpsters. A few doors down a guy in a soiled apron smoked a cigarette in an open doorway. Through slitted eyes, he watched them pass.

The girl led them to the end of the block, took a sharp right down a narrow street, then hooked left. Mark and Decker trotted behind her, guns held down by their sides. At any moment Mark expected to feel bullets tearing through him from behind. The few people they passed took them in, then quickly looked away. Didn't want to get involved, Mark gathered. He'd seen the same thing in Iraq and Afghanistan, people so acclimated to violence they went about their everyday lives as if it wasn't happening all around them.

The girl set a good pace, weaving with the confidence of a native through a maze of crumbling adobe buildings. After five solid minutes of running she ducked under the metal fence surrounding a dilapidated warehouse. Decker and Mark followed. She eased aside a door that dangled on its hinges and came to a stop in the middle of the room.

It was an old factory, long abandoned by the look of things. In the far corner a rat scratched at something in an oily puddle. It glanced up at them, then returned its attention to lunch.

"Where are we?" Decker asked.

It was a good question. They'd taken so many turns that even with his infallible sense of direction Mark would be hard-pressed to find true north.

"El Eden," the girl responded.

"Is that still in Mexico City?" Mark asked.

"You really were kidnapped, weren't you?" The girl examined them more closely. "You're in Iztapalapa. It's one of the *delegaciones*."

"The ninth borough," Mark said, remembering the map he'd studied prior to the mission.

"Shit, we barely moved at all." Decker barked a short laugh.

He was right. The rescue mission had been launched in the southern section of Iztapalapa. They were probably less than two miles from where this all began.

"Thanks for getting us out of there," Mark said. "Now we gotta get back to our friend."

"I didn't hear about any Americans getting kidnapped recently." Her eyes narrowed. "And you don't look like *turistas*."

Decker was tearing open the packaging for the phone they'd taken from the store. He squinted at the instructions. "Do I need a code or something for this thing?"

"It only works if it's activated at the register."

"Crap," Decker said.

The girl drew a cell phone out of her jacket pocket and tossed it to him.

"Thanks," he said. "What's your name, anyway?"

"Isabela Garcia," she said. "Who are you calling?"

"A friend."

Mark waved him over, keeping an eye on Isabela. "I don't think we should call Tyr," he said in a low voice.

"Why not?" Decker's brow furrowed.

"Because there's a leak. The mission went south because someone set us up. Until we know who, I don't trust the organization."

"Then how the hell do we get out of here?" Decker asked dubiously.

"We call my brother," Mark said. "He's got his own K&R firm, he can help." He didn't add that they hadn't spoken in years. Jake could be a jerk sometimes, but in a situation like this he'd put his personal feelings aside. At least, Mark was hoping he would.

"All right." Decker handed him the phone. He jerked his head toward Isabela. "What do we do with her?"

"We wish her the best and send her home."

He started to dial, but was interrupted by Isabela. Arms crossed over her chest, she said, "You're here for Cesar Calderon, aren't you?"

The room erupted in smoke and blinding lights. Flores squeezed his eyes shut. His ears rang, which he took as a good sign. A real grenade would have separated them from his head. A flashbang, then. Thank God for small favors.

Shouts all around him. Flores squinted to see through the tears streaming down his face. Latino men in a motley assortment of camouflage streamed through the door, bandannas tied over their mouths. They were brandishing automatic weapons. He groaned—déjà vu all over again.

Sock was facing the wall. He'd dropped the gun and crossed his hands behind his head. One of the guys kicked his knees in from behind, then leaned over and whispered something in his ear. Sock replied in a low voice. The man glanced up, saw Flores watching. He walked over, swinging his gun back as if it were a bat.

A thousand stars exploded in Flores's head as the butt of it made contact with his skull.

"What now?" Jake asked.

They'd emerged on the outskirts of Iztapalapa, in a

neighborhood labeled San Miguel Teotongo on the map. The blood trail they'd been following had petered out on the other side of the tree line. Either Mark's team had made more of an effort to cover their tracks, or somehow they'd managed to stem the bleeding. There was a third option, that whoever had been spilling so much blood was abandoned, but knowing his brother Jake doubted it. One thing Mark had always taken seriously was the precept to leave no man behind. Syd had someone in her network checking local hospitals just in case.

They were back to square one.

"Maybe they already made contact with Tyr," Jake said. "We could call them directly and ask."

"I doubt they'd tell us anything," Syd snorted. "Besides, my guy there said he'd call if anything changed. And I haven't heard from him yet."

"We could canvass the area," Fribush said.

"And what, ask if anyone saw a bunch of injured Americans stumbling around?" Syd shook her head. "We stay out here, we risk running into the Zetas looking for them. We need to regroup."

"If one of them is bleeding, they'd start by trying to patch him up," Jake said thoughtfully. "We could scope out the pharmacies."

"Good." Syd spun on her heels. "Let's get back to the cars."

Maltz had reported their position via radio a few minutes before. Syd led the four of them through a dusty lot and around an adobe building that was in the process of melting back into the earth. She stopped short, and Jake nearly crashed into her.

"Christ, Syd," he grumbled. Then he saw what had stopped her. Kelly and Maltz were next to one of their cars, hands on their heads. They were surrounded by more than a dozen men bearing automatic weapons.

Syd reacted before he did, an H&K materializing in her hands. She shoved Jake back, ducking down beside the building. Kane, Fribush and Jagerson followed her lead, guns ready. Jake fumbled with the Glock tucked in his ankle holster.

"You think they saw us?" he asked.

As if in response, a spray of bullets sent chunks of masonry jumping off the building a few feet away. Jake scrambled back. Kelly yelled something, and his jaw clenched. If they were hurting her...

"Zetas?" Syd asked.

"Couldn't tell." Jake grunted.

"Kane, you and Jagerson circle around. Fribush, see if you can get up high, find a nest to snipe from."

"This is nuts, Syd. There are at least a dozen of them," Jake protested.

The other men exchanged glances. Kane shrugged, then the three of them trotted toward the rear of the building.

"They'll kill Kelly and Maltz," Jake said. "You're setting us up for a bloodbath."

"We don't have a lot of other options."

"We have one." Jake dropped his gun. Before Syd could stop him, he stood and rounded the corner, hands held high.

"No dispare!" he called out, hoping that was the polite way to ask them not to shoot.

Two of them kept their guns trained on Maltz and Kelly, the rest swiveled, aiming for his chest. Jake stopped ten feet away. *"Soy* Jake Riley," he said. *"Americano."*

A tall black man stepped forward. He lowered his gun

slightly, but kept his finger on the trigger. "Good for you," he said. "Now maybe you can explain what the hell you're doing here."

"What about Cesar Calderon?" Decker raised the LMT, pointing it at Isabela's chest.

She looked back at him defiantly. "Everyone knows he was kidnapped. Los Zetas have him."

"Lady, we don't know what you're talking about," Mark said. "Now why don't you—"

"They have my father, too," she said. "That's what the cocaine was for. I was trying to raise the ransom money."

"Sorry to hear about your dad," Mark said. "But we've got to get back to our friend."

"They'll kill him now, because of you." Her chin quivered. "They'll know I helped you. You've ruined everything."

"Tell you what," Mark said. "I'm going to call my brother, and he might be able to help."

"The way you helped Calderon?" she spat.

"That's not very nice," Decker commented.

"I heard what you said…you don't trust your own organization."

"Yeah, well, my brother's part of a different one," Mark said. "And him I trust. Tell us where we can reach you, and we'll make sure someone helps your father."

"I know where they are keeping Calderon," Isabela said. "Take me with you, and I will tell you."

"Lady—"

"It's not safe for me here now," she argued. "I cannot go home, they will be waiting there."

"What about relatives?"

"There's no one besides my father. If you do not take me, I will be killed," she said flatly.

"Crap." Mark rubbed his forehead with one hand. He'd done missions all over the globe, in places as far-flung as Panama and Bali. He'd thought nothing could get worse than the disaster that was Somalia. Yet none of his missions had ever gotten as messed up as this. What he'd give for a nice little underwater raid.

"Fine," he said, after processing it for a minute. Decker started to object, but Mark cut him off with a sharp look. "She's right, we can't leave her."

He moved in close, lowering his voice and filling it with menace. "But if it turns out you're lying, and you don't know where Calderon is, or if we find out you're working for the Zetas, I'll put a bullet in your head myself."

Isabela's eyes widened and she nodded once, stiffly. Mark stepped back and dug the plastic bag out of his pocket. One of the morphine bottles had shattered, but everything else remained intact. He flipped open the phone and dialed. Stepping away from the two of them, he waited as it rang.

"I need to talk to Jake Riley. Tell him it's his brother."

Decker and Isabela watched him, standing in silence a few feet apart.

"No, the other brother." Mark's brow furrowed at the response. "What the hell is he doing in Mexico City?"

Nine

Flores awoke with a throbbing headache. He groaned and shook his head to clear his vision.

He was in the back compartment of a large truck. Wherever they were going, the road was bumpy as hell. He'd been stuffed between two rough burlap sacks, probably to keep him from flopping around while unconscious, which struck him as surprisingly courteous. His hands were bound again, this time behind his back.

Shit, Flores thought with a sinking feeling.

Two other men occupied the space with him, both dressed in military fatigues and bearing LMTs. One couldn't have been more than eighteen years old. The other was the guy who tried to blow up the van that morning.

The older man noticed he'd awoken. His eyes narrowed under the brim of his khaki cap, but he didn't say anything.

"Mi amigo," Flores tried. *"Con la herida de bala. Y el otro. Dónde están?"*

There was no response.

"Adónde vamos?" Flores asked.

The man jerked his head toward the kid. He stumbled

over, bracing himself against the side of the truck as it bounced. Reaching Flores, he held up a roll of duct tape.

"Cállete," he said.

The message was clear. Flores fell silent. The compartment was stuffy enough without having to struggle to breathe. They weren't worried about him crying for help, since they didn't insist on gagging him. They just weren't interested in conversation.

They drove for hours, the road worsening until their pace slowed to a crawl. At one point they ascended so steeply he had to wrap his legs around one of the sacks to avoid being thrown against the rear door. Flores had never been prone to motion sickness. But riding in that windowless compartment, head still pounding from the blow he'd received, more than once he almost gagged up the tacos from that morning.

When they finally came to a stop, Flores felt a wave of relief. It dissipated as soon as the door slid open and he saw where he was.

Judging by the sun's angle it was midafternoon. Light sheared through reams of barbed wire, stretching as far as he could see in either direction. Long lines of metal pens extended away from him. They looked like kennels—but instead of dogs, people were clustered in each. Most were filthy, their clothing worn to rags.

Next to the drug trade, kidnapping was one of Mexico's biggest industries. Tyr had given a seminar when he first signed on, including a PowerPoint presentation filled with photos of jungle prison camps like the one he now faced. Captives were kept there for months or years as negotiations for their release dragged on. Thanks to the squalid living conditions, some of the hostages died long before their relatives managed to scrounge up a ransom payment.

At least in Mexico City, there was a chance that Tyr would track them down and rescue them. Here, Flores harbored no such delusions. It would take an army to free anyone from this camp.

A shove from behind sent him flying. With hands bound, there was no way to catch himself. Flores landed hard in the dirt, his knees bearing the brunt of the impact.

A pair of boots appeared an inch from his nose. Flores followed them up to find the van passenger staring down at him. He'd pegged him as a hard guy, someone you'd never mess with in a bar fight. He looked plenty pissed now.

"Sígame," he said.

Flores stumbled to his feet and followed him along the dirt road. No point playing hero, he had to survive long enough to figure out an escape plan. For some reason, they were keeping him alive. He couldn't imagine why, but as long as it worked in his favor he wasn't about to question it.

People lined up at the pen doors as they passed, hands clutching the chicken wire. They watched his progress, but no one said a word. There were men, women, children of all ages.

They were in the mountains somewhere, a swath of land reclaimed from the jungle. It was even hotter here than in Mexico City, Flores's shirt instantly soaked through. His eyes panned from side to side, taking in his surroundings. They passed a guard tower manned by two men, then another soldier on foot patrol. The guy slammed the butt of his rifle against random cages as he passed, causing the inmates to shy back. As Flores walked, he mentally composed a map of the facility.

The passenger finally stopped in front of a pen identical to the others. Six feet high, maybe ten feet long, eight feet wide. He nodded for the guard accompanying them to open the gate, then motioned Flores inside.

Flores took a deep breath and walked in, head bowed. The door swung shut behind him and was rebolted. A double lock, he noted. The chicken wire wasn't thick, but a hundred feet away stood another guard tower constructed of rough-hewn beams. He watched as a muzzle scanned the pens in a long arc, then swept back. The guards seemed to be on top of things. Still, they couldn't always be vigilant. He'd suss out their rotations, try to determine possible escape routes. Figure out the pen's weaknesses and how to exploit them. Then at the first opportunity, he'd slip away. Flores had years' worth of training, and it was a hell of a lot easier to survive in a jungle than the desert. One way or another, he told himself, he was making it out of here.

"Hatching a plan?" a voice behind him asked in English.

Startled, Flores spun around. A man ducked out of the sheltered rear of the pen. His clothes hung off him in shreds, and a thick beard draped down to his chest. Despite that, Flores recognized him immediately.

"Cesar Calderon," the man said, extending his hand. "Nice to meet you."

Ten

"I'm Jake Riley, CEO of The Longhorn Group."

Jake caught a flash of recognition in the black man's eyes. He was tall, nearly six-three, muscles bulging out the sleeves of his camos. He glared down at Jake.

Jake started to lower his arms, but the gun muzzles weren't coming down. He ended up with them in front of his chest, palms forward.

"You're clearly lost, Mr. Riley," the guy said. "Museums are on the other side of town."

"You're from Tyr," Jake said. "Right?"

"Jake—" Kelly called out.

"We're all on the same team here." Jake chanced a small step forward.

The man cocked an eyebrow. "Last I checked, I didn't work for The Longhorn Association."

"Group," Jake said. "The Longhorn—"

"Whatever. I don't give a shit what you're doing here, you're in our way."

From behind him, Syd called out, "Take it down a few notches, Brown."

Frowning, the man shifted his aim. "Syd Clement. Should have known."

"Miss me?"

Jake turned slightly. Syd was edging out from the side of the building. Despite the odds her gun was drawn, zeroed in on Brown's chest. She approached slowly, placing her feet like she was walking a tightrope.

"She with you?" the guy asked, talking to Jake but keeping his focus on Syd.

"That depends," Jake replied. "How do you two know each other?"

"Kiev. She nearly got my client's kid killed."

"The girl was fine, Brown. I can't believe you still even remember that."

"No thanks to you," Brown retorted. "Syd nearly blew the whole raid. Told the head guy about it in advance, just so he'd let her at his hard drive."

"National security was at stake." Syd shrugged.

"Yeah, so to hell with everyone else. They had five hostages, including our girl," Brown told Jake. "If I hadn't moved up the start time of the operation, they all would have died. Fucking CIA."

"Never been a big fan of them myself," Jake said. "I was FBI."

"They're even worse," Brown said. "Even you can do the math, Syd. Drop the gun."

"I got a whole unit ready to pick you off." Syd jerked her head toward the nearest building. Jake looked up and saw Fribush aiming down at them. He lifted his free hand in a wave.

"Great," Jake muttered under his breath.

"There are five more just like him," Syd said. "You won't even be able to tell where the shots are coming from."

"They start firing, you're out a CEO," Brown said.

Syd shrugged. "They grow on trees, especially in this economy."

"We're looking for Mark Riley," Kelly called out. She'd lifted her head, but her hands remained on the roof of the car. "And we know you are, too."

"So?" Brown said after a minute.

"So we should help each other."

Brown tilted his head back and laughed openly. "Then we can all join hands and sing a song. This ain't the Scouts, honey. You should leave this to the people who know what the fuck they're doing."

"Good point. Any advice on how to lose a whole unit?" Syd said.

Brown looked pained. "Wouldn't have happened on my watch."

"Sure it wouldn't. Sounds to me like someone at Tyr sold them out. Maybe you're next."

A van turned down the street. They all shifted their attention to it. Jake waited for the driver to pull a one-eighty when he saw the firepower on display. When the van continued forward, he frowned.

"What the—"

The street in front of them was suddenly torn up, bullets ricocheting off the pavement.

"Kelly!" Jake yelled, scanning the chaos for her red hair.

Everyone had scattered, breaking for cover. A member of the Tyr unit had taken a hit. He writhed on the ground, clutching his leg. Brown charged forward and grabbed him under the armpits, dragging him off the road.

Jake finally spotted Kelly cowering beside the nearest rental car, Maltz beside her. He bent over and said something in her ear, then grabbed her hand. Maltz slid open the car door and shoved her inside.

Jake paused for a second, deliberating. For the moment, Kelly was as safe as any of them. Safer, maybe, if they could get to the backup weapons in the car. Syd had raced behind the closest building. He followed her, wishing he'd held on to his gun.

The van was approaching fast, gaining speed. When it was less than a hundred yards away, Fribush and Jagerson returned fire from their rooftop sniper nests. Their bullets tore gaping holes in the van. The windshield shattered, but the occupants didn't stop firing. Worse yet, the van continued accelerating.

Jake watched as the van suddenly veered crazily from side to side. It was going nearly fifty miles an hour when it hit the car Kelly and Maltz were in, climbing onto the trunk before flipping over and crushing the roof.

Jake was on his feet and running before the tires stopped spinning.

"Jake!" Syd yelled from behind him, but he didn't stop. The van rested on its side across the roof of the car, hood slanted toward the ground. Jake saw a bloody hand trying to force the side panel open from the inside. Belatedly he realized that there were probably still armed men alive inside. And in all the excitement, he'd neglected to collect his gun.

Something whistled past his ear. There was a smattering of fire from behind him. Someone inside the van yelped in pain.

Syd came up alongside him.

"Thanks," he said.

"Later. You check the car, I'll cover you." Syd squeezed

off a few rounds into the side of the van. The bloody hand flopped down.

Jake dropped to his knees beside the rental car. The top had been completely crushed by the weight of the van, every window shattered. "Kelly!"

Jake tried to open the car door, but as he pulled on it the van groaned, shifting slightly. "Christ," he muttered, skittering back. The van swayed, then stilled. Jake moved forward again, warily trying the front passenger door. If he could maneuver into the car, he could help them out of the backseat….

His hand was on the door handle when Kelly called his name. She walked out of the alley across the street.

"How the hell…"

"We went straight through the car." Kelly ran up and wrapped her arms around him. "Michael thought it would be safer over there."

Jake buried his face in her hair and dug a hand into it. Maltz stood silent a few feet away. "Thanks," Jake said over her head. Privately he thought, *Michael?*

"No problem." Maltz nodded. "Any survivors in the van?"

The Tyr unit had reemerged from the shadows. Two of them attended to their fallen comrade, tightening a tourniquet around his leg to staunch the bleeding. The rest edged toward the van, guns up and ready.

"Ayúdenme!" A voice pleaded from the interior.

On a three count, four members of the Tyr team shoved the van hard. The front left fender hit the ground first, followed by the rest of it. It kicked up a cloud of dust as it settled.

"Sal!" Brown called out. *"Y no lo matamos."*

After a minute, a Mexican in army fatigues crawled

out the hole where the windshield had been. Shakily he stood, arms high.

"I hurt!" he called in a thick accent. "Hospital."

Brown walked forward and grabbed him by the collar. "Trust me, my friend, you'll hurt a hell of a lot more when we're done with you."

Eleven

Kelly stood next to Jake, watching the Tyr team mobilize. They were organizing in almost complete silence, as if the assignments were being transmitted telepathically. She had to admit they looked impressive. Matching uniforms, even. Two of them stood guard over the guy who had climbed out of the van.

"They're taking him?"

"Looks like it," Jake said.

"What are we going to do about it?"

"I'm still working on that," Jake said. His cell phone rang. He fumbled with it, frowning at the caller ID.

"Who is it?" Kelly asked.

"Work."

"What, now?"

He shrugged. "Must be important. They're not supposed to bother me unless something directly related to the case comes in."

Jake stepped away to answer it. While he was speaking, Syd joined her. They watched as the survivor's hands were zip tied behind his back. "How'd Tyr get the jump on you two?" she asked without looking at Kelly.

"They came up from behind while we were waiting for you."

"Huh," Syd said. "I gotta have a chat with Maltz about that."

"He didn't do anything wrong," Kelly said defensively. "There were too many of them. Anyway, we were handling it before you showed up."

"Sure you were," Syd said. "You had everything under control."

Kelly was about to retort but Syd had already turned away, eyes narrowed.

The Tyr team was melting back into the spaces between buildings. Two of them cradled the injured team member in their arms. Two others escorted the new captive away. The rest were gathered around Brown. Syd marched over to him. Warily, Kelly followed.

"Going somewhere?" Syd asked, arms crossed.

"Even in this neighborhood, the *federales* will show up at some point," Brown said without bothering to look at her. "Time to move out."

"Bullshit," Syd said. "You're sharing him."

"Or what, your team will take us out?" He smirked. "I think that ship sailed, Clement."

"This is ridiculous," Kelly said. "If we pool resources, we all get what we want."

"Who's your friend?" Brown asked, finally making eye contact.

"FBI," Syd said dismissively.

"That explains it," Brown said. "Didn't realize they were making them cuter."

"She's engaged." Syd jerked her head toward Jake. "To him."

"Yeah?" Brown eyed Kelly. "I don't see it."

"I know, right?"

"Excuse me?" Kelly interrupted. "Can we finish discussing what we're going to do here?"

"Nothing to discuss, lady," Brown said. "We'll drop you a line when we recover our hostages. Have a nice flight home."

Jake reappeared, slipping an arm around her waist. Kelly could tell by his expression that something had happened, but it was hard to say if it was good or bad.

"Let's go," Jake said to Syd.

Her hackles rose. "Screw that. I'm not letting them—"

"We don't need them," Jake said. He rubbed Kelly's back reassuringly.

"This is bullshit, Jake."

"Seriously, Syd. Let it go." He stepped away from Kelly and grabbed Syd's elbow, steering her toward their sole remaining rental car.

"What's going on?" Brown asked.

"None of your concern, apparently," Kelly said.

She followed Jake and Syd, sensing the weight of Brown's eyes on her back.

Syd continued protesting as Jake propelled her into the passenger seat. "Radio Jagerson, Fribush and Kane, tell them to meet us at the corner of Maria Eugenia and De Los Angeles. It's about a click away."

"This is crap, Riley," she grumbled. "We could have taken them."

Despite that, she picked up the radio and relayed the instructions.

Jake held the rear door open for Kelly and she climbed in. Maltz slid in the other side. He glanced at her, and she shrugged. Jake climbed into the driver's seat and pulled away. Brown remained stock-still in the middle of the street, watching them leave. As they turned the corner, Jake said, "I told you, we don't need them."

"Are you kidding? They've got someone to interrogate. That guy might tell them where your brother is."

"That's what I'm saying, Syd." A grin split Jake's face as he said, "I don't need anyone to tell me. I already know."

"What?"

"We're on our way to meet Mark now. Then we can get out of this shithole," Jake said, "and Brown can do whatever the hell he wants."

Twelve

"I know who you are," Flores said. "I actually work for you."

"Really?" Calderon's eyebrows shot up. "In what capacity?"

"Special Ops."

Calderon laughed sharply. "Let me guess," he said. "You're here to rescue me."

"It's a long story," Flores replied uncomfortably. The irony of the situation wasn't lost on him. As far as he knew, Kaplan was dead, Riley and Decker were captured or killed, and Sock…who the hell knew where Sock was? What he'd witnessed earlier didn't bode well for the guy's innocence. And the fact that Sock wasn't here rendered him all the more guilty in Flores's eyes. If there was another Tyr unit in the country, they were probably still scouring Mexico City for them. All in all, he had no good news to offer.

"I'll get us out of here," Flores finally replied. With a sinking feeling, he realized that encountering Calderon complicated his escape plan a thousandfold. Alone, he'd easily survive a few weeks in the jungle. But Calderon had to be in his late fifties, and the weeks he'd already spent in captivity had clearly taken a toll. He was gaunt, emaciated. He'd only slow Flores down. He flashed back on Maryanne's face again.

"That's all right, son." Calderon patted his shoulder awkwardly. "We've had lots of practice getting people back from places like this. I'm sure Linus Smiley is on top of it."

"I'm sure he is, sir," Flores said. He debated how much to tell him about his suspicions. Calderon was already in bad shape, he decided. No need to worry him, especially when there wasn't a damn thing they could do about the situation.

"I'm surprised they haven't come for proof of life, though," Calderon mused. "I have to say, if I was on the other side of this, I'd be wondering what the hell is going on. I'm guessing the board isn't taking it well."

"I wouldn't know, sir," Flores said.

"No, of course you wouldn't." Calderon smiled wanly. "Well, at least now I have someone to pass the time with. Do you play chess?"

Flores shook his head.

"Then this is the perfect opportunity to learn." Calderon went to the rear of the pen. After scrounging around for a minute, he produced a rolled up piece of felt. Carrying it back, he carefully unfurled it. Squares had been drawn on in chalk. Some of the pieces were recognizable, others were just chips of wood.

"I haven't had time to carve the entire set," Calderon said apologetically. "And part of me is hoping I won't get the chance to finish. You should see the one I have at home. Mahogany, with—"

"They gave you a knife?" Flores interrupted, his mind immediately clicking through the possibilities.

"I traded for some cigarettes. It's not very sharp," he

said. "Some of the guards are better than others. If you need anything, I can discreetly ask around."

"Thanks," Flores said.

"Not a problem. Now, let me show you how to set up the board. Chess takes a minute to learn and a lifetime to master…"

Flores tuned out Calderon's chatter as he watched him fastidiously arrange the motley pieces on the felt. There was something off about the guy. Maybe it just stemmed from spending weeks in this hellhole, but still—this was a man who had developed a reputation as the master of K&R work worldwide. Flores would never have guessed that he'd spend his confinement patiently awaiting a rescue—playing chess, no less. Wouldn't he want to seize the opportunity to help plan an escape? What the hell was going on here? Flores's mind shifted back to their failed raid. Maybe Sock had sold them out on orders from above. Maybe the entire thing was a setup. But why?

"Your move," Calderon said with a grin.

Syd leaned against the wall nearest the door observing the reunion. It was far from warm, despite the circumstances. Of course, if she ran into a family member out in the field, it would probably go down the same way.

They were in a dingy motel room at the intersection of Maria Eugenia and De Los Angeles. The neighborhood hadn't improved much from where they spent the morning, and this motel was no exception. In comparison, the place they stayed in yesterday was practically a Four Seasons. Cement flooring peeked through worn patches in the brown rug. The bed sloped distinctly to the right and sported a comforter that didn't appear to have been laundered since the Kennedy administration. Music blared from a battered clock radio that Jake had set to something tinny to cover their discussion. Mark winced when he turned it on, but didn't say anything. There was a funky smell, too—funny how cheap motel rooms all shared the same tang of cigarette smoke, stale food, body odor and something else she couldn't quite pin down.

Eight of them packed into the space made it all the more comical. Maltz, Jagerson, Fribush and Kane had finally excused themselves, said they'd keep an eye out for hostiles. Syd suspected they just needed some air.

The Feeb sat on the bed rubbing her leg, looking even more agitated than usual. Syd watched her fidget. What could possibly be eating her now? They'd accomplished what they'd set out to do and emerged unscathed. In her book, that counted as a win.

Mark Riley was better looking than Syd had expected. About an inch taller than Jake, with more muscle packed on a similar frame. Same blue eyes, hair almost completely gray, but otherwise they could have passed for twins. Right now they even shared the same pissed-off look. *Ah, family,* she thought with a sigh. *Always a drag.*

"You're not hearing me," Mark growled.

"I heard you just fine," Jake retorted. "Your men weren't there when you got back, so you're assuming the Zetas caught up with them. But maybe they had to move because their location was compromised, and they had no way of letting you know. Maybe they managed to get in touch with Tyr, and they're already on a plane home. You're making a lot of assumptions here."

"Kaplan was there," Mark argued. "Still warm. And the room stank from a flash bang."

"Fine." Jake rubbed his eyes wearily. "So the Zetas got them again. Or someone else did. What the hell can you do about it?"

"I'm not leaving them here," Mark said.

"They have my father, too," the girl chimed in. "I know where they've probably taken them."

Syd eyed her. Pretty thing, a little mousy but with good bone structure. Somehow she'd already managed to wrap Mark Riley around her little finger, that was clear.

"What was your name again?" Jake asked.

"Isabela," she said, drawing herself up. Syd smirked at the gesture. It was impossible to look imposing when you were five-four, but she gave her credit for trying.

"No offense, Isabela, but I came to get my brother back. Mission accomplished. Now I just want to get the hell out of here." Jake plunked down on the bed beside Kelly.

"Well, I'm staying." Mark glanced at the other surviving member of his team, who nodded. "Decker, too. If you could loan us some weapons—"

"Jesus Christ." Jake exhaled deeply. "These guys beat you before, and that was when you had a full team. Two of you going after them like this is suicide, it won't matter if we give you bazookas."

"I'll take a bazooka," Decker interjected. "You got any?"

"No, but we can lend you a few AKs," Syd said.

"That'll work," Decker said. "Much appreciated."

Jake shot a glare at her. "You're not helping."

She shrugged. "They're going whether you want them to or not."

"At least tell me you'll join up with the rest of your guys. Brown had two units with him," Jake said. Decker and Mark exchanged a look. "What?"

"Not sure we can trust Tyr," Mark finally responded. "That's why I called you."

Jake examined a bare patch of floor by his feet. "Where

do you think they're being held?" he finally asked, raising his eyes.

"Jake," Kelly said warningly.

"They have a prison camp in the Veracruz mountains. It's about two hundred miles northeast of here," Isabela said. "I know they have my father there."

"How do you know?" Syd asked.

Isabela turned, appraising her. "A friend with information on Los Zetas told me."

Huh, Syd thought. Despite her mousy appearance, the girl had a certain look about her that Syd recognized. And it wasn't that of a scared novice in way over her head. She wondered why the hell Isabela was so gung ho for them to raid this camp.

"A prison camp," Jake said. "So we're talking dozens of guards, at least."

Isabela glanced at Mark before replying. "Probably more," she said. "It's inside one of their main bases."

"Fantastic," Jake said. "How the hell are you gonna grab your guys and get out without a dozen bullets in your back?"

"We'll come up with something. I've done it before," Mark reminded Jake. "Hell, I was doing this sort of thing when you were still in high school."

"Yeah, and look how well that worked out for you," Jake said.

Mark didn't reply, but his hands clenched into fists. Syd wondered again what the hell they'd been fighting about all these years. Whatever it was must be juicy.

"There's nothing I can say to stop you?" Jake sounded bone-weary.

"Nope."

"You should go with him," Kelly said. "Or at least let them have Kane and Jagerson."

"I'll go." Syd jumped in. Jake threw her a look. "What? I've got nothing better to do."

"Did you hear the part about this being a suicide mission? They're not even sure their guys are there," Jake argued.

"Yeah, well. I love to travel, and I've never seen that part of the country before."

"I can't commit any of my people to this," Jake said. "If they go, it's voluntarily."

"I'll ask them," Syd offered. She strolled outside, the silence behind her thick enough to cut with a knife. It was a relief to close the door. Times like this reminded her why she'd cut off contact with her own family.

Syd strolled down the cement path in front of the rooms, her guard up. Dusk had fallen, and with it dozens of neon signs flared to life down the street. Theirs was still the only car in the parking lot.

"Hey," someone said in a low voice.

She turned to find Maltz tucked into an alcove that once housed a vending machine, stray wires still dangled from the wall.

"Where are the others?"

"Fribush crashed out in the car and Jagerson and Kane went for a beer. Figured if anything went down they'd be close enough to hear it. How's it going in there?"

"Remind me never to host them for Thanksgiving," Syd said.

Maltz made a sound that she recognized as his version of a laugh. "Close call today," she said. "How you holding up?"

"I've had closer."

His eyes were cast in shadow. Still, Syd detected a shift in his voice. "Here's the deal," she said. "Riley Senior wants to go looking for his men. He thinks they're in a prison camp crawling with Zetas up in the mountains. They're looking for volunteers."

"You going?"

Syd grinned. "How could I not?"

"Then I'm in."

"You sure?" Syd asked. "Odds aren't good."

"Gotta die sometime, right?" Maltz said.

"Hopefully not tomorrow," Syd said. "I got a hell of a 401K going now. You do, too."

"My dog will live well, then."

"You have a dog?" The thought was preposterous.

"Sabine. She's a French bulldog."

An image of Maltz strolling along behind a tiny white dog popped into Syd's head and she cracked up.

"Go ahead and laugh. She's tough as they come."

"I'm sure." Syd wiped a tear from her cheek. "It's good to have you back, Maltz. We get out of this, I'm buying you one of those doggie purses to carry her around in."

"I'm man enough to handle that."

"I figured. Stay here, I'll go check with Kane and Jagerson."

"They'll come," Maltz said.

"I know." Syd paused, wondering for a second if she'd completely lost her mind. She'd nearly gotten Maltz killed once before, and now she was dragging him into something that was really none of their business. If nothing else, that made her a lousy boss.

"Don't worry about it," Maltz said, as if reading her mind. "I'd be going anyway. You don't leave a man behind."

"These aren't our men," Syd reminded him.

"Might as well be."

"Yeah, I guess you're right."

Fribush was snoring in the reclined passenger seat of

their rental car. Opting to let him sleep, Syd walked down the block toward the bar. A beam of yellow light from the open door bisected the pavement. The jukebox inside sputtered out songs she recognized from her teens. *Christ,* she thought. *It's like entering a goddamn time machine.*

Kane and Jagerson sat on adjoining bar stools, the only patrons inside. In front of them two bottles of beer sweated beads of water. They fell silent as she approached. They were an odd pair. Kane was enormous, easily six-four, with a protruding brow, dark hair and big ears. Jagerson was smaller but wider, with close-cropped blond hair, freckles and green eyes. They couldn't have looked more out of place if they'd tried. It was no wonder the locals cleared out when they entered.

"Hiya, boss," Kane said. "All set in there?"

Syd ran down the situation for them, keeping her voice low. She knew from experience that whatever one decided, the other would follow.

"When do we move out?" Kane asked.

"Tomorrow at dawn," Syd said. "Tonight we'll need to resupply for the jungle."

"I'm on it," Kane said, sliding off the stool. Jagerson dumped a handful of pesos on the counter and they followed her out into the night.

The man's head snapped back from the blow. Blood streamed down his cheek from a cut below his eye. Linus wrinkled his nose in disgust. "Are you sure this is necessary?" he said. "I heard that torture doesn't work."

"This isn't torture, sir. It's the fine art of persuasion," Ellis Brown said.

The two of them stood in the far corner of the room observing the proceedings.

"What if he's telling the truth? He might not know where they're keeping Cesar."

"If he doesn't know, he can lead us to someone who does," Brown said. "It's all about climbing the food chain."

The man moaned. Linus had arrived ten minutes into the interrogation. His flight to Mexico City had been delayed twice en route. He was climbing out of his skin with frustration by the time the taxi dropped him off a few blocks away. Brown had secured an abandoned building on the outskirts of the district. Apparently the unit moved their base daily so as not to attract attention.

In spite of himself, Linus was secretly thrilled to be here. He was one of the few Tyr employees without any military- or covert-operations experience. His years at the Agency had been spent compiling reports. He'd managed to claw his way up the ladder via sheer force of will, by being better at his job than everyone else. Linus knew that some viewed him as a glorified pencil pusher, which irked him to no small degree. Part of the reason he got on a plane was to prove he was as capable of this sort of thing as Cesar.

Unfortunately that meant bearing witness to displays such as this.

The man assigned by Brown to administer punishment drew back his fist again, fingers wrapped around a set of brass knuckles. As he swung in with an uppercut, Linus winced in anticipation. The prisoner took the blow on his chin. It knocked loose one of his teeth, sending it skittering across the floor.

"Where are they keeping Cesar Calderon?" he growled again in Spanish.

"No sé," the man replied, wheezing from the effort.

Brown motioned the interrogator over and whispered

something in his ear. The man nodded, then strolled back and bent over to look directly in the prisoner's eyes. "Who do you work for?"

Something akin to relief passed over the man's bloodied features. "Fuentes," he said. "Vicente Fuentes."

"Fuentes?" Linus frowned. "Isn't he with the Sinaloa Cartel?"

Brown hesitated a moment before replying, "Yessir."

"I thought the Zetas ran the Gulf Cartel."

Brown didn't answer. Emboldened, Linus walked forward. "Ask him if he's part of Los Zetas."

The prisoner's attention shifted to him. At the word "Zetas," his eyes widened and he jabbered excitedly in Spanish.

"What's he saying?"

"He claims he's not one of them, sir," the interrogator translated.

"So why the hell did they attack your unit?"

The prisoner was still chattering away. A cuff from the interrogator shut him up. "He says there's a turf war, they assumed we were Zetas. They have orders to shoot any they see on sight."

"Let me get this straight," Linus said slowly, enunciating each word as he turned back to Brown. "We're interrogating someone who probably has no connection whatsoever to Cesar's kidnapping."

"We're not a hundred percent certain the Zetas have him, sir. That was just the buzz we heard." Brown looked uncomfortable.

"Good Lord." Linus removed his glasses and took a cloth out of his jacket pocket to polish them. "Cut him loose."

"All due respect, we can't do that, sir."

"Why not?"

"Whatever cartel he's with will come down hard on us."

The prisoner's gaze shifted back and forth between them. He said something, then repeated it more forcefully.

"Now what?" Linus grumbled.

"He's saying there's a Zetas prison camp in the jungle near Veracruz."

"Fine. He'll take us there." Linus waved a hand to quell Brown's next words. "Sounds to me like the only lead we have. Your search of the city hasn't produced any results, so they're probably being held somewhere else."

"We haven't completed that search, sir," Brown argued.

"Do you think you ever will? It's been days, and you haven't found any sign of Cesar or the rest of the team."

Brown appeared enraged at this usurping of his authority. "It's hard to say, sir," he finally replied. "They might keep moving them."

"Or maybe they were never here to begin with. Time to explore other options." Linus strolled to the door feeling rather pleased with himself. Maybe now the board would appreciate what he brought to the table. Cesar might return as the public face of Tyr, but clearly he wasn't enough of a big-picture visionary to move them forward into the future. That required a whole different skill set, one Linus had mastered.

All in all, things were turning out better than expected.

Thirteen

Flores awoke in the dark. Someone was whispering nearby, and his senses immediately went on high alert. He was lying on a mat of moldering leaves, with a ratty towel functioning as a blanket. He waited for his eyes to adjust: Calderon was squatting at the opposite end of their pen. Who was he talking to?

Flores crept forward, straining to overhear. He hadn't paid much attention yesterday to the prisoners on either side of them, and no one had gone out of their way to initiate contact. Calderon had explained that people came and went so frequently, there was generally little effort at communication. Plus rumor had it there were Zetas spies everywhere, prisoners who exchanged information for special treatment. Best to keep to yourself, he'd advised.

Yet Calderon was hunched by the far wall of their pen, and Flores could discern a figure on the other side.

Their whispers suddenly ceased. Calderon's head whipped around, the whites of his eyes visible. *"Hola compadre,"* he whispered.

"Hola." Flores moved closer. On the other side of the wires hunched a small figure with a thick beard. Although

his lips weren't moving, steady chatter emanated from him. Confused, Flores looked down: a small transistor radio was clenched in the man's hands.

"Every night relatives send messages to loved ones who have been kidnapped," Calderon explained, keeping his voice low. "You never know who will be on, or when, so we take turns with the radio."

"Oh," Flores said. Funny this hadn't been mentioned before. A radio could potentially provide a huge advantage.

"This is Ramon Tejada." Calderon gestured to the man in the next pen. "His wife was on the other night so he's listening, hoping she'll return."

"Where did the radio come from?"

Calderon shrugged. "One of the guards traded for it awhile back. They figure it's harmless. Even if we could reconfigure it to signal out, it would only transmit in this region. And no locals would be willing or able to help."

Flores was no radio tech, but that sounded right. Still, there was some comfort in discovering that they weren't completely cut off from the outside world.

They sat and listened in silence as a teary-voiced woman told her daughter Ana Martinez how much she loved and missed her, how hard they were working to raise the money to get her back home.

"Is she here?" Flores asked after a minute.

"Who knows?" Tejada's voice was weak, quavering. "There are probably a half dozen Ana Martinez's in here." He punctuated his words with a hacking cough. Flores moved back a few inches.

The voices of one forlorn relative after another trickled out of the tinny speakers into the night, name after name: Carlos, Maria, Adriana, Ernesto. Tears that could fill a well of sadness. Flores caught himself listening for

Maryanne's voice, which was ridiculous. Even if she knew he was missing, which she probably didn't, there was no way she'd be aware of this call-in show. Still, it was hard to quell the hope in his heart.

There was a moment of silence, then a radio announcer with an obnoxiously cheery voice announced "Radio Aro-Am." There was a click, then silence: Ramon had shut it off.

"Lo siento, señor," Calderon said. *"Posiblemente mañana."*

Ramon only grunted, which sparked another coughing fit. Flores followed Calderon to the other side of the pen, where their sleeping pallets were squeezed under a low-hanging tarp that served as their shelter.

"That cough." Calderon shook his head. "He's had it for weeks now. Not good."

Flores was more concerned about the prospect of catching it. Illness would render an escape nearly impossible. And he was guessing the Zetas weren't big on handing out antibiotics.

"We should get some sleep, *amigo,*" Calderon said, lying down. "Tomorrow is another day."

"You don't seem worried, sir."

"Why would I be worried?" Calderon sounded puzzled.

"Well, they haven't taken any proof of life from you, even though you've been here for weeks. And then our team got snatched. Tyr probably sent in another unit, but they have no way of finding us…" Flores's voice trailed off.

There was a long moment of silence before Calderon spoke. "I've been doing this a long time, Enrique. There's no fixed playbook for negotiations."

"Yeah, but by now—"

"I'm too valuable for them to risk losing," Calderon interrupted.

He sounded so sure of himself that Flores hated to burst his bubble. "But, sir. The rest of us—I mean, the way it went down. It seems like someone told them to expect us."

"You're implying that someone at Tyr doesn't want me released," Calderon said.

"It had occurred to me, sir."

"It's not outside the realm of possibility." Calderon seemed to weigh his words before continuing. "The same thought had occurred to me. But if someone at Tyr conspired to get me out of the way, then why am I still alive?"

It was a good question, one Flores didn't have the answer to. "It just seems like something else is going on here, sir."

"Something else is always going on." Calderon shifted onto his side, facing away from Flores. "It's late, go to sleep. Dreams are the only respite from this place."

Flores lay still for a long time, looking up at the stars through a gap in the plastic tarp. He thought again of Maryanne, wondered if she could feel the baby kicking yet. As he drifted off, the radio clicked back on next door, the steady murmur of despair lulling him to sleep.

"I can't believe you're doing this." Kelly lay on the bed, facing away from Jake. It wasn't cold in their motel room, but she clutched the sheets to her anyway.

"Kel, I've got to. There's no other way."

He reached out and rubbed her shoulder. She didn't respond to his touch.

"So I'll stay, too," she said.

He hesitated before answering. "You can't."

"We've been through this before—"

"This time is different," he said. "We're going into the jungle. It's going to be a lot of trekking across rough terrain."

"I can manage," Kelly protested.

"Not in the shape you're in, and we both know it."

"This is because Syd doesn't think I can handle it."

"No, it's because even if you were healthy, I wouldn't want you along. It's just too dangerous. Hell, I don't even want to go," Jake said wearily. "And if something happened to you, I'd never be able to forgive myself."

Kelly threw off the covers and sat up. Her left foot landed on the carpet. She avoided looking at where the stump of her right leg ended at the edge of the bed.

Jake wrapped his arms around her from behind. She let him, but remained rigid. He buried his face in her hair anyway. "When you were in that hospital bed last summer, all I could think was that I wasn't there to protect you."

"I don't need protecting."

"Bullshit. Sometimes we all need it."

"Well, you won't be there to protect me if you go," Kelly said. "What if something happens to you?"

"If you tell me not to go, I'll stay."

Kelly debated. When it came down to it, she really didn't want Jake to go. This was the craziest thing she'd ever heard of, the group of them heading off into the jungle, trying to chase down an army of well-trained mercenaries. He'd been right to call it a suicide mission.

By the same token, Kelly knew that if she stopped him, and something happened to Mark, Jake would never forgive her. Not even if it meant he survived. Every time he looked at her, he'd be seeing his dead brother. And although she felt guilty admitting it, Jake's departure left her free to pursue her own case.

"Go with your brother," she said.

"Kelly…"

"But don't get yourself killed," she said fiercely.

"I won't. I promise."

He pulled her back down on top of him. Kelly buried her face in his chest, felt the steady rhythm of his heartbeat against her ear. She tilted her head to kiss his neck. Jake's breath quickened as she nuzzled his ear, then nibbled his lower lip.

"I don't know if we have time," he said, glancing toward the clock.

Kelly didn't answer. She moved forward, breasts inches from his lips. Lifted her hips and drew him into her. His lips parted and he let out a small gasp. "Oh, God…"

Kelly started slowly. It had been so long, and it felt so good that for the moment she forgot about her leg, forgot about him leaving, forgot about the way she sometimes caught Syd looking at him. For now, he was all hers.

He arched his pelvis up, matching her movement. Put his hands on her hips to guide her, driving her faster. Kelly let her head fall back. As they got close she leaned forward again, her body lined up with his, lips inches from his mouth.

"You're so beautiful," he said. "I love you so much."

Kelly didn't answer, just watched as he threw his head back and moaned. One way or another, she knew this was goodbye.

JANUARY 31

Fourteen

"Crap." Syd swore as she slipped on a pile of rotting leaves. "I hate the jungle."

"Right there with you, boss." Maltz extended a hand to help her up.

Jake didn't say anything. He was already second-guessing the decision to accompany them. Kelly was behaving strangely, too, which didn't help. First, she initiated sex last night. Not that he was complaining, but even before her injury she'd never been the first to make a move. And the way she'd looked at him as he closed the door that morning—it was like she never expected to see him again, even if he survived.

He shook it off. No matter what, he couldn't afford to be distracted. Kelly was probably already on a flight back to New York. She'd be safe, that was the important thing.

That morning they'd exchanged their rental car for two jeeps. The road into the mountains wound for hours, the surrounding foliage growing greener and thicker as the city receded in the rearview mirror. At times they slowed to a crawl, edging around potholes, going off road in places where the pavement had failed. They'd only passed a handful of other cars, mostly trucks, farmers headed toward the city and buses overloaded with passengers. As far as he could tell, they hadn't drawn any attention: just another group of adventurous tourists on their way to visit the ruins at el Tajín. In truth, they passed that turnoff and headed south instead, weaving up into the mountains. Mark was in the lead car, Isabela navigating. An hour or so past the turnoff, they pulled over to the side of the road.

"We have to go the rest of the way on foot," Isabela had explained. They hid the cars, covering them with brush for camouflage. Hopefully they'd still be there when they got back. If they got back, that was.

"How much farther?" Syd grumbled as she lost her footing again.

"A few more miles, I think," Isabela replied.

"Great," Syd said. "Three more miles of mud."

"Good for your skin, boss," Maltz offered.

"Go to hell," Syd said.

"We should pipe down," Mark said. "Might be patrols."

At that they fell silent.

Jake had to give Isabela credit, for someone with no training she was holding up pretty well. Mark and Decker helped her over the toughest spots, but she usually refused their assistance. It was nasty going, too. The ground was uneven, rocky and wet. By the end of the first hour they were all soaked through and caked in mud. Blisters throbbed on Jake's feet, and his arms ached from continually batting away the swarms of no-see-ums determined to feast on him. All in all he figured this was the perfect site for a prison camp. No one would come here voluntarily.

Someone suddenly pushed him from behind, sending him sprawling.

"Hey!" Jake protested, knee-deep in mud.

Mark had landed on top of him. He clamped a hand over Jake's mouth and shoved his head down.

Jake was wrestling him off when he heard voices. This section of the jungle was so thick, Kane had been leading the way with a machete. Now Jake was grateful for the coverage it offered. He nodded, showing that he understood, and Mark released him. Ahead of him Kane, Fribush and Jagerson were pressed flat to the ground. Syd and Maltz were behind him with Isabela. He couldn't see Decker.

The voices continued approaching: definitely male, speaking Spanish. At first Jake thought they were arguing, then one of them laughed out loud. The smell of cigarette smoke wafted past. *Shit,* Jake thought. Looked like Isabela's estimate of the camp's location was off.

He sensed movement and turned to find Syd signaling to their men. Mark shook his head vehemently and gestured back. Jake made a mental note to sign up for a Special Forces hand-signals class if he came out of this alive. It was like being stuck with a group of pitchers and catchers, he never knew what the hell they were talking about.

Mark suddenly rolled off him and vanished into the wash of greenery. Jake turned to raise his eyebrows at Syd, only to discover that she and Maltz had disappeared, too. He and Isabela were left mired in the mud. She wore an expression of abject panic. Jake tried to look reassuring, but part of him wondered if they'd just been abandoned.

He buried his head in the moss as one of the men approached. The Mexican was no more than twenty, dressed in camo pants and a Metallica T-shirt. The guard stopped on the other side of a patch of giant ferns, an arm's length away. If he glanced down at the ground, there was no way he could miss seeing Jake.

Jake willed himself invisible. He tried to regulate his breathing, but it still sounded unbearably loud.

The guard unzipped his fly, letting loose a stream of urine two feet from Jake's head. As he pissed he focused back over his shoulder, still talking to his friend. They both broke into guffaws: must have been a hell of a punch line, Jake thought.

Something rustled a few feet behind him: Isabela. The guard started at the noise. He took a step toward it, then barked in surprise. Jake jerked his head up: Isabela had leaped to her feet and was bolting back the way they had come, black ponytail swishing across her back. The guard stepped through the ferns, swinging a rifle to his shoulder. He was less than a foot away, so focused on Isabela's retreat that he didn't notice Jake.

Isabela tripped and went flying, landing on all fours in the mud. The guard aimed for the center of her back.

"Wait!" Jake jumped to his feet.

Startled, the guard swung his weapon around. At the sight of Jake, his eyes narrowed.

Jake held up both hands. The second guard came around a tree, still zipping up his pants. He was older, with a nasty scar bisecting his face.

They jabbered back and forth, then the older guard tore through the undergrowth in pursuit of Isabela.

The younger guard prodded him with his gun muzzle. Jake stood and crossed his hands behind his head. The guard jabbed him hard in the back to propel him forward.

Great, Jake thought. Apparently he'd found the perfect way into the camp: as an inmate.

* * *

Kelly dialed again, staring out the motel-room window as she waited for an answer. By now she had the number committed to memory. Ten calls in the past few days, and each time she was redirected to a voice-mail system where a bland female voice announced that Global Investigations was currently on another call, and to leave a message. Either they were the busiest P.I. organization Kelly had ever encountered, or it was one guy who didn't bother checking his messages. Based on the area code, the firm was located in New York. Which made sense—she vaguely recalled that Lin Kaishen's father had been some sort of diplomat with the UN. The family had hired Global Investigations to continue following up leads on Stefan Gundarsson after the FBI closed the case. Kelly's boss at the time, a smarmy so-and-so named Bowen, declared that the family refused to accept the truth because they were Chinese and had no respect for American police work. Privately Kelly thought they had good reason to doubt that the FBI had done its job. She wished the file provided more information on why the P.I. was convinced that Stefan was still alive, but there had only been a short report written by the agent who fielded the call. "Global Investigations claims to have evidence that suspect Stefan Gundarsson survived and is living in Mexico. Kaishen family requests that field agents follow up." A note scrawled at the top read: Case Closed, Do Not Pursue.

A click, and the voice-mail message started to play again. Kelly hung up, frustrated. She cracked the window and lit a cigarette. Jake didn't know that she'd fallen back into the habit. She'd been careful to hide it from him, never smoking in their apartment, sneaking drags on the roof or by the service entry to their building. She knew he'd never tell her to stop, but hadn't wanted to deal with the weight of his disapproval.

Kelly inhaled deeply, causing the embers to flare. She tried not to stare at the tangle of sheets on the bed. God, she hoped Jake came out of this all right. But she'd let him go because this was what they did, who they were. Which was precisely why she was so focused on Stefan. She needed closure on this case, once and for all.

She held the smoke in her chest for a long moment before releasing it. Perhaps she should just head to the airport and try to catch a flight home. She felt the darkness starting to encroach upon her, the almost overwhelming sense of futility and purposelessness that she'd struggled with ever since waking up in that hospital bed.

Maybe she was so fixated on the possibility that Stefan was alive simply because without a case to pursue, she really didn't have a reason to go on anymore. When she'd first met Jake three years ago, she'd been at the top of her game. Her professional reputation was spotless, her solve rate the envy of her peers. Since then she'd lost a high-profile case, her lower leg and very nearly her life. The FBI didn't want her back. Jake was staying with her out of a misguided sense of obligation. Her entire family was dead. Aside from Jake, there was no one in the world who cared if she lived or died. She didn't even have any real friends.

Ironically enough, she'd met Jake while pursuing Stefan. Her therapist would probably have a field day with that one. Kelly dropped the cigarette into a half-full water glass. She rubbed her eyes, suddenly exhausted.

Her phone rang. She fumbled for it, knocking it off the windowsill. Recognizing the number, she scooped it up and answered just before it went to voice mail.

"Hello?"

"This is Mike Caruso at Global," a voice thick with a Brooklyn accent said. "Got a few messages from you."

"Right, hello." Kelly cleared her throat. "I wanted to find out more about your investigation for the Kaishens."

A pause, then he said, "I take client confidentiality seriously. Can't share details."

"You called the FBI with a tip a few months ago," Kelly pressed. "I'd like to follow up on that."

He laughed. "You got some nerve. It's thanks to you people they fired me."

"The Kaishens fired you?"

"Yeah, after one of you douchebags told them I wasn't reputable. All because of some bullshit DUI they dug up. I still got an outstanding bill for expenses."

"I'm truly sorry to hear about that," Kelly said, her voice conciliating. "I was the lead on the original case."

"Well, I'm not in much of a mood to help. Bye."

"Wait!" Kelly exclaimed. "How much do they still owe you?"

"Three grand, give or take," he said after a brief silence.

Kelly was willing to bet the real figure was much lower, but she was in no position to bargain. "I can get you the money if you tell me what you found."

"Yeah?" Another pause. "Cash, in my account. I'll tell you what I know when it gets here."

"I'm in Mexico now, I can't send it until I get back," Kelly said. "Please, Mr. Caruso. This is important."

Another long pause, then he sighed. "You bastards better not screw me over again."

"I won't, I promise. How did you find Stefan Gundarsson?"

"Same as always, I followed the money." A hint of pride

in his voice as he said, "I was the third P.I. they hired, the other two didn't turn up jackshit."

"But his personal accounts were seized." Kelly's brow wrinkled. Maybe this was just a scam.

"Sure they were, but you folks forgot about his so-called church. Couldn't touch that cash, it was protected under some bullshit federal law for houses of worship. That account got cleared out by one of the Moonies drinking his Kool-Aid."

It made sense. They hadn't kept tabs on Stefan's devotees, and he'd had hundreds when he vanished. "So why Mexico?"

"The guy got a cashier's check when he closed the account, then a few days later his credit cards showed charges in Mexico City. So I headed south. Tracked him to a dive hotel. And guess what? He conveniently turned up dead, victim of a 'mugging' the same week he got there. He'd been stabbed."

Kelly sucked in a breath. Stefan had always preferred knives. "But maybe he just saw an opportunity and ran with the money."

"Yeah, except the money never turned up. And someone was still using his cards for a few weeks after he bought it. So I checked out some of the other charges. Found some folks who had seen a guy matching Gundarsson's description. Trust me, there aren't a lot of guys like him running around down there. I told the Kaishens, and they called you people. And then they fired me. Said that 'my services were no longer needed,'" he scoffed. "Tell you what, you folks did your job better, you'd have this guy."

"I can't believe they just gave up," Kelly said. She'd met the Kaishens briefly. They'd been stricken by their daughter's death.

"What I can't figure is why you're so gung ho now," Caruso said. "It's been months since I called that in."

"I was…on another case. I just found out about this recently." Kelly paused. "So do you think there's a chance he's still here?"

"Maybe. Easy to get lost in Mexico. But after he offed that guy, he'd be nuts to stick around."

Kelly's heart sank. He was right, the chances of Stefan remaining in the area were slim, especially if he'd gotten wind of the fact that someone was tracking him. "Can you think of anywhere I should start looking?"

A pause as Caruso thought it over. "Lot of bookstore charges, guy was a reader. Mainly the ones that sell foreign language books. Try them, you might get lucky. But I gotta be honest, I doubt it."

"Thank you, Mr. Caruso. This has been extremely helpful."

"Yeah, sure. Just make sure to send the cash."

He hung up.

Kelly realized she was twisting her engagement ring around and around with her thumb and forced herself to stop. It was a long shot, but she was already here. If she headed back to New York, all she could do was sit around an empty apartment waiting to hear if Jake was okay.

Kelly took a deep breath and went through her things. She still had her go-kit, along with an H&K sidearm and extra magazines. She could leave everything else, it was better to travel light. If she uncovered any sign that Stefan was still alive, she'd contact the FBI and wait for backup. Catching him would be a huge accomplishment, maybe enough to get her back on active duty.

She shrugged on the backpack and headed out the door to find an internet café.

Fifteen

"We need to get moving." Linus impatiently paced the narrow channel between the bed and the bathroom. "This is ridiculous."

"It would be ridiculous if we went out there unprepared." Brown sat calmly at the motel room desk, playing a game of solitaire. Their departure had been delayed when they couldn't get some equipment that Brown deemed essential to their mission. What those things were, he hadn't shared. Linus suspected he was stalling to save face. Now it was nearly dusk, and there was no sign that they were leaving anytime soon.

"Shouldn't you be doing something?" he finally exhorted.

As Brown slowly stood, glowering down at him, Linus was struck by the realization that anything could happen to him down here, and Brown could spin it however he wanted. His own men could riddle him with bullets and blame the Zetas, or they could claim that he never showed up. He swallowed, hard. "Sorry, I'm just—"

A knock at the door interrupted him. Brown opened it a crack after checking through the curtain. One of his men stood there looking agitated. They exchanged a few words in low voices, then Brown shut the door again.

"There's a complication," he said, frowning.

"Another one?" Linus couldn't contain his exasperation.

"I'll be right back," Brown said, strapping on his sidearm.

"I'll come with you," Linus insisted.

Brown looked ready to object, then shrugged and said, "Suit yourself."

Linus followed him along the corridor and down two rooms. Brown knocked on the door to Room 17. It opened.

This motel room was identical to the other: a sagging queen-size bed, a desk marred by years-worth of accumulated abuse and a rickety chair. Two members of the Tyr team stood at opposite ends of the room. A large man dressed in ratty jean shorts and a soiled T-shirt tilted back in the chair, feet on the bed opposite. At the sight of Brown he slowly rose to his feet. He looked familiar, but it took Linus a second to place him.

"Wysocki," Brown said. "So you finally made it home."

"Hey, boss." Wysocki's arrogant smirk faded slightly at Brown's approach.

"Where's the rest of your team?"

"Dunno." Wysocki shrugged. "Kaplan got himself shot, so Riley and Decker went out for meds. They were taking a long time, so I left Flores with Kap and went out for food and a phone. Came back, and everyone was gone. Waited awhile for Riley and Decker, but they never showed. Then I called you."

"Funny you didn't call as soon as you got away." Brown's eyes narrowed.

"I was under orders."

"Whose?"

"Riley's." Wysocki lowered his voice. "I think he might've been in on it, sir. We were ambushed at the site. The Zetas had a mole."

"So who planned the escape?"

"Mostly Decker and me, sir. Man, I hope Decker's okay. Riley might've just handed them all over to those assholes again." Wysocki glanced at the other men in the room. "Heard you were headed into the jungle after them. I'd love to come along."

"I'm not sure—" Linus interjected.

"We're already down one man," Brown said. "Suit up, Wysocki."

With that he turned and left the room.

Something flashed across Wysocki's face. Linus couldn't be sure, but it looked like triumph. He scurried after Brown, who strolled back to their room as if he hadn't a care in the world. Brown plunked back down in the chair and shuffled the deck of cards.

"I know he's one of your men," Linus said, "but what makes you think—"

"I don't trust him, either. Friends close but enemies closer, right?"

"I suppose. But what if he reveals our plans to the Zetas?"

"He'll be under surveillance the whole time, without a functioning radio. If he is working with them, he could be a valuable source of intel."

"What about Riley?" Linus asked. "I know he hasn't been with Tyr long—"

"As far as I'm concerned, every one of those men is a liability," Brown said. "When we find them, they'll be treated as hostiles until proven otherwise."

* * *

Flores scraped the bottom of his plate with a rusty spoon, making sure to get every last morsel of the sparse cornmeal. He definitely preferred the hospitality of the Zetas' city branch. The food was a hell of a lot better, and there had been more of it. With these rations, no wonder Calderon was a sack of bones.

Calderon had already finished and was carefully rinsing his plate and spoon. They were only allotted two small water bottles apiece per day, so every drop was precious. Suddenly one of the guards appeared outside their pen.

"Venga conmigo," he said, gesturing toward Calderon.

Calderon stood, his expression tough to read.

"What do you think they want?" Flores asked.

"Tough to say. Proof of life, possibly? This might be the beginning of negotiations." Calderon smiled thinly. "Hopefully I will return with good news for both of us, *amigo.*"

"Good luck." Flores shook his hand, then watched as he was led down the aisle.

Next door, Ramon Tejada monitored Calderon's departure, but he didn't say anything.

Flores paced as he waited. He'd already quietly begun planning their escape, familiarizing himself with the guards' shifts, analyzing the strengths and weaknesses of the camp from what he could observe from their cell. That morning Calderon had mentioned that periodically army helicopters skirted low overhead. It was the only time the guards seemed distracted, he claimed. Perhaps enough to mask their escape, if they timed it right.

But what if they were actually moving him to a different pen? If Calderon didn't come back, Flores would be forced to leave without him. Anything else was too risky. Not a decision he relished making.

A siren blared, and there was a commotion at the end of their row. A line of guards appeared. In ragged formation they trotted forward, each breaking off to stand in front of a different pen. One stopped directly across from Flores. The guard raised his rifle to his shoulder and aimed for his chest.

Flores's heart nearly stopped. His mind raced as his field of vision narrowed to the guard's finger, watching pressure increase on the trigger. He'd never know his child. His body would likely never be found. Maryanne would have no idea what had really happened to him. He wasn't going to get a chance to say goodbye.

"Tranquilo, amigo," Ramon muttered in the next pen. "It's a drill."

"What?" Flores examined the guard facing him. The man had frozen, as if awaiting an order.

"They do this a few times a week. It's to prepare the guards, in case the camp is ever invaded. They're to make sure none of the prisoners survive." Tejada's words dissolved into another coughing fit.

"So how do we know this isn't going to be the time they shoot us?"

"We don't."

Flores shifted his head. Tejada hadn't moved at the guard's approach. He remained seated near the door, face tilted up to catch the thin ray of light that sliced across his cell.

The siren issued a staggered series of bleats, and the guard outside Flores's pen lowered his weapon. A moment later, he trotted back toward the end of the row, falling in line with the other guards.

Flores breathed out hard and wiped a line of sweat

from his brow. He resolved to be long gone before the next drill.

More coughing from next door. Flores turned to see Tejada bent double, hacking into a soiled handkerchief. *"Cómo estás?"* Flores asked.

Tejada waved a hand. After a moment, the fit passed. He took a sip of water, then collapsed on a pile of matted leaves. Despite his condition, he produced a cigarette from the pocket of his shirt and lit it. Lying on his back he nursed it, a thin trail of smoke rising like a wraith above his head. "This place is hell," Tejada said after a moment. He shifted to squint at Flores. "And you're living with the devil."

Before Flores could ask what he meant, Calderon reappeared, the guard shoving him from behind. The door swung open and he stepped back inside. Calderon looked shaken, face pale, hands trembling.

"What happened?" Flores asked. "Did they take a proof-of-life photo?"

Calderon sank into a crouch, clutching his knees to his chest. "No, my friend," he said in a voice barely above a whisper. "They wanted something else."

"What?"

Calderon didn't reply. Flores figured he was waiting for the guard to leave, but the door to their pen hadn't been closed yet.

"Venga conmigo."

Flores turned to find the guard pointing at him.

Sixteen

Jake grunted as the guard delivered a sharp kick to his ribs. He'd slipped again, and apparently falling wasn't permitted. The guard yelled, waving his free arm wildly for Jake to get back up.

"Not my fault," Jake said through gritted teeth as he slowly rose to his feet. "It's damn slippery."

The only response was another jab in the back from the gun muzzle. It wasn't helping that the second guard hadn't reappeared. As he propelled Jake forward, the guy cast glances back over his shoulder, obviously increasingly worried. They'd already traveled about a half mile. Jake wondered where the hell this camp was, and why the guards wandered so far afield to take a piss. Maybe they were assigned the outer perimeter, or some prisoners had escaped and they'd been tracking them down.

The jungle was even thicker here, enormous ferns rising up to meet dangling vines. Steam covered everything, a fine mist that wrapped around trunks and dripped off leaves.

A sudden crashing sound behind them, something large tearing through the undergrowth. They both froze.

"Hector?" The guard called after a second.

There was no response.

The guard shouldered his rifle, aiming at some rustling bushes a dozen yards away. *"Quien es?"* he called out. *"Sal de ahí!"*

There was no response. The jungle had fallen silent. A bead of sweat rolled down the inside collar of Jake's shirt. *Syd and Mark,* he thought. *Has to be.* His relief at the fact that they hadn't abandoned him was accompanied by annoyance: what the hell had taken so long? Counting Decker and his team, they had six people trained to intervene in this exact situation.

The guard swiveled back around, pointing his gun at Jake's head as he spat out a stream of commands. Jake's Spanish was limited to finding bathrooms and ordering beers, but he got the gist of it.

Still, he shrugged in response. *"No hablo español."*

The guard stepped closer, jabbing the weapon threateningly. "They come out," he said, "or you die."

"I don't know who you're talking about," Jake said slowly. "I'm alone."

The guard hissed in frustration and muttered to himself. He prodded Jake in the chest, nudging him forward. Jake turned slowly and kept walking, eyes scanning either side of the narrow path. It was a sea of green and gray.

Wait…he caught a flash of something brighter to his right. Jake covertly focused on it as he walked.

There was definitely something out there that didn't belong in a rain forest.

Jake took a deep breath. He let his left foot slide out on the next patch of leaves, dropping to his belly in the mud.

A sharp crack from the right, and something wet hit his back. Looking up he saw the guard lurch sideways, a bullet hole near his hairline. Jake grimaced. More rustling, and Syd and Mark emerged side by side through the trees, followed by the rest of the group. Jake was relieved to see Isabela among them. At the sight of the guard's body she went pale and averted her eyes.

"Took you long enough," Jake muttered.

Syd jerked her head toward Mark. "He wanted to let them take you all the way into camp, figured that would be the easiest way to find it."

"Gee, thanks," Jake said. "I'm glad cooler heads prevailed."

"We would have gotten you out," Mark said without looking up. He was patting down the guard's pockets, relieving him of a hunting knife and ammunition.

"Remind me not to come save you next time." Jake stood and brushed himself off as best he could. He avoided looking at the guard, too.

"Guess we're even now," Mark said. "Not that you really saved me."

Jake opened his mouth to retort, but Syd interrupted. "The camp can't be far, can we hold off on the arguments? It's almost dark. We need to find a safe place to regroup."

"Agreed," Mark said. "Let's move out. Follow close. Stay a little off the path, but in sight of it. Decker, you take the rear."

"I got it," Maltz interjected.

Mark appeared ready to argue, then thought better of it. Syd led the way, tacking off the path twenty feet, then beating a trail parallel to it. Mark stayed close on her heels.

Jake followed him into the brush. It was harder going off the path. They weren't using the machete anymore, wary of leaving a trail. He followed in Mark's wake as carefully as he could, but he swore his brother was intentionally setting branches to snap in his face. He yelped when one hit his cheek, drawing blood.

Mark glanced back and raised an eyebrow. Jake just glowered and motioned for him to keep going. As he watched his brother's broad back move smoothly through the trees, Jake couldn't help but remember being in this exact same formation many times before. Throughout their entire childhood, he'd followed Mark. The gullies and sagebrush surrounding their house had been their personal playground, host to endless rounds of cowboys and Indians. At school, he'd taken over as quarterback when Mark graduated and relinquished the position. The only place he hadn't followed him was into the Navy SEALs.

They'd always been close, much closer than he and Chris ever got. Chris was definitely the odd one out in a family of adrenaline junkies, a nerdy kid who preferred books to BB guns, the school year to summers. Meanwhile Mark and Jake had been nearly inseparable, sharing a bedroom and constantly getting into trouble—nothing serious, but the local cops knew them by sight.

And then Mark left, and everything changed.

Mark suddenly stopped short and held up a closed fist. Jake halted a foot behind him. Finally a signal he recognized: the military gesture for "Freeze."

Mark dropped to the ground and crawled forward. After a second Jake followed, figuring what the hell, he had chosen to be here. No reason he shouldn't be privy to whatever Mark had seen. He inched forward, sodden clothes chafing uncomfortably against his skin as he came up alongside Mark and Syd.

They were on the edge of a small cliff. The path the guard had been leading him down transformed into a series of switchbacks that descended at least a half mile to the valley floor. And tucked inside the valley was the prison camp.

Mark scanned it through a pair of binoculars. Jake held out his hand for them. Reluctantly Mark passed them over.

Jake adjusted the focus. His heart sank at what he saw.

Isabela had told them the camp was big, and connected to a military base. But either she hadn't known, or hadn't accurately conveyed, the size of the thing. Jake had been picturing something far more ad hoc, similar to the FARC camps in Colombia. The FARC were masters of building temporary bases, leaving a trail of abandoned shelters strewn through the jungle as they played cat and mouse with the Colombian army.

Apparently Los Zetas had no such qualms. The prison camp sprawled off into the distance. It was huge, covering a few hundred acres. The tree canopy shielded it somewhat from overhead view. Still, there was simply no way the Mexican army was unaware of its existence, Jake thought. Syd was right: Los Zetas had to be aligned with powerful people in the government.

Syd and Mark edged back from the lip, staying on their bellies. Jake followed. Ten feet away, Mark stood. He walked back into the underbrush, then squatted down. "All right, we've got our visual," he said. "We'll regroup a few clicks away, then do our recon tonight."

"How the hell are you going to find your men?" Jake asked. "It's a lot bigger than I thought."

"We'll find them," Mark said.

"My father, too," Isabela interjected.

"Right," Mark said, meeting her eyes. "We'll try to find him, too."

"And then how do we get them out? I saw guard towers,

dogs…" Jake turned to Syd. "Even you have to admit, this is crazy. We're not dealing with a few guys at an outpost here. They probably outnumber us a hundred-to-one. Plus they know the terrain, we don't."

For the first time in recent memory, Syd looked hesitant. Not a good sign.

"We need to create a distraction, get some guards out of the camp." She turned to Maltz. "Kind of like what we did in Syria."

Maltz was already shaking his head. "Jake's right, there are too many of them. Won't work."

"We could fly in more men," Kane suggested. "Pull some teams off other jobs."

"That'd attract too much attention," Mark argued. "We're already here. We've got surprise on our side."

"Surprise won't be enough," Syd said. Mark started to argue, but she cut him off. "Jake's right, we go in like this, it's a suicide mission. And I for one am not in the mood to die. Or to end up in some godforsaken Mexican prison camp."

They stood in silence for a moment.

"What about the Tyr team?" Syd said after a pause. "We could join forces."

"Don't trust 'em," Decker chimed in.

"Maybe if we had more C4," Maltz said, thinking aloud.

"Getting in is easy," Syd said. "It's getting out that's the problem."

As they debated, dusk swept in from the uppermost branches, bringing with it a slight chill. Jake shivered in his wet clothes. Isabela looked as miserable as he felt. He wondered again what the hell he'd been thinking. He should be on a plane home with Kelly right now. Mark seemed dead set on getting himself killed. Beyond that, he'd made it clear that he'd prefer having no help. Now Jake had put the lives of his business partner and some of his best employees at risk.

"We've got another problem," Maltz said after a minute. "Chances are they'll come looking for the guys we took out."

"He's right," Decker said. "We stashed them pretty good, but still—"

"They'll find us," Syd finished. "We should fall back to a safer location to figure out a plan."

"I think we should stay," Mark said.

"No way, not all of us. I'm pulling my men," Syd turned to Jake. "Right?"

Jake nodded. "There were a few motels in that village we passed through, we can book some rooms and try to keep a low profile while we regroup."

Mark's face clouded. Before he could say anything, Decker laid a hand on his arm. "She's right, Riley. You and me can scout the camp. But all of us, together—there are civilians here."

Mark's gaze settled on Isabela. "You should head back with them," he said, sounding defeated. "We'll gather as much intel on the camp as we can."

"Here." Syd handed him a radio with a fat antenna. "Stay in contact and use the satellite encrypted channel to report what you find. Maybe you'll spot a weakness we can use."

"We're leaving?" Isabela interrupted. "What about my father?"

"I'll get him out," Mark said. "I promise."

Isabela looked ready to argue, but before she could speak a siren blared from the camp.

Syd cocked her head to the side. "Far as I'm concerned, that's our cue to go."

* * *

Kelly sat on a park bench rubbing her leg. All of the walking today had exacerbated her condition. She considered popping a Vicodin, but decided against it. On the off chance that she did find something, she needed to be sharp. Unfortunately, so far she'd had no luck.

An internet search had turned up five foreign-language bookstores in Mexico City. She'd started with the two that focused on European languages. Unfortunately they'd proved fruitless. Neither owner recognized Stefan's photo.

According to the P.I., the money had arrived in Mexico City almost three years earlier. Even if Stefan had been a regular at the time, they might not remember him. Or maybe some of the bookstores he frequented had closed in the interim.

Still, Kelly dogged on. After all, she mused, it wasn't like she had anything better to do. The next store was on the eastern side of the city, not far from where they'd spent the past few days. She stopped for lunch in the Zona Rosa before heading back to the grim and dangerous section of town.

Kelly checked her watch: nearly 3:30 p.m. No matter what, she didn't want to be walking around there after dark. Time to get a move on.

It took nearly a half hour for her cab to weave its way through the glut of traffic. The heat wave was holding fast, the sidewalks thronged with people in T-shirts milling in and out of stores. The neighborhoods deteriorated as they drove. Entire blocks were boarded up, gangs of young men hung out on apartment building stoops. Kelly swallowed hard. Maybe this had been a mistake.

The cab pulled up to a lone storefront in the middle of a devastated block. Kelly peered out the window—it was hard to tell if it was even open, it looked just as dingy and abandoned as everything else.

"Espere, por favor," she said, handing the driver some cash.

He looked around nervously, but nodded.

A tinny bell rang when she opened the door. The interior was dark, books stacked on every available space. A tiny man scurried out of a back room and approached her with a toothy smile. *"Sí, señora?"* he said hopefully.

"Hola. I'm looking for someone." Kelly dug Stefan's file photo out of her backpack. The man's face fell at the realization that she wasn't a customer after all, but he took it from her and adjusted his glasses on the bridge of his nose.

"Why are you looking for this man?" he asked, his English formal but succinct.

"His family has been trying to find him," Kelly said. She'd opted against identifying herself as an FBI agent, figuring that wouldn't endear her to the locals.

"I see." He extended his arm out to squint at the photo.

"He might have come in a few years ago," Kelly said.

"As you can see—" he swept his arm in an arc "—my customer base is small. If it weren't for the internet…" He shook his head. "I don't know why I keep the store open anymore."

"I'm sorry to hear it." Kelly fought to keep the impatience from her voice. "So, do you recognize him?"

He eyed her. "You don't look like family."

"I'm a family friend."

"I doubt that. This man—" he jabbed the photo "—he is not one to make friends."

Kelly's heart leaped. "So you do know him?"

"He hasn't come in for months. But yes, he used to be

one of my best customers." The man sounded regretful. "I ordered the *Berlingske Tidende* regularly for him, along with some other texts. Then one day, he stopped coming in." He peered around the store, as if perhaps the reason why lay hidden in its shadows.

"Do you have any idea where I might find him?" she asked.

He sighed. "I do, but it is very dangerous. No place for a lady."

"Please," she said. "It's very important."

He regarded her for a long moment. "You must promise not to go there alone, or ever at night."

"Of course," Kelly lied.

"Very well, then. I could never understand it, since clearly he was a man of some means. One book alone cost nearly four thousand pesos. But from what he said, I gathered that he lived in Bordo Poniente, among the *pepenadores*."

"Where's that?" Kelly asked.

"The city dump." His nose wrinkled. "Less than a mile away. You can smell it quite plainly when the wind blows from the east. But I must warn you, *señora,* it is enormous. Finding one man in there will be difficult. And it's one of the most dangerous places I know."

Coming from someone living in this neighborhood, Kelly guessed that was saying something. *"Gracias, señor."* She reached out to shake his hand. His eyes widened when she handed him a five-hundred-peso note.

"Please, be careful," he called after her.

Kelly was already out the door, bells tinkling in her wake.

Flores tried to stay calm as he was led along the row of pens. They'd bound his hands in front of him with a zip tie, not something they did to Calderon, but he was probably considered more of a security risk. Other prisoners glanced up from their meal trays as he passed. Some appeared envious, others disinterested. Apparently it wasn't all that unusual for prisoners to come and go. He scanned each cage in passing for Sock and Kaplan.

Flores wondered what was going on. Had Tyr negotiated his release? Did they even know he was here? What had shaken Calderon so badly?

They reached the end of the row and emerged into some sort of main corridor. The camp was more massive than he'd imagined. There was an exterior fence on his right. Long lines of pens extended into the distance on his left. He counted off twenty rows before the guard ordered him to halt.

They were standing in front of the sort of prefab trailer used by managers at construction sites. The guard stepped forward and rapped twice on the door. After a moment, it swung open and Flores was shoved inside.

He staggered up the steps, knocking his knee hard against the metal. Flores swore as he caught himself. He managed to climb the last step to enter with a shred of his dignity intact.

The inside was sparsely decorated. Sheets of paper were taped to the wall: mainly guards' schedules, from what he could make out. No windows. An enormous locked cabinet piqued his interest. Weapons cache, maybe? Filing cabinets flanked it on either side.

At the far end, an enormous man sat behind a large metal desk. Rolls of flesh bulged out the collar of his camouflage jacket. He wore an absurdly small beret on his head and an ugly sneer on his face.

"Siéntese." The man gestured to the folding chair opposite him.

The guard nudged him forward. Flores sat down.

"What's your name?" the obese man asked in English.

Flores debated for a minute: name, rank and serial number were even permitted in the military. He only had one of those anymore anyway. "Flores. Enrique Flores."

"*Hola,* Señor Flores. I am General Gente. Are you thirsty?"

Flores shrugged. He was, in fact, dying of thirst, but figured this might be their way of messing with him.

Gente nodded to the guard, who brought over a Dixie cup filled with water. Flores used both bound hands to raise it to his lips. Clean water. It tasted unbelievably good. He drank it in one gulp and set the cup down on the desk, hoping they'd refill it.

"So, Señor Flores," the general said after watching him drink. "I understand you came here to rescue Señor Calderon."

Flores didn't respond.

"He already told me as much." Gente waved a hand. "But did he tell you why he's here?

Apparently Flores wasn't expected to hold up his end of the conversation, because Gente continued without pause. "You were a military man, like many in your line of work. That we have in common." The folds of flesh surrounding his mouth shifted slightly as he attempted to grin. "I very much enjoyed my time in your country, Señor Flores. Best training in the world. One thing Americans have always understood is how to turn men into soldiers."

It was hard for Flores to picture Gente surviving basic training, never mind the grueling punishment undergone by elite units.

"The thing about soldiers," Gente continued, "is that they are instruments serving a larger purpose. You might have thought that, after leaving the military, your days as a pawn were over. You would be mistaken, my friend."

Chess again, Flores thought. *What is it about chess in this place?*

"So you are probably unaware of our previous...arangement with Señor Calderon."

"Was it for a larger pen? Because if so, I have a complaint to lodge," Flores said.

Gente chuckled. "I appreciate a sense of humor. We don't see it much with our guests." He leaned forward, crossing his pudgy hands. "Señor Calderon came to us a few years ago with a proposal. He saw an opportunity for a mutually beneficial relationship."

Flores's mind raced. The thought of Calderon colluding with this cartel was repugnant. He reminded himself that you could never trust an interrogator. They would say anything while attempting to extract information. Turning prisoners against each other was a time-honored tradition, one he'd been advised about during training. He hardened his features, opting to play along. "What kind of arrangement?"

"There's an inherent problem with your line of work, my friend." Gente leaned back, causing his chair to creak in protest. "You rely on others' misfortune. If people are not kidnapped, Señor Calderon has no opportunity to ride in and play hero, no? And if we kidnap someone without significant resources, well..." He held his hands palms up and grinned. "Hardly worth the effort, *ve?*"

Flores shrugged, acknowledging the point.

"So." Gente's eyes glinted as he said, "Señor Calderon shared a list of your clients. We were provided with names, schedules, security information. Once they became our guests, he negotiated their release and the insurance companies paid their ransom." He jabbed the desk with his finger. "Señor Calderon was the savior who rescued them from evil kidnappers. His clients were relieved to have their employees returned unharmed, and we got paid. Everyone was happy. *Entiende?*"

Everyone but the poor schlubs who spent months suffering in camps like this one, Flores thought. He had to admit, it made sense. Kidnappings had spiked in recent years—even in a bad economy, Tyr was doing well. It was one reason he'd joined up. At the enlistment meeting, they'd even given a little speech, bragging about being recession-proof. The cardinal rule of the K&R industry, the one they hammered home, was that client lists were sacred. If it was known that a business had taken out insurance, their employees obviously made more tempting targets for kidnappers. After all, a large insurance company could muster bigger ransoms than most individual families could afford. For that reason, security companies like Tyr never advertised their client list—even employees weren't privy to them. If Calderon really had shared that information with a kidnapping cartel, he'd betrayed everything the business stood for. Not that he would have. It didn't take a genius to see the obvious flaw in what the general was saying.

"So why'd you kidnap him, if he was identifying targets for you?"

"Señor Calderon betrayed us." Gente's features darkened. "A rival organization offered him a larger cut if he shared the list with them instead. He decided to take it."

"Why are you telling me this?" Flores finally said.

"Because if you're planning to help him escape, I hope this would dissuade you."

"How could I escape?"

Gente chortled. "Please, Señor Flores. I very much

doubt there's a camp that could hold you, should you set your mind to it. But be aware, you will have to travel many miles before you are out of our territory. And I will not take it kindly."

"Why didn't you just kill us?" Flores asked. "If Calderon betrayed you, why bother keeping him alive?"

"Because we're hoping to reestablish a relationship with your company."

"I'm just a pawn, remember?" Flores said. "Not much I can do."

"I'm aware of that. I feel badly keeping you here. But you are now a bargaining tool. And, I hope, someone who can provide unique assistance. Should you agree to help us, I can have you across the border by this time tomorrow."

"Help you how?" Flores asked. The offer sounded too good to be true—which meant it was probably some sort of setup.

A knock at the door. Gente appeared irritated by the interruption, but nodded for the guard to open it. Another man in fatigues poked his head in.

"Han llegado, General."

Gente's expression brightened. "So sorry, Señor Flores, this is a busy day."

Flores stood. "Thanks for the water."

Gente held up a hand. "Sit. We still have time to discuss what you can do to secure your freedom."

Seventeen

Jake stripped off his pants and looked around for a place to hang them, finally draping them over the ancient TV in the corner. The cuffs dripped muddy water onto the matted green carpet. He was in another crappy motel room, nearly as bad as the last. Not that he cared: right now, all he wanted was to scrub off the dirt and get five solid hours of sleep. Although, after all he'd been through, the temptation to just drop into bed was overwhelming, shower be damned. From the look of things, the sheets had already seen their share of filth.

Hours earlier they'd filed back into the jungle wrapped in silence, leaving Mark and Decker behind. As the shadows grew, they quickened their pace. Still, most of the way they were forced to stumble through the dark, afraid to use flashlights. Jake had never been so wet and muddy in his entire life.

After making it back to the jeeps, they drove to a town ten miles down the road, an enclave filled with the sort of souvenir shops that sprouted like mushrooms near tourist attractions. Shabby taco stands and motels sporting a variety of pyramid motifs dotted the landscape. This time of year, there were few other cars. They had eaten in silence, the only customers in an open-air restaurant. As Jake choked down rice and beans, a dog wandered in and nonchalantly pissed on the leg of their table. Which pretty much summed up the entire experience for him so far.

He was about to turn on the shower when there was a knock at the door. Jake wrapped a towel around his waist and opened it. Syd leaned against the doorjamb. She'd already changed, her blond hair was still wet.

"I was just about to chip the mud off," Jake said.

She came in, closing the door behind her. "Want to borrow my chisel?"

"Girls don't have chisels. Even I know that," Jake said.

She grinned at him. "You'd be surprised."

Jake was suddenly hyperconscious of his nudity. He took a step back, gesturing to the only chair in the room. "Have a seat."

Syd eyed it. "That thing looks like it could walk on its own. No, thanks."

"So what's up?" Jake asked. He was a little discomfited by the way she was looking at him, like a cat appraising a meal.

"What's that scar from?" she asked finally, pointing to his chest.

"Mark, actually." Jake looked down at the rough circle. "Shot me with a BB when I was twelve."

"On purpose?"

"Yup. I told him he couldn't aim for shit." In spite of himself, Jake smiled a little at the memory. They'd been out squirrel hunting with their Christmas presents, matching BB guns. They both kept missing, goading each other about it. But Mark was the one with the temper.

"So he shot you?"

"What, he doesn't seem the type?" Jake raised an eyebrow, and she laughed.

"Ah, sibling rivalry."

"I don't even know if you have any brothers or sisters," Jake said. "You never talk about your family."

She stiffened almost imperceptibly before saying, "Nothing to tell."

"C'mon, let's have it. You've seen my scar."

"We should try to come up with a plan."

"See? Whenever I ask, you change the subject."

"Why do you want to know?" Syd stepped closer. It was a small room. She was a foot away, the bed right behind him.

"Just curious," Jake said, suddenly overly aware of his breathing. He tried to force his mind back to Kelly, but she suddenly felt infinitely far away, more a memory than a reality.

Syd reached out and ran a fingernail around the ridges of the scar, outlining it. Her gaze never left his face. His body responded to her touch. Jake readjusted the towel and edged back until the hem of the comforter brushed his heels.

Syd half smiled. Her hand was still on him. She trailed her fingers down his chest. Jake sucked in his breath as they grazed his belly button and kept going.

"It's a bad idea."

"That's what you said back in Livermore," she reminded him, stepping closer. "Only then, you were more convincing." One deft tug and his towel fell to the floor. Both of her hands were on him now. He tried to object as she sank to her knees, but as she took him in her mouth his head dropped back.

"Oh, God," was all he could manage.

Her tongue was all over, teasing him. He fell into the

rhythm, her hands running up and down his legs, setting the small hairs on end.

He was getting close when something started beeping. Syd pulled her head away.

"That's the radio," she said, getting up.

"Leave it." Jake put his hands on her shoulders, but she resisted. She kept her body close to him, rubbing her breasts against his chest as she dug the radio out of her pocket.

Mark's voice crackled through. "We've got some intel for you. I can transmit it."

"Great," she said. "The satellite uplink is open. Send what you've got."

"Roger. Check back when you've read it."

Syd set the radio down on the table and turned back to Jake.

He had retrieved the towel and wrapped it back around his waist. "So, uh…you should probably…"

Syd was unbuttoning her shirt. "Oh, we've got time. At least ten minutes until the transmission comes through. The satellite reception here is for shit." The shirt slipped to the floor.

"Syd—"

"I know, you're engaged." She unzipped her pants, and they dropped next to her shirt. She approached slowly, wearing only light blue panties. "If you want me to stop, I will."

She put both hands on his chest and pushed. Jake fell back onto the bed. As she mounted him, she nuzzled his ear and whispered, "You're already dirty, so we might as well have some fun."

FEBRUARY 1

Eighteen

Kelly winced as she slipped again. She shone the flashlight on her elbow: blood. Crap. She panned the light around the ground until she found a relatively clean area to set down her backpack. It took a minute of digging through it to find the first-aid kit. She had to give Syd credit: the woman knew how to pack a go-kit. Inside Kelly had also found a flashlight, duct tape, a thin rope, energy bars and water. Sadly nothing she could cover her nose with. Even after five hours of exposure, the stench was relentless and unremitting. It felt like all manner of terrible creatures had crawled inside her nose and set up camp.

Kelly rolled up her sleeve, wincing as the fabric peeled away from the cut. She doused the wound with antiseptic, figuring this was an ideal place to catch a staph infection. Kelly bandaged the cut as best she could one-handed and pulled the sleeve back down, then drew in a deep breath. She'd have to be more careful. Fatigue affected her more since the accident. Her coordination went right out the window when she didn't get enough sleep. And tonight was definitely one of those nights.

Kelly had concluded that this must be the main dump for Mexico City. The bookseller hadn't been kidding, it was sprawling. In places the refuse was stacked several stories high. It was like walking through a garbage version of Manhattan. She picked her way through carefully, grateful that she still wore the combat boots Syd had given her. They were ugly, but perfect for navigating this mess. The air was so torpid with rot it was hard to breathe.

It was nearly dawn. Kelly had been searching for hours without encountering any sign of Stefan. She had come across dozens of rats, cats, a few feral dogs that forced her to skirt around, waving her flashlight menacingly as they growled at her. Most upsetting had been the realization that people actually lived here. When the bookseller mentioned *pepenadores,* she wasn't sure what he meant. But less than an hour into her search she'd spotted movement out of the corner of her eye. Kelly swung around, gun ready. Her flashlight revealed a child of no more than ten rummaging through the piles of trash. He held up a hand against the glare, then scampered away. She followed him with the beam as he disappeared into a stack of rusted metal. Kelly cautiously approached, then shone the light inside. Five sets of eyes stared back at her, all wide with fright.

"Lo siento," Kelly had said, backing away as she lowered her weapon.

They had only been the first of many. Apparently a significant portion of the city's population couldn't even afford the run-down housing she'd seen over the past two days. As she navigated the dank corridors among the trash mounds, she became adept at spotting ramshackle shanties cobbled together. Snores or arguments issued from a few. Others appeared empty, but she could sense the presence of people inside. People who were probably as afraid as she was, clutching something to defend themselves with. Stefan was undoubtedly not the first predator to stalk this ground. The few denizens who materialized at the shanty entrances gaped at her. She'd never felt more out of place.

Kelly got back to her feet, weaving slightly. She was exhausted, starving and filthy. What was she doing? She didn't even speak enough Spanish to ask anyone she encountered about Stefan. He could be fast asleep in one of the shanties she'd already passed by, and she'd never know it. She should go back to the motel, or to the airport. She could call her old boss at the FBI, try to persuade him to send a team of investigators. But the only new lead she had was slim at best, and the P.I.'s report had been ignored before. Unless she came up with something solid, chances were the FBI wouldn't act. Better if she could give them an exact location, something to work off of. And for that, she had to stay the course. She moved forward.

Kelly tripped again, nearly landing on the jagged top of a rusty can. One thing was certain: Mexico City was not a recycling mecca.

A strange noise broke the silence. Kelly froze, straining her ears. It repeated, faintly. There was no mistaking it, someone was screaming. With renewed energy, she made her way toward the sound.

Mark settled into his bivy sack and closed his eyes. He hadn't slept for nearly twenty-four hours, but couldn't manage to drop off. He shifted, careful not to make any noise. He and Decker had ensconced themselves in the nook of a cliff. It was the perfect spot, ground cover rendering it invisible from above and below. The only danger was rolling off. They'd each tied a hand to a root jutting out from the dirt beside them. Chances are it wouldn't hold them, but at least if they started to roll the arm tug would wake them. And hopefully no more guards with bladder problems would stumble past.

Decker had crashed out almost immediately. That was something they were conditioned to do: given a safe opportunity during a mission, grab some shut-eye. It could literally save your life, and was a hell of a lot more effective than pills at keeping your brain sharp. Not that Mark hadn't gone the pill route on occasion; they all had. But given a choice, he preferred sleep.

Tonight it eluded him. They'd spent the hours since dusk casing the camp, making the most of the cover of darkness. As Mark gazed at the swaying trees above him, intertwined branches forming a dark ceiling, he reflected back on what they'd seen.

None of it had been good.

They hadn't been able to locate any of their men, including Calderon. The camp covered over a square mile by his estimation and was cleverly constructed in two parts, an outer circle surrounding an inner one. The outer circle was penetrable, surrounded by a low chain link fence. The problem was that it was composed entirely of guard barracks and training grounds. Apparently this was where the Zetas trained and stationed the bulk of their forces. Even at two in the morning there had been active patrols, two men each and no more than three minutes between each pass. If that wasn't enough security, every hundred feet there was a guard tower, complete with generator-fed lights and sirens.

So to access the prisoners' holding pens, you had to infiltrate that outer circle, getting past the guards and patrols. It wasn't impossible: he'd already gone back and stripped the fatigues off their kills, just in case they ended up needing them. But both he and Decker would stick out like sore thumbs in there. If Flores was still with them, he would have had a shot posing as a guard. As things stood, however, there was no way.

They'd also witnessed something that turned out to be a drill. The siren that had sent Syd and the others scurrying away had summoned hundreds of guards armed with automatic weapons. Each took a position outside a pen, gun ready. Mark's guess was that if a competing cartel or police force actually did raid the camp, orders were to shoot the prisoners. The guards stood there for a full five minutes before the siren issued a staggered series of bleats, obviously the all clear.

So a small force was no good, and a small army would be even worse. He'd sent the intel to Syd, hoping she'd come up with something. Because based on what he'd seen, there was no way in hell they were getting anyone out of there.

After everything that had happened, he felt personally responsible for Flores and Sock. The prospect of being forced to abandon them rankled him.

Mark shifted onto his side and squeezed his eyes shut again, trying to find sleep, but his mind continued to race. He should have been more insistent about sending Jake home. It had been a conscious decision, going to work for Tyr rather than The Longhorn Group. He knew that if Jake ever got wind of it he'd be pissed, but figured that was a small price to pay. Despite what Jake thought, it hadn't been a decision he arrived at lightly, or out of revenge. This line of work, bad things happened. Mark never wanted to leave his blood on his brother's hands. Which made him showing up here even worse.

Decker snored slightly, and Mark dug an elbow into his back. The noise subsided. Decker grumbled once, then the snoring recommenced. Mark watched a line of ants give them a wide berth. They balanced leaf cuttings above their heads as they marched along the cliff edge, then vanished over the side. He closed his eyes again and prayed for Syd to come up with a plan.

Michael Maltz shifted in his chair. Holding any position for too long hurt, it didn't matter if he was standing, sitting, or lying down. All night long he awoke every hour or so, the pressure from even the softest mattress felt like spikes against his damaged joints.

He watched as Jake and Syd pored over the sheets of paper spread across the table. It was nearly 0400. Based on the intel from Mark Riley, Syd had scrawled out some diagrams, enlargements of images Mark emailed her: primitive maps of the compound, a rough sketch of guard stations, the works. Didn't matter, Maltz thought. He'd spent the bulk of his career doing this sort of snatch-and-grab operation. It was what he was trained for, what he was best at. And he'd been doing it long enough to recognize an impossible situation when he saw one. The camp might as well be Fort Knox. They weren't getting in there without cluster bombs, drones, the works. Anything less would turn into the Alamo.

Syd and Jake weren't ready to admit that yet, although he could tell they saw it. They'd spent the past half hour arguing, hashing out details of one plan after another. Each was ultimately rejected as unfeasible.

Syd leaned over to examine a drawing on the far side of the table, her hip brushing Jake's. Riley jumped like he'd been shocked, and Maltz thought, *huh.* Not that it was surprising. Syd tended to get what she wanted, and she'd wanted Riley for a while. Maltz didn't really get why. Riley was a decent enough guy, but Syd could do better. Had done better, that he'd seen. But then, he'd never been accused of understanding women.

Shame about the fiancée, though. She seemed nice enough.

"We could try a variation on Operation Jaque," Jake said.

Syd tilted her head to the side, thinking it over. Jaque was an operation led by the Colombian army a few years earlier. A relatively small unit had successfully rescued three U.S. contractors and a slew of high-ranking Colombian officials by posing as humanitarians. They choppered them right the hell out of there. But that had been an ad hoc camp, run by a bunch of kids with visions of Che Guevara in their heads. "I don't think the Zetas give a crap about their prisoners' well-being," she said. "And they're supposed to be a hell of a lot smarter than the FARC."

Maltz pushed off the arms of the chair, lumbering to his feet. "We get hold of some C4, punch a hole in the perimeter here." He jabbed at the map. "And here, and here. Then we have a few guys in uniform infiltrate."

"Won't work." Jake was already shaking his head. "Mark said they line up to shoot prisoners if there's any sign of trouble."

"Then we just need better intel. You know where your guys are, you get to them first."

"And what about the other prisoners? We're just going to let them be massacred?"

Maltz shrugged. "You see another option?"

"Either way, we need Riley and Decker to get the exact coordinates of the friendlies." Syd brushed a strand of hair out of her eyes as she bent over again. Maltz caught Jake watching her, and flashed him a broad grin. Jake flushed and looked away. "Mark said he'd try to get closer today. Not much we can do until then except gear up. Maltz, I'm sending you and Kane back into town to scare up some more firepower. Pablo should be able to spare a few M203 grenade launchers. Try to get a Barrett fifty sniper rifle, too."

"Gotcha. Anything else?"

Syd thought for a second, lips pursed. "Would a helicopter be too much to ask?"

"Probably. But I'll see what I can do."

"If not, then an up-armored Hilux—something big."

"Sure." Maltz left. He felt someone at his heels, and turned to find Jake following him from the room, as if the guy was scared to be left alone with Syd. Maltz had to smile at that. Wise man.

"I want to thank you for staying." Jake fell in step beside him as he walked back toward his room. "You and the other guys didn't have to."

"Not a problem," Maltz said. "Anything for Syd."

"Still, thanks." He fell silent. Maltz stopped outside his door and waited. "The thing is," Jake continued, "I can't see any way for this to work."

"That's 'cause it can't," Maltz said.

"Yeah, you're right." Jake looked past him, toward the neon sign mounted in front of the motel that featured a constantly erupting volcano. "My brother's going to get himself killed."

"I wouldn't worry about Mark. Guys like him can handle themselves." Maltz turned the knob and flicked on the light in his room. "I gotta wake Kane. Hold tight until we get back."

Cesar Calderon awoke to something sharp pressed against his throat. He opened his mouth to yell, but fingers clamped down, stifling him before he could make a sound.

"Relax, *señor*."

It was Flores, his new cell mate and, apparently, employee. Calderon shut his eyes and sighed. The minute they'd reopened the gate last night, ushering Flores back in after his meeting with Gente, he'd known it would come to this. There had been something different about the young man's expression, a hardened look. They'd made him an offer, and he'd accepted.

"Gente wants you to kill me," Calderon said.

The pressure on his throat eased. He could make out Flores's silhouette against the chicken-wire ceiling. He didn't respond.

"Please make it quick." Calderon grabbed Flores's wrist to draw the knife closer.

"Why would I kill you?" Flores asked after a pause.

"Because they'll release you. I don't blame you. If the situation was reversed, I'd do the same. But I'd prefer not to suffer if possible."

Calderon closed his eyes again, determined not to see death coming. He uttered a silent prayer, pictured his wife, Thalia, and felt a pang of sorrow. He should have given her children. He wondered if notification would be immediate, or would months pass before the news reached her? Hard to say how the Zetas would play this. He used to consider himself an expert on his opponent. That had been his gift, sizing up the man on the other side of the phone line, discerning when he was bluffing, the best time to make an offer. Now, when it mattered most, he appeared to have lost that particular skill.

A trickle of blood down the side of his neck distracted him. His breath came in shallow gasps.

"My wife is pregnant," Flores finally said softly.

"Felicitaciones." Calderon swallowed hard. "There is no other option for you, then. You must return to her."

Still, the young man waited. Calderon frowned. Better

to have his throat slit in his sleep than to suffer through this. "They will kill you if you do not complete the task," he finally said. "I know Gente. He is as good as his word."

"How do you know him?"

The question was sharp, accusing. Calderon half smiled at the vehemence of it. "Let me guess. Gente told you we were collaborating."

"Do the other prisoners know? How many are here because of you?" Flores spat.

Calderon sighed. "They're supposed to cover this in our training. A seasoned kidnapper will say anything to get you to help them."

A pause, then Flores replied, "He could have just threatened me with death."

"Yes, but this gives you an opportunity to absolve your conscience. If what he said was true, and you believed it, you would feel justified killing me, wouldn't you? Especially since I'm the only reason you're here."

"I guess so." Flores sounded uncertain, but still wary. A roving spotlight caught the tip of the knife, making it glint. It was the one he'd used to whittle his chess pieces. Clever.

Calderon's lips tweaked. Strange that he could smile in such a situation, but there it was. It was fitting that he was about to be murdered by an employee wielding his own tool against him, the knife he had gone to such great lengths to procure.

"What were you thinking, anyway, taking a business trip to Mexico? A guy like you has a bull's-eye on him."

"So I should just stay home? How long have you been working for us, Enrique?"

"Six months."

"Then you've met some of the other men, heard about the jobs they were working. Europe. North Africa. The former Soviet bloc nations. South America. Silicon Valley. East Asia. Where could I travel without risk of being kidnapped?"

"Nowhere, I guess."

"Exactly. I took the appropriate precautions, but as you yourself learned," he said pointedly, "Los Zetas are far better trained than some of our other adversaries."

"And here you are."

"Yes. Here I am." Calderon sighed.

After a long pause, Flores spoke again. "They told me you cut a deal for more money with a competing cartel."

"Did they? Well. That would have been clever of me." Calderon folded his legs and clasped his wrists around his shins. "So, what now? You kill me, and they set you free?"

"Something like that." Flores twisted his wrist, sending the knife in a slow arc. "What I can't figure out is why they want me to do it. They could shoot you themselves."

Calderon half smiled. "You're not the only one Gente offered a deal. When he called me in, he proposed forming a collaboration with Tyr for client lists and information. If I refused, he'd kill me. That's why there haven't been any negotiations, no proof of life. If I agreed, he said they'd make it appear as if I escaped on my own."

"What did you say?"

"No, of course. Such a deal would compromise everything I've built Tyr to stand for." Calderon rubbed his eyes with his thumb and forefinger. This was taking too long, dawn was breaking. "We must come up with a plan."

Flores scoffed. "What, other than killing you?"

"Clearly you're not going to be able to do it, *amigo.*

Soldiers these days…" Calderon shook his head. "They can bomb a village to oblivion, but are unable to kill a man face-to-face. That's what happens when warfare is conducted at a remove. But if you don't complete the task, we both have a problem."

Flores lowered the knife. "Fine," he said after a minute. "What do we do?"

"General Gente is first and foremost a businessman," Calderon said. "I'll request a meeting to tell him I've changed my mind."

"You seriously think that will change anything? That he'll just let us go free?"

"No, but it buys us some time. Hopefully enough for you to get us out of here."

Nineteen

Kelly skirted mounds of trash the size of large hills. She paused frequently, shifting course a few times as she tried to pinpoint the source of the screams. They had increased in volume, then abruptly abated. The last had been a few minutes ago.

The first rays of dawn were breaking over the dump, casting everything in an oddly ethereal glow. Kelly spun slowly, trying to get her bearings. She was relatively certain the screams were coming from the west. She had the disconcerting realization that she had no idea how to get out of this maze, but shoved it away: she'd figure that out later. Now, she had to find Stefan—if it even was him, and not some other thug trolling the dump for victims. In a place like this, crime was probably a way of life. If the *federales* didn't respond quickly to an incident like their shootout in Iztapalapa the other day, it was hard to imagine they'd police the city dump. All the more reason to be careful, she reminded herself.

Kelly switched her grip on the H&K. Her fingers ached, but she didn't dare holster it. She pivoted in a slow circle. The silence was broken by a fluttering of wings: vultures, soaring past above her. She repressed a shiver.

The morning air was damp, and she was only wearing a thin Gore-Tex shell over her T-shirt.

A clattering, off to her right.

Kelly picked her way carefully, trying not to make a sound as she circled another mountain of trash. On the opposite side, about fifteen feet away, stood another shanty. She approached slowly. Despite the cold, a trickle of sweat slid down her back. The door hung open. It appeared abandoned, but something was off.

Kelly nearly jumped out of her skin as a loud crackle pierced the morning stillness. Glancing down, she cursed silently: she'd stepped on an empty potato-chip bag. She lifted her foot to step over it. Chanced a quick look over her shoulder—and saw a giant fist approaching at warp speed.

Kelly tucked her chin in time to temper the impact, but the force of the blow still knocked her to the ground. She landed hard on something sharp and gasped. Above her loomed an enormous figure, face cast in shadow by the sun rising behind him. The gun had flown from her hand when she fell. Kelly scrambled toward it. The man anticipated the move, lunging forward and kicking it away.

He turned and grinned at her.

"Agent Jones. Lovely to see you again."

Ellis Brown was not a happy man.

It had taken far too long for them to get their asses out here. Someone had cleared out their usual local arms dealer, and he had a pretty good idea who that was. Goddamn Syd Clement and her pissant outfit. He'd been forced to make do with inferior equipment, which rankled him. He'd given his men orders to shoot on sight if they encountered the other team, but so far there hadn't been any sign of them.

Making matters worse, the closer they got to the site of this supposed prison camp, the more the cartel guy clammed up. All night long he'd led them on a wild-goose chase, up and down two other mountains before claiming this was the right one.

Either the camp didn't exist and this was just a stalling technique—or he was leading them to his cartel's den to be slaughtered. Both good reasons why Brown hadn't wanted to rush in half-cocked. Linus Smiley showing up had thrown a wrench in the works. Snide little bastard began issuing orders, as if he had a clue what to do in the theater. Boy Scouts had more military training than that sniveling pencil pusher. Brown took comfort in the fact that Smiley appeared completely miserable. His fancy khaki outfit was soaked in mud, and he'd badly twisted an ankle five minutes in. He limped along at the rear, followed by the last of Brown's men.

Brown wiped sweat off his face with the back of his arm. What he'd always admired about Cesar Calderon was that, like any good commander, he understood how to hold the reins. There were times when you had to give your men some slack, allowing them to do their jobs unimpeded. Cesar would never have shown up in the middle of a mission, undermining his authority with his men. Brown had been sorely tempted to put a bullet in Smiley's skull last night. If they didn't recover Cesar, and Smiley took over Tyr…he didn't even let himself think about it.

The cartel guy stopped short, and they all paused. His hands were zip tied in front of him. They'd cleaned him up a little in case they encountered any *federales* on the drive here, but he still looked like hell, his face a mass of hamburger. He turned to Valencia, the team member acting as his translator, and jabbered something.

Valencia looked askance at Brown. "He says this is wrong, too. Thinks it might be the next hill."

"Tell him he's this close to spending a few quality hours with a blowtorch," Brown snapped.

"Maybe we should head back to that town we passed," Smiley said in a quavering voice. "I could use some sleep before we tackle another—"

"We'll sleep after we find the boss." Three long strides forward and Brown towered over the cartel guy. The Mexican shied away, but Brown grabbed his jacket, yanking him close. "Listen, you little shit, I'm done screwing around. I don't know what you're trying to pull, but if this story about a camp isn't complete bullshit, you're going to lead me there. And if you don't, I'll start by slicing off your tongue."

The guy's eyes went wide, and Brown smelled urine. He glanced at the telltale stain on the guy's pants and grinned. "Guess you don't have to translate that," he said to Valencia.

"No, sir." Valencia stood slightly to the side.

"Tell him he has five minutes to give us a location. Any longer, we tie him to a tree and have some fun with him."

Syd lay on her back, hands crossed behind her head as she examined the concrete swirls comprising her ceiling. A mass of papers surrounded her on the bed. Not that she needed them anymore; after going over them for hours they were fully committed to memory. Unfortunately, there wasn't anything there she could use.

She rolled onto her stomach and dangled her feet off the side of the bed, sighing. Funny, usually she would appreciate a challenge like this. Syd loved being out in the field, facing seemingly insurmountable obstacles. But for some reason, what happened with Jake last night had taken her heart out of the operation.

Syd let her mind wander back over it, remembering the details. The way his tongue tasted when he kissed her. His hands, the rough skin around the knuckles. Going in, she hadn't really expected anything to happen. But in the aftermath of the jungle, with all that adrenaline still churning through her body…she'd learned a long time ago there were only two surefire ways to dissipate it: fighting or sex. And she generally preferred the latter option.

Strangely it wasn't working. The adrenaline was gone, but she still couldn't sleep. Syd knew it had probably been a mistake—Jake was the type of guy who would read more into what happened than it actually meant. Right now he was probably castigating himself, she thought with a snort. Seducing one of the other team members might have been a smarter move, although in this day and age that opened her up to a sexual-harassment suit. She laughed at the thought—how had she of all people ended up in a job where that was a possibility?

The fact that she couldn't stop thinking about Jake was seriously starting to irritate her.

Syd raised her toes up toward the ceiling in a stretch, then brought them down, landing on the floor. She used the momentum to fall forward in a plank position and pumped out twenty push-ups. Sitting back up, she eyed the shower curtain bar, wondering if it would hold her weight for pull-ups. Probably not. Yoga, maybe?

She ran a hand across the back of her neck, massaging out the kinks. Dawn was breaking, the light below her curtains was shifting from blue to yellow. Mark and Decker were probably holed up somewhere grabbing some sleep. It would be more dangerous for them to case the camp during daylight hours, but they intended to try. Maltz and

Kane were en route to the city to re-up on supplies now that she had a better idea what the operation required. For the moment, there was nothing she could do.

So why the hell couldn't she sleep?

She considered knocking on Jake's door. Maybe he'd be up for a game of cards, she told herself.

Syd quickly dismissed the idea. In reality, she knew exactly how he'd respond to her showing up. It would be awkward, him stuttering out a bunch of platitudes that amounted to "go away." All because he was hung up on a redhead who had been useless even before she lost her leg.

Syd flopped back down on her mattress. It was ironic: the one time she didn't want to be alone, there was no one who wanted to be with her.

Brown lay on his belly glaring through a pair of field binoculars. His little pep talk had worked. The cartel guy had drawn a map with shaking hands, swearing on his mother's life that it would lead to the Zetas prison camp. And lo and behold, much to Brown's surprise, the camp actually existed.

While he and Delano did some recon, the rest of his men were stationed a half mile back. Brown had taken the abduction of Cesar Calderon as a personal affront. The man had given him a job despite his spotty service record. Calderon had trusted him when most men in his position wouldn't. If Brown had to march into that camp personally and kill every last motherfucking Zeta encountered, he'd do it, and happily.

Based on what he was seeing, that might be what it was going to take. Brown had never actually had to deal with a Zetas camp before. Most of those cases were solved by Calderon over the phone. Now he understood why that seemed to be company policy. The place was a goddamn fortress.

His unit had already been reduced to fifteen able-bodied men after their run-in the other day. Combine that with the shit equipment, and the fact that one of those men was Sock…they might as well turn around and head back now.

"Remind me again why this is a snatch and grab?" Delano asked. "Seems like the perfect case for a ransom." He was lying on his stomach beside Brown, holding up his own pair of binoculars.

"Ours is not to reason why, my friend." But Brown had wondered the same thing. He'd heard through the grapevine that Tyr hadn't even been sent proof of life, which was unprecedented. It got him thinking. Maybe a ransom had been requested, and Smiley refused to pony up. Smiley showing up here had only fueled his suspicions. If the situation had been reversed, he had no doubt that Smiley would already be home golfing, yet another of Cesar's success stories. And the fact that Smiley had sent in another team first, led by an unseasoned leader, spoke volumes.

Brown intended to correct that mistake now. If Cesar was still alive, he was getting him home. And then they'd both deal with Smiley.

"We should send Valencia in as a guard. He's got the best shot."

Brown grunted in response. Delano was right. He had a few native Mexicans on his team but Valencia would be the best option. He had one of those faces people never glanced twice at. They'd have to try to match the Zetas' camo as best they could, though from what he could see it looked pretty standard. There were enough guards down there that they couldn't possibly all know each other by face. They'd wait for a shift change, then send him in on a quick recon mission. With any luck, the Tyr men were all being housed close together. If not, then Calderon was the priority. Once he was out, they'd save Flores, Riley and Decker if they could.

Brown scanned the camp one more time, making a mental note of how many guards were in each tower, how many were making rounds. "Okay." He lowered the binoculars. "Let's—"

Delano was frozen, staring at something behind him. Brown rolled slowly onto his side. His eyes followed the barrel of a rifle up to find a big guy gazing down at them.

Twenty

Kelly nearly passed out as another punch knocked her head back. Stefan had lifted her off the ground with one hand, and was beating her senseless with the other. The few kicks and punches she'd landed glanced off him, as disregarded as a gnat on an elephant. Her head throbbed. The temptation to succumb to the darkness was almost overwhelming. She wouldn't be able to sustain many more blows.

Stefan's grip on her throat tightened. He wrapped his other hand around the first and squeezed. Stars clouded her vision. Kelly clawed at his hands, but his grip was steel. He drew her close, his face inches away, fixated on her eyes as they bugged out of her head. He had an odd expression, a mix of stark curiosity and fascination. Kelly struggled, her chest contracting desperately for air. Everything tunneled down until all she could see was Stefan's grinning face floating in a red haze.

That galvanized her. Kelly's right leg shot back. She launched it forward, putting all of her hip strength behind it. Her prosthetic foot was made of energy-storing carbon fiber capable of producing a hundred pounds of cubic pressure, all of which she now directed at Stefan's torso.

She felt the reverberation of the kick in her hip. Stefan gasped and his hands released.

Kelly dropped to the ground coughing, her hands reflexively checking her neck. It felt raw, bruised, like she'd swallowed a razor blade. She stumbled backward, out of reach.

Stefan was writhing around, clutching his stomach. Kelly's expression hardened. She lifted her leg again, from the hip the way Brandi had shown her in countless therapy sessions. Kelly brought the metal foot down hard on Stefan's right knee. He yelped and drew it protectively toward his chest, then tried to roll away. She focused on his right hand. He jerked it away an instant before her foot connected.

Stefan's face hardened. His hand snapped out, grabbing her ankle and pulling.

The sudden move knocked her off balance. Kelly stumbled and fell. He held fast. Kelly gritted her teeth as her stump twisted unnaturally in the prosthetic socket, straining against the pins.

"I see you've undergone some changes, Agent Jones," Stefan spat. "Tough couple of years?"

Something inside Kelly snapped. All the rage and frustration she'd kept bottled up for months surged to the surface. Her other leg swung around, delivering a solid blow to Stefan's jaw. His head shot back. She used the momentum to roll to her stomach, then lashed out with a donkey kick to his nose. There was a satisfying crunch, and the pressure on her prosthesis released.

Kelly scrambled to her feet. Stefan clutched his nose and struggled to stand, growling at her in Danish.

She couldn't see her gun, but spotted a length of rusty rebar ten feet away. Kelly lunged toward it, hearing him right behind her. She reached out, snatched it up and whirled back around. She didn't have time to aim, so the first blow glanced off his shoulder. Kelly hopped back, getting a few feet between them. Stefan faced her in a wrestler's stance, hands loose by his sides, knees slightly bent. His nose canted to the left, bright red blood flowed from it down into his mouth. He didn't seem to notice.

Kelly kept her elbow close to her side. The danger of wielding a weapon against a stronger opponent was that he could rip it away and turn it against her. She had to land some crushing blows without getting close enough for him to seize the advantage.

It hurt to breathe, as if his hands were still wrapped around her throat. Her stump throbbed, and her vision was slightly blurry. Kelly blinked to clear it. Stefan feinted forward, and she dodged left. The motion sent another stab of pain shooting up her spine. She gritted her teeth and wiped a bead of sweat from her eye.

Stefan was smiling again. It was the same look he'd given her the last time they'd faced off, nearly three years earlier. He'd come close to killing her that night. She still had nightmares about it from time to time.

He feinted again. Kelly swept the rebar in an arc, but he dodged back quickly and it grazed his knuckle.

Stefan cocked his head to the side. "Before I kill you, I'm curious to hear how you found me." That same voice, heavy with a Danish accent, overly formal.

"I was already here. Finding you was a bonus." It hurt to talk, but she wanted to keep him off balance. Kelly watched his eyes closely, waiting for them to indicate that he was about to strike again.

"Vacationing in Mexico City?" His eyebrows shot up. "Couldn't afford Cancún on a government salary? That's a shame. I hope you enjoyed yourself."

"It was great," Kelly said. "It'll be even better once I arrest you."

He barked a laugh. "You always had a certain charm, Agent Jones. It almost makes me forget that, thanks to you, I nearly died in a river."

"I was hoping you had."

"Yes, well. Sorry to disappoint." He lunged again. Kelly anticipated the move this time. She brought the rebar down hard on his forearm. He groaned, and she seized the opportunity to crack him across the kidneys. Stefan dropped to one knee.

Kelly danced back again, momentarily forgetting the pain in her leg. "I should probably mention I don't officially work for the FBI anymore."

Stefan opened his mouth to respond, then shifted his gaze to something past her shoulder. Kelly wasn't about to fall for that stunt. She lifted the rebar, preparing to slam it across his forehead.

At the sound of voices behind her, Kelly froze. She couldn't understand what they were saying, but it belatedly occurred to her that Stefan was the local here. It was possible he'd managed to recruit new protégés willing to step in and save him.

"Sorry we didn't have more time to catch up. Lovely seeing you again." He sneered. Then he gained his feet and started running.

It took Kelly a second to recover from the unexpected move. She started after him, her go-kit bouncing against her back as she ran. She only got ten feet before a familiar sound brought her skidding to a stop.

The bullet shredded the top of a plastic bag a foot to her right, sending up a puff of white confetti. Kelly slowly raised her hands and turned to face the new threat.

Two men in black uniforms, black baseball caps and

Kevlar vests stood about twenty feet away. Both had automatics leveled at her chest.

"*Now* you show up?" Kelly said. "You've got to be kidding me." One of them shouted at her in Spanish. *"No hablo!"* She chanced a glance back over her shoulder. Stefan had vanished. At the realization that he'd gotten away again, her shoulders slumped. Suddenly she was bone-tired. Kelly swayed, a move that made the already skittish cops even more agitated.

Kelly didn't care. She carefully lowered herself to the ground, perching on her backpack. One of the cops approached slowly, keeping his gun trained on her, asking what sounded like the same question over and over again.

"He got away," she said dully, running her hands through her hair, mindless of the filth coating them. "I can't believe you let him get away."

The other cop had disappeared into Stefan's shanty. He stumbled back into view a minute later, bent over and vomited.

The two *federales* engaged in a few minutes of animated conversation, then shifted their attention back to her. Kelly couldn't understand what they were saying, but she didn't like the look on their faces. She'd seen it before, the universal expression of cops facing down a really bad guy. *"Soy policía,"* she attempted.

It didn't seem to make a difference. One leveled his rifle at her chest while the other approached her. He wrenched Kelly to her feet, twisting her arm painfully behind her. She struggled against him, suddenly panicked. Every terrible thing Syd had said about the Mexican police force rushed into her mind. They committed kidnappings, extortion, car theft, burglary, even rape.

"What the hell?" Kelly demanded, trying to keep the fear from her voice.

He forced her to the threshold of the shack. When she saw what was inside, Kelly's stomach turned and she nearly threw up.

Lying in a coagulating pool of blood on a pile of rags was the body of a young boy, or what was left of him. All the skin had been stripped from his body. Long pieces of it hung from a clothesline draped across the room.

"This wasn't me," Kelly gasped, fighting for air. "It was him, the man I was fighting…"

They either didn't understand or didn't care. A pair of handcuffs slapped down on her wrists, and they led her away.

"Well, goddamn." Brown's face split in a grin. "If it isn't Mark Riley."

Mark didn't return the smile. When he and Decker had first spotted the Tyr unit, they'd fallen back to discuss their options. Not knowing who to trust, they'd decided their best move was to observe from a distance. When Brown split off from the rest of the group, it presented them with the perfect opportunity to get some questions answered. With that in mind, he kept the LMT's barrel aimed at Brown's chest.

Brown's smile faded. "You got some sort of Stockholm Syndrome, Riley? We work for the same people."

"Someone ratted us out." Decker materialized beside Delano. "Zetas were waiting when we showed up."

Brown's eyes narrowed. "Well, it sure as hell wasn't me."

"You and Calderon are buddies, right?" Mark cocked his head to the side. "Funny that you weren't in charge of this snatch and grab."

"Smiley's decision, not mine." Brown grunted. "Hell, I wanted to come. He said I was still needed on the Colombia job."

"He's with you," Mark said. "Why?"

"Dunno. Thought that was kind of strange myself." Brown eyed him. "We got Sock back there, too."

"Wysocki? How the hell did he get away?"

"Said he left Kaplan and Flores and went for some food. When he came back, they were gone."

"But he decided not to wait for us?" Decker said.

"Yeah, that struck me as kind of strange, too. Plus he showed up without a scratch on him," Brown replied.

"That son of a bitch." Decker spat on the ground.

"Kaplan's dead," Mark said. "We found his body when we got back."

"Sorry to hear that. We worked together a few times, he was a good man." Brown shook his head. "This has turned into one giant clusterfuck, that's for damn sure."

"Why'd you take Sock along?" Mark asked.

"Figured it was the only way to keep an eye on him. Listen, we're both navy men. You mind lowering that weapon?"

Mark hesitated a moment, then dropped the barrel down. Decker kept his up. At a glance from Brown, he shrugged and said, "I'm a marine. That navy shit doesn't fly with me."

In the canopy above them, the sudden rustle of birds taking flight. They all froze, then Mark waved for everyone to follow him farther into the undergrowth. There was a small clearing in front of a giant ceiba tree. Brown settled down on one of the enormous roots, using it as an ad hoc bench. "Damn, I'm tired. Ran around all last night trying to find this place. You know your brother's here?"

After a second, Mark nodded.

Brown squinted up at him. "He seemed dead set on getting you home. Yet here you are."

"Never leave a man behind," Mark responded. "We think Flores is in there."

Brown nodded. "I know it's not company policy, but I'd have done the same. Any good intel yet?"

Decker and Mark exchanged a glance. After a pause, Mark begrudgingly acknowledged, "We did some recon, but couldn't figure out a way in."

"It's tight, all right," Brown agreed. "And you don't exactly look native. We're going to send in Valencia."

"That's a good choice," Decker said. "I worked with him in Ecuador."

"Yeah, so. We figure he'll get a bead on Calderon, see if he can locate Flores, too. Then we get them the hell out of this taco stand."

"You got fifteen guys, not including Smiley," Mark said.

"Oh, we're not including him. Men only." Brown grinned. "I'm sending him back to town to wait this out."

"And I wouldn't take Sock if I were you."

"Wasn't planning on it. Especially now."

"So that's fourteen of you against a small army," Decker noted.

"Well, we got a little inside info you're probably not privy to." Brown smirked. "Seeing as how you don't trust us anymore."

"What kind of information?"

"We should probably come to some sort of arrangement first," Brown said. "I could use more manpower and equipment, and thanks to your baby brother, you've got access to it."

"In exchange for what?" Decker asked.

"Am I wrong, or don't you two technically still work for me?" Brown's eyes narrowed. Decker raised the barrel of his gun again. "Right now, I'm only interested in saving my own ass."

"You two could have headed north, crossed the border by now. You came here to try to complete the mission, right?"

"Mostly to save Flores. Calderon would have been a bonus."

"If you did some recon, you already know there's no way you're getting anyone out alone," Brown said. "I don't trust Sock or Smiley any more than you do. But this is my operation. You decide to trust me, we can help each other."

Mark thought it over. Brown was right, even if Syd and Jake came up with some sort of genius plan, it was unlikely they'd even get so far as infiltrating the camp. And without knowing where Flores was being held, they might as well just pack up and leave. "Fine," he finally said. "But I want Sock handled."

"Trust me." Brown grinned again. "It will be a pleasure."

Jake paced back and forth in the motel room. He'd spent the past few hours futilely attempting to get some sleep. Maltz and Kane had pulled out a few hours earlier, headed back to Mexico City for heavier artillery. Syd was in her room, ostensibly trying to catch a nap in their down time. There hadn't been any more news from his brother. For the moment, he had nothing to do except beat himself up for betraying Kelly.

He fell back on the bed, going over it again. What the hell had he been thinking? Even if Kelly weren't in the picture, sleeping with his business partner counted as the dumbest thing he'd ever done, and he'd done some insanely stupid things in his life. The fact that he'd cheated on Kelly when she was at such a low point made it even worse. He'd never cheated on anyone before—hell, this was the first time he'd been in something that qualified as a real relationship. And he'd just blown it. Typical.

Jake watched a cockroach wander across the ceiling. The dark stains that mottled the stucco occasionally camouflaged its small body, then it reappeared. The truth was, he was lousy at every type of relationship. He and Mark had been best friends growing up, and now they weren't even on speaking terms. He had lots of acquaintances, mostly guys he could grab a beer with. But people he could actually talk to? For the past few years, there had only been Kelly. He wondered how the hell that happened. He was in his mid-forties, and for all intents and purposes, he was utterly alone.

In retrospect, the falling out with his brother marked the beginning. Their father took off when they were kids; aside from sending crappy Christmas presents, he was completely out of their lives. Their mom got a job as a secretary at the local army base and worked her ass off for twenty years, doing her best to give them a good life. Not that they'd appreciated it at the time. He and Mark had given her more than a few gray hairs. Still, the four of them had been close, a tightly knit unit.

Then a decade ago their mother was diagnosed with breast cancer. Jake had taken a leave from work, flying home to be with her during each round of chemo. He and Chris had taken shifts caring for her. Unfortunately the treatment at the base was less than subpar. Jake had fought the establishment, trying to get approval for a transfer to a civilian hospital. They refused, and she died a few months later.

Of course, none of that had been Mark's fault. What pissed off Jake was that through all of it, his brother hadn't even made the effort to visit. He sent postcards from wherever he happened to be deployed, most arriving weeks after the postmark. It nearly killed Jake, seeing their mom's face light up when one was delivered, the way she devoured what was usually just a few sentences about the food and weather. His mother claimed that she didn't expect any of her sons to stop their lives on her account. She was so excited when Mark finally sent word that he'd be home for Christmas. Unfortunately she only lasted through Thanksgiving.

During the funeral Jake had seethed as Mark stood there, eyes concealed by a pair of sunglasses. After they both had a few drinks, it came to blows. And they hadn't spoken since. Until now, that is.

Yet he'd flown to Mexico the minute Mark was in trouble. Jake wondered if his brother would have done the same for him. Probably not.

A knock at the door jarred him out of his reverie. He opened it to find Syd standing there, looking worried.

"We should talk," she said.

"Yeah, I was thinking the same thing." Jake stepped back to let her move past him. She settled into the only chair, leaving him to perch awkwardly on the bed. "Listen, about last night—"

"Oh, Christ, not about that!" Syd rolled her eyes. "I heard back from Mark. They've run into some complications. Could be a good thing for us, or it could turn into a shit sandwich."

Jake flushed, but said, "I don't think that's a real expression."

"Whatever, you know what I mean. Anyway, they ran into the Tyr unit. He thinks it's a good idea to partner up."

"What? Mark was the one who said they couldn't be trusted."

"I know, but Brown offered some information in exchange. He's got a guy who can infiltrate the camp, figure out where the friendlies are. Mark doesn't think he'll be able to narrow it down without that intel."

"I don't know." Jake had a bad feeling. An already complicated situation just kept getting worse.

There was another knock at the door.

Syd's eyebrows shot up. "You expecting someone? I didn't think they had room service here."

Jake crossed to open it. Syd slipped to the side, drawing her sidearm. "You can never be too careful," she said in response to his look.

Jake opened it a crack. Isabela was standing there. "Can I come in?" she asked.

"Jeez, Jake. The bed was barely even cold yet," Syd muttered as he slid back the bolt and opened the door.

"What?" Isabela looked puzzled.

"Just ignore her," Jake said. "You need something?"

"I have information," Isabela said. Her demeanor had brightened considerably since last night.

"What kind of information?"

"I know how we can get into the camp," Isabela said. "But it has to be tonight."

Twenty-One

Every time someone passed by their pen door, Flores's head jerked up. He kept waiting for a guard to usher them out for another tête-à-tête with the general. Although he figured it was equally likely they'd be shot inside the pen to serve as an example to other prisoners.

Yet the morning passed uneventfully. Lunch trays were brought, then taken away. Calderon had exchanged a few words with the guard, requesting another audience with General Gente. And still, nothing. Flores was climbing out of his skin.

Calderon, on the other hand, was almost preternaturally calm. He'd suggested a game of chess to pass the time. Flores had agreed, since there wasn't anything else to do, but sitting there facing a tiny board only made him edgier. Flores still hadn't figured out the damn game, but whenever Calderon gestured that it was his turn he moved a piece somewhere. So far he was down ten games and counting.

"You must concentrate, *amigo*." Calderon grinned as he swept another of Flores's pieces from the board.

"What if he doesn't care that you've changed your mind?" Flores said.

"Then we will be killed," Calderon said flatly.

"Great."

"It is out of our hands." Calderon glanced up at him. "Some things you cannot control."

"And some things you can." Flores jumped to his feet. He'd cased the perimeter of the pen in its entirety. There was a weak section in the back, near where they slept. The chicken wire wasn't buried as deeply into the ground there, and the wires were looser—he assumed that a previous tenant had worked away at them. It was the best way out, somewhat sheltered from the guards' view by the tarp. Calderon's knife was dull, but with enough muscle power behind it he should be able to fray the wires until they tore. What he wouldn't give for a pair of wire cutters.

Flores still wasn't sure how he felt about Calderon. There were holes in his story, but Gente's version didn't make complete sense, either. He suspected both of them were mixing truth and lies. Part of him was tempted to make a break for it and leave the guy to rot. But that would be condemning him to death, and he didn't feel right about that. Holding the blade to Calderon's throat that morning, he'd just felt dirty. He kept seeing Maryanne's face, and in the end he hadn't been able to go through with it. Hopefully that would be a decision he wouldn't regret.

He was down on his knees, examining the surrounding wire for weak points, when a shadow fell across the pen. Flores's heart leaped into his throat. He slowly stood and turned around. A guard was on the other side of the door, gun drawn. Calderon had frozen, one hand still clutching a chess figurine.

The guard appeared uncertain. He raised the brim of his hat an inch. Calderon exhaled sharply and rose to his feet.

"What?" Flores asked, coming up alongside him. "Is he going to bring you to the general?"

"No, *amigo*." Calderon kept his voice low, but the excitement was unmistakable. "He is one of ours."

Kelly was in a dark place. Ripples moved across the ceiling, like it was made of water. She was so cold. Dampness clung to her skin, her clothes sopping wet. The air reeked of something burning.

"Hello? Is anyone there?" she called out.

The silence was broken by a flutter of wings. Something brushed against her, and she reared away from the oily silk of feathers.

There was someone in there with her. She felt their presence, heard their steady breathing. Footsteps echoed through the gloom, sure and steady, as if they knew exactly where to find her. She felt for her gun, but it was gone.

An icy grip suddenly closed around her arm.

Kelly shot up, breathing hard. She wiped a hand down her face, trying to shake off the nightmare. Glancing around, she realized that the one she'd awoken to was in a way much worse.

She was in a dingy holding cell. When the *federales* had brought her in that morning they'd done the usual, fingerprinting her, taking mug shots, then shoving her in a cell with a motley assortment of other women, mostly prostitutes based on their appearance. They'd taken her in with a glance, then left her alone.

It was odd to be on the other side of things for the first time.

A short while later she'd been ushered into an interrogation room. A red-faced cop whose uniform strained at the seams barked at her, an unintelligible mishmash of

Spanish and English. When it was clear she had no idea what he was saying, he finally slammed her FBI badge down on the table and sat back, arms crossed.

She shrugged. *"Soy policía,"* she repeated.

That only served to irritate him further. He exploded in another tirade, spit flying as he leaned over her. Kelly kept her expression stony. When he finished, she simply said, *"Teléfono."*

He stormed out of the room. Kelly remained there alone for ten minutes, then another cop came and led her away. She tried to impress on him the importance of allowing her a phone call, but apparently that right wasn't automatic in Mexico. She knew next to nothing about their judicial system. Kelly wondered how long they'd be able to hold her, and if they'd actually gone so far as to charge her with anything. More than that, she wondered where Stefan was now. And how many other people he'd manage to kill before she got the hell out of here.

Even though she'd requested a telephone, she honestly wasn't sure whom to call. Jake was probably in the middle of the jungle somewhere. Her former boss at the FBI, ASAC McLarty, wouldn't want to touch this with a ten-foot pole. The sad truth was, there was no one else.

But no matter what, she intended to stop Stefan. And to do that, she'd have to get out of here.

Kelly sat up, unhooked her prosthesis and massaged the spot where her leg ended. They'd originally taken it, probably assuming it could be used as a weapon. But after a thorough inspection, they'd returned it to her.

Her whole right side throbbed from the fight this morning. Kelly winced as she encountered sore spots—Brandi would not be pleased, she thought with a grim smile. With all the abuse her body had suffered in the past few days, she'd probably set herself back months' worth of physical therapy. Everything was bruised and sore. Her head ached from lack of sleep and the beating Stefan had given her, and it still hurt to swallow. But all in all, she felt okay. In fact, oddly enough, she felt a hell of a lot better than she had for a long time.

An image of Stefan's expression when he realized he was losing the fight popped into her mind. Tough not to feel good about that. Even unarmed and missing a leg, she'd almost beaten him. That was something to be proud of.

Approaching footsteps echoed off the concrete floor. Kelly wondered if they'd finally managed to locate a translator. Or maybe they were going to let her make a phone call after all. A guard appeared, fussed with a key ring, then unlocked the door to her cell.

"Where are we—"

Kelly froze at the sight of the man accompanying him.

Twenty-Two

"Why do we have to attack tonight?" Syd asked.

"Can I come in?" Isabela stood uncertainly on the threshold. She'd showered and changed into some clothing Maltz had rustled up for her. With her hair down, she was actually quite attractive. No wonder she'd easily managed to enlist Mark's help.

"Sure." Jake stepped aside. Isabela entered and looked for a place to sit. She ended up leaning against the wall by the television.

"I called some contacts," Isabela said.

"Not the Zetas." Syd's voice was hard.

"No, of course not. I know some people who work for the Sinaloa Cartel."

"Isn't that one of the rival cartels?" Jake asked.

"It's *the* rival cartel," Syd said, eyes narrowing. "The Zetas took over the Gulf Cartel after Osiel Cárdenas was extradited to the U.S. in 2007. They formed a partnership with some former Sinaloa members, the Beltrán-Leyva brothers. Now the two cartels are sworn enemies, responsible for most of the uptick in violence. It's interesting that you seem to know all these guys."

"We all grew up together in el Eden," Isabela said

defiantly. "The cartels were the only option for most of the local boys."

"And you became a pharmacist. Interesting."

"This information could save Mark's friends, and my father," Isabela retorted, chin raised. "You think I would risk his life?"

"It remains to be seen if you even have a father, never mind one in the camp," Syd said. "We only have your word on it."

"Why else would I be here? I am in as much danger as the rest of you."

"She's right, Syd. I can't figure out a reason for her to lie about all this," Jake said.

"That doesn't mean she isn't," Syd retorted, but she settled back into the chair. "So what's the information?"

Isabela said, "Recently Los Zetas had a few shipments seized. Their top men think they have a mole."

"There's a lot of that going around," Syd commented. Jake silenced her with a sharp look.

Isabela continued, "The general called all Los Zetas commanders back to the camp, so he can figure out who is the traitor. Luis says the Sinaloans found out about this and they plan to raid the camp now. They are going to execute the leadership and take over their prisoners."

"A power grab," Jake said. "If they take the camp and eliminate the top guys, they've effectively seized their base of operations."

"Exactly," Isabela said.

"And your friend just called up and told you this?" Syd asked.

"Luis was the one who first told me my father was being held there."

"That was nice of him," Syd said.

"Prisoners will die during the raid," Isabela retorted. "Luis wanted to prepare me for bad news."

"This is such a crock." Syd rolled her eyes. "If a major cartel was planning a raid, don't you think we'd have seen some of them rolling through here by now? There's only one road."

"They are already waiting on the other side of the mountain," Isabela insisted.

"You have to admit, Isabela, it sounds awfully convenient," Jake said slowly. He held up a hand to fend off her protests. "I'm not saying I don't believe you, but it's a huge coincidence."

"What reason would I have to lie about this?" Isabela asked, challenging them with her eyes.

What reason indeed, Jake wondered.

"Good to see you, Valencia," Calderon said.

Valencia nodded and lit a cigarette. "Not much time, sir. Do you know where the others are?"

"I don't know if Kaplan survived," Flores said. "I think it's just us." For the first time since this nightmare began, he felt a ray of hope. They hadn't been forgotten. Hell, they might even get out of here alive.

They stood near the entrance to the pen, keeping their voices low. Flores glanced over—next door, Ramon Tejada was taking an interest in their conversation. From what he'd observed, interactions with the guards were limited, and their pen had clearly gotten more than the usual share of attention the past two days.

"What's the plan?" Flores lowered his voice and moved closer to the door.

Valencia blew smoke toward the treetops before saying, "This is recon. No plan yet."

"If we don't get out by tonight, they'll kill us," Calderon said urgently.

"They might kill us sooner," Flores said. "Things have gotten complicated."

"Complicated how?"

"They're trying to get Calderon to work with them, arranging kidnappings," Flores said. "He's going to tell them yes to buy some time, but either way one of us probably won't be walking out of here."

"Huh." Valencia's eyes flicked over to Calderon. "I'll let Brown know."

"Oh, thank God. I was hoping Ellis would be here," Calderon exclaimed.

"We're doing what we can, sir. Be ready to move." With that, Valencia shifted away.

Flores and Calderon watched him leave. Valencia kept his head down as he strolled past the pens. As he circled the guard tower, a soldier barked something down at him. Flores froze, terror gripping his heart. Valencia had to make it out, had to let the others know where to find them. He felt the hope deflating.

Valencia said something in response, and there was a cackle of laughter from above. Valencia ground out his cigarette under a boot heel, turned the corner and disappeared. For a long moment, they both remained silent. When a few minutes passed without the sound of gunfire, Flores let his shoulders relax.

Calderon turned to him, expression jubilant. "You see, *amigo?* Now all we have to do is stall for time."

Flores was about to reply when a shadow darkened the door of their cage. He looked up to find another guard staring in at them, the same one who had escorted him to see the general. The guard fumbled with the lock, then the door swung open. He pointed at Flores.

"*Venga conmigo,*" he said gruffly.

Twenty-Three

"Fancy meeting you here, Jones."

Kelly blinked back tears. "How did you find me?"

Her former partner, Danny Rodriguez, stepped into the cell. He forced a smile. "The boss got a call that one of his agents was locked up down here for murder. Imagine his surprise when he heard it was you."

"McLarty sent you?"

"Not exactly. I was in L.A. working a case, and heard the news through the grapevine. Figured I'd come bring you a cake with a file in it. Sorry I didn't get here sooner, I caught the first flight out." His eyes wandered down to her leg, and she realized her prosthesis was still off. She quickly reached for it, sending it tumbling off the cot to the floor. "Here, let me—"

"I've got it," Kelly said sharply. As soon as the words left her mouth, she regretted them. She leaned over and scooped the prosthetic off the floor, busying herself with strapping it back on. Rodriguez kept his eyes averted, as if she were putting on a bra, not a leg. She felt a flare of rage, then tried to temper it. He was just trying to be courteous. Rodriguez had visited a few times during her recovery period, but eventually stopped showing up.

Probably because she was just as surly with him as she was with everyone else.

"So." Rodriguez leaned back against the bars. "You missed my wedding."

"Sorry about that," she mumbled. "Congratulations."

"Thanks." Rodriguez held up his ring hand. She caught a flash of gold. "It was a lot of fun. Shame you weren't there."

"I wasn't up for it."

"Yeah, I understand."

Rodriguez appeared to have aged a decade since she last saw him. He no longer looked like an unseasoned rookie. There was an air of confidence about him now. Even his face looked leaner. He'd finally lost the last of his baby fat, and the beginnings of worry lines creased his eyes.

"Thanks for coming," Kelly said. "I've been trying to explain what happened, but they didn't bring in a translator."

"What the hell are you doing here, Jones? Aside from killing kids, I mean."

"It wasn't me."

"Yeah, I figured." Even though he said it, she detected some doubt. Kelly could hardly blame him. When an agent went through what she had, they never came back whole. It wasn't beyond the realm of possibility that she could have lost it. Had their positions been reversed, she'd probably be wondering the same about him.

"Remember Stefan Gundarsson, from the college case? He's here."

"Stefan's dead." Rodriguez's brow wrinkled.

"He's not. I saw him."

"That how you got so messed up?" He waved a finger in a circle, taking in her appearance. Kelly realized how she must look: beaten, bruised and reeking of garbage. No wonder Rodriguez was sticking to the far side of the cell.

"There was a lead in one of those files you gave me that claimed he was living down here. By the time I found him in the dump, he'd already killed the kid. But he's still out there, Danny."

His eyebrows shot up—she never called him by his first name. "First things first," he said after a second. "Let's get you out of here."

"You need to call it in. I can work with a forensic artist—he's modified his appearance slightly. His hair is short now, and he's clean-shaven—"

"Jones, relax. We gotta make sure you don't end up a permanent resident of the Mexican prison system, then we can deal with other matters."

Kelly could tell by the way he said it that he didn't believe her. "I saw him, Danny. He's here."

Rodriguez didn't respond. He walked out of the cell and spoke to the guard in a low voice. The guard nodded once, then started to slide the door shut.

"Wait!" Kelly cried, lurching toward the door. A wave of panic washed over her as it closed.

Rodriguez held up both hands placatingly. "It's okay, Kelly. Trust me, I'll have you out of here as soon as I can."

The click of the latch seemed to resonate. As their footsteps faded down the hall, Kelly sank back down on the cot. For some reason, now she felt even more alone.

Mark clicked off the radio with a frown. They were still hunkered down in the knoll. Brown wanted the deal sealed before taking them back to the main group.

"What?" Brown asked.

"Syd said yes. And there's another thing."

"Christ, seems like there's always another thing," Decker grumbled.

Brown waved a hand impatiently to silence him. "What?"

Mark was still turning the information over in his head. It didn't sound like Syd believed Isabela, but forced to choose between the two of them, he leaned toward trusting Isabela. He knew those CIA types. Syd seemed capable enough, but her lack of faith in intel she hadn't personally confirmed was hardly surprising. "We've got this girl with us whose father is being held down there. She claims that a rival cartel is planning to move on the camp tonight."

"Which cartel?"

"The Sinaloans."

Brown bellowed a deep laugh. "Well, there goes our inside information."

"So it's true?"

Brown grinned. "I got a Sinaloa goon back at our staging area who told us the same thing."

"That's how we found the camp," Delano chimed in.

"Yeah?" Mark rubbed his chin. "Two separate sources. I wonder if your guy knows what time the raid is supposed to go down?"

"We'll see. And since we're buddies again—" Brown's grin widened "—I'll give you first crack at him."

Flores shifted in his chair. The general glared at him contemptuously. "I'm disappointed in you, Señor Flores. I thought we had a deal."

"I figured you'd call Calderon out. Did you hear he wanted to talk to you?"

"*Sí.*" Gente's hands tapped together in front of his

mouth. He had the swollen, dimpled knuckles of a child. "I have nothing left to say to Señor Calderon. You were supposed to do the talking for me."

"Oh," Flores said, subdued. So it looked like that part of their plan was a dud. Now that Calderon had finally caved, it was funny that Gente wasn't jumping at the chance to strike a deal. Didn't make a hell of a lot of sense. But then, nothing about this made sense anymore.

"He told you he was innocent." Gente leaned back, causing the chair to groan woefully. "And you believed him."

"I can't figure out why else you'd keep him alive," Flores said. "His story made more sense than yours."

"And what was his story?" Gente's lips kept tugging up at the corners, as if he wanted desperately to smile but the weight of his cheeks prevented it.

"That you wanted him to strike a deal releasing client lists, and he refused. That's why you wanted me to kill him."

"He refused?" Gente cocked an eyebrow.

"That's what he said."

"I understand, *señor.* After all, he is your employer. And you're right, we have kept him alive. But then, he still has some powerful friends in the government here. If we killed him, it would send the message that no one is safe."

"I'd think you'd want that. Make them scared of you."

"Not really." Gente rocked slightly. "A certain level of government assistance is necessary to keep our operations flowing smoothly. If they saw us as a threat, they might take actions that wouldn't benefit us. That is why you—" Gente jabbed at the table with a meaty index finger "—must kill him."

"And if I say no?"

Gente regarded him in silence for a moment. "Part of me admires your blind loyalty, even to a man as undeserving as Cesar Calderon." He practically spat the name. "If he is not dead by tomorrow morning, then both of you will be shot during an escape attempt. This is a gift I'm giving you, soldier," he said. "I could easily stage such a thing and guarantee your deaths. But I would prefer that you live. You remind me of myself at your age."

Flores swallowed a slew of retorts to that comparison. "I'd do better with a gun."

"I'm sure you would." Gente laughed out loud. "And I'd bet you'd take a few of my men with you."

"Give me another chance." Flores tried to sound earnest as he said, "I'll do it tonight."

"How will you do it?"

"I'll put a pillow over his head so I don't have to see his eyes when I drive the knife through it."

The response seemed to satisfy the general. "Very well. But if Calderon sees another dawn, I will have you both killed. And it will not be quick or painless."

Twenty-Four

As she stepped outside, Kelly felt the pressure in her chest ease. She inhaled deeply—even the smog tasted good after stale prison air. "Thanks, Rodriguez. I owe you one."

"You owe me a hell of a lot more than one," he grumbled good-naturedly. "Did you know that seventy percent of the cops in this town only made it to third grade? They're not a fun bunch to deal with."

"What did you tell them?"

"I told them you were a hardened criminal who was already wanted for similar crimes in the U.S., and that we'd make sure you never saw daylight again."

Kelly examined his face to see if he was kidding.

He shrugged. "Hey, it worked, right? Part of the deal was that I get you on the first flight out. So let's grab a cab."

Kelly sifted through her backpack to make sure everything was still there. Her wallet was shy a few hundred pesos, and her pill bottle was gone. That would usually send her into a panic, but for some reason the loss actually made her feel calmer. She still had enough cash to get by for a few days. Her expensive new cell phone was gone, too. She considered trying to get it back, but thought better of it. Chances were she wouldn't need it anyway. "I can't go."

Rodriguez breathed out hard, sending his lips flapping. "I knew it."

"We have to head to the dump and interview some of the people living there. One of them might know where Stefan is."

"Absolutely not." Rodriguez's grip was firm on her elbow as he steered her toward the curb. "You get caught again, I doubt they'll let you out. And they'll probably throw me in there with you."

"You don't have to come," Kelly said. "You can go back, try to persuade McLarty to send backup."

"I told you, Jones, I already ran it by him. He can't spare anyone right now."

"He didn't believe me, did he?" Rodriguez didn't answer. Kelly stared him down, but he didn't shrink under her gaze. He had grown up, she realized. Which probably didn't bode well for her. "I'm telling you, he's here," she insisted.

"Jones, you've been through a lot the past seven months. I mean, with the accident—"

"It wasn't an accident. My leg got blown off by a grenade," she retorted.

Rodriguez shifted, clearly uncomfortable. "Anyway, you've been under a lot of stress."

"Not enough to make me start seeing things, Rodriguez. We never found Stefan's body."

"The M.E. thought it probably got caught under something in the river."

Kelly blew out air, exasperated. "It's been three years… don't you think some sort of remains would have turned up by now? Didn't you see the report last fall from the P.I. the Kaishens hired? Stefan's money ended up here."

Rodriguez sighed. "I knew I shouldn't have gotten you those files. That case isn't even technically ours. If the field office in charge didn't follow up on it, there was probably a reason."

"They didn't even bother looking into it. Maybe because he wasn't stateside anymore, so ASAC Bowen figured he could shunt the problem off on Mexico."

"C'mon, Kelly. You don't honestly believe—"

"I'm telling you, the P.I. was right. Somehow Stefan survived the shooting and came here. And now he's killing people again. What he did to that kid was one of the worst things I've ever seen."

"I know. The *comandante* showed me the pictures."

"So?" Kelly asked. "You want to just let him keep doing that?"

She could see him weighing what she'd said. "We don't have any jurisdiction here."

"I know that."

"You're not officially on duty right now. And I'm supposed to be back in L.A. by tomorrow morning. I could catch hell for getting involved in this."

"Then get on a plane." Kelly marched away from him, headed into the throng of people. It was twilight, the streets were packed. Horns blared as cars pumped out choking clouds of exhaust. She felt Rodriguez at her shoulder.

"Don't be like that, Jones. You know if there was any way—"

"I know. Listen, you've done enough." She raised her hand to flag down a cab. It inched through the traffic toward the curb. "I'll be fine. Just do me a favor. If I don't make it home, tell Jake what happened."

"Christ, don't say that."

The cab parked at an angle. Kelly opened the door and awkwardly climbed in, dragging her bad leg behind her. She leaned over to pull the door shut. "Goodbye, Danny."

He half raised a hand in a wave.

The cab edged back into traffic. They'd gone less than five feet when someone banged on the trunk. The passenger-side door was flung open, and Rodriguez clambered inside.

"I'm going to regret this," he grumbled.

"I said you didn't have to come." Kelly had to fight to repress a grin. Despite her bravado, she hadn't been optimistic about tracking down Stefan without assistance.

"I've heard your Spanish, Jones. You couldn't get help finding the bathroom."

"Thanks." She settled back into the seat and gazed at the orange moon hovering over the volcano on the city's edge. For the first time that day, she had a good feeling.

Jake nearly fell again. They'd had an easier time making their way back through the jungle, maybe because this time they knew where they were headed. It was less damp than before, too, making it less slippery. Still, his boots were already soaked through.

It felt good to be on the move doing something, however. Syd and Mark had been exchanging terse radio communications all afternoon. Apparently Isabela's tip about the rival cartel raid had panned out, confirmed by some guy the Tyr group was holding prisoner. Jake had decided that the less he knew about that, the better. After this experience in the field, working the office side of the K&R business was suddenly vastly more appealing.

Syd and Mark figured that the ensuing confusion would

be their best shot at springing Calderon and Flores. Apparently there hadn't been enough time to track down Isabela's father, or the Tyr spy simply hadn't bothered. Her jaw had tightened at the news, but Mark assured her that he'd personally go in after him. It had been tough to convince Isabela to remain at the motel, but on that point Syd refused to budge. Jake couldn't blame her for that. He wasn't as innately suspicious as she was, but something about Isabela's story was a little too convenient.

Jake wasn't holding out much hope that they'd be able to save any of the prisoners. Still, the plan had evolved from a suicide mission to one where it was only extremely likely they'd all be killed. So things were looking up.

He hadn't been able to get in touch with Kelly. She should already be back in New York. It worried him that she wasn't answering either their home phone or her cell. With any luck they'd be across the border by sunrise, and he'd arrive home tomorrow afternoon. Jake hadn't decided yet what to tell her about the incident with Syd. In reality, his cheating unearthed a much larger problem in their relationship. And the time had probably come for both of them to face it.

Of course, there was a good chance he wouldn't survive long enough to have to deal with it. It was an oddly comforting thought.

Jake pushed it out of his mind. Right now, he had to focus on the task at hand—getting through this jungle maze without being shot. He was following Fribush's wide back. Syd was ahead of him, with Jagerson bringing up the rear. The strap of an AK-47 chafed his shoulder. Under the Kevlar vest, sweat pooled down his back.

Kane and Maltz were still in Mexico City scrounging up supplies. Hopefully they'd make it back in time for the raid. Their plan required a few dozen well-trained men—at the moment, they had twenty. And after their earlier experience with the Tyr team, Jake wasn't ruling out the possibility of friendly fire.

Fribush suddenly stopped and dropped to one knee. Jake did the same, breath catching in his chest. The bushes ahead of them parted.

"Don't shoot," a voice called out. Mark materialized, Decker at his heels. He looked exhausted, Jake noted, but had that familiar glimmer in his eyes, as if they were about to light the wick of a cherry bomb. He saw Jake and smiled. "Glad you came," he said. "Brown's unit is back this way."

Jake fell in step behind him. The fact that for the first time Mark seemed happy to see him raised a lump in his throat. He reminded himself why he was angry with him, but for some reason none of that seemed to matter anymore. They were partnered up again for the first time since they were kids. He had to admit, it felt good. The truth was, he'd missed him.

They followed Mark a quarter mile into deeper undergrowth. Branches tore at Jake's face and hands as he pushed through them.

Suddenly they emerged in a small clearing packed with men checking weapons. They all stopped to examine the newcomers. Judging by their expressions, many weren't thrilled with the new partnership arrangement.

Jake recognized Ellis Brown from their earlier confrontation. He was standing over a guy tied to a tree. The guy's head hung forward, face covered in blood. At the sight of them Brown broke into a smile and approached, arms held wide.

"So the Littlehorn group is here."

"Longhorn," Jake corrected him.

"He's messing with us, Jake," Syd said. "Enemy of my enemy is my friend, right, Brown?"

"I'll take what I can get out here." He gestured to their rifles. "I figured you were the ones who bought up every AK-47 in town."

"You know me…I've never been a girl to pass up a good sale." She tucked a stray blond hair behind her ear.

"Any more where those came from?"

"I might be able to spare a few," she said coyly.

In fact, Fribush had a duffel bag filled with them slung over his back. They had decided as a unit to hold on to the weapons until they were certain Tyr wasn't planning some sort of bait and switch.

Syd jerked her head toward the prisoner. "So he confirms the cartel raid rumor?"

"Yup. And a couple of my guys scouted the far side of the camp. A few clicks southeast they spotted at least a hundred men hanging around waiting for something. And I doubt it's a Shakira concert."

"Any idea what time they're moving in?"

"This guy doesn't have any idea—believe me, if he knew he would have told us. Riley says the shift change happens around midnight, so that would be my guess. But we thought there might be an easier way to find out for sure." Brown's eyes drifted over to Jake.

"What?" Jake asked. The way Brown was regarding him induced a distinctly bad feeling.

"Apparently the Zetas snatched Cesar because they want to strike a deal with him," Brown said. "My guy didn't have time to get the details. But we were thinking that you could approach the Sinaloa cartel, offer them something similar."

"You want me to make a deal with a drug cartel? For what?"

"Clients," Mark replied. "Tell them you'll offer inside information on who they should target."

"That's insane. I'd never do that."

"Neither would Cesar, that's why he's rotting down there," Brown growled.

Jake's head reeled. "You want me to approach a group of armed soldiers who are about to raid their rival's prison camp and offer them a deal? They'll shoot me on sight."

"I doubt it," Brown said. "They'll be curious enough to hear you out first. Probably. And we'll have a few snipers in the bushes covering you. Truth be told, the Sinaloans don't strike me as the A-Team. I'm kind of doubting they'll manage to take the camp."

"So why contact them at all?" Jake asked.

"It's a good idea, actually," Syd said. "Makes it less likely they'll shoot at us. And we'll be approaching from the other side. Having us on board actually improves their chances. If the bosses over there are savvy, they'll understand that."

"No way," Jake said. "I'm not making a deal with those guys."

He caught Mark looking at him with disapproval and felt a flare of rage. All the good feelings he'd had a second earlier dissipated. He wondered if Mark had even blinked when Brown suggested Jake risk his life.

"I'll go," Syd said.

Jake shook his head. "Not this time, Syd. Longhorn belongs to both of us. We're not going to compromise it."

"What about Calderon and Flores?" Mark demanded.

"They don't deserve to be shot in a pen in the middle of the jungle. Isabela's father, too."

"Sorry, but there's no way. It's a bad idea."

"Jake—" Syd laid a hand on his arm.

He shrugged it off. "I'm not letting you talk me into it. You want to take part in this raid, fine. But not like this."

Jake could see her looking for an angle that would convince him. "Okay," she finally said. "We'll do it your way. But it's a hell of a lot more dangerous."

"So be it." Jake turned to Brown. "I'm guessing you've still got men watching the other cartel?"

Brown looked at Syd as if asking approval, then slowly nodded. "They'll radio in as soon as the Sinaloans start to move."

"All right, then. And you know where Calderon and... what's his name?"

"Flores," Mark said heavily.

"Right, Flores. So you know where they are. The minute we find out the raid is on, we head in. If we're lucky, we'll be able to free them during the initial confusion. We've got two more men coming with heavier artillery, hopefully they'll get here in time."

"If that's how you want to play it," Brown said. "I still think—"

"I don't care what you think," Jake interrupted. "You want to use my people and our resources, those are the terms."

"Agreed," an unfamiliar voice chimed in. A small, weasely man emerged from behind a tree. He walked forward, hand extended. "Linus Smiley, vice president of the Tyr Group."

Jake eyed the extended hand, then ignored it. "So are we all on the same page?"

Smiley started to reply, but Brown interrupted. "Yeah, why not."

"All right, then."

A soldier trotted up to Brown and said something in a low voice. Brown's face darkened, and he swore.

"Now what?" Syd asked.

"Wysocki got away," he said to Mark.

"Who the hell is Wysocki?" Jake asked.

"No time for that." Mark slung his LMT back over his shoulder, face grim. "We can't let him get down to camp to warn them."

Twenty-Five

Sock was hauling ass down the mountain, half sliding on his back to get to the bottom before they shot him.

Getting away had been easier than expected. When Brown showed up in camp again, Sock knew he was in for it. Brown had already been treating him like a mole, not even allotting him a radio. Now that Riley and Decker had materialized, the jig was up. Brown assigned two guys to watch him at all times, even when he took a piss. Once everything settled down, Sock knew he was in for the beating of his life, or worse. Riley probably blamed him for the whole operation going tits up. And hey, he'd be right.

In the past Sock had worked a couple of jobs with the two goons watching him, Hayward and Figuarello. They weren't the best Tyr had to offer—he knew it and they knew it. The fact they hadn't bothered tying him up confirmed their incompetence. When the new group showed up in camp, it provided enough of a distraction for him to bolt.

Luckily Sock had heard enough about their plans to give the general a reason to save his ass. Initially he'd intended to sit this one out. Gente had gotten squirrelly lately, claiming Sock didn't have enough power in the organization to prove helpful anymore. And they both knew what that meant—once Sock wasn't valuable, he'd better hightail it stateside or there'd be an extra hole in his head to spit out of. And he hadn't been paid nearly enough to deal with that.

Still, this was fresh intel. A rival cartel raid—that was something he could take to the bank. He just had to make it down there without getting shot.

Sock slid another few feet before regaining his footing, grabbing branches to slow his descent. The camp was less than a hundred feet away. He felt a surge of adrenaline. After all the bullshit of the past week, being forced to hunker down and play victim with the rest of his pathetic unit, having to go back in when Gente decided he still needed ears on Tyr…now it was all going to pay off. He'd collect enough greenbacks to set himself up nicely somewhere new. He already had his eye on beachfront property in Honduras. Just a little bit farther and all his money troubles would be behind him.

Kelly shifted uncomfortably, trying not to let the smell get to her. They were hunkered down inside one of the tiny shanties in the dump. Rodriguez was murmuring in Spanish with a tiny, wizened woman. She looked sixty but it was hard to tell; under all those layers of filth might lurk a thirty-year-old woman. The absence of teeth caved in her lower jaw and Kelly could tell it took some effort for her to form words. To his credit, Rodriguez leaned in to listen, despite the stench emanating from the woman's rags. The walls shifted with shadows from the light of the single candle she'd lit, making them appear alive.

This woman was the third person who had agreed to speak with them. Initially every *pepenador* they approached had scampered away. One had become enraged, waving his arms and berating them with what even Kelly could tell was a stream of epithets. After that encounter Rodriguez had wisely led them back to civilization for what he called, "critical supplies." When they returned armed with bottled water, gum and snack food, doors were suddenly flung open. But most of the *pepenadores* claimed to be oblivious to the fact that a giant white man was killing children in their midst. A few had scrutinized Kelly, recognition in their gaze.

Then this woman had waved them into her shanty. After greedily accepting a bottle of water and an energy bar, she launched into a monologue that Rodriguez interrupted with occasional questions. Finally he stood and bowed his head. *"Muchas gracias, señora."*

Kelly followed him back outside. The moon had climbed in the night sky, casting their surroundings in an orange glow. If anything the smell was even worse out here; the open air did little to dissipate it.

"Christ, no wonder you reeked." Rodriguez held a handkerchief to his nose. "Couldn't you stumble across a killer who was holed up at the Hilton?"

"What did she say?" Kelly asked impatiently.

"She confirmed that a man they call the White Devil showed up about a year ago. Right around that time, kids started disappearing."

"And they didn't do anything about it?" Kelly asked.

Rodriguez shrugged. "Most of the kids here are on their own. Runaways, orphans. You gotta understand, Jones, these people are in survival mode. *Pepenador* literally means garbage person or scavenger. They don't have time to worry about anyone but themselves. And they figured there was a chance the kids either returned to families if they had them, or found another way to survive."

"Why was he called the White Devil?"

"Apparently he did some weird stuff—weird even for this crowd. Chanting, rituals. Set up an altar outside his shanty and slaughtered animals on it. Then he didn't even eat the animals, which really threw them. They steered clear of him after that. A few of the families even pulled up stakes and moved farther away."

"Does she know where he might have gone?"

"Nope. Her friend saw him leave out the exit to the north at dawn, running from the cops. I'm guessing that's when they grabbed you?"

Kelly nodded.

"Well, she says he hasn't been back since. They're watching for him now, after what the police found. A few of them are pretty riled up. If he's smart, he won't come back."

"Nice of them to show some concern now," Kelly grumbled.

"It's not really surprising, Jones. To be honest, the cops at the station couldn't get rid of you quick enough. I get the feeling that unless some of the dead kid's relatives show up, they'll bury this thing. And she didn't have any idea who the kid was. Chances are they'll never ID the body."

"Jesus," Kelly said. The fact that a child could die so horribly, without anyone caring enough to initiate even the most basic investigation, was beyond horrifying.

"Life is viewed differently down here, Jones," Rodriguez explained. "Justice, too. We live a pretty cushy life, all things considered." As soon as he said it his posture changed. He'd obviously suddenly remembered her injury, but the words were already out.

"Let's check out where he was living," Kelly mumbled.

"Yeah, okay." Rodriguez followed as she wove between

the dark tiers. "After that, though, we're finding a hotel. I'm gonna need a few hours in the shower."

"At least you believe me now," Kelly said after a minute. Rodriguez didn't respond. "You do believe me, right?"

"I believe you saw someone down here. Maybe it was Stefan, maybe just someone who looks like him. Either way, he sounds like a bad guy."

"It was Stefan," she said firmly.

It took a half hour of wandering to locate Stefan's shanty. They stood silent in the doorway, flashlights playing across the interior. Aside from the removal of the boy's body and skin, it was exactly as she'd left it that morning. The shack was assembled from scavenged sheets of corrugated metal. The layers of cardboard comprising the floor were dark brown and stiff with blood. A pile of rags in the corner probably functioned as a bed. Kelly repressed a shudder at the sight of the clothesline, still draped from one side of the room to the other like a morbid Christmas garland. Aside from that, the only furniture was a rickety table dead center in the six-by-six-foot space.

"Christ, that's a lot of blood," Rodriguez murmured, running his flashlight beam across the muddy trails.

"I can't believe they didn't even bring a crime-scene unit out here," Kelly said. There was no indication that aside from arresting her and removing the boy's remains, the cops had done any investigating of the shanty itself. No fingerprint powder anywhere, no sign that blood-stained samples were removed. Apparently Rodriguez was right: the boy's murder would garner no more attention than if he'd been a pigeon that inadvertently struck a window and died.

"What's all this?" Rodriguez asked, examining the far wall. "Looks like crazy-person wallpaper."

Kelly played her flashlight across it. She recognized some of the characters. "Runes," she said. "Remember? That was Stefan's thing in the other case."

Rodriguez let out a low whistle. "Huh, maybe it really is him. Hell of a coincidence otherwise."

"No one seems to understand that I lost my leg, not my mind," Kelly grumbled.

"Well, let's not pretend you were a picture of sanity before this." Kelly raised an eyebrow. He held up his hands defensively. "I'm just saying, you've always been extremely driven. That's why you were so good. You have this ability to focus on a case to the point where you shut everything else out."

Kelly was going to retort, but the words struck home. He was right. Ever since joining the Bureau, she'd focused more on her solve rate than on her life. Which is why, when the job was gone, she'd discovered there wasn't much of a life to go back to. "Driven isn't the same as crazy," she finally replied.

"It is when it makes you do crazy things. Like chasing a lunatic through a dump in a foreign country."

"Point taken," she said. "Of course, that means you're probably crazy to help me."

"Don't remind me." Rodriguez grinned at her. Tears suddenly smarted behind her eyelids. Kelly blinked them back, surprised. He noticed. "You okay?"

"I'm fine. Sorry." Kelly shook her head. "Just tired, I guess."

"Well, you've had a hell of a day. Maybe we should get you to a hospital. They never checked you out after that beating." He sounded concerned.

"No hospital." The mere mention induced memories of the constant hum of fluorescent lights and the cloying smell of disinfectant. If she had her way, she'd never set foot in a hospital again.

"You sure?"

Kelly nodded.

"Okay, then. So, getting back to our guy here." Rodriguez turned his attention to the wall, squinting. "In the campus case he was spelling something with the girls' bodies, right?"

"VIDAR, using the runic alphabet. It was an old Norse legend, something about a wolf." A series of photographs flicked through Kelly's mind. Stefan's earlier victims had all been young, mostly college students, their bodies positioned strangely, legs bent off-kilter to spell out letters from a runic dictionary. Stefan had believed that some ancient book he'd stolen would provide the key to raising the dead, among other things. Apparently ritual sacrifice was a necessary component to the plan—but she'd managed to stop him before he claimed his final victim. And who knew, maybe he'd been right, she thought. After all, rising from the dead was a feat he'd managed to pull off in the end.

"Jesus!" Rodriguez yelped, leaping to the side.

A rat scampered past and raced out the door. Rodriguez shuddered. "I hate rats. I ever tell you that, Jones? Snakes, spiders, bring 'em on…but rats? I'm thinking it's time for that shower."

"One second." The rat had emerged from the stack of bedding in the corner. Kelly went outside and grabbed a long gearshift that jutted up from one of the stacks. Back inside the shanty she prodded at the bedding, sifting through it. Something solid rested at the bottom. She tried to get a purchase with the stick, but whatever it was refused to budge. Giving up, she dropped to her good knee.

"Oh my God, you're not going to—" Rodriguez clamped his mouth shut with a pained look as Kelly dug her hand into the center of the pile. After a second of groping around, trying not to picture Stefan sleeping there, waiting to feel another rat's teeth biting down on her hand, Kelly found it: the hard corner of a book. With a small cry of triumph, she yanked it out.

"I had three heart attacks while you were doing that," Rodriguez said.

"Shine the light over here." Kelly held up the book.

"I'm really hoping you have hand sanitizer in that pack. You know how many diseases rats carry?" Rodriguez muttered. He shifted the flashlight beam so that it illuminated the cover.

It wasn't what Kelly had been expecting. When Stefan vanished, an ancient text had disappeared at the same time. This wasn't that book. Instead it bore the cheap laminated cover of a self-published novel, with a crudely drawn image of a Norse ship above the words *Vikings in Mexico*.

"Quality bedtime reading," Rodriguez said.

"I didn't think Vikings made it anywhere near here." Kelly flipped through the pages. The margins were covered with scrawled notes, nearly every page was filled.

"That's because they didn't," Rodriguez said. "It's ridiculous. Probably written by some nut job."

"Well, another nut job might have believed it," Kelly noted. She poked through the bedding again, but didn't come up with anything else.

"Please tell me we're done here," Rodriguez said. "A few more minutes and I might never eat again."

"Take pictures of the walls. I can try to decipher the runes back at the hotel," Kelly said.

Rodriguez snapped a few shots with his camera. Kelly

looked them over: they were clear enough for her to make
out the scrawlings.

"So are we good?" Rodriguez asked.

"Yeah. Let's get out of here."

Twenty-Six

Jake cursed again as he slipped and slid another ten feet. His face was covered in scratches from where branches had torn at his flesh. Mark's flashlight bounced along twenty feet ahead of him—Jake hadn't seen him fall yet. Apparently he'd inherited all the balance.

Nearly the entire Tyr contingent had taken off down the mountain, running full bore. Jake had followed without stopping to think it through. Mark was still fast as hell, he'd give him that. The rest of the group, Decker included, was charging along behind them. He'd managed to stay within a hundred feet of his brother by sheer force of will, but it felt like his lungs were going to burst from his chest. Jake kept waiting to hear gunfire—it was inconceivable that they wouldn't be heard by this "Sock" character they were pursuing, or worse yet, by another Zetas patrol.

Jake surmised that Sock was the mole who sold out Mark's mission in the first place. Why the Tyr folks kept him around after discovering that was frankly beyond him. It was funny, when he and Syd established The Longhorn Group, they'd modeled it almost entirely after Tyr, the gold standard of Kidnap & Ransom firms. Now that he'd seen them in action, he was wondering if they wouldn't have been better off emulating the Keystone Kops.

Up ahead, Mark suddenly skidded to a stop. Jake pulled up short. Someone slammed into his back a second later, sending him sprawling with a grunt. Syd rolled off him.

"Christ, Riley, a little warning next time," she grumbled, reaching for an AK-47 that had skidded a few feet away.

Jake got back to his feet. He extended a hand to help her up, but she dismissed it with a withering look. Ever since their encounter, she'd been almost nasty to him. Either Syd was just as uncomfortable about what had happened, or she didn't care for his reaction to it. He wondered what she'd been expecting. Anyway, this wasn't the time or place to deal with it.

Jake followed her, bent nearly double as they approached Mark. His brother had hunkered down next to an enormous fern. On the other side of it, the moon lit up an enormous man with blond hair sheared close to his head. His hands were in the air. Two Mexicans were brandishing assault rifles at him. The prison camp fence was less than fifty yards away. Jake glanced up to the nearest guard tower and spotted the barrel of a large machine gun.

"Shit," Mark said with resignation. "He got to them."

"Maybe not," Syd said in a low voice. "It sounds like they have no idea who he is."

Sock was speaking loudly in broken Spanish. Whatever he was saying didn't seem to be registering. The two guards moved closer, shouting. Sock slowly lowered to his knees. One of the guards stepped forward, then turned his head to say something.

Fast as lightning, Sock grabbed the barrel of the gun and yanked it from the guard's grasp. The strap still hung from the guy's shoulder, and he was whipped to the ground. Sock switched his grip on it quickly, jamming the butt against the base of the guy's throat, pinning him. He yelled something to the other guard, who didn't seem to know how to react.

"What's he saying?" Jake asked.

"He's claiming to be friends with a General Gente. He's demanding to be taken to see him," Syd said in a low voice.

"We can't let that happen." Mark raised his gun to his shoulder, aiming for the back of the Sock's head.

"The noise will alert the camp," Syd warned.

"I know. No avoiding it now, though."

Jake started to protest, then shut his mouth. If this guy Sock was the reason most of Mark's team ended up dead, it was his call to make. Still, Jake wasn't a fan of shooting a man down in cold blood. And alerting the camp to their presence eliminated the element of surprise they were counting on. Of course, if Sock got to this general, that was a wash anyway.

A rustling behind them. Jake jerked his head around. Decker and Brown appeared, also bent low.

Brown took in the situation, including the guard tower. "Hope to God they don't have thermal sights up there," he said, focused on the muzzles pointed down at the scene below. "We'll light them up like a Christmas tree."

"If they did, we'd already be dead," Mark murmured in response.

"So what're you waiting for?" Brown said in a low voice. "Shoot that asshole."

Mark didn't respond. His finger moved the trigger back an increment. Jake recognized his brother's expression: he was girding himself for something he didn't want to do. He'd seen it countless times growing up. It seemed like no matter what was asked of him, Mark's instinctive reaction was always to resist. That defiance even applied to minor tasks like mowing the lawn or taking out the trash. It was why his decision to enlist had always puzzled Jake. He couldn't comprehend his obstinate older brother signing up for a job where he'd spend his life following orders.

A quick spurt of machine-gun fire, and suddenly the blond guy's head was gone. Mark seemed surprised. He glanced down at his weapon, then at Decker.

Decker lowered his gun and shrugged. "Bastard deserved it."

The guards took a second to recover. Once they did, they sprayed the surrounding jungle with gunfire. More rounds erupted from the tower, tearing the ferns surrounding them to shreds. Jake scrambled back. He must have set branches swaying, because suddenly all the gunfire zeroed in on their location.

"Run!" Syd yelled, already sprinting back up the mountain.

Kelly was flipping through the book when there was a knock at her hotel-room door. She opened it to find Rodriguez standing there, face shiny and red from a good scrubbing.

"Jeez, Jones." His nose wrinkled. "You decided to skip the shower?"

"I wanted to go through this first, see if it might give us a lead on Stefan." Kelly self-consciously took a step back.

Rodriguez held out a hand for the book. "Let me take a crack at it. And please, get in the shower. I'm starving, and there's no way they'll let us into a decent restaurant with you smelling like that. Or even an indecent open-air one. It's that bad."

"Fine." Reluctantly Kelly handed over the book. Rodriguez plopped down in a chair, and she went into the bathroom. Over the noise of the shower, she heard occasional exclamations. It was shocking how much filth came off her. The water only ran clear after ten dedicated minutes of scrubbing. It was tough to balance without a handicap bar; she dropped the soap a few times and almost fell out of the tiny stall trying to retrieve it. It was funny that today she'd actually been less aware of her injury than usual. Despite the pain, having something else to focus on made it fade into the background. Yet a simple shower drove the point home. She wasn't whole anymore, and never would be again.

Kelly laid a towel on the toilet seat and sat on it while she dried off and strapped her prosthesis back on. Rodriguez had scrounged up some clean clothes for her. The T-shirt was a size too small, the pants too large, but she rolled up the cuffs and examined herself in the mirror. Purple bruises were emerging on her face, and her throat still showed the ghosts of Stefan's hands in bright red marks. She swallowed hard, once again feeling the life being choked out of her. Kelly shook it off. She ran a brush through her hair and went back into the bedroom.

"The guy who wrote this is nuts," Rodriguez declared without looking up. "I mean, man, you should read the stuff in here. And he's treating it like the Gospel."

"I know," Kelly said. The book was a pseudohistorical text. Based on a single claim that one of the Aztec kings had red hair, the author posited that the Vikings had made their way to the Mexican peninsula during the tenth century.

"It says that they found longboat hulls in Baja. Is that true?" He looked up at her.

Kelly shrugged. "I have no idea. But obviously Stefan

thinks it's true. There's a lot of stuff like that. But so far I haven't found anything that might tell us where he's headed."

"Huh." Rodriguez flipped forward another few pages, then his eyes widened. "Did you see this?"

Kelly leaned in to peer over his shoulder. On the right hand side of the page was a drawing of a temple. At the top, one figure stood over another. The caption read, "Ritual Sacrifice during *Tlacaxipehualiztli* (6 March–25 March)."

"The Aztecs practiced a lot of ritual sacrifice," Kelly said. "They used to throw kids into volcanos."

"Right, but look at what he's holding up."

Kelly leaned in. The image was fuzzy around the edges and she had to squint to make out the details. "It looks like a jacket."

"Unless I'm wrong," Rodriguez said, "that's human skin."

Twenty-Seven

Kelly felt a rush of excitement as she examined the image. "It says this is a sacrifice to Xipe Totec. Do you have your computer?"

"Back in my room. I kind of doubt we'll get a wireless connection here, though," Rodriguez said. "The phone in my room doesn't even work."

"We have to try." Kelly skimmed the margin notes. Unfortunately most were in Danish, the cribbed handwriting so small she could barely make out the text. "We'll have to translate this, too. And find out where that pyramid is."

"So you think Stefan is copying ancient Aztec sacrifices now?" Rodriguez raised an eyebrow. "That kid he killed didn't have any of the same wounds as the college girls. That would mean he's totally broken from his M.O."

"I know, it's not textbook," Kelly said. "But it's still a form of ritual sacrifice. Maybe that's all that matters to him, having a larger justification for killing his victims."

"It's still a stretch, Jones. If he's that crazy, maybe he even thought that dump was an Aztec pyramid."

"Or maybe the pyramid used to be there." Kelly hoped not, though. She knew that Stefan was insane, but at least in the past that insanity had been grounded in reality. He'd probably been using the dump as a base to practice—it perfectly suited his needs, with an endless supply of potential victims and little risk of interference by the authorities. If this was anything like his previous scheme at the university, he was building up to something larger. Their best shot at catching him lay in figuring out what that would entail.

"All right," Rodriguez sighed. "I'll get my computer. But the deadline still stands—if we don't have a better lead by tomorrow, we're out of here."

"Of course," Kelly said. "Keeping my bag packed just in case."

"Funny," Rodriguez said. "Be ready to go in five. We'll probably have better luck getting WiFi at the restaurant anyway."

Kelly grabbed her backpack and scanned the room to make sure she wasn't leaving anything behind. She had a funny feeling they wouldn't end up coming back tonight. For the first time in a long while, she felt a familiar spark, that sense of a case about to break open. It was a sensation she'd almost given up on ever experiencing again. She had no intention of leaving without seeing this through. If lying about her willingness to go home tomorrow kept Rodriguez here a bit longer, so be it. In the end, she'd find a way to get Stefan with or without his help.

Running uphill was a hell of a lot harder than coming down. On the plus side, Jake wasn't slipping as much. But the whole time he kept expecting to feel the hot burn of a bullet penetrating his back. He'd seen the damage that an automatic weapon inflicted on human flesh. In a place this isolated, there was no surviving that kind of wound. If one of them got hit, they'd have to be left behind.

Syd was still ahead of him, and he could hear the rest of the group following. He'd lost all sense of bearings, and prayed that Syd knew where the hell she was going. The gunfire must have put the Zeta camp on high alert, who knew how many units would be combing the jungle for them now. They'd have to move the whole team back and regroup, if not retreat entirely. Without the element of surprise on their side, Jake couldn't conceive of any way they'd be able to pull off the invasion.

Syd vanished behind a tree. He followed, almost slamming into her when she stopped dead.

"We've got to stop meeting like this," she commented, pushing him back with one hand.

"Why are we stopping?"

"Because I don't think they're following us anymore."

Jake listened. Gunfire still crackled below them. "I still hear it."

"Yeah, but that's not close." She cocked her head to the side. "Sounds like it's coming from the far side of camp."

Mark suddenly passed the tree. Syd let out a low whistle. He spun in his tracks and spotted them. "Decker and Brown are headed back to base to regroup," he said. "We should join them."

"I don't know if we have time. Listen."

Mark's eyebrows knit together. "Crap," he said. "The other cartel."

"They probably heard the gunfire, figured that was their cue to start the raid," Syd said.

"I'll call Brown on the radio," Mark said, pulling it off his belt. "We better get in there now if we want to save anything but corpses."

Twenty-Eight

Flores was in the back of the pen, working away at the chicken wire with the knife when the firing started. He'd initially tried to dig down to where the wire was inserted in the soil, but whoever constructed their cage did an annoyingly good job of it. Two feet down and he'd still encountered nothing but wire mesh. The only way out was to slice through, separating the wires one by one, which was extremely time-consuming. Three hours in, and he'd only managed to separate four wires in a straight line. His hands were a bloody mess from rubbing against the sharp edges.

At the first burst of gunfire, he froze. Was Tyr coming for them? Or had the unit been discovered?

"What's going on?" he asked. Calderon had the side of his face pressed against the bars, trying to see down the line of cages.

"No sé," he replied. In the neighboring cage Tejada suddenly started hacking. *"Silencio,* Ramon!" Calderon snapped.

Tejada's shoulders shook, but he kept his mouth closed as he coughed.

"Why aren't they coming?" Calderon sounded puzzled.

"In the drills, they always come within a minute or two."

"Maybe the general isn't sticking by his word," Flores said. "Could be he decided to use this as a cover to kill us."

Calderon snorted. "Don't kid yourself, *amigo*. He can shoot us whenever he wants. No, this is something different."

"Whatever it is, we gotta get a move on." Determined, Flores went back to the task at hand. A pair of white eyes shone from his left, regarding his handiwork.

"Take me with you," Tejada begged. "Please, or they will kill me."

"Absolutamente," Flores lied. The truth was, he'd be lucky to get himself and Calderon out of here in one piece. He sawed away, and another set of wires split. Flores pried them apart with his fingers, then started on the next one down.

"All right, here it is." Rodriguez tapped at the keyboard one-handed while holding a taco in the other. A trail of salsa dribbled down his chin.

They were ensconced in a restaurant a few blocks from their hotel in the Chapultepec-Lomas district. The area was decidedly more upscale than the other sections of Mexico City Kelly had seen so far. The few cars passing by at this late hour were mostly foreign-made, Toyotas with a few Lexuses and Mercedes scattered in between. The streets were cleaner, and even the smog seemed less pervasive. In spite of that, Danny had declared three other restaurants too sketchy before settling on this one. Part of a hotel bar, their meal even came complete with a free wireless connection.

"Man, this is good," Rodriguez said appreciatively,

holding back the taco to eye it. "Just like Momma used to make."

Kelly had only managed a few bites of her enchilada. She was itching to find a lead to pursue, keenly aware of Stefan's trail fading by the minute. By now, he might even have snatched another victim. "You were saying?" she asked impatiently.

"The guy who wrote the book has a website with more information. Xipe Totec, aka 'our lord the flayed one,' was a life-death-rebirth deity. He's usually represented wearing a flayed human skin. The flayed skins of sacrificed victims were believed to have curative properties when touched. Mothers even took their children to handle such skins in order to relieve their ailments." Rodriguez made a face and set his half-eaten taco back down on his plate. "So much for dinner."

"What else does it say?"

"Xipe Totec flayed himself to give food to humanity. It was supposed to be symbolic of the way maize seeds lose their outer layer before germination. After twenty days the priests took off the skins and placed them in caves. Must have been pretty ripe by then."

"What about the sacrifice, and the pyramid?"

Rodriguez continued as if she hadn't spoken. "There's an Aztec calendar here with each deity and what kind of sacrifice they got. To kick off the New Year on February 2, they committed mass drownings. Next month, the flaying, then victims were shot with arrows and had their hearts yanked out while they were still alive…it says here that in 1487, the Aztecs sacrificed eighty thousand prisoners over the course of four days. That's insane. How was anyone left?"

"The temple, Rodriguez."

"Right. Okay, sacrifices to Xipe Totec were made

during the month of *Tlacaxipehualiztli,* starting around March 6." He looked up. "That's over a month away, so Stefan's timing was off."

"Unless he was just practicing," Kelly said grimly.

Rodriguez shuddered. "Makes me appreciate Catholicism."

Kelly read over his shoulder. "It says Xipe Totec was associated with the Great Pyramid of Tenochtitlán. Where's that? Is it still around?"

"Holy crap," Rodriguez said. "Jones, it's right here. The Aztec city of Tenochtitlán was built on an island in Lake Texcoco, the site of present-day Mexico City."

Jake smeared some more mud on his face. Under close inspection it would never hold up, but he was hoping that from a few feet away, in the dark, a Zeta guard would be fooled.

"Nice," Syd said.

"You're not going to do the same?" he asked, eyeing her.

Aside from tucking her blond hair under a cap and dressing in camo, Syd hadn't done anything to alter her appearance. "No reason to bother," she said. "I doubt there are any female guards down there. The Zetas aren't known for their forward-thinking gender policies. If I get spotted, they'll shoot me whether I've got crap on my face or not."

She had a point, Jake thought, taking her in. Even in the somewhat loose-fitting camouflage, she was obviously female. "Don't worry about me, champ. I'll be fine." She winked at his look of concern.

As always, Syd was never in a better mood than at the outset of an extraordinarily dangerous operation. Jake wished he could share her enthusiasm. They were about to go up against highly trained mercenaries, while trying to avoid the other mercenaries shooting at everything in sight. They had to penetrate to where the hostages were being held, in the middle of what sounded like the final stand at the Alamo.

And that was the easy part. Somehow, they had to get back out.

Kane and Maltz still hadn't made it back from town, so they were forced to rely almost exclusively on a bunch of guys from a competing company, who so far hadn't impressed Jake with their level of skill. All things considered, he would have preferred stepping into an active volcano. The odds of survival were probably roughly the same.

Another rocket flared across the sky above camp. Jake watched its flickering descent. Sputters of automatic gunfire below them, a deafening cacophony that lit up the night like sparklers. The bulk of the fighting was centered on the south side of camp.

Mark came to stand beside them. "We're infiltrating in teams of three. Brown and his guys are going after Calderon and Flores. Decker and I will cover them, then we'll try to find Isabela's father."

"We never got a lock on his location," Syd protested.

"I know. But I promised I'd try."

"Where do you want us?" Jake asked.

Mark turned to look at him. "I'd feel better if you covered us from here."

"Bullshit," Syd said.

"Syd, you're a walking target in there. And Jake, we both know this isn't your sort of thing."

"You can't go in there without someone watching your back," Jake argued.

"It's not a put-down. I just don't think—"

"I can handle myself. And you said you can't trust these Tyr guys. They might put a bullet in your back just because they can."

Mark looked ready to argue the point, but he was interrupted by Brown's voice crackling out of his radio. "In position. We're a go in two."

"Roger that. Heading for the east gate." Mark clicked off. He examined Jake for a long moment before saying, "Fine, you're on with me and Decker. Syd, hang back with the sniper rifle. We're going to need a good shot to help us on the way out."

Syd nodded curtly. Jake was about to walk away when she abruptly threw her arms around him. "Take care of yourself, partner."

"Always." He gently eased her off, then followed Mark down toward the camp.

Twenty-Nine

"So we just need to find out where that temple used to be located," Kelly said.

"Maybe." Rodriguez scrolled through the site. "Although it says similar sacrifices were made in other Aztec cities like Tlatelolco, Xochimilco and Texcoco."

"Stefan was focused on Tenochtitlán," Kelly said, shaking her head. "That's why he came here in the first place. Admit it," she said with a grin. "This feels right to you."

"You know—" he examined her "—that's the first time I've seen you smile since…well, you know."

Kelly's smile vanished as quickly as it had appeared.

"I just meant—"

"It's okay," Kelly said quickly. "I know. And I'm really sorry that I missed your wedding. Truly."

Rodriguez shrugged, but his cheeks were pink. "No problem. It was hectic, anyway—three hundred people screaming at each other in Spanish. You would have been miserable."

"You kidding? That's practically my second language now." Kelly smiled again, and Rodriguez grinned back. "So let's find out where this temple used to be."

"That sounds an awful lot like we won't be sleeping tonight," Rodriguez grumbled. But he typed some words into the search engine. "Here's something. 'An island city, five miles square, Tenochtitlán was surrounded by Lake Texcoco. Three causeways led into the city. Canals were used as streets and people traveled everywhere by canoe. With palaces, gardens, fountains, aqueducts and sewage collection on large barges for use as fertilizer, Tenochtitlán was more advanced than any city in Europe. Looming over it all was a great pyramid with bloodstained temples on top.'"

"Does it say where the pyramid was located?"

"I'm working on it." He hit a few more keys, and a large topographic map materialized onscreen. "Says here that maps of Tenochtitlán are only accurate to a certain point—most of them come from archaeological exploration and Spanish records. But this is a mock-up of the ancient city." Kelly leaned in. The map was scrawled on old parchment, squiggly black lines delineating streets and houses. "After the conquest of the Spaniards, the Great Pyramid of Tenochtitlán was mostly destroyed. It was located dead center in the city."

"That sounds easy," Kelly said.

"Not exactly. We've got to find out what the original borders of Tenochtitlán were. If I were back at the office, we could print out an overlay…"

"No time," Kelly said. "Keep digging."

Rodriguez blew out hard, making it clear he wasn't enjoying himself.

"I can take over if you want," she offered.

"No, it's fine. Wait…here we go." Another page popped up. This one had a photograph of an archaeological site.

Kelly read aloud, "'More than four hundred years later the base of the pyramid was found during rebuilding after major earthquakes. The dig has gone on since 1978. The pyramid ruins lie to one side of the cathedral built by the Spanish next to the Great Marketplace. The site can be visited using a series of overlooks and footpaths.' This is it, we need to get here."

"Now?"

Kelly nodded, and his shoulders slumped. Rodriguez scooped up the last of his taco and jammed it in his mouth, chewed three times, then swallowed. "The things I let you talk me into." He shut the laptop and pushed his chair back. "We're making a stop first."

"We don't have time—" Kelly said impatiently.

"Listen, Jones. I've only got my sidearm and ten rounds. And unless I'm mistaken, you're still unarmed. I'm not going after anyone like that."

"It's nearly midnight, how do you expect—"

"You're forgetting that I've got family here, *chica*." He winked. "Time to pay a visit to Tío Pablo."

Beads of sweat ran down Flores's face, but he persisted. The shots were getting closer. Personally he planned to be long gone by the time the battle arrived. He had assumed that Tyr would stage a late-night snatch and grab, flying under the radar to sneak them out during a shift change. But from the sound of it they'd sent a large enough team for an all-out assault. The company manual never mentioned that type of operation.

The ground shook as a grenade exploded nearby. Screams and cries followed it. Flores gritted his teeth. He could feel Calderon at his shoulder, breathing hard.

"We must hurry, my friend," Calderon said.

"I'm going as fast as I can," he snapped.

Next door, aside from occasional coughing fits, Tejada had fallen silent. He sat with his arms wrapped around his knees, rocking back and forth. The motion made the light in their pen shift.

Flores yanked the last two wires apart, pushing them out and away so they would cause the least amount of damage when they crawled through.

"Is that wide enough?" Calderon asked dubiously. The seam in the wires extended from about a foot off the ground to the bottom of the pen. The wires were spread two inches apart, gaping open like an inverted mouth.

"We're about to find out," Flores said. He pulled some of the filthy matting they used as bedding over his head to protect it, then carefully pushed through. His head just cleared the space. Flores could feel the upper wires straining, tearing at the bedding. One caught the back of his right hand and he winced. He shifted the hand to free it, then eased his shoulders through. The wires snagged at his clothing, but if there was enough room for his shoulders, the rest of his body would follow.

"You did it, *cabrón!*" Calderon snarled exuberantly. "Let's go!"

Flores wiggled forward on his belly, an inch at a time. He was halfway through when there was a commotion at the front of their cage. He froze, shifting his head to see behind him.

One of the Zetas guards had materialized at their door. He was aiming right for them.

Thirty

Jake kept to the shadows as he followed Mark and Decker. They were entering the camp through the main gates on the eastern side. A pothole-riddled road wove away from the massive wooden fence, disappearing into the jungle. He glanced up at the guard tower they were skirting, wondering why no one was shooting at them yet.

"They must have pulled everyone south to act as reinforcements," Mark said, as if reading his mind. "But there are probably still hostiles covering the pens."

Decker was on point, sweeping the barrel of his LMT from side to side as he moved ahead of them. They slipped inside, initially sticking to the interior wall. The camp was composed of a motley assortment of dwellings, some obviously prefab, others built on-site from raw wood. They passed a long building, probably guard barracks. A light rain started to fall.

"The rain's good cover," Decker said in a low voice. "Finally we get a break."

Jake kept glancing back, braced for someone to start peppering them with rounds. They passed quickly through the section of camp where the guards lived and trained. Decker stopped abruptly, holding up a fist. After waiting a few beats, he charged across an open space, down the long aisle that marked the beginning of the prisoners' section. A moment later, Jake and Mark followed. They made it across without encountering any guards.

"Hell, this is almost too easy," Mark murmured.

They approached what looked like an endless row of kennels constructed out of chicken wire. The smell was terrible here, sweat and piss mingled with rotting leaves. As they passed along the row, a chorus of voices kicked up. Stark-white eyes stared out at them, fingers clutching the wires. *"Señores!"* they cried out. *"Por favor!"*

"Christ, we might as well have brought a bullhorn," Decker said, agitated. "They're gonna bring guards running."

Jake agreed, but there was no way to silence the prisoners. The noise shot along the line of pens like the wick leading to a bomb, increasing in volume until a single excited proclamation stood out. *"Americanos!"*

"Calderon and Flores are two rows down," Mark said. "Brown should be coming up on them." The plan had been for Brown to enter from the next gate over, the one closest to Calderon's holding cell. That way if one of their groups attracted fire, it would distract the guards enough to allow the alternate team to slip inside.

Mark was moving faster now. Jake broke into a trot to keep up with him. The radio on Mark's shoulder suddenly crackled. "This is Alpha team. Hostiles at the North Gate," Brown said in a low voice.

"Roger," Mark said. "Beta team clear. We're almost at the target."

"Roger that. We'll double back and come in after you."

The radio fell silent.

So it's down to us, Jake thought. They turned the next

corner at a dead run. According to their intel, Flores and Calderon were being held a few hundred feet down and to the right.

A sputter of gunfire a few rows over. Someone screamed. A second passed, then more rounds. The scream was abruptly silenced. Mark and Decker slowed. Jake matched their pace.

"Sounds like some of our friends hung around to execute prisoners," Decker said.

At the sound of the shots, the murmur surrounding them ascended to a fever pitch. Prisoners threw themselves against the wires, clawing at the pen doors in their desperation to escape. Jake gritted his teeth and kept going.

They turned down the last row. Twenty yards away, a guy in fatigues braced an LMT against his shoulder as he aimed into one of the pens.

"Alto!" Mark shouted, sighting his own weapon.

The muzzle of the gun swiveled toward them.

"Get down!" Mark shoved Jake hard. He flew through the air, rolling a few times before slamming against the metal side of a pen.

A sputter of machine-gun fire, and Mark dropped to the ground.

Flores froze, his legs still inside the cage. Every fiber of his being screamed for him to squeeze all the way out and run for his life. But if he did that, Calderon would be killed. And in spite of everything, he didn't know if he'd be able to live with that.

Of course, chances were the guard would shoot them both anyway.

"Métanse!" the guard yelled, pivoting the gun back and forth between them.

Calderon locked eyes with Flores. His held a look of infinite sadness. *"Vaya con Dios, amigo,"* he said before turning away.

"Wait," Flores protested, but Calderon was already walking toward the entrance to the pen. He kept his hands held high, chin jutted up. The guard shifted as if anticipating an attack, although the door remained locked. The barrel of his gun aimed directly at Calderon's chest. His body shielded Flores, at least for the moment.

Flores channeled the adrenaline coursing through his veins. He dug his elbows into the dirt, clawing his way forward. His hips shifted through the opening. The sheared wires rended his pant legs as he dragged himself out. As his feet cleared the gap, gunfire erupted behind him. Without looking back, he leaped up and ran like hell.

"Mark!" Jake cried out.

Decker was already firing. The guard's body was buffeted by bullets, making him jump and twitch like a rag doll. His rifle went off in a sputtering arc, bullets ripping into the trees overhead as he toppled over.

Jake crawled to his brother. The impact of the bullet had thrown him on his side. His eyes were closed, and he didn't appear to be breathing.

Jake's hands shook as he rolled Mark onto his back. He couldn't see any blood.

Decker squatted next to him. He reached out a steady hand, feeling for a pulse. Then he shook him.

"Hey!" Jake cried.

Mark suddenly shifted, and his eyes popped open. He looked up blearily.

"What happened?"

"Got your bell rung," Decker said brusquely. "Looks like your vest stopped it, though."

Mark lifted his head. There was a quarter-sized hole in the front of his shirt. He stuck a finger in and tapped his vest. "Good thing they weren't using hollow points," he said.

"Good thing," Decker agreed. "Scared the piss out of your brother, though."

"Yeah?" Mark shifted to look at Jake. "I didn't think you'd be shedding any tears over me."

"I just wasn't in the mood to carry you." Jake cuffed his shoulder.

"I'd feel the same way." Mark grinned.

"We better keep moving," Decker said.

"Sure." Mark winced as he staggered to his feet, shrugging off help. He looked down the line of pens, getting his bearings. "Should be twelve pens down."

"Crap," Decker said. "That's where the guard was."

Thirty-One

Kelly sat in the corner nursing a mug of coffee. It was lukewarm and weak, with a greasy film that probably portended a serious case of Montezuma's revenge down the line. But she didn't want to offend their host, so she gambled and took a few sips. It didn't actually taste that bad. There was a hint of something...cinnamon, maybe? At least she hoped that's what the floating brown flecks were.

She examined Rodriguez's Uncle Pablo over the lip of the cup. He was tiny, birdlike, the few sparse hairs on his head carefully combed across the top. An enormous moustache dominated his face, as if overcompensating for his baldness. Bright red pants were cinched above his waist with a belt, and he wore white leather loafers with black socks.

Apparently Pablo spent his spare time stocking weaponry. Once Rodriguez explained the reason for their late-night visit, he led them to a back room that was an NRA member's wet dream. Wooden shipping crates were crammed into every available space, some stacked nearly to the ceiling. Pablo flung open the closest crate to reveal

a stack of gold-plated AK-47s. A second held grenades.
A third, handguns.

Kelly didn't ask where all the artillery came from, or
why he was in possession of it—she figured she was better
off not knowing. She watched Rodriguez sift through the
crates, appreciatively examining a rifle scope as they discussed terms in Spanish. From what Kelly could gather,
although they qualified for a friends and families dis-
count, none of this stuff came free. Which was a little
worrisome. Thanks to the *federales,* she had less than a
few hundred dollars on hand, and she doubted Rodriguez
had much more. She suspected this wasn't the kind of deal
sealed with an AMEX card.

She caught Pablo eyeing her. He said something to
Rodriguez in Spanish. Danny's brow darkened. The two
of them started arguing. Rodriguez was easily a full head
taller than his uncle, but Pablo still jutted his chin forward
and shouted back. Kelly wondered if there was anyone
else in the house. Personally she thought arguing with
a guy who owned this much artillery was a bad idea. It
struck her again how different things were down here,
how she could simply vanish. No one would have any idea
where to start searching for them. She wondered if Danny
had told anyone where he was going. Probably not—or
if he had, they would have no idea that their night ended
with a stop at Uncle Pablo's.

They were interrupted by a sudden pounding from the
front of the house. Pablo smiled, exposing a line of gold
teeth. He said something in Spanish, then swept out of the
room, brushing her shoulder with his hip as he passed.
Kelly shied away from the contact.

"What was that all about?" she asked in a low voice,
relieved to finally set the coffee mug aside.

"Nothing," Rodriguez said, but he looked enraged.

"Why does he have all this stuff?"

"He's the biggest arms dealer in town," Rodriguez said without meeting her eyes.

"Oh." Kelly was taken aback. That kind of association could prove career-ending at the Bureau. After a second, she added, "Don't worry, I would never tell McLarty."

"I know you wouldn't," he said. "Otherwise I never would have taken you here."

Kelly held up a finger and they both fell silent: a conversation was being conducted in low voices in the other room. "You don't think he'll come back armed, do you?"

"I wouldn't put it past him," Rodriguez muttered. After taking in her expression, he said, "Relax, Jones, I'm messing with you. My mother is his favorite sister, and I'm her only son. He could never get away with killing me—the whole family would come down hard on him."

Kelly wanted to point out that the whole family had no idea they were there, but she held her tongue. "Is he your mother's favorite brother?"

"He's no one's favorite anything." Rodriguez glowered. "And after what he just said, he's officially off my Christmas-card list."

"What'd he say?"

"You're better off not knowing."

"Okay." Kelly decided to leave it alone. She took in the array. "What can we afford?"

"One LMT and two handguns. Or two handguns and a grenade."

Kelly's right leg twinged at the mention of grenades. She'd avoided looking at them since entering the room. "The handguns are all we need," she said. "We'd attract too much attention with the LMT anyway."

"Agreed."

Pablo entered the room again as if on cue. Kelly suspected that he spoke more English than he let on.

"Qué pasa?" Rodriguez asked, his grip tightening on the rifle in his hand.

Kelly suddenly realized that Pablo wasn't alone.

"More customers," Pablo said with a thick accent, flashing the shiny grin again. He stepped aside to reveal two hulking figures. One of them stepped across the threshold into the room.

"Maltz?" Kelly asked, astonished.

"Ms. Jones." Maltz swept the room with his eyes, taking in Danny and the open boxes of weapons. "Thought you headed home."

"No, I got…delayed."

"Uh-huh." His eyes narrowed. Maltz said something in rapid-fire Spanish to Pablo, who shrugged but shrank under his gaze.

"Who the hell are you?" Rodriguez asked.

"I could ask the same," Maltz said. Kane filled the doorway behind him.

"They work for Jake," Kelly said.

"Jake's down here? You didn't mention that." Rodriguez sounded annoyed.

"It's complicated. He's working a case." Kelly turned to Maltz. "Danny used to be my partner."

"Okay." Maltz kept an eye on Pablo the whole time he questioned her. "You two are a pretty long way from the airport. Jake know you're here?"

"No," Kelly said flatly. "How's it going with the operation?"

Maltz shrugged. "We're here to re-up on equipment. Figured *mi amigo* Pablo could help. We'll wait for you to finish up." He nodded to Kane, and they stepped back into the other room.

Once they left, Pablo turned back to Danny and rattled something off in Spanish. Once again, Kelly felt herself at a deficit. She was sick of not knowing what everyone was saying.

Rodriguez pulled a roll out of his back pocket and palmed off a few hundreds. Pablo counted them, then raised an eyebrow. Rodriguez forked over one more, and they were the proud owners of two new Glocks. Pablo leered at her one last time before disappearing into the other room.

"I'd prefer an H&K," Rodriguez said, sighting down the scope.

"I would, too." Kelly shuffled the slide a few times to check the spring and pulled the trigger to dry-fire it. "They look clean, though."

"No way to test them, we'll have to take Tío Pablo at his word." Rodriguez eyed her. "Why didn't you call Jake to bail you out?"

"Because he would have tried to make me go home," Kelly said.

"Smart man. How come he can talk you into things and I can't?"

"He wouldn't have been able to. I just didn't feel like having that fight." Kelly glanced at her watch: it was nearly midnight. "We should get going."

They exited through Pablo's living room. Crude paintings of nude women dotted the cheap wood paneling, and the maroon shag carpet had seen better days. Despite the ramshackle appearance of the house from outside, the room held thousands of dollars' worth of electronic equipment. An enormous flat-screen TV dominated one wall, with a complicated array of video game consoles and stereo equipment trailing from it. Two Barcaloungers faced the TV. Maltz perched on the edge of one, Kane stood beside him. Pablo occupied the other. They all fell silent when Kelly and Rodriguez entered.

"All set," Kelly said. "Good luck with your mission."

Maltz stood and came over to her. Kelly flushed at his proximity.

"I don't feel right leaving you like this," he said in a low voice. "Seems like you're up to no good."

"I've got her back," Rodriguez said.

Maltz looked him over. He didn't seem reassured. "I'm guessing you don't want me to tell Jake that we ran into each other."

"That would be best, thanks." Kelly swallowed hard.

"You sure you're okay here?" Maltz probed her eyes. She nodded once, and he stepped back. "Good luck," he said.

"Thanks." Rodriguez ushered her out of the room before adding under his breath, "We'll need it."

Flores peered cautiously around the edge of the pens. He was next to what appeared to be a barracks building, long and narrow with windows set high along the side. He'd managed to make it this far without encountering any guards, except for a dead one an aisle over. Other prisoners cried out to him, but he ignored them. He hated doing it, the memory of Calderon's sacrifice fresh in his mind. But he had to get out of here, back to Maryanne. One man traveling alone had a shot at escaping. If he added anyone to that equation, the risk increased exponentially. Flores figured that from the sound of it, Tyr had the Zetas on the run anyway. Hopefully the casualties wouldn't be too high.

There was a gate about fifty feet away on his right, guard towers flanking it. To get out, he'd have to get past those towers and across an open expanse. Beyond the clearing he could see the edge of the jungle, where the road plummeted into darkness. The Zetas had cleared a hundred-foot swath surrounding the camp, forming a sort of no-man's land.

This was probably where they'd brought him in. The heavy fighting was coming from the opposite end of camp, leaving this his only option.

A light rain was falling; Flores blinked it out of his eyes as he watched for movement. Nothing: no gun muzzles, no sign of any guards. It struck him as odd that the Zetas would have pulled men off their stations, especially if they were under attack. Maybe Tyr had already cleared this sector. But then why weren't their men holding it down? He wondered how the battle was progressing, how many of his Tyr buddies were back there fighting. Now that Calderon was dead, there wasn't much point hooking up with them—they'd raise a lot of questions he wasn't prepared to answer, like how he'd let Calderon die after everything they'd done to try to save him. He was better off forging ahead on his own.

If he managed to get past the gates alive, Flores could make his way through the jungle parallel to the road, following it all the way back to Mexico City. From there, he'd have to find his way home—not easy, but not impossible, either.

But first, he had to get through without being shot.

Odd that the gate had been left open, but that worked in his favor. He couldn't detect anyone in the guard tower, but that didn't mean it was empty. For all he knew it was a functioning sniper's nest. He scanned the ground around him and spotted a rock a few feet away. Scrambling forward as silently as possible, he scooped it up and tossed it near the entrance.

Nothing.

He'd have to risk it.

Flores started forward, then jerked back when he sensed movement in his peripheral vision. Keeping low, he edged forward. On his left about fifty feet away, two guards were loading up a Toyota Hilux. He breathed out, hard. Lucky break—if they'd seen him, he'd be dead for sure.

The guards were clearly in a hurry, loading file boxes in the rear of the truck. Someone he couldn't see barked an order at them. Flores frowned: he knew that voice. General Gente was apparently ducking out of the battle, abandoning his men. *Typical,* Flores thought. All that talk about his elite training, and at the first sign of trouble Gente headed for the hills. He'd served under commanders like that and had nothing but contempt for them.

He edged forward as they moved out of his line of sight. Gente's trailer was ten feet past the Hilux. The soldiers disappeared inside.

Flores could chance it, running for the exit before they reappeared. The gate was tantalizingly close. Less than a minute and he'd be free. In a few days he'd be back in Maryanne's arms.

That would be the smart thing to do. But then, no one had ever accused him of being a genius.

Mentally apologizing to Maryanne for what he was about to do, Flores flipped his grip on the knife so that it was clenched in his fist, blade forward. Bent low, he double-timed it, running as quickly and silently as possible, heart pounding in his chest.

The guards re-emerged from the trailer. Peering under the truck bed, he could see their boots. Their chatter didn't abate. Hunching down beside the truck's rear left tire, Flores listened. They sounded agitated, babbling about Sinaloan bastards getting the jump on them.

"Why the hell are we even bothering with this crap?" one grumbled in Spanish.

"Three more and we're done. Hurry up so we can get out of here," the other replied.

The sound of retreating footsteps. Something heavy dropped into the truck bed, the Hilux rocked slightly in response. Flores glanced around the edge of the tire. A guard was with his back to him. An LMT dangled from his shoulder strap.

Flores came up behind him. Belatedly the guard spun, reaching for his weapon. Flores already had a hand across his chest, blocking the move. Before the guard could make a sound Flores slit his throat, jerking the knife across his neck from left to right. As he dragged him back to the other side of the truck, the man's hands grasped futilely at the wound. He gurgled plaintively, jerked a few times, then went still.

Flores dropped the body into the truck's shadow and waited. He checked the LMT, making sure it had a full clip and was ready to fire. It felt good to be armed with more than a whittling knife. The heft of it in his hands was reassuring.

Less than a minute later, the other guard called out for help. Flores watched the man's legs from beneath the truck—he appeared to be staggering.

"Come get a box, you lazy bastard!" the guard yelled.

Flores straightened to peer over the lip of the truck bed. The guard had stacked three boxes on top of one another, apparently determined to finish the job in a single trip. *Thank God for small favors,* Flores thought grimly.

He stepped forward. The guard couldn't see him over the towering boxes.

"Take the top one, I can handle the other two," the

guard grunted. Obligingly Flores knocked the top box off the stack. The guard's expression rapidly shifted from relief to shock. Without hesitation, Flores fired a series of rounds into his face. The rest of the boxes toppled down as the guard stumbled back. He made it five feet before dropping to the ground.

Flores heard an oath and swiveled. Gente filled the doorway of the prefab trailer. The fat man glowered at him, then spun around and slammed the door.

Flores charged forward. He fired off rounds, blowing the cheap handle off the door before kicking it in. The door suddenly sputtered, chunks of wood flying as Gente shot at it from inside. Flores leaped back, cursing. He took cover behind the rear of the Hilux. He could empty his clip into the side of the trailer, but it might be armored along the inside. For all he knew Gente had a full arsenal in there, and he had to conserve rounds if he wanted to make it out alive. He should just leave, get out of here before the gunfire brought more Zetas running. The gate seemed to call out to him, an irresistible lure.

"I thought you had trouble killing men face-to-face, *señor,*" Gente called out from the interior. He sounded unfazed.

His tone sparked rage inside Flores. "I got over it," he yelled back.

"I'm surprised you're still here," Gente replied. "I thought you were smarter than that."

"Well, you thought wrong," Flores muttered.

"Is Señor Calderon with you?"

Flores didn't answer. Gente chuckled again. "*Bueno,* the bastard didn't make it."

"He was a hero."

"You still think so, *amigo?* One of those boxes holds files. Open the one marked Tyr."

Flores didn't have to look hard. The box he'd knocked out of the guard's hands had spewed a comet trail of files. He edged forward. The headings were written in a cribbed hand, hard to make out in the dark. He dragged a few toward him, then scrabbled back to the shelter of the truck. Most were guard schedules, disciplinary files…apparently the Zetas had retained the military zeal for bureaucracy along with their actual training.

Sorting through, his eyes locked on one labelled Tyr.

He knelt on one knee and flipped it open with his right hand, using his left to keep the LMT aimed at the side of the trailer. Inside, he could hear Gente panting, still fighting to catch his breath.

There were subfolders inside, each with a name. Flores flipped open the topmost one. Inside, the blueprint of a house had been sketched out by hand. The next page held names and dates. He was shocked to recognize one of them: Wysocki. Rain smudged the ink.

"Damning, isn't it?" Gente called out.

"Doesn't mean jackshit. You could have gotten all this from Wysocki."

"Take the flash drive. On it you will hear Calderon selling his own clients' freedom."

There was a flash drive tucked into a pocket inside the folder. Flores scooped it out and crammed it in his pocket. "Shame I didn't bring my computer."

Gente laughed again. "Come inside, you can use mine."

Flores scanned the truck bed for something that would drive Gente from the trailer. There were markings on the outside of one box. Carefully keeping the trailer door covered, he reached out his free hand and dragged it toward him. Popped the top and looked inside. What he saw made him smile.

"I'll need more men after this," Gente said. "You could be my second-in-command. I can make you a wealthy man."

Flores dug inside the box. It sounded like Gente was moving around in the trailer, probably preparing some sort of ambush. Maybe he really did have some training. "Interesting offer," he called back, then he yanked out the pin with his teeth. "But where you're going, I don't think they're hiring."

Flores counted to three, then tossed the grenade inside the trailer door and raced for cover behind the truck.

A shout of surprise. Gente appeared in the doorway, his face panicked. He made it down the first step, and then the entire trailer erupted. Flores covered his head to protect it from the debris raining down. Some of it was stained dark red.

Flores cautiously looked up. The rear half of the trailer was gone, the rest was a smoldering ruin. There was a dark pit where Gente had been standing, the stairs had disappeared entirely.

"All right, then," he said. Scooping up the other guard's LMT, he checked the truck. A set of keys rested in the ignition.

With a grin, Flores climbed inside and started the engine.

Thirty-Two

Mark and Decker overtook Jake as they raced down the line of pens. The fallen guard lay askew, arms and legs flung out, his rifle on the ground beside him. The rain clouds parted briefly, moonlight casting the blood-stained ground dark gray.

"Stand back," Mark said. A shadow shifted inside the cage. Mark held his gun inches away from the lock and squeezed the trigger once. The metal blew apart and the door swung wide. Mark ducked his head inside.

"Christ, I hope this is the right pen," Decker muttered.

A figure stepped forward into the light.

"It's the right one," Mark said. "Mr. Calderon, we're here to save you."

Calderon was shaking. "Just in time," he said unsteadily. "They were about to kill me."

"Where's Flores?" Mark asked, peering around him.

"Already gone."

"He left you? Doesn't sound like Flores."

A noise sounded in the pen next door. They all spun, guns ready. A tiny man, white hair wild, threw himself against the bars of his cage. Jake jerked back as he sputtered at them in Spanish. *"Ayúdenme!"*

Mark looked at Calderon. "This a buddy of yours?"

"There are no friends in here," Calderon replied. It was hard to see his eyes in the dark, but his tone was flat.

"Your call," Mark said.

Jake didn't wait for a response—he might not be able to save all the prisoners, but this one he could manage. He motioned the man back with his gun and shot off the lock. The prisoner fell out of the pen and dropped to his knees, grabbing at Jake's pant legs as he said, *"Gracias"* over and over.

"No problem," Jake interrupted, reaching out a hand to help him up. "Can you walk?"

"Sí, señor." The man scrambled to his feet, then bent over, racked by coughs. Even fully upright, he barely reached Jake's chest.

"He's your problem," Mark said before turning back to Calderon. "Which way did Flores go?"

"Out the back. He cut a hole in the pen. Please, we should really—"

"How long ago?"

Calderon shrugged. "Minutes."

"Probably already out the exit." Decker was facing away from the pen, keeping an eye on their back. "What now, Chief?"

"Isabela's father." Mark turned back to Calderon. "We need to find another prisoner, Francisco Garcia. Any idea where he might be?"

"Is he a client?" Calderon asked.

"He's a friend of a friend."

"Then I don't see why—"

"This is part of the deal, Mr. Calderon."

"I know Señor Garcia," the little white-haired man interrupted. "He's being held by the rear gates."

"Which gates?"

The man pointed south, where the worst of the battle raged.

"Great," Decker said. "It couldn't be easy."

"Decker, take Calderon out the gate we came in," Mark said. "Jake, go with him."

"You'll need someone to watch your back," Jake said.

Mark weighed the suggestion. Something exploded nearby, the tang of sulphur wafted toward them.

"Take him," Decker said. "You'll need backup more than I will."

"Fine," Mark said. "Let's go."

It was nearly 1:00 a.m. Kelly peered out the window as Rodriguez paid the cabdriver.

"I don't see a temple," she said.

"I had him drop us off a few blocks away. Figured better safe than sorry," he replied.

The Templo Mayor was located in el Centro, a section of town thronged by tourists during the day, but deserted at this late hour.

"We should do a quick check of the grounds once we get there. If we don't see Stefan, we'll find a place to watch for him. Maybe there's a hotel with a good sight-line," Rodriguez added hopefully as he ran a hand through his hair. "I could use some shut-eye."

Kelly took him in. His suit was badly rumpled, and removing his tie had revealed a salsa stain on his shirt. He looked exhausted. "Thanks for doing this," she said, suddenly moved. In retrospect she'd been a terrible friend, shunning him during her months of recovery and missing his wedding. Yet here he was marching into a dangerous section of Mexico City with her in the middle of the night, chasing after a serial killer. She'd never had a friend willing to do anything like that. Except for Jake, she reminded herself.

"Sure." Rodriguez forced a smile. "And if we don't find him tonight, tomorrow I'll see if McLarty can arrange for some cooperation from the local authorities."

"What makes you think he'll believe me now?"

"Because now it's not just you saying it. Let's get going."

She followed Rodriguez as he broke into a trot, taking a left down the next block. He didn't stop moving until the street dead-ended on a public square. He motioned for her to follow him into the archway of a building.

Rodriguez eyed her. "Just so we're clear, the goal here is to arrest him."

"Of course," Kelly said, surprised. "What did you think I was going to do?"

"Nothing. But I know you've got history with this guy. You went after him on your own, without telling anyone. I just want to make sure we're on the same page."

"I was just following up a lead. If I got a fix on him, I was going to call McLarty."

"All right. But no cowboy shit, got it?"

"Got it."

He motioned toward the square and said, "It's this way."

Flores gunned the engine and the truck leaped forward. He spun the Hilux in a tight circle, kicking up gravel. For a second it bogged down in the mud on the side of the road, but he shifted into four-wheel drive and it lurched free.

"Gotta love a Hilux," he muttered through gritted teeth. This one appeared armored, which was a bonus, and had a nearly full tank of gas. The Hilux was a workhorse, the vehicle of choice for this sort of potholed terrain. If he was lucky, it would take him all the way to the border without breaking down.

Flores tore through the open gates, braced for a sputter of gunfire from above—even if the sides were armored, chances were the roof wouldn't be. When nothing happened, he released a lungful of air. Looked like he was home-free.

Just as he was thinking it, the side of the truck was suddenly pummeled by gunfire. Flores swerved, trying to avoid it, but a shot pinged the car door inches from his left knee. The driver's-side window cracked and he ducked. He reached out his right hand, trying to grab the LMT, but it had slid to the floor of the cab.

Flores kept his foot on the accelerator as he leaned over to retrieve it. Unfortunately the sudden motion sent the truck off the road. It slammed hard into a ditch. He pressed the gas. The front tires spun uselessly in the mud.

"Damn it!" He slammed his fist against the steering wheel.

"No se mueva," said a voice. A gun muzzle pressed against his ear.

He raised his hands, hopes shot to hell.

"Flores?"

He turned to find Decker standing there. The big man's face split in a grin and he lowered the rifle. "Holy shit, am I glad to see you."

"Me, too. Want a ride?"

"Hell, yeah." Decker turned and waved someone over. "Get in."

The passenger door opened. At the sight of Cesar Calderon, Flores's jaw tightened.

"Hola, amigo." Calderon slid inside and clapped a hand on his shoulder. "I'm glad you made it out alive."

"Yeah, me, too." Flores looked away from him, focusing back out the windshield. "Where are the others?"

Decker slid in beside Calderon and slammed the door. He kept the muzzle of his LMT aimed out the window. "Riley's going after another prisoner. Think you can get out of this ditch?"

Flores opened the door a crack. The front tires were mired in mud, but the rear ones were free. "I think so."

"Thank God, I wasn't looking forward to hoofing it out of here. Let's blow this joint."

Flores threw the truck into Reverse and ground down on the accelerator. After a second of protest, it broke free and fishtailed back onto the road. As he drove away, Flores glanced back in the rearview mirror. The gates of the camp receded into the distance.

"Where to?" he asked after a minute.

"There's a motel about an hour's drive due north." Decker clicked on his radio. "We have the package, en route to rally point two."

After a second of static, a woman's voice replied, "Copy that."

Flores surreptitiously examined Calderon. It was hard to reconcile the man who had saved his life with the one who had apparently put so many others at risk. But he still only had Gente's word for it. He had to hear what was on that flash drive.

"Everything okay, Enrique?" Calderon asked.

Flores shifted his gaze, looking directly at him. Unless he was mistaken, there was a shrewdness in the man's eyes now.

"Just glad we made it out alive." Flores turned his attention back to the road.

"Amen to that," Decker said. "Hopefully Riley will, too."

Thirty-Three

They were an odd trio, Jake allowed. Mark was in the lead, pausing occasionally for whispered instructions from Señor Tejada. The small man wasn't thrilled to be along for the ride. He wheezed with every breath. Thanks to the lengthy confinement, his muscles had atrophied to the point where he could barely walk, never mind run. Jake kept expecting him to keel over.

As they got closer to where the main battle raged, Tejada became increasingly agitated.

"Señor," he finally said, grabbing hold of Mark's sleeve. "Please let me go back to the others."

"You're the only one who knows where Garcia is being held," Mark said.

"But, *señor…*"

"If you don't like it, I can stick you back in your cage."

At that, the small man fell silent.

Jake was thankful that the constant din of prisoners begging for release had faded; this close to the action, most had withdrawn to the rear of their pens. He could barely make out shadows as they passed, people attempting to curl into themselves and disappear. A few still called out for help, but it happened less and less frequently. Not that it would matter anymore. The perpetual *rat-a-tat* of machine-gun fire overrode everything. His team could run screaming the whole way and chances were no one would hear them. The air was thick with smoke. The ground shook beneath his feet: grenade explosion. It was followed by screams.

They turned down another row to find carnage. Body parts still clothed in the tattered remains of camouflage were scattered about. Blood trailed out the doors of many of the pens, some of which stood open. Either the Zetas had started executing prisoners, or they had been collateral damage during the fighting.

"Jesucristo." Tejada crossed himself.

"Stay close," Mark advised, but Tejada didn't need any persuasion, he was practically tripping over their heels.

Another explosion, so close Jake's ears contracted from the pressure. Tejada might have the right idea. Saving Isabela's father had been more appealing on the other side of camp.

Bullets suddenly tore up the ground twenty feet away from them. Dirt clods sputtered up in a steady line, heading their way.

"Take cover!" Mark yelled, vaulting sideways.

Jake lunged for a break in the pens, dragging Tejada with him. They fell on their sides. Tejada was racked by coughs, choking for air. Wide eyes stared at them from inside the pen.

"Dónde está Francisco Garcia?" Jake asked.

A pause, then a quavering female voice said, *"Una fila más."* A finger poked out of the chicken wire, pointing right.

"Gracias." Jake tried to remember how to say, "Stay calm, help is coming," but decided the lie wouldn't serve

either of them. He hauled Tejada back to his feet. "You heard the lady. We gotta go that way."

A helicopter swept past overhead. Jake ducked back into the shadows as a spotlight illuminated the aisle between the pens. It panned about, clearly looking for something.

"Who is that?" Tejada asked, perplexed.

"No idea, but I'm guessing not a friend."

"Jake!" Mark called out.

"We're over here."

Mark appeared across the aisle. "I'm cutting back… maybe the next row is clear."

"Okay. We have to get over there somehow, though."

"I know. Gotta avoid a chopper now, too." He looked at Tejada. "Maybe you two should head back."

Tejada looked hopeful, but Jake shook his head. "No way. I'm not leaving you."

"This isn't my first rodeo, Jay-Jay. I've done this before."

It had been years since anyone called him that. "I'm backing you up," Jake said firmly. "And we need him to help us ID Garcia. Everyone in here will probably claim to be him."

"Yeah, I thought the same thing." Mark scanned down the row. "All right. But stay on me."

"You got it."

They jogged back the way they'd come, Tejada scrambling to keep pace. At the end of the row, they jigged left and headed down a parallel aisle. The damage was less severe, but the ground was still stained with blood.

The helicopter swept past again. It flew low, nearly skirting the pens. Jake ducked instinctively.

"Holy crap," Mark said.

"What?"

"It had army insignia on the side."

The helicopter jarred to a halt two aisles away. Hovering, the spotlight fixed on something. A fifty-caliber machine gun pummeled the ground. At this proximity, the noise was deafening.

"That's the aisle Isabela's father is on!" Mark shouted to be heard over the din.

"Mark, we've got to turn back. There's no way—"

"Which pen is Garcia in?" Mark asked fiercely.

Tejada gazed back blankly. Mark grabbed him by the shoulders. "Give me some direction and I won't have to take you along."

"Pen nine. Count from the back of the row," Tejada stuttered.

"Okay." Mark turned to Jake. "Get him out of here. I'll meet up with you."

Without another word Mark sprinted away, headed straight for the spot beneath the chopper. Jake hesitated. Tejada was so petrified he was literally shaking. There was no way he could subject him to that kind of assault. Mark disappeared around the next corner. "C'mon," Jake said.

"Please, *señor*. I can't—" Tejada's cheeks were streaked with tears.

"I know. We're heading back."

Tejada cast a quick look toward where Mark had disappeared. Without another word, he fell in behind Jake.

As they headed back the way they came, Jake felt like he was moving through cement. Half a dozen times he spun, prepared to race back to help Mark. Each time, the sight of Tejada's raw terror stopped him.

They had almost reached Calderon's empty pen when a massive explosion threw them to the ground. Jake rolled on his back. Over the tops of the pens, right where Mark had vanished, a huge fireball roiled.

"This is déjà vu all over again," Rodriguez grumbled.

Kelly didn't respond. She'd forgotten how sulky Rodriguez got on stakeouts, especially when he didn't have snacks. Not that she blamed him. She was second-guessing the line of reasoning that led them here, too. What seemed like a stroke of genius last night at the restaurant now just felt like a stretch. They'd been hunkered down in the shadows near the main entrance to the Templo Mayor museum for nearly three hours and hadn't seen any sign of Stefan.

The ruins of the Aztec temple encompassed a full city block. It was a sunken labyrinth, rough-hewn stone passages descending in tiers. The way they were constructed reminded her of sea jetties, small dark rocks held together by concrete. A modern building stood off to one side: the museum, Kelly guessed. In the center rose a flight of crumbling stairs, all that remained of the original temple.

"I'm calling it," Rodriguez said, checking his watch. "Nearly dawn, rush hour starts soon. Even Stefan's not crazy enough to try anything then. Let's head back to the hotel and grab some sleep before calling McLarty."

"Just a little longer," Kelly pleaded, but she suspected he was right. The links seemed much more tenuous upon reflection. But then, this was the only lead they had.

"Maybe he's waiting until…what was that date again?" Rodriguez stifled a yawn.

"March 6. Maybe." That was more than a month away. Hard to imagine Stefan would wait that long to seize another victim, especially since he knew Kelly was in

Mexico. Of course, he might be assuming she was still locked up, so perhaps he felt safe enough to stick around. "He could have gone back to the dump," she offered.

"They'll kill him if he does," Rodriguez said. "Seems like a stretch, anyway."

"You're right." Kelly blinked back her exhaustion. Her entire body had stiffened up after hours of sitting in the same position, combined with the beating she'd received yesterday. Despite the half dozen Advil she'd swallowed, her right leg throbbed.

"Well, we can't hang around here until March," Rodriguez said. "I've got to get back to L.A. and find out if I still have a job."

"I understand," Kelly said, defeated.

"That sounded like you aren't planning on coming with me." Rodriguez's eyes narrowed. "That wasn't our deal."

"If McLarty agrees to send backup—" Kelly froze. Something had darted across her sight line, headed for the locked entrance to the museum. "Danny, look."

He followed her eyes. "Could be anyone," he said. "You want to get closer to check?"

Kelly didn't need to get closer, she recognized Stefan's gait. But she nodded.

They approached the temple from the street lining the western side. A long wall separated the museum from the road, topped by a metal banister. The stones cast long shadows in the moonlight. While Kelly watched, a dark shadow vaulted the banister and disappeared into the darkness below.

"That's him," she said.

"He's alone. That's a good sign." Rodriguez seemed uncertain. "The temple grounds are private property.

We could call the *federales*. There's probably still trace evidence on him from the boy."

"You said it yourself, justice is different down here," Kelly argued. "Either way, we should try to get him off the streets tonight, before he kills anyone else."

"I suppose it'll be easier to extradite him if he's already in custody," Rodriguez said. "All right, we go in, but I'm taking the lead. And if anyone asks, we arrested him on the street."

"Of course." Kelly followed Rodriguez as he darted across the plaza toward the banister. He looked over the side, then jerked back. "Christ," he said. "The things I let you talk me into. That has to be a twenty-foot drop."

Kelly peered over. The temple ruins stretched away from them for over an acre. The archaeological excavation had carved out deep stone-lined troughs leading from one ruined structure to the next. Some had doors allowing entry while others were mere mounds of stone. Tarps stretched above a few, including the original stairs leading up the side of the temple pyramid.

"Where'd he go?" she whispered.

"Who knows? It's a maze down there." Rodriguez sighed. "Sure you want to do this?"

In response, Kelly threw her good leg over the banister. She eased her prosthetic after it, then lowered herself until she was hanging by her arms. Taking a deep breath, she let go.

Kelly landed hard, keeping her right knee bent so that her left ankle absorbed most of the fall. She winced as pain shot up her good foot—that was all she needed, to have both legs compromised. She rolled her foot and the throbbing eased.

Rodriguez dropped to the ground beside her with a muffled curse.

"You okay?" she whispered.

"That wasn't as easy as you made it look," he grumbled.

Kelly waved him silent. She'd heard a noise off to their left. She pulled the Glock out of her waistband and made sure a round was chambered. At a nod from Rodriguez, she headed toward it.

The moonlight cast shadows, throwing off her depth perception. Kelly stumbled and nearly fell more than once. The stones that remained from the original plaza were held in place by concrete, creating rough paths between low rock walls. Here and there she found herself on a more modern walkway, but it was constantly interrupted by uneven cobblestones. They reached a dead end.

"I'll climb up, see if I can spot him," Rodriguez offered.

She nodded. With a grunt, he heaved himself up on the parapet. His head swiveled from left to right. Suddenly he ducked back down.

"He's near the temple steps," he said. "Follow me."

They stayed low as they trotted forward. The channel they were following widened into a plaza. Rodriguez paused.

"Pretty exposed here," he whispered.

"What's he doing?" Kelly asked.

"Hard to tell. He's still alone, though."

Kelly turned that over in her head, wishing they'd done more research on the temple. She'd assumed that Stefan intended to murder another victim on the steps, the way they'd seen in the picture, but even he wasn't crazy enough to do it right out in the open. There must still be enclosed areas scattered around the temple grounds. Maybe his next victim was already concealed in one.

"Hang on." Rodriguez cautiously peered over the lip of

the wall. "All right, he's going into one of the chambers. Probably only one way in, so we can corner him there."

Kelly nodded again. She fought down a tremor of fear at the thought of facing Stefan again. Her whole body still ached from the beating he'd given her. But this time she had Rodriguez with her, and she was armed. Unless Stefan had more surprises up his sleeve, he wasn't getting away.

Mark raced across the next aisle. Bullets tore up the ground in front of him. He dived and rolled, squeezing off a few rounds as he scrambled for cover between two of the pens. Mark checked his ammo: running low. He needed to conserve enough to get them back out.

It was eerily silent here. He peered inside the pen he'd landed next to. Dead eyes stared back from the depths of the cage. He swore under his breath—if the Zetas had summarily executed this row of prisoners, it might already be too late for Isabela's father.

The chopper swept past again, and he pressed closer to the bars. The spotlight panned the ground inches from his feet and kept going. Mark edged forward, maneuvering around more bodies clothed in fatigues. It was impossible to tell whether they were Zetas or Sinaloans. From the sound of it, everyone was firing wildly at anything that moved.

Still, the worst fighting had shifted over a few aisles. He eased along the row, counting. In a few of the pens people were still alive, but barely, panting hard as they bled out. One pleaded for help in a raspy voice. It killed him, but Mark didn't respond. He couldn't risk drawing fire. Based on the wounds he could see, most of these people were beyond help anyway. He'd passed four pens so far, five to go. Hopefully inside he'd find someone alive.

As he reached the seventh pen, a figure turned the corner and tore down the aisle toward him, gun blazing. Mark lifted his LMT, aiming for the guy's chest.

Suddenly the man stopped short, frozen in the spotlight descending from above. His body jerked and danced as a stream of bullets tore through him. He staggered a few steps, then dropped.

Mark pressed himself to the ground. He held his breath, praying for the chopper to keep going. It hovered for a second, then turned to make a pass down the next row. The sound of gunfire continued.

"Jesus," he said, breathing hard. After a second, he forced himself to crawl forward. Six pens. Seven. The eighth pen appeared empty. Mark treated the chicken wire like a tow rope, pulling himself along it. Coming up beside the ninth pen, he drew a small maglight off his vest and shone it inside.

A man lay on his side. His chest rose and fell as he squinted into the light.

"Francisco Garcia?" Mark asked. The man opened and closed his mouth, trying to say something. The ground around him was drenched with blood. Above the churning rotors and gunfire, Mark discerned a familiar whistling noise, one that sent a chill racing along his spine.

He leaped up and started running. Got less than three yards before the missile exploded behind him. The shock wave lifted him off his feet, sending him hurtling through the air. Mark lost hold of his weapon, arms and legs churning for a purchase as a blast of heat seared his back and his ears popped. He crashed into something solid and a piercing pain shot through him. He managed to choke out three breaths before slipping away.

Thirty-Four

Jake got to his feet unsteadily. Tejada was praying again, a steady murmur. He tugged at Jake's sleeve, desperate. "*Señor,* we must go," he said.

"Mark—" Black smoke rolled over the tops of the pens. As the cloud reached them the smoke made his eyes water, clouding his vision and constricting his throat.

"*Por favor, señor.*"

Jake was frozen. Childhood memories flooded his mind. His brother holding the back of the seat as he learned to ride a bike. Teaching him to shoot a gun. Handing him his first beer. Sneaking him a dirty magazine. He took a step toward the destruction.

The missile had sparked a fire along the line of pens. As the smoke around them blossomed and grew, the cries from trapped prisoners increased in intensity. Jake blinked and looked around. For a second he'd forgotten where he was, what he was supposed to be doing. His mind was an utter blank.

The sight of a terrified face pressed against the wire of the nearest pen brought him back. It was a woman, hands red and worn, face streaked with soot and tears.

"We've got to get these people out," he said, dazed.

Jake waved the woman back and aimed his sidearm. On the second try he hit the lock and it sprang off. The woman slammed against the door. She scurried away, vanishing around the corner.

Jake moved on to the next pen.

"Señor!" Tejada yanked at his arm, trying to drag him away. Jake shook him off. He shot the next lock. The teenage boy inside shoved his way out and fell to the ground, trying to kiss Jake's boots. Jake ignored him, moving along to the next one.

"Riley!" someone cried. Jake barely processed the voice. He was in the zone. Mark might be dead, but he'd be damned if he was going to let all these other people die, too. It was wrong to leave them behind. He squeezed the trigger. There was a click: the clip was empty. He popped it out and started to reload. Someone grabbed his arm again, more forcefully this time. He whirled, ready to punch out whoever was trying to stop him. Caught himself when he saw Syd.

"What the hell, Jake? We've got to get out of here. Where's Mark?"

"There's a fire," he said. "I'm getting them out."

"But—"

"They'll die."

Syd turned toward the approaching fire. "Okay," she finally said. "I'll take the next row over."

Tejada had disappeared, but Jake barely noticed. The fire was gaining momentum, increasing in intensity as it raced along the tree canopy. The light rain had been replaced by hot embers drifting down from above, singeing his hair and skin. He barely noticed. His whole life had been reduced to aim, shoot. Aim, shoot, reload.

He finished one line of pens. There was a steady stream of prisoners pouring down the aisle now. Some clutched each other as they attempted to run, tears streaming down their faces. Syd had freed nearly everyone on the other side. Jake crossed to the next row without bothering to check and see if there were any hostiles waiting to engage him—he no longer cared. He turned the corner safely and started freeing the next line of pens. People pressed past him, a filthy horde almost indistinguishable in their layers of dirt, fleeing barefoot through the heat and smoke. Aim, shoot. Aim, shoot, reload.

Jake was forced to stop when he dug through his pouch in vain for more ammunition. He turned to ask Syd for some, and found himself face-to-face with Ellis Brown. He looked positively enraged.

"What the hell is this?" he demanded. "My men have been pinned down for nearly a half hour! Where's Riley?"

"I need more ammo," Jake said dully.

"I asked you a question."

"Lay off, Brown," Syd said, appearing beside them.

They were interrupted by a bellowing loudspeaker. Syd and Brown fell silent, listening. Jake tried to discern what was being said, but his Spanish was rusty and the bullhorn distorted the noise.

"Shit." Syd turned to him. "Jake, we've got to go."

"Not until we get them out," he said with determination.

"The army is on their way in, Jake. They'll save the rest. But we need to get clear before they show up."

Brown was already barking orders at his men, heading for the exit at a trot. A military-personnel carrier came screaming around the corner, nearly running them over. Brown froze, then raised his hands in the air.

"Don't worry, Brown, he'll only shoot if I tell him to," Syd said cheerfully.

The passenger door of the truck swung open, and Kane stuck his head out. "We miss the party?"

Syd grabbed hold of Jake's sleeve. "We need to go," she said forcefully. "Now."

"But Mark—"

"Jake, if you don't get in that truck I'll shoot you and have Kane throw you in anyway. Your choice."

Jake hesitated another minute. The fire was increasing in force, but most of the pens in its direct path were empty. For the moment, the rest of the prisoners appeared safe. Without another word, he turned and followed her.

The truck was an old army flatbed covered by dark green canvas. He peered in the back. The benches lining either side were filled with Brown's men, some looking much the worse for wear.

"We'll ride in the cab," Syd said.

Kane let them squeeze inside, then took the seat closest to the window. He cradled a rocket launcher, the business end of it poking out the window. As soon as the door closed Maltz shifted into gear and the truck lurched forward.

"Couldn't find a chopper, boss," he said apologetically.

"This'll do." Syd kept her eyes focused out the windshield as she reloaded her H&K. "What about the way we came in?"

"Mexi army was up our ass the whole way here. I'm guessing that way is already blocked," Maltz said. "Looks like we won't miss the action after all."

"Stick to the periphery, the fire is mostly in the center of camp." Syd pulled open the canvas flap separating them from the rear cabin. "Brown, we're headed into the hot zone. Get some of your men working point."

"Roger," Brown said. At a nod, two of his men took up positions in the back of the truck, weapons covering the road to their rear. The rest slashed some holes in the canvas sides. They jutted their guns out through the gaps after dropping to one knee on the floor of the carrier.

Maltz spun the steering wheel right and the truck swerved, nearly going up on two wheels as it took the next corner. A stream of epithets issued from the flatbed.

"A little warning would be nice!" Brown hollered.

"Sorry," Maltz muttered. "Haven't driven one of these in a while."

Jake noticed sweat beading on his forehead. The sight wasn't reassuring.

They emerged on the road lining the camp's perimeter. Jake winced as they bumped over a pile of fatigues. Maltz did his best to avoid them, but the road was littered with bodies. No one said anything. Aside from the roar of the fire it was silent, the gunfire had abruptly ceased.

"The rest probably took off into the woods," Syd guessed.

Kane grunted his assent. "Army sent them running."

"Funny that the army showed up now," Syd commented. They passed a row of pens that were lit up like a torch. Fire danced along the rooftops. As they crossed the next aisle, a machine gun sputtered at them. Jake instinctively hunched his shoulders, trying to duck, but in the tiny truck cab there was nowhere to go. A bullet pinged off the windshield, pocking but not shattering it.

"Bulletproof. Thank God for small favors," Syd said.

Maltz gunned the engine, and the truck forged ahead.

"Everyone okay back there?" Syd called out.

"Be a lot better if the ride was smoother," Brown grumbled.

"Feel free to walk," Syd said. "Your choice."

There was no response.

Maltz turned right again. The exit gates were a few hundred yards away.

"Almost there," Syd said. Jake barely dared to breathe.

Suddenly the whump of rotors was overhead. The same helicopter Jake had seen before swept past, spun and lowered down to face them, blocking the exit. The spotlight zeroed in on the cab, blinding them. Jake held up a hand to block the glare. Maltz slowed, then came to a stop.

Kane pointed the rocket launcher forward and glanced questioningly at Syd. Her lips pursed.

"Hold off, they're not firing on us yet," she said, laying a hand on it. She called into the back, "Brown, we've got company!"

A pause, then Brown said, "What do you want to do?"

"It's a Bell 206 armed with missiles. Stand down for now."

Someone barked orders in Spanish through a bullhorn. Ropes unraveled from the chopper and dark figures slid down them. Within minutes they were surrounded by men in uniforms labeled PGR, brandishing automatic weapons.

Jake felt a flare of rage. This was the helicopter that had killed Mark. These people were responsible for his death. He reached past Kane and turned the door handle.

"Jake, wait—" Syd protested.

He ignored her. Slinging his legs over and climbing out, he started to lift his sidearm. The bullhorn blared again. The voice sounded angry. Jake ignored it. He marched straight toward the helicopter, prepared to fire.

"Jake, no!" a voice shouted.

Jake froze, disoriented. This time the protest was coming from the helicopter. Another figure appeared in the door and slid down a rope, then came running toward him. He lowered his gun when he saw who it was.

"Isabela?"

Syd was half out the truck cab, prepared to cover Jake and most likely get mown down, when lo and behold the pharmacist appeared. Syd frowned. Isabela wore the same black uniform as the men surrounding them, a PGR patch on her sleeve. At an order from her, they lowered their weapons—some more reluctantly than others.

"What the hell is going on?" Maltz asked, perplexed. "That the chick Riley showed up with?"

Brown's head poked through the canvas. "Still holding back here?"

"Looks like it," Syd said. "Hang on, I'll be right back."

She climbed down and slowly approached Jake and Isabela, keeping her sidearm ready. "So," she said. "Looks like you weren't telling us everything after all." Syd glanced at Jake, finding it overwhelmingly hard to resist saying "I told you so."

"My apologies." Isabela's meek demeanor had vanished. "I was working undercover in the pharmacy, trying to infiltrate Los Zetas distribution system. Mark nearly ruined months of work."

"You should have told us." Jake sounded enraged. Syd's grip on her H&K tightened.

"I wasn't sure I could trust you."

"PGR works for the Attorney General, right?" Syd said.

"Yes. We handle anything narcotics-related."

"So that intel about the rival cartel raid?"

"Our operatives within the Sinaloa cartel spent months convincing them to attack. When you showed up, we realized if anything went wrong we could blame the Americans. So we changed the timetable." Isabela surveyed the wreckage around them. "It worked. We probably set both cartels back years."

Jake spat out, "You sent my brother on a suicide mission." His fists were curled in tight balls, jaw clenched.

"It was important. The man he was rescuing was one of our best agents." She looked around. "Where is Mark? In the truck?"

"He was killed by a rocket from your helicopter," Jake said. "The fire nearly took out every prisoner here, too."

Isabela waved an arm, and the men surrounding the truck headed away from them in twos. "They'll save as many as they can. We already have units opening pens on the north side." She regarded him. "I'm sorry about Mark."

"He only went back because he thought he was saving your father. And a lot of those prisoners were executed."

Isabela shrugged. "It was a calculated risk. We had other lives to worry about."

"Not ours, apparently," Syd said. "Since you made sure we'd go in first."

Isabela appraised her. "Yes, but you were going in anyway. This created the distraction you needed, otherwise none of you might have survived. Did you free Calderon?"

Syd eyed Jake, who looked ready to empty a clip in Isabela's head. Which she'd be in favor of, if it wouldn't get them all killed. She stepped in between them. "We got our guys," Syd said. "I doubt yours made it, though."

"That is a shame. Garcia was a good man." Despite her words, Isabela didn't appear particularly dismayed by the loss. She looked past them. "You are sure Mark is dead?"

Jake whirled around. A two-headed beast shrouded in soot and blood and dirt was approaching through a haze of smoke.

Kane slid out of the cab and raced to help ease the second man to the ground. The other figure straightened, and Jake's heart leaped. It was his brother.

"Mark!" he yelled, running forward.

Mark took a step, then faltered and dropped to the ground.

Thirty-Five

"What are these things?" Rodriguez asked, running a hand over the bumpy white wall they crept along. The building Stefan had entered was still fifty feet away. They'd opted to get as close as possible before risking the open plaza. That meant winding through a jagged maze that just cleared their shoulders. They stayed low, trying to move silently.

"They look like skulls," Kelly said. Rodriguez jerked his hand away. "Ritual sacrifice, remember?"

"As if this place weren't creepy enough," Rodriguez muttered.

Kelly waved a hand to silence him. They were almost at the end of the row. From here, they'd have to cross a wide plaza leading to the chamber Stefan had vanished into.

"Ready?" she asked.

Rodriguez nodded, and she set off at a trot. Her right leg screamed with every step. Long lines of pain shot up her hip and into her lower back. Kelly gritted her teeth and tried to ignore it. Painfully aware of the gravel crunching underfoot, she panned her Glock from side to side. The shadows were impenetrable. Had Stefan heard them? Was he waiting to pounce?

It felt like an eternity before she reached the small opening Stefan had vanished into. It appeared to be one of the less excavated sections of the ruins. No concrete buttressed the floor, and the entry was a three-foot-tall slit in the mottled stone.

"Ladies first," Rodriguez murmured.

Taking a deep breath, Kelly eased her way inside. Darkness swallowed her completely. She had a flashlight in her pack, but didn't dare use it. The floor sloped down at a slight angle, as if they were descending into the bowels of the earth.

"What is it with you and tunnels?" Rodriguez muttered in her ear.

Kelly didn't reply, although she'd been wondering the same thing.

She felt her way along the rough wall, hoping the bumps under her fingers weren't more human skulls. It was hard to gauge distance, but after what felt like fifty feet she detected a glimmer up ahead. Kelly slowed her steps, trying to creep soundlessly toward the light source.

The tunnel they were in terminated abruptly at a larger chamber. Kelly stopped just shy of the entrance. A shadow suddenly darkened the doorway. She drew back and held her breath. After a moment, it disappeared.

In a low voice Rodriguez said, "Let's take him now."

Kelly nodded her assent. She crept forward, a foot at a time. More shadows flickered and danced across the walls—the light must be from candles.

Kelly peeked her head into the room, then frowned. She felt Rodriguez at her shoulder.

"What's wrong?"

"He's gone."

"What?" Rodriguez poked his head up alongside hers. The chamber was wider than Kelly had expected, a rough oval twenty feet in diameter. There were no other visible exits.

"Where the hell did he go?"

Kelly stepped into the room. It was empty save for a candle guttering in a glass jar. Faded murals lined the walls, pocked by small enclaves holding heaps of bones. A thin layer of dust hovered above the dirt floor. Kelly held a finger to her nose, fighting off a sneeze.

"Man," Rodriguez said. "This guy really is magic. How does he keep doing that?"

"Not magic. There has to be another way out," Kelly said with determination. Stefan was flesh and blood—their fight had proven that. She thought back to their encounter at the university years earlier. "Check for trapdoors."

"Yeah? That seems a little…unlikely," Rodriguez said. "This is an archaeological excavation. Professionals have been all over this site. If there were a secret entrance, they'd probably have found it by now."

"Maybe not. Stefan could have stumbled across something in his research."

"All right." Rodriguez sounded dubious, but he moved across the floor, scuffing up small clouds of dust with his shoes. Kelly moved along the opposite wall, scanning the floor for any discrepancies.

They met at the far side of the room. "Nothing," Rodriguez said, mystified. He thought for a moment. "I saw something on the Discovery Channel last month, about a temple in Pacal. There were four stone plugs in the floor and a hidden stairway underneath that led eighty feet down. No plugs here, though."

"There are these." Kelly went to the nearest inset in the wall. It was shallow, no more than a foot deep. Inside lay a stacked skeleton with a head on top.

"That's odd." Rodriguez pointed to the skull. "A dog?"

"A wolf," Kelly said, recognition dawning. The first time she'd encountered Stefan, he'd been enthralled by a wolf myth. Finding a wolf skeleton here had to be more than coincidence.

"Is there anything beneath it?" Kelly reached her hand in, sifting through the bones.

"I bet you just messed up decades worth of research," Rodriguez said. She drew her hand back out. "Anything?"

Kelly shook her head, frustrated. Her eyes shifted to the candle. It waved back and forth, sending a stream of oily smoke back toward the tunnel. She frowned.

"What is it?"

"The candle should be flickering the other way, from the wind coming in the doorway."

"Huh." Rodriguez ran his hands along the mural opposite the door. Stopping, he licked his palm, then held it up. "It's coming from here," he said.

Kelly came to stand at his shoulder. The mural they faced portrayed an exotic beast with an elaborate tail and glowering eyes. She bent to examine it. The eyes weren't painted on: they were small holes, drilled straight through the chamber's rock wall.

"Well, he didn't fit through those," Rodriguez said.

"You remember anything else from that special?" Kelly asked.

"God, I was half asleep…" Rodriguez ran a hand over his face. "They were talking about how the Aztecs might have used sound, some sort of harmonic thing."

"Like music?" Kelly said.

"Yeah, the rocks were tuned to a specific frequency. Or something like that."

"I didn't hear Stefan making any sounds."

"Some of them were beyond human perception, like dog whistles." Danny shrugged at her skeptical look. "Hey, you asked. I wasn't the one who made it up."

"How the hell did he get out of here?" Kelly said, frustrated.

"I have an idea." Rodriguez slung the backpack off his shoulder. "But it'll probably get us both arrested again."

"What is it?"

Rodriguez unzipped the pack and dug through it. After a second, he withdrew a beige brick and held it up for her to see. "I snagged this from Uncle Pablo."

"Is that C4?" Kelly asked.

"Yup. Your call, Chief. Is this guy worth making us enemies of the Mexican state, and archaeologists everywhere?"

Jake raced to his brother's side. Mark lay on the ground, completely still. Jake rolled him over and checked for a pulse: it was there, but barely. Streams of blood ran down his cheeks. More flowed from cuts along his arms and legs. Pieces of wood and shrapnel jutted out from the tattered remains of his Kevlar vest. Jake tugged at the Velcro sides, trying to get it off, but Syd stopped him.

"We don't know if any shrapnel penetrated," she said. "The vest might be the only thing keeping him from bleeding out."

Jake swiped a hand across his forehead. Isabela was a few feet away, deep in discussion with one of her men. "Hey!" He stood abruptly and shoved the guy aside, getting in her face. "You got a doctor here?"

"Field medic," she said. "He's looking over our man first."

The guy Mark had been carrying lay a few feet away. One of the army soldiers was tightening a tourniquet around his leg. "Well, he just dropped into second place."

Isabela's eyes narrowed. "Garcia was imprisoned here for months. He's been shot."

"And my brother saved him. Now call over that medic."

Her jaw tightened, but after a second she barked an order. The medic trotted over to Mark's side. Jake took a knee beside him, watching the shallow rise and fall of his brother's chest.

The medic checked Mark's vitals, then probed a few of the larger pieces of shrapnel with his hands. He looked up and met Jake's eyes. It didn't take a translator to tell what he was thinking.

Jake yelled for Isabela. She approached warily.

"Where's the nearest hospital?" he asked.

"Fifty miles away." She eyed Mark. "But the one in Mexico City is better equipped for this sort of trauma. That is where we are sending Garcia."

"Take Mark, too."

"We are in the middle of an operation—"

"Our team can help with the cleanup," Jake said forcefully. "Now do the right thing by Mark. You owe him."

Isabela said something to the medic. He rattled off a reply. A shadow crossed her face. "Mario says he probably would not survive the journey," she said. "It would be a wasted trip."

"You don't know my brother," Jake said. "Now load him on the chopper."

She cocked her head to the side. "I really am sorry, but

I do not have the authority to do that. My first responsibility is to my men. I can make sure that Mark is loaded on the next trip, but we have other casualties."

"Please," Jake said. "You can save him."

Isabela hesitated, then called over two of her men. They approached the stretcher. "Your people will stay as long as we need them," she said sharply. "And they will follow my orders."

"You got this?" Jake turned to Syd.

"Sure, partner. I got this." She squeezed his shoulder. "He's going to be okay."

Jake didn't answer. He wrapped his arms around Syd and drew her to his chest. Then he trotted after the stretcher.

"The buses will be arriving shortly," Isabela said. "You will help me load the former prisoners on, make sure none of the Zetas try to join them."

"Got it," Syd said, but her eyes were focused on the chopper as it lifted off the ground and ascended into the night sky.

Flores turned into the parking lot, bringing the Hilux to a stop in front of Room 12. He drew a deep breath. After everything that had happened in the past few days, this tranquil motel with adobe walls shedding white paint seemed surreal. It was going to take a while for normal to seem normal again.

"I got to piss like a racehorse," Decker announced, throwing open the door and stepping out.

Beside him, Calderon stretched his arms up, face splitting in a grin. "Strange, isn't it? I can't wait for a shower, *amigo*."

"I bet." Flores got out and went around to the back of

the truck. He grabbed a wool blanket and spread it over the truck bed.

It took a second to realize that Calderon had followed. His eyes narrowed as he took in the boxes. "What are these?"

Flores shrugged. "Don't know. But some of it looks like ordnance, probably better to keep it covered." As he tucked the blanket around a box in the far corner, he discreetly swept the Tyr folder beneath it.

"Perhaps we should—"

"Cesar!"

A small man whom Flores recognized as Calderon's subordinate burst out the door of Room 14. "Thank God you're all right!"

Calderon extended his arms. "Linus, my friend. Good to see you."

"Yes, well…" Linus's nose wrinkled. Rather than a hug, he awkwardly patted Calderon's outstretched arms.

Calderon laughed. "I smell that bad?"

"No, of course not. Well…let's get you inside. You can shower in my room. I have a change of clothes, too. They might be a little…"

Flores leaned against the bumper, listening to their voices recede. The door to Linus's room shut behind them. After a moment, Decker came to join him.

"Here." Decker tossed him an energy bar. Flores tore open the package with his teeth and devoured it. "I got more where that came from," Decker said. "Or we can head down the road, it's early but maybe that taco place will open up if we ask nicely."

"We'd have to take Calderon," Flores said.

"Yeah, and Smiley. Why? What's eating you?"

"There a computer here I can use?"

"Sure. Wireless is spotty, though." The door to Room 12 remained ajar. Decker led him inside and directed him to a Toughbook perched on a table in the corner. "Help yourself."

Flores dug the flash drive out of his pocket and stuck it in the USB port. Before he clicked on it, he paused. "You might not want to hear this," he warned Decker.

"That's like waving a red flag in front of a bull," Decker snorted. "Play it."

After another second of hesitation, Flores opened the file.

"I was just starting to panic," Smiley called over the sound of the shower. "There's a board meeting scheduled this Friday."

"Don't worry, Linus. We'll be ready for them."

"I hope so. They'll have some tough questions. I was thinking that in light of everything that's happened, some restructuring might be in order."

Calderon shut off the tap. The water had been lukewarm, but after months without bathing, it had felt as luxurious as a Roman bath. "What kind of restructuring?"

"It was a bitch finding you, Cesar. And damned if anyone in the government down here had a clue. I couldn't even figure out who to call. It occurred to me that maybe we should have more cross-departmental involvement. Make sure the Central America guys know something about what's going on in the East Asia department. That sort of thing."

Calderon repressed a flash of irritation as he dried off. "I'm too tired to discuss business, Linus."

"Of course. Maybe on the flight home. I chartered a plane, once the rest of the team gets back we can—"

"I'm anxious to get home." Calderon appeared in the

doorway. Linus's clothes were almost comically small on him. He rubbed his hair with a towel as he continued. "By now Brown has everything well in hand. They can follow us on another flight tomorrow. I expect to leave in five minutes."

"Yes, sir," Smiley said, chastened. His neck flushed red as he moved about the room gathering up his things.

A knock at the door, then Decker opened it. "We're gonna grab some chow down the street."

"Actually we're leaving in a few—"

"All due respect, sir, it's been days since I had a decent meal. And the airport is five hours away, easy. I need to fill my gut to make that drive."

"Very well," Calderon said, peeved. "But make it quick."

"Can't leave you alone, sir, not with Zetas still running around out there. You'd best come along."

Calderon was about to argue, then thought better of it. "I could use a good meal," he said. "Linus?"

"Of course."

The three of them headed out into the night. After a second, the truck door closed and Flores fell in step with them.

"Be good to have a hot meal, eh, *amigo?*" Calderon said. "Not like last night."

Flores didn't answer.

The other motels flanking the narrow road were dark, their neon signs still. Without them on, the surrounding jungle seemed closer, as though it was on the verge of opening a dark mouth and swallowing them whole. Smiley cleared his throat. "Must be the off season," he said.

"Mexico's too dangerous for tourists these days. Hell, you could even get kidnapped," Decker joked.

Flores laughed sharply. They continued in silence, until Calderon said, "What was your name again, soldier?"

"Decker. Rodney Decker."

"I'll make sure you get a promotion when we get back to headquarters, Rodney." Calderon scratched his neck. "Funny, the bug bites feel worse after a shower than they did before. What I'd do for some Calamine."

"We might be able to get some at the airport," Smiley said.

Calderon took in their surroundings. "This is almost as remote as the camp." He shook his head. A few hours ago, his sole priority had been staying alive. Now he was already burdened by the thought of meetings, conference calls and the myriad responsibilities awaiting him. In an odd way, his captivity had provided a respite from all that.

"What's so funny?" Decker demanded.

"Oh, nothing. I just have a lot to do when I get home." Calderon waved a hand dismissively.

"Yeah, I'll bet." Decker examined him. "When they asked you to cut a deal and sell out clients, you said no, right?"

"Please," Smiley snorted. "That's really—"

Calderon looked Decker dead in the eye. "Of course I said no. That's why they kept me so long without demanding a ransom."

"Huh." Decker dropped his gaze back to the road. It was becoming increasingly overgrown the farther they went from the motel.

A ribbon of fear spiraled up Calderon's spine. He was a good liar, renowned for spouting convincing fallacies during a hostage negotiation. But he got the sense that the man beside him wasn't falling for the act.

"Last case I worked for you was a tough one. Little girl got snatched and killed," Decker finally said.

"Jennifer Esposito?"

Decker nodded. "I was the first one in the room, right after they pulled the trigger. We killed the bastards, but still…" He shook his head. "It got to me, you know? Pretty little girl. Shouldn't have died that way."

"Yes, well. It's a dangerous country," Smiley said.

"Her father was a client?" Flores interjected. He'd slipped behind them.

"The company he worked for was." Calderon cleared his throat. "How much farther is this place? Perhaps there's some food back at the motel. Then we could just get on the road."

"Here's the thing I don't get," Decker said, ignoring the question. "I talked to the girl's bodyguard, and he said the reason the Zetas took them by surprise was that somehow they had the alarm code. How do you figure they got that?"

"Alarm company, maybe? I honestly don't know."

Decker shook his head. "Nope. It was a rotating code. He said the only people who knew it were the Espositos, him and one other guy. Tyr set it up. And the bodyguards seemed straight to me."

"What are you insinuating?" Linus asked sharply.

"Nothing." Decker jerked his head toward a dirt trail leading away from the main road. "It's that way."

Calderon was hyperconscious of Decker and Flores behind him as they followed the trail. The trees reached together overhead, forming a dark canopy.

Linus suddenly exclaimed and staggered back. "Oh my God!"

"What?" Calderon edged past him. They were on the overhang of a cliff. Past the lip of it he caught a glimpse of sky, stars fading into the horizon. He sighed. No wonder these idiots had gotten caught by the Zetas. No sense of direction. "We've come the wrong way."

"Looks right to me," Decker said.

Calderon felt a jab in his back, pressing him forward. "What are you doing?"

"Gente taped your conversations. We heard the deal you made." Flores's voice seethed with rage. "You lied to me."

"What?" Smiley protested. "That's insane. Cesar would never—"

"A lot of men risked their lives coming down here after you." Decker stepped forward. "And a lot of them died."

Smiley held up his hands. "Let's all just take a minute. Those tapes can be manipulated—"

"Is that what happened?" Flores demanded. "They fixed the tapes? And the codes? The blueprints?"

"Cesar…" Smiley turned to face him, doubt in his eyes. "It's not true, is it?"

Calderon considered proclaiming his innocence, but clearly somehow they'd stumbled across proof. At this point, his best bet was damage control. "In the end, we saved lives. Most of our clients secured release in a few weeks, some a bit longer. That was the beauty of it. They all survived. It's rare we can say that in this business."

"Oh my God." Smiley appeared horrified.

"Don't judge me, Linus. You know the pressure we were under. The board demanded that we improve the bottom line. And this arrangement worked."

"I had no idea." Smiley turned back to Flores and Decker. "Please, you have to believe I didn't know."

"So why'd they take you?" Decker asked.

"I terminated the agreement."

"I don't get why they didn't kill you," Flores said. "I sure as hell would have."

"Initially Gente thought there was a chance of reestablishing the status quo," Calderon said. He was suddenly exhausted, as if he'd run a marathon. My God, the havoc he'd wreaked. All for a bit of guaranteed glory and a larger bonus. And now he'd trade everything for his life.

"And you said no? Bullshit," Flores spat.

"It's true. I don't expect you to believe me, but it is. The Esposito case was the final straw. She was just eleven years old." Calderon's heart seized at the memory. "They were supposed to take her father, but he wasn't home when the team went in. He'd woken up with a toothache and booked an emergency appointment at the dentist. So they grabbed his daughter instead. I initially decided on a compact with the Zetas because they were professionals. Lately, however, they were allowing amateurs into their ranks. Anyway, the company's insurance didn't cover Jennifer, so the ransom demand couldn't be met."

"And you let her die?"

"No, I tried to save her." Calderon turned to Decker. "I sent in your team. I even offered my own money. The general didn't care. Once he realized she wasn't insured, he killed her, partly to cover up the mistake his men had made. That's when I told him I was done."

"That sounds like a load of crap," Decker noted.

"Well, that's what happened," Calderon said. "You want to kill me, fine. But you've got a pregnant wife, *amigo*—"

"I'm not your *amigo*," Flores growled.

"And Decker, I could make you a full partner in the firm. No more going out in the field unless you want to."

"I feel sick." Smiley had gone pale. "All these years we've worked together, Cesar. I thought I knew you."

"Shut up, Linus," Calderon snarled. He turned back to Flores and Decker. "We'll start off with a six-figure bonus. What do you say?"

Flores and Decker exchanged a look.

"That's a lot of money." Decker scratched his chin thoughtfully. "Hell, I've never even seen that much money."

"He did save my life," Flores pointed out.

"Still, there's Kaplan."

"And Monroe, Black…hell, a lot of guys died for this sorry bastard."

"Don't be foolish, gentlemen." Calderon's eyes narrowed. "If this comes out, Tyr will cease to exist. You won't have jobs at all. There's only one smart choice here."

"He does have a point," Decker said.

"Yup. What do you think, Decker? You feeling smart today?"

Decker eyed Calderon thoughtfully. Smiley had wrapped his arms around himself and was rocking back and forth. The wind picked up around them, a few raindrops started to fall.

"Probably start pouring in a minute." Flores glanced up at the sky. "We should be getting back."

"So we have a deal?" Calderon asked hopefully.

The shove took him by surprise. The ground beneath his feet suddenly disappeared. "Wait! You work for me!"

Calderon's fingers clawed at the air as he tumbled down, legs working as if he were attempting to swim back up. His body hurtled end over end. The last thing he saw was the branches of a tree reaching up to embrace him.

Decker peered over the cliff edge. Calderon's body had come to rest in the uppermost branches of a giant ceiba. It swayed slightly, then stilled. "Guess I'm still a dumb shit," he said, turning back to Flores.

"Guess so."

"Still hungry?"

"Starving."

They started to walk back toward the road.

Linus Smiley had dropped to his knees, hands covering his head. Hesitantly he called after them, "What about me?"

"What about you?" Decker yelled back. "You want to follow him?"

"No," Smiley said in a small voice. He cleared his throat. "Aren't you worried?"

"That you'll tell?"

Smiley couldn't see their eyes in the dark. He nodded once.

"You're not that stupid. See ya."

As they vanished into the trees, the clouds opened up and a warm rain started to fall.

Thirty-Six

"You're sure about this?" Rodriguez asked as he finished attaching the blasting cap to a small wad of C4. They'd decided to err on the side of caution, concerned about a cave-in.

"I'm sure," Kelly said, although that was the last thing she felt. The very sight of the C4 had opened a hole in her stomach, memories of hurtling through the air, pain everywhere as fire erupted around her. But if she was going to die, perhaps it was only fitting that this time she set the bomb. "Do you know what you're doing?"

Rodriguez shrugged. "We got a little bit of explosives training in basic. I'm no demolitions expert, but C4 doesn't exactly require a college degree." He pushed the putty into a small fissure in the wall, then stepped back and crossed himself. "My mother will never forgive me," he muttered as he backed away.

They withdrew into the tunnel leading to the chamber. Rodriguez hesitated, holding the detonator.

"What?" Kelly asked.

"I was just thinking, there has to be another way. Stefan got through there somehow."

"If there is, we don't have time to find it," Kelly said

firmly. "He might have stashed another victim back there."

"Okay. But if we die, I'm holding you personally responsible." Rodriguez nodded, and Kelly plugged her ears. He pushed the detonator button.

The resulting explosion was smaller than she'd expected. A cloud of smoke and dust rolled out of the chamber, making her cough. Kelly waved a hand in front of her face to clear the air. Her head pounded, ears smarting from the concussion.

"How long do you think we have until that brings someone running?" Rodriguez asked.

Kelly didn't intend to stick around to find out. She edged back into the chamber. The dust was slowly settling. A gaping hole punched through the mural, about two feet high and a foot wide. Rubble dotted the floor surrounding it.

"Another blow to Aztec civilization," Rodriguez muttered.

Kelly stuck her head through the hole. The air on the other side was cooler and laden with condensation. There was an odd smell, metallic and musty at the same time. "Can you get my flashlight out of the pack?"

He handed it to her, and she turned it on. Past the wall was another tunnel, similar to the one they'd entered the chamber through, but slick with water. She panned the light along the sides, then probed the depths. The light vanished into the darkness. Stefan was nowhere in sight.

"He probably heard the explosion, so we'll have to be careful," Kelly said. Rodriguez handed her the backpack, and she dropped it through the hole. She pushed her shoulders through, wiggling awkwardly as she dragged her legs behind her. Rodriguez pressed on her good ankle and she fell through, catching herself with her hands as she dropped to the floor. After considerable grunting, Rodriguez followed. They both stood.

"Dios mío," Rodriguez said. "How did they not know this was here?"

Kelly didn't have time to wonder about that. Stepping carefully, she made her way down the tunnel. It reminded her of the passages where she'd first pursued Stefan. But those tunnels were beneath a college campus, in existence for a few hundred years at the most. This was clearly much, much older. More murals lined the walls. Rivulets of water coursed down them, making the images appear to weep. Up ahead, she detected a distinct noise. "Is that water? It sounds like—"

"A river." Rodriguez panned his flashlight down. The tunnel floor descended at a steady angle, almost like a ramp. And at the bottom, water lapped at the stone.

Kelly descended the ramp slowly, struggling to keep her footing on the slick surface. "It is a river," she said, astonished, when she reached the bottom.

The tunnel ended abruptly and the ceiling shot up almost thirty feet. The walls were painted with more murals streaked green and brown from condensation. The air hung heavy with mist. The ramp Kelly was on turned into steps that descended into the water. It was impossible to tell how deep the river was, but it rushed past at a steady clip, vanishing into a hole in the wall on her right.

Rodriguez panned his light across the chamber. "Great, an underground river. Just what I was hoping for. I don't see any boats."

"I think we'll have to swim." Kelly was already briskly stripping off her pack.

Rodriguez rubbed his chin with one hand. "One problem with that, Jones. I'm not exactly a great swimmer."

"You can't swim?"

"I grew up in the barrio. Swimming lessons weren't an option."

"That's okay. You stay here, I'll go check it out." Kelly tucked her Glock inside the backpack and raised it above her head. Getting wet shouldn't prevent the Glock from firing, but if possible she'd prefer not to test that theory.

Rodriguez started to follow suit.

"What are you doing?"

"Coming with you."

"That's ridiculous," she said. "If you can't swim, you can't swim."

"I can't let you do this alone. Hell, we've come all this way." Rodriguez grimly unlaced his shoes.

"We don't even know how far this goes," Kelly argued.

Rodriguez paused. "You just reminded me of something else on that show."

"What?"

"These tunnels they found in Guatemala. Apparently they went underground for nearly 800 kilometers, across almost the entire country."

"See?" Kelly said. "No way you're swimming that far. And if you start to drown, I might not be able to save you. I don't float that well myself these days," she said ruefully, glancing at her foot.

Rodriguez still held his shoe. Kelly could see him deliberating. "Look," she said. "Get to the U.S. Embassy, see if there's someone there who can help." She glanced at her watch. "It's nearly dawn. Pretty soon someone's bound to discover the new hole we made. It would be better if you weren't around when that happens."

"True," Rodriguez said. "But what if this does stay underground for miles? I don't want to lose a partner to hypothermia."

"I'll be fine. I've done almost nothing but swim for months now."

"We could go to the embassy together, scare up some reinforcements."

"Stefan came down here for a reason. I promise, if I find him, I'll just monitor him until you get back. But this river might come out somewhere else in the city, and I don't want to risk losing him again. Try to find a boat so you can catch up." Kelly slipped into the water. It was chillier than she'd expected. Her teeth immediately started to chatter. She held the backpack high above her head until the water reached her waist. Taking a deep breath, Kelly lay down, wincing at the shock of cold against her skin. She held the backpack up with both hands, bracing the flashlight alongside it to illuminate the hole in the wall. Kelly stretched her legs out in front of her, pointed downstream. As she floated away, she waved one hand back at Rodriguez.

"Damn it, Jones," he said with resignation. "Don't get yourself killed."

She chose not to reply.

Jake held Mark's hand. The medic hovered over him, injecting medication into his IV line, eyes continually checking the portable monitor beside the gurney.

Garcia appeared stable. The tourniquet had staunched the flow of blood from his leg, and his color was slowly returning.

"How's Mark doing?" Jake finally asked.

The medic either didn't speak English, or thought it best not to answer.

The chopper suddenly banked sharply. Out the cockpit window, a stream of lights appeared. They had to be close, Jake gathered, they'd been flying for nearly an hour.

Suddenly, the monitor started flashing. Mark's body jerked uncontrollably.

"What's happening?" Jake asked, panicked.

The medic shoved Jake aside as he fumbled through his medical kit. "Seizure."

Jake could only watch powerlessly as Mark twitched and contorted. The medic dug out a portable oxygen mask and set it over Mark's mouth. The monitor bleated once, then settled into a steady monotone drone.

Mark fell still.

"We must…" The medic squeezed the bulb of the oxygen bag, then motioned for Jake to take it. Jake tried to recall his CPR training as he watched Mark's chest rise and fall. The medic nodded his approval, and Jake squeezed again. The defibrillator machine whined as it charged. Three beeps indicated it was ready.

"Hands, please," the medic said, pushing the oxygen bag away. He attached one electrode to Mark's shoulder, then yanked up the bottom of his shirt to attach the other to his lower left abdomen. He pressed the button. Mark's body contracted once, hard, in response to the electric current. They both watched the monitor. It didn't change.

The medic nodded for him to squeeze the airbag again. Jake pumped twice, then pulled it away.

The helicopter continued to bank. Through the cockpit window, Jake saw the outline of a building rushing up to meet them through the smog. The medic pressed the button again: Mark's body jumped. The monitor continued to drone.

As the helicopter righted itself and started to descend, Jake began praying.

FEBRUARY 2

Thirty-Seven

She owed Brandi a debt, Kelly thought as she drifted downstream. She was much more comfortable in the water than she would have been before starting physical therapy. Not that it was pleasant. The water was cold and brackish. Slimy things kept brushing up against her. As soon as she swept through the hole, something icy slid across her leg. Kelly jolted away, nearly losing her pack and flashlight. She caught both just in time. She struggled to remain calm. This would be a hell of a time to have a panic attack.

The tube narrowed. The ceiling was about three feet above her head, and she had five feet on either side of her. A hundred feet in, the current gathered speed. The roof seemed to be sloping down, walls narrowing to a point in front of her.

Kelly took a deep breath. The walls here were bare. Steam rose off the river, curling up and around her like wraiths determined to drag her underwater. The reason the current was quickening suddenly became apparent: at the very edge of where her flashlight penetrated the gloom, she saw another hole in the wall. The river raced toward it.

Kelly felt oddly unafraid. She swept along, fingers cramping from her death grip on the flashlight and backpack. The river gained speed. The rift appeared far too small for her to fit through, yet she remained buoyed by an overwhelming sense of peace and calm. It certainly wasn't where she'd expected to die, or how, but it was oddly fitting. Her original showdown with Stefan had started underground and ended by a river. Apparently history was repeating itself.

Ten feet from the opening.

The hole was larger than she'd initially perceived, the stone edges surrounding it worn smooth. Water churned at the entrance, small whitecaps sloshing among the brown.

Five feet.

Kelly panted a few times to empty her lungs, then drew in a deep breath right before the torrent sucked her down.

The rushing current nearly yanked the backpack and flashlight from her grip. Kelly clutched them to her chest, hugging them tightly. Her left knee banged against something and she nearly opened her mouth to gasp in pain. She drew her legs in to her chest. The water spun her, it was impossible to tell which way was up anymore. Her flashlight caught odds and ends of stone, most just before she smacked into them. Something hit her chin as she shot past, then her elbow. It felt like the channel was narrowing even more. She curled into a ball, trying to make herself as small as possible. Her lungs started to burn.

Kelly fought the urge to breathe in. She wondered how long she'd been under. Thirty seconds? A minute? She'd never tried to hold her breath for an extended period. She had no idea how long she could last.

Suddenly Kelly felt herself rising, buoyed by the air

reserve in her chest. She fought her way up, clawing at the water with her free hand. Kelly exploded out of the surface, exhaling hard, choking as some water shot into her mouth. She sucked in air greedily. The flashlight shone up from below. Kelly tried to take a stroke with her right arm, kicking her left leg to maneuver herself back into a floating position.

But something was wrong, she wasn't moving. She tried again, then switched her grip on the light so that it pointed down.

Her prosthetic foot was wedged into a crevice between two rocks.

Water pressure built up behind her, driving her head down. Kelly had been white water kayaking a few times, and knew this was how most people drowned. She sucked in another gulp of air and dived below the surface. She struggled to free the prosthetic, but her hands kept sliding off the slick polyurethane foam cover. She jerked with her hip, but that only sent shooting pains through her stump.

Kelly broke the surface again, gasping. The current seemed stronger, determined to defeat her. She spit out water as she struggled to breathe. She was drowning slowly. She didn't have a choice. She'd have to abandon the prosthetic and go after Stefan with one leg.

There wasn't much time left. Already she felt sluggish. Her arms were tiring and she was beginning to feel sleepy, a clear sign that hypothermia was setting in. She shrugged the backpack over her shoulders—it was already soaked, no point trying to keep it above the surface any longer.

Sucking in a deep breath, Kelly dived again. She struggled to unfasten her prosthetic. The silicone liner was rolled tightly over her stump. Her hands slipped, the liner refused to budge. Just as she was starting to panic, worried that the water had somehow created an airtight seal, it slipped off. She was free.

Kelly shot forward quickly. She stretched her left leg out in front of her as the current bumped and jostled her. The top of the chamber was inches above her head, her nose almost skimmed it. Kelly drew in deep breaths, holding the air in her lungs for a few seconds each time.

Suddenly, without warning, she was sucked back underwater.

Rodriguez pressed the buzzer again, irritated. It was just before dawn. There should have been someone watching the gate to the embassy. Apparently security wasn't as tight as he would have expected.

It was a full five minutes before footsteps approached from the other side of the gate. A door opened and closed, and a bleary-eyed guard appeared in the window of the guardhouse.

"Buenos días, señor," he said with a yawn.

Rodriguez pressed his badge against the window. "I need to get inside, now."

The guard blinked at the ID, unimpressed. A metal drawer slid open in front of Rodriguez. The guard motioned for him to drop his credentials inside. He drew it back to him, picked up the case and examined it. Rodriguez tapped a finger on the narrow metal ledge. "Any day now," he muttered.

The guard held up the ID, comparing the photo to Rodriguez's face. Apparently satisfied, he put the ID back into the drawer, along with a green pass. "Everyone is still asleep, Señor Rodriguez," he said. "You'll have to wait."

Rodriguez jabbed a finger toward the phone beside the guard's right hand. "Wake them up," he said. "Or I'll go do it myself."

Thirty-Eight

Kelly broke the surface, sputtering. She shook her head to clear water from her eyes, treading to keep herself afloat. It was pitch-black, and the flashlight had been ripped from her hands. It felt like she'd been through the spin cycle of a washing machine. Her lungs ached, her head throbbed from the cold and her teeth wouldn't stop chattering. The temptation to close her eyes and drift off to sleep was almost overwhelming. She forced herself to focus. Where the hell was she now? And more importantly, where was Stefan?

The thought of encountering him while unable to walk snapped her awake.

Kelly twisted in a full circle, trying to get her bearings. In the dark, it was impossible to tell which direction she'd come from. The steady press of the current had suddenly dissipated: she must be in an eddy. There was a noise off to her left. She spun to face it, squinting hard. In the distance, she detected a faint glow.

Kelly took a deep breath, dived down, and fumbled along the floor. The river was shallower here, in places her fingers brushed against rocks. Using a breaststroke, she felt her way along the bottom, praying to come across the smooth surface of her prosthetic, or the metal of her flashlight. But she encountered nothing but mud and pebbles.

She tried three more times before giving up. They could be right beside her and she'd never see them in the dark. Kelly fought the urge to scream in frustration. After everything she'd come through to get here, she'd arrived incapacitated.

But going back was not an option. Most importantly, she had to get out of the water before hypothermia induced loss of consciousness. Kelly chewed her lower lip. She was out of choices. It was move forward, or die right here and now.

She pushed a strand of hair from her eyes, flipped onto her stomach and swam toward the glow, her good leg kicking behind her. The light was about a hundred feet away. As she got closer, Kelly saw the rim of a shoreline. The sandy banks sloped up at a steep angle to an archway set into the wall. The area surrounding it was painted with murals similar to the ones in the cavern: elaborate red, yellow, blue and black swirls.

What appeared to be candlelight flickered from the archway. An inflatable raft was beached on the small spit of land.

Kelly dragged herself out of the water. The bank was gritty silt, sand mixed with coarse pebbles. Pushing with her left leg and crawling with her arms, she managed to get herself completely on shore. She flipped over on her back, exhausted, and shrugged off the pack. Her shivering increased. If anything, she felt colder than when she had been submerged. Her body was losing heat fast, she had to find a way to warm up. A breeze emanated from the archway. Kelly willed her teeth to stop chattering as she dug through the pack for the gun. It was soaking wet. She slid out the clip and checked it. Muddy, but Glocks were designed to fire under the worst conditions imaginable.

Kelly crawled to the boat. There was a paddle tucked inside, but no dry clothing she could put on to warm up. She braced the paddle under her right armpit and got to her feet, using it as a crutch. It was awkward holding both the paddle and the Glock, but if Stefan suddenly appeared she needed to be ready.

Kelly strained her ears, listening for sound coming from the archway, but the air was still. She was tempted to find out where it led, but the incline was steep and her muscles throbbed from cold and fatigue. Her fingers and toes were going numb. If Stefan was in there, she'd be forcing a confrontation. Shivering the way she was, her aim would be off. There was a chance he'd manage to get the gun away from her, and then she'd be at his mercy.

But if she took the boat, he'd be stranded. Kelly could paddle farther down the river and wait for Rodriguez to arrive with backup. The current wasn't as intense here; she should be able to make her way back upstream. Under the circumstances, that seemed like her best option.

Kelly was limping toward the boat when a voice behind her said, "You're not planning on stealing my raft, are you, Agent Jones?"

Kelly was so startled she nearly dropped the gun. She carefully edged her body around.

Stefan was framed in the archway. He leaned against the wall, arms crossed over his chest. She noted with no small amount of satisfaction that his face was as bruised and beaten as hers, nose still canted to the side.

"I can't figure out how you got a raft through there," she said. "Impressive."

"Practice." He grinned down at her. "Looks like you had some trouble."

Kelly flushed. She clenched the paddle tight against her armpit, then bent her elbow, aiming the Glock at his chest. Her standing leg quivered from fatigue and her hands shook badly from the cold. She gritted her teeth and tried to steady them. "Get down on your knees," she said.

Stefan appeared unconcerned. He remained where he was. "I have to say, your tenacity is remarkable. Most government employees aren't nearly this diligent."

"I mean it, Stefan. You're under arrest."

He laughed. "I have to ask, Agent Jones. How do you intend to get me out of here? Say that I comply with your request. You'll have to restrain me, get me in the boat and somehow maneuver it while holding a gun on me. Do you honestly think you're capable of that in your condition?"

"My partner will be here soon."

"Ah, I see." He rubbed his chin. "Strange that he's not here now."

"He went for help."

"And yet you told me that you're no longer with the FBI. Which begs the question, under whose authority are you arresting me? This is not United States territory." He stepped toward her.

Kelly fought the urge to hop back. She jutted up her chin. "Right now, this Glock gives me the authority." She clenched her jaw to stop her teeth from chattering.

"Hypothermia." Stefan took another step forward. "I had the same problem on my first journey here."

"I'll shoot," Kelly warned.

"Go ahead." He rushed forward.

It took Kelly a second to react. Her first shot went wild,

ricocheting off the wall to his left. The second and third were closer, but she still missed.

Five feet away from her Stefan dodged right. Her fourth shot caught the sleeve of his shirt. He reacted with a growl, leaping forward, his hands grasping for her.

But now he was nearly at point-blank range.

Kelly squeezed the trigger.

Nothing happened.

Stefan's face split in a grin. Kelly squeezed the trigger again and again, panicked. The magazine held thirteen rounds. She should have nine left.

Stefan backhanded her across the face, sending her flying. Her head smacked the rubber side of the boat. The Glock slipped from her grasp.

She rolled off. The paddle had fallen by her heels. Kelly snatched it up and knocked it against his legs, trying to sweep them out from under him. He grunted at the impact, but didn't budge.

Kelly spotted the gun on the other side of the boat. She scrambled for it, heaving her body over the gunwales and into the raft. Panting, she pushed hard with her good leg, scrabbling for a purchase against the slippery rubber sides. The gun was only a foot away. Kelly lunged for it.

Her fingers were about to close on the handgrip when her head was jerked back. Kelly yelped in pain. Stefan hauled her up in front of him by the hair. She kicked at him, but the blows didn't seem to make a dent.

"Nice try," he said.

Kelly clawed at him, aiming for his eyes. Her fingernails raked his cheeks, drawing blood, but he completely disregarded her attack. He marched over to the wall, dragging her with him. Kelly flailed at him, resisting.

He drew her head back and slammed it into the wall. Shards of darkness danced before her eyes, and something hot ran down her face. Blood, she thought blearily.

She tried to get her hands in front of her, pushing back off the wall, but he was too strong. He bashed her head against the rock again, and again. The swirls of the mural spun up to meet her, going fuzzy right before impact.

And then everything went black.

Thirty-Nine

Jake perched on a rickety chair. The seat was rough and chipped, and one of the front legs was shorter than the other. No matter how he tried to balance, it insisted on wobbling. He finally gave up and rocked slightly back and forth, the tempo illustrating his agitation.

Back in a hospital waiting room. Again. He'd spent most of the past seven months in rooms like this one, waiting for Kelly to heal. And now his brother hovered on the brink of death. They'd managed to stabilize Mark briefly as the helicopter landed, but he crashed again as they wheeled him toward the O.R. Jake hadn't been able to tell what they were saying, but based on the doctor's expression, the outlook wasn't good.

His cell phone rang. Jake pulled it from his pocket, frowning when he didn't recognize the number. Syd had already called to say that the fire was almost extinguished, and they'd managed to save the majority of prisoners. She and Isabela were waiting for transport vehicles to haul everyone back to Mexico City to be reunited with their families. They'd rounded up some surviving members of the battling cartels. He asked Syd what she thought the army planned on doing with them, and she professed not to know. He had a feeling that in the end, they were better off that way.

He debated, then clicked the phone open.

"Jake?"

It took a minute to place the voice. "Rodriguez?"

"Yeah, it's me."

"This isn't a great time." Jake rubbed the stubble on his cheek.

"I know, Kelly told me you were in the middle of an operation. I just—"

"You talked to Kelly? When?" Jake had already tried her phone twice that morning. It still went straight to voice mail.

"Not long ago," Rodriguez said evasively. "That's why I'm calling…."

As Rodriguez explained, Jake's fists clenched. He couldn't believe that Kelly would do something so stupid, not after what she'd been through this past year, what she'd put them both through. He flashed back on her expression the last time he saw her. He should have recognized that look she got when focused on a case.

"Where is she now?" he interrupted, the chair bobbling a few times as he stood.

Kelly slowly opened her eyes. It took a minute to remember what had happened.

She was in an enormous cave. It was cathedral-like, the ceiling soaring a hundred feet above her head. Thick candles were set at intervals around the space, their flickering marking a cadence along the walls. The murals here were astonishing, gloriously rendered images of mythical creatures with gaping mouths and intertwined limbs.

Stefan was nowhere in sight.

Kelly tried to sit upright, then dropped back down

with a gasp. Her head pounded as if it were still being hammered against the wall. She rolled onto her side and squeezed her eyes shut, choking back bile as she willed the pain to subside. After a few deep breaths, the throbbing abated slightly. Still, her vision swam.

She realized with a sinking sensation that her hands were bound behind her. She inhaled deeply, trying to calm the familiar flutter in her chest marking the onset of a panic attack. Kelly concentrated on her breathing. After a few minutes, the sensation dissipated.

All right, she thought. *I'm probably going to die down here. But maybe there's still a way to take him with me.*

She rolled back over to scan the room. It felt like rope bindings; she might be able to burn them off. A candle flickered about ten feet away. Gathering herself, Kelly rolled. The action induced a wave of nausea. Ignoring it, she rolled again.

"Oh good, you're awake. For a moment I thought I'd killed you."

Kelly froze. Stefan was ducking out of a low tunnel on the far side of the room—probably the one leading to the river.

"You must be cold," he continued. He rustled through a pile of things in the corner: Kelly made out tools, tarps, sundry other items. With an exclamation, he drew out a ratty wool blanket. Crossing to her, he draped it over her.

Kelly considered shrugging it off, but the truth was she was still freezing. And it provided her with cover as she tried to loosen her bonds. "What is this place?"

"Amazing, isn't it?" Hands on his hips, he gazed around proudly, as if he were personally responsible. "You should feel honored. Only the highest priests were granted access to this chamber. You and I are the first to have seen it in nearly five hundred years."

Kelly followed his eyes—she had to admit, it was impressive. The murals here were pristine, probably nearly as bright as the day they were painted. "How did you find it?"

"It took some time, I'll admit." Stefan settled down on his haunches. "I have to say, Agent Jones, seeing you again took me by surprise. But after thinking it over, I think it's oddly appropriate you turned up. Don't you?"

"More like bad luck."

"That's right, I keep forgetting you lack in faith." Stefan rubbed his chin thoughtfully. "Don't you think this surpasses any sort of coincidence, the two of us meeting up here, under such similar circumstances, years later? Once again underground, by the water."

"I was following up a lead claiming you were still alive," Kelly scoffed. "It wasn't exactly magic."

"Ah—" he held up a finger "—but then your gun failed on you. Was that a coincidence, too? Or divine intervention?"

"More likely cheap ammo," she said. "The gun dealer wasn't exactly reputable."

"And you found me here."

"You left your book back at the dump."

"Still, impressive." He eyed her. "How did you manage to penetrate the outer chamber, if you don't mind my asking?"

"C4." She took some pleasure in the expression of horror on his face. "How did you do it?"

"There was a switch located behind the eyes. It merely required sticking the appropriate instrument through the holes." He appeared disappointed. "And you think I'm a monster. Those murals were nearly a thousand years old.

Granted, it took me months to uncover the secret, but still. No need to resort to such extreme measures."

"How did you even know the tunnel was there?"

"Same as you, I'm guessing. The wind told me." He winked at her. "I researched the Templo Mayor extensively. Legends claimed it was constructed on top of caves filled with primordial water, home to Huitzilopochtli, the ancient god of fire who occupied the center of the earth. I realized that if the Aztecs knew about those caves, there might be remnants of their civilization down here." He pointed to the murals surrounding them. "Don't you see? It's all outlined here, the exact steps to take."

"What are you planning?" Kelly asked. She couldn't make out anything in the murals but a slew of random images.

"I initially came here out of necessity," Stefan said thoughtfully. "Driven by you, of course. But then I stumbled across the most wonderful book, a book that proved I was meant to be here all along."

"So you decided to skin a child?"

"Everything has a reason and a purpose, Agent Jones. I came to realize that the rituals I was seeking were much older than anything in the *Raudhskinni*. And it's not the easiest thing in the world to skin someone. I needed practice, to do it correctly when the time came."

"You're insane," Kelly said. "None of those rituals accomplish anything. You're just looking for excuses to murder people."

"Again, that's your lack of faith talking." He shrugged. "We'll have to agree to disagree."

"What's the ritual supposed to accomplish?"

"There's more than one, of course. The gods don't just hand out immortality."

Kelly's head throbbed. In a tired voice she said, "Think

it through, Stefan. If those rituals actually endowed immortality, wouldn't the Aztecs still be running things?"

"There are examples in the book," he said excitedly. "Native tribes in the mountains that shun modern society. Some members are rumored to be a thousand years old." His eyes glinted. "Many of them have red hair. Descendants of Quetzalcoatl, God of the Aztec and Olmec people. He arrived from across the sea and taught them to raise corn and build structures. That's why they called him Quetzalcoatl, you see. It means 'the culture bringer.' This is where our cultures intersected. And that is why my arrival here was more than mere coincidence. I will complete the rituals, then join them. Together we will raise civilization from the ashes."

Kelly opened her mouth to argue with him, then realized it was pointless. It was like trying to reason with a child. At least he didn't seem to have another victim down here. Unless she was about to fill that role. "So are you planning on skinning me?"

"Oh, no." Stefan barked a laugh. "You wouldn't be appropriate at all. You're far too old for that ritual, and I'm guessing probably not a virgin, either, eh?"

Kelly didn't reply.

"I will kill you, eventually. But your skin is safe for the moment."

Kelly dreaded his response to the next question, but forced herself to ask, "Do you have another victim?"

"You provided an unfortunate interruption of my original plans." Stefan glanced at a large watch on his wrist. "The specific time, date and location of the rituals are critical for success. So I'm afraid we're going to have to wait a bit."

"Sorry, there's someplace I've got to be," Kelly said.

Stefan laughed again. "Ah, Agent Jones." He tapped her left foot with his hand. "You've finally found your sense of humor. That's good to see."

Forty

"I can't believe you let her go in there alone." Jake fumed as he panned a light across the subterranean river. Threads of vapor rose off the surface.

"Hey, she didn't leave me a choice. It was either follow her and drown, or go for help. You of all people know how she can be," Rodriguez said pointedly. "Hell, I'll be lucky not to get arrested for defacing a cultural site."

"Still, you should have tried to stop her." Jake's light came to a halt at the hole in the wall. "Jesus. Or at least tried to find a boat."

"Yeah, because those are easy to find at four in the morning." Rodriguez snorted.

"Well, we've got one now." Jake eyed the tiny inflatable raft the embassy had lent them. It looked like a kid's toy. He suspected they'd appropriated it from their swimming pool. With any luck it would remain afloat. "Let's get going."

Rodriguez grumbled as he tightened the straps of a tiny life jacket, the only one they'd been able to locate. One of the embassy hacks was back on the surface, trying to convince some enraged archaeologists that the destruction of the mural had been necessary for national security.

Jake doubted that argument was working. Still, it bought him and Rodriguez time to go after Kelly. As soon as the *federales* showed up, that window of opportunity would close. They had to get moving.

Jake eased the boat into the water. It bobbed a few times. He held it still while Rodriguez climbed in. The bottom almost immediately filled with water, and Rodriguez hissed. Without giving him a chance to protest, Jake climbed in and pushed off.

Taking the flimsy rubber paddle in both hands, he guided them toward the wall. He needn't have bothered, because as soon as they slipped into the current the boat was propelled there. Rodriguez kept the light directed straight forward, illuminating the path. He clutched a dry bag to his chest, face drawn and pale.

"Get a grip, Rodriguez," Jake muttered. "It's probably only a couple of feet deep anyway."

Before Rodriguez could answer, they were sucked into the hole. It was a long tunnel. The raft bounced off the walls a few times. The current gained speed, the water slipped away quickly beneath them. Something sharp pressed against his leg from beneath the raft, and his mouth tightened. With the luck he was having lately, they'd sink before finding Kelly, and he'd have to save Rodriguez. Although the way he felt about him right now, that wasn't his highest priority.

"Jesus," Rodriguez said loudly. "We'll never make it through there!"

Jake looked ahead. The tunnel was narrowing to a point. Rodriguez was right; the raft was probably too large to fit through.

"Lie as flat as you can," he ordered, "and hold on to the sides."

Jake got low, pressing his back against the floor of the

raft, knees tucked down. It sank an inch lower and water sloshed over the sides, the cold making him shudder. Rodriguez's head crammed against his legs. He lowered the flashlight. They were suddenly hurtling into darkness.

Rubber scraped against rock, and they jarred to a stop. His body rocked slightly from the impact. The raft was caught on something.

"We're stuck!" Rodriguez called out, panicked.

Jake could feel the pressure building up behind them. More water poured over the sides, drenching his shoulders. If they didn't get free soon, the boat would sink.

"Hang on," he said, unclipping the flashlight from his belt. He reached over the side and scanned the light around. They were blocking an even narrower opening inside the tunnel, impeding the progress of the water.

"I'm going to shove us off," he said. "But the boat might puncture or go down. If it does, get away from the raft and keep your feet up. Don't try to stand."

Jake pushed hard with his right arm: nothing. He tried again, this time using both hands, the flashlight dangling from a strap around his wrist. With a lurch, the boat spun free. Jake dropped back to the floor, rapping his head hard against a rocky outcropping on the way down. He winced, barely processing the pain. There was a ripping sound as the raft shot through the hole.

"We made it!" Rodriguez's head popped up, outlined by the glow from Jake's flashlight. His eyebrows knit together. "What's that sound?"

Jake sat back up and panned his light along the outside of the raft. There was a long slit in the rubber right above the waterline. Air was hissing out at an alarming rate. "I've got bad news."

Rodriguez was beside him in a flash, the sudden motion nearly capsizing them.

"Careful," Jake warned, but Rodriguez ignored him.

"Crap. You bring any duct tape?"

"Don't be—" Jake caught himself. Syd had packed their go-kits. And if he knew Syd, there was a roll of duct tape tucked inside his. He fumbled for the bag. The zipper resisted his first few tugs.

"We're sinking," Rodriguez noted apprehensively, clenching the dry bag to his chest. "Do you think this bag floats?"

"Shine your light over here so I can see." Jake pawed through the contents of his backpack. The inside of the bag was suddenly illuminated. Jake sorted through energy bars and loose ammo until his hand closed around something circular. He yanked it out: a roll of silver duct tape.

"Wow. You really take that Boy Scout motto to heart," Rodriguez said.

Jake didn't answer, busy peeling off the outer wrapper. He yanked off a long line of tape, tearing it with his teeth. "Hold the hole closed."

Rodriguez set his bag down on the floor of the raft. Reaching both hands over the side, he squeezed the ragged edges together. Jake managed to tape a section. He tore off another strip of tape, and they repeated the process. Five strips later, the hole had been sealed.

"We're still taking in water," Rodriguez said.

He was right. The raft had lost too much air. With their combined weight it barely cleared the surface. A steady stream of water slipped over the side.

"Start bailing," Jake said.

"With what?" Rodriguez demanded, palms open. "Any chance you have an air pump in there?"

"Nope." Jake started scooping with his hands. He

quickly realized it was a losing battle. He dug through the pack again, but there was nothing better to bail with.

"Brace yourself," he finally said, slinging his arms through the loops of the pack.

"For what?" Rodriguez asked, his voice filled with dread.

"We're going to have to abandon ship."

Stefan had finally fallen silent after what felt like an hours-long monologue about the Aztec calendar, Vikings and what he planned on doing with his immortality. Apparently he'd been hungering for someone to talk to. He addressed her as though she was an old friend. It was bizarre.

Kelly had tuned him out after a few minutes. She lay flat on her back trying to loosen the bindings around her wrists. It was difficult. Her fingers were still numb and the rope was wet. Every time she felt one knot release, she discovered another. Stefan hadn't taken any chances.

She prayed he'd leave her alone for a while, so she could try to burn through the ties. Stefan appeared supremely confident that he had the upper hand, which worked in her favor. The fact that he hadn't killed her yet was puzzling, but it gave her hope.

Hope. Kelly nearly laughed out loud. Because one thing had struck her as she lay there in arguably the most perilous situation she'd ever faced: she wasn't ready to die. Despite the uncertainty of her future, she wanted the chance to experience it. So she'd lost her lower leg. Lots of people had suffered the same injury and gone on to lead productive lives. In the past few days she'd proven that she was still capable of most of the things she could do before the accident.

"You're smiling," Stefan noted. "Why?"

"It's funny that I had to end up here to get some clarity," she finally replied.

Stefan squinted at her. "Perhaps there's hope for you yet, Agent Jones. You see, there are no coincidences in life. You end up precisely where you're supposed to be for a reason."

"I keep forgetting that you were a preacher of sorts," Kelly said. "Nice sermon."

He shrugged. "A bit trite, I'll admit, but the reason platitudes are clichéd is because they're so frequently true." He glanced at his watch again. "Almost time."

Kelly's stomach constricted. He stood and brushed off the seat of his pants. Her hands clenched into fists as she braced herself for whatever was coming.

Stefan's lips curled into a thin smile. "Don't worry, Agent Jones. It will only hurt for a moment."

Syd watched as the remaining prisoners were loaded on to a bus. The surviving cartel members had been rounded up and were sitting in a circle, feet in front of them, hands behind their heads. A few were led off to the barracks building Isabela had requisitioned for interrogations. Occasional screams emanated from it. Syd had already decided that whatever was happening in there was none of her business.

She glanced at her watch impatiently. Jake should have called by now with an update on Mark. There was a tug at her sleeve. Syd instinctively yanked her arm away and spun. A wizened elderly woman was looking up at her. She had to be less than four feet tall.

"Qué quieres?" Syd snapped.

"Gracias, señora." The woman's lips cracked wide in a toothless smile. *"Gracias por habernos salvado."*

"De nada." Syd watched the woman shuffle off,

gingerly mounting the bus stairs with the assistance of one of the PGR soldiers. Funny. She could count on one hand how many times she'd been thanked for her work in her life. Back when she was with the Agency, it was more likely she'd be put on a death list.

Isabela emerged from the barracks. After spotting Syd, she headed over.

"We're pulling out," Syd said. "It seems like you've got things under control."

"More or less," Isabela agreed.

"Don't take it personally, but I hope we never see each other again."

Isabela laughed. "In our line of work, you never know." She watched as the bus doors swung shut. The engine started with a growl. Cheers erupted inside as it rattled toward the gate.

"So you really think this will make a difference?" Syd asked, skeptical.

Isabela shrugged. "It is like battling the Hydra. You stop one cartel, a dozen others appear. But for these people it made a difference. And we might have gained a few weeks of peace. Los Zetas were particularly dangerous, thanks to their training and level of organization. So whoever takes their place might not present such a challenge."

"Seems futile," Syd noted.

Isabela smiled thinly. "*Es México.* Most of our humor revolves around the futility of it all." She shuffled her feet, avoiding Syd's eyes as she asked, "How is Mark?"

Syd shrugged. "No idea. Jake hasn't called. He's at the Hospital Ingles in Mexico City if you want to check up on him."

"I will." Isabela extended a hand. "Sorry for the… confusion."

"Making sure my people don't encounter any trouble at the border would mean more than sorry at this point," Syd said.

Isabela nodded. *"No hay problema.* It will be handled."

"Great. *Adios."* Syd mock saluted, then headed for the gate.

Forty-One

Kelly steeled herself. But rather than come after her, Stefan headed back to the corner where his supplies were stacked.

Kelly watched, her stomach filled with dread.

Stefan rummaged inside a large duffel bag. Apparently satisfied with the contents, he hauled it over one shoulder and came back to her. Stopping five feet away, he dumped it on the ground. "Here is where we part ways, Agent Jones."

"Are you going to try to kill me?" She eyed it, wondering what was inside.

"Try?" He barked a laugh. "It would not be difficult in your current condition. But I'm on the verge of an important ritual—I can't directly sully my hands." His eyes lingered on her throat. "Although it's a shame, since it would undoubtedly be enjoyable. You'll have to reconcile yourself to a much slower demise, I'm afraid." He looked regretful.

"You're not doing the ritual here?" she hedged.

Stefan seemed surprised. "Of course not. These things can't be done underground." He gestured to the chamber. "This is where priests cleansed themselves before performing the rituals. The murals say as much."

Kelly doubted any of that was true. "You can't possibly be planning to kill someone back at the Templo Mayor. It's in the middle of the city."

His eyes glinted as he said, "Goodbye, Agent Jones. It was lovely chatting with you." He nodded, turned and walked away.

Kelly was taken aback. Was it possible that he was just going to leave her there? Her heart leaped at the thought. Perhaps he had underestimated her, and assumed she wouldn't be able to free herself. Rodriguez would hopefully be showing up soon with help. The bonds around her wrists had loosened slightly. Reinvigorated, she tugged at them. Her hands separated a fraction of an inch.

At the entrance to the tunnel, Stefan stopped and held something up, showing it to her: a stick of dynamite.

Kelly's heart sank.

He called out, "I hope for your sake the air runs out quickly." Then he whirled and vanished from sight.

He was going to cause a cave-in, trapping her here. Kelly cast her eyes around the chamber. It might not survive the blast, the entire ceiling could come crashing down. Even if it held, how would anyone find her? Panic set in, a vise grip tightening around her chest.

Kelly rolled over. After struggling for a minute, she swung her good leg under her and sat. Using her foot, she pushed herself backward toward the tunnel, but her progress was slow. She made it five feet, then ten. Maybe she could get out in time. Stefan probably wasn't familiar with explosives; there was a whole host of things he could have done wrong....

Kelly was ten feet from the entrance when an explosion

ripped into the room. It began as a rumble on the far side, then a torrent of rocks and flames spewed from the tunnel mouth.

They both froze at the sound of an explosion. "What was that?" Rodriguez asked. "Earthquake?"

"I don't know," Jake said, but his stomach filled with dread. Stefan was ruthless. During the campus case, he'd beheaded a man he considered a friend. The thought of what he might be doing to Kelly right now was almost more than Jake could bear. "Stay with the boat if you want," he said, getting up on his knees. "I'm going in."

Before Rodriguez could stop him, he dived over the side. Even though he was already drenched, the shock of the water hit him hard. He spit out a mouthful, pulling a face at the foul taste.

"Christ, Riley," Rodriguez called out. "Be careful."

Jake was already swimming, the current swept him along. He held the flashlight in his right hand, so the light panned up and around in an arc as he swam. After ten strokes, he shone it in the direction the river was flowing. There was another opening up ahead, even smaller than the one that had torn their boat. He was racing toward it at a steady clip. Five feet away, he took a deep breath and dived beneath the surface. The water roiled, his flashlight illuminating rocks on either side. Jake did his best to avoid them, pushing off with his hands, but one still clipped him hard on the shoulder. He kept his legs locked out straight behind him, resisting the current's efforts to drag him down. After less than a minute, he broke the surface, gulping air. *Rodriguez isn't going to enjoy that,* he thought…but the life preserver should bear him back to the surface. As long as he didn't panic, he'd be fine. The current ebbed. Jake shone the light around.

He was in a larger chamber, similar to the first one they'd entered. The walls were covered with drawings. It looked like there was a spit of land on the right. Jake made for it, carving a path through the water with strong strokes. His knees brushed bottom and he stood. Jake staggered on to dry land, shivering.

There were drag marks on the ground—someone had managed to get a boat there, although after what they'd come through he had no idea how.

Movement caught his eye. Jake panned the light toward it. A few feet away, something flesh-colored bobbed in the shallows. His heart clenched. Part of him didn't want to see what it was, especially not after the explosion they'd heard. He approached slowly, as if it might attack.

Kelly's prosthetic. A wave of relief washed over him, replaced almost immediately by concern. What the hell had happened down here?

Jake swiveled. There was a pile of rubble against the far wall. Coming closer, he saw dust settling around it. The air hung thick with a pungent chemical smell.

He pressed his ear against the rock closest to him.

"Kelly?" he called out.

A long moment passed. Then he heard Kelly's voice, faintly calling for help.

Kelly strained her ears. For a second, she thought she'd heard Jake. She waited, then shook her head. Ridiculous. He was miles away.

The blast had snuffed out the candles, leaving her in the dark. The right side of her body felt hot. She'd probably suffered some burns. Chunks of stone had fallen off the surrounding walls, one landing what sounded like inches from her head, but her fears of a larger cave-in proved unfounded. All things considered, it could have been worse.

At the thought, Kelly laughed. She was stuck in a forgotten Aztec chamber hundreds of feet below Mexico City. Hard to imagine a worse scenario.

Kelly managed to reach the tunnel entrance. From what she could tell, the only way out was now a wall of stone. She took a deep breath and forced herself to relax, organizing her thoughts. First things first: she had to free her hands.

Kelly made her way back to Stefan's supply pile. Facing away from it, she managed to unzip the closest duffel bag and reached in, praying it didn't hold something awful, like human skin. Her fingers fumbled across what felt like more rope, then a water bottle, a small shovel…something caught her finger and she inhaled sharply. Carefully she felt her way along it: a knife. She leaned forward, straining her arms as she moved her wrists back and forth. The knife nicked her wrists a few times, but after a minute the rope loosened.

Kelly yanked her wrists apart as hard as she could, and the last of the rope gave. She shook out her hands to get the blood flowing again. It was a small victory, but having her hands back made her feel better.

Now she had to find some light.

A few more minutes of groping through Stefan's stash produced a box of kitchen matches and a large candle. She lit it on the third try. The wick flickered to life, sweeping the shadows away. Kelly nearly cried from relief. She turned back toward the tunnel.

What remained of the entrance was nearly a solid wall of stones. Still, some looked small enough for her to move. She had nothing to lose by trying. Kelly dug through the pile and extricated a shovel. Holding it in her right hand, the candle in her left, she made her way back across the room, supporting her weight on the shovel handle. It took five minutes of arduous effort to get there. She panted from the exertion as she examined the cave-in. Stefan's dynamite had done its job well. The center of the tunnel had collapsed completely, leaving only a few feet clear on her side—and who knew how much damage the far end had sustained. The entire outer chamber might have come down. Maybe Stefan had accidentally buried himself in it. Comforting thought, but she doubted it. Not with her luck.

Kelly found one stone at the top that looked small enough to move. She worked on it for a minute, wiggling it back and forth, grunting slightly from the effort. It finally gave, triggering a small avalanche of rubble. Kelly hopped back, narrowly avoiding having her foot crushed. She'd have to be more careful with the next one.

Getting back into position, she slid her hands into the cracks around a rock the size of a basketball.

Kelly stopped and cocked her head to the side. This time she had definitely heard something. Maybe Rodriguez had finally arrived with help—if he wasn't in jail for setting off an explosive at the Templo Mayor. She pressed her ear against a large boulder dead center in the tunnel. A scratching sound, murmured conversation—there was definitely someone on the other side. Her heart leaped—maybe she'd be getting out of here after all.

"Hey!" she called out.

A pause, then a muffled response.

"I can't hear you," she yelled. "Can you get me out?"

Another muffled shout through the wall. The voice sounded male.

"What?" Kelly moved closer, closing her eyes to try to hear better.

She couldn't be sure, but it sounded like they were yelling for her to get out of the way.

Rodriguez appeared, huffing as he staggered toward Jake.

"Thanks for the help back there," he said. "I almost drowned."

"I figured the vest would save you." Jake dug frantically at the wall of rocks. "Give me a hand. I think Kelly is on the other side."

"How the hell did that happen?" Rodriguez stepped back and perused the wall.

Jake didn't answer. His fingers were already cut and bleeding, his breath came in short gasps. He slid his fingers into the cracks surrounding a particularly large piece of rubble, pushing with his foot against the rock below it as he heaved. After a second, it shifted. He hauled it out, dumping it on the ground next to the three he'd already removed.

"It'll take forever to get her out that way." Rodriguez surveyed the damage.

"You got a better idea?" Jake snapped.

"Actually, I do." Rodriguez dropped the dry bag to the ground. Sifting inside, he brought out a chunk of gray putty. "I happen to have some C4 left."

Jake examined it. "I don't know much about munitions." He scanned the ceiling. "We don't want to bring this down on top of us."

"We start with a little and work from there," Rodriguez said. "Either way, it's easier than digging through this mess."

"She might be pinned in there. Blowing it up might kill her," Jake said.

"That's a risk," Rodriguez agreed. He rubbed his chin.

"I'm just worried that our *federales* friends will be here soon, and they'll be less interested in helping than arresting us. If we were home, I'd say wait. But here…"

Jake thought about it. Rodriguez was right. Plus they had no idea how much air Kelly had left. They had to chance it. He pressed his mouth to the wall and yelled as loud as he could, "Kelly, get back and take cover!"

As soon as she heard the order to get clear, Kelly scrambled away from the tunnel mouth and shielded her candle. Rodriguez probably had some C4 left, hopefully enough to penetrate the rubble. A puff of dust coughed out the entrance. Kelly held up the light. There was no discernible change on her side of the rock wall.

"It didn't work!" she called out.

"Stay back, we're trying again." The voices were more distinct. Kelly stayed to the side of the opening, knees curled in to her chest. She covered her ears with her hands and squeezed her eyes shut.

The rumbling was louder this time. More chunks of rock broke free from the ceiling above, one landed with a crash in the center of the room. A smaller one bounced off her head, scraping her cheek on its descent.

She ignored the pain, scrambling forward as soon as the rumbling ceased. Still no change, but she distinctly heard voices on the other side. She called out, "Did it work?"

As if in response, the rock wall facing her suddenly shifted. One of the smaller stones at the top drew back and a hand appeared.

"Oh, thank God." Kelly exhaled. She crawled up the wall with her hands, getting unsteadily to her feet.

The wall crumbled before her. The roof of the tunnel seemed stable enough, but the quicker she got through it the better. When the rubble was cleared to shoulder height, a head poked over the top. At the sight of her, Rodriguez's face flooded with relief.

"Jesus, Jones. The situations you get yourself into."

"We've got to hurry," Kelly said. "Stefan has some sort of ritual planned."

"One thing at a time." Rodriguez passed something through the gap. "This should help."

Kelly almost cried with joy at the sight of her prosthetic, a sentiment she never would have imagined a few days ago. Leaning against one of the larger boulders, she refastened it. Despite the pain in her stump, it reinvigorated her. "I'm coming over," she called.

Kelly eased herself into the opening. She froze as the movement sent smaller stones shifting beneath her. A pair of strong hands grabbed hold beneath her armpits, yanking her through just as the rocks gave way.

"Thanks," she said, looking down as she brushed herself off.

"Anytime."

Kelly raised her eyes slowly to find Jake staring down at her. He didn't look pleased. "How did the mission go?" she asked tentatively.

"Later. Right now I want to know what the hell you were thinking."

"We should really—"

"You didn't even call to tell me what you were up to."

"I...lost my phone," she said weakly, figuring this wasn't a good time to bring up her brief stint in jail.

"You can get a phone in any corner store in Mexico City. You managed to call him." He jerked a thumb toward Rodriguez, who stood off to the side looking wildly uncomfortable.

362 · *Kidnap & Ransom*

"I didn't, actually. McLarty called Danny."

"So you decided to go after this lunatic alone, even though—"

"Even though what?" Kelly demanded, eyes narrowing.

He wasn't backing down, though—she saw it in his eyes. "Even though you're crippled now. You can't do the things you used to do. Christ, look at yourself. You're beat to hell." He reached out a hand and gingerly wiped her bleeding cheek. She winced.

"I almost had him," Kelly retorted, trying not to flinch at the word "cripple." She scanned the spit of land: the raft was gone and she couldn't see her gun anywhere. Stefan had a fifteen-minute head start, minimum.

"We can fight about this later," she said. "Right now we have to get out of here."

"Back in there?" Rodriguez asked, shivering. His suit hung lank, pant cuffs dripping around his ankles.

"Unless you two found another way out," Kelly said, looking back and forth between them. Jake was clearly enraged, she recognized the set of his jaw.

There was a groan overhead. They all froze, eyes drawn upward.

"I don't like the way that sounded." Rodriguez examined the ceiling. "Believe me, I hate to say it, but Kelly's right. We have to get out of here."

"Let's go." Kelly avoided Jake's eyes as she marched back to the water's edge.

He didn't reply, but she heard him fall in behind her. Without giving herself time to think about it, she waded back into the current.

Forty-Two

Kelly shuddered as the water licked at her shoulders. Jake floated behind her; Rodriguez paddled clumsily in the rear. The current carried her toward another opening in the wall. Jake shone a flashlight forward, illuminating it. It was wider than the one they'd entered through.

"How long is this river?" Jake asked. "It feels like we've gone miles already."

"We're probably not even outside the city yet," Rodriguez called from the rear. "I think it's leading south. It'll probably meet up with the Panuco River. Most of the city's water drains into there."

Kelly reached the end of the chamber first. Another rumbling sound from above, and an enormous piece of the ceiling detached and fell into the water with a resounding splash. Rodriguez yelped. The force of the wave swept her into the darkness beyond.

She fought to keep her legs up, panicked at the thought of getting her foot trapped again. Something brushed against her, then grabbed her arm. She lashed out at it.

"Ouch!"

"Sorry," she said. "Where's your light?"

"It went out," Jake said flatly.

"Oh." For some reason, Kelly wasn't as terrified as she should have been, whirling through this black pit, buffeted by the wake caused by rocks tumbling down behind them. At least this time she wasn't alone.

"No going back now," Rodriguez said. "Sounds like the whole roof caved in. I hope no one tries to come after us."

"Light up ahead," Jake said.

He was right: Kelly made out a gleam in the distance. The current was slowing, too. The tunnel narrowed. Unexpectedly, light glinted off the walls on either side, momentarily blinding her.

It took a minute for Kelly's eyes to adjust. When they did, she almost couldn't process what she was seeing, it was so completely unexpected.

Syd glared down at the floor. She didn't know what to make of the situation. She'd arrived at the hospital a half hour before, only to discover that Jake had left. The nursing staff had no idea where he'd gone. Syd had an inkling. At a time like this, there was only one reason for him to leave his brother's side. Kelly must have gotten herself into some sort of trouble, and Jake went to save her.

Much as Syd hated to admit it, the thought bothered her. Not that she expected the other night to mean anything. They'd both just been letting off steam in the middle of a tense operation. She'd done the same dozens of times all over the world, couldn't even remember half the men's faces now. On the ride back to Mexico City, she'd prepared a speech in case Jake thought it meant more. *Gotta think of the business,* she'd say brusquely. *Probably better that it not happen again, just a one-time thing.*

The fact that it hadn't even occurred to him to call with an update on Mark was peeving, however. And she wasn't much in the mood to give that speech anymore. She'd prefer to shake him hard and demand to know why he was wasting his time with Kelly. The Feeb had been irritating enough before she lost her leg. Syd figured Jake was sticking with her out of pity, that sooner or later it would fall apart of its own accord. But that was taking longer than expected.

Not that she cared, she reminded herself. None of her business either way.

She looked up to find Maltz standing beside her. He'd emerged from the battle unscathed, which was a relief. She still felt guilty for what had happened to him last summer.

He ran a hand through his hair. "Jake's gone, huh?"

Syd shrugged. "Not my problem."

"Sure," Maltz said. "Nurse says Mark'll be out of surgery soon. You want coffee?"

"Please. Cream, no sugar." Syd sank down in a chair. Her eyes smarted as she watched Maltz limp down the hallway. Raising a hand to her cheek, she was startled to discover it was wet. Hurriedly Syd wiped away the tears.

Forty-Three

"Holy crap," Rodriguez said.

Kelly was inclined to agree. "Where are we?"

The underground river had terminated in a long, metal tube that shot her out into the open. She was now floating in the middle of a canal. Twenty feet away, a brightly painted flat-bottomed boat filled with people drifted along, guided by what appeared to be a gondolier. After what they had just been through, surreal didn't even begin to describe it.

"Believe it or not, I actually know," Rodriguez groaned. "Lago Xochimilco."

"Lago what?" Jake swam a few strokes to pull up beside them. The gondolier had swung his boat around and was paddling toward them. A few of the passengers were snapping photos.

"Lago Xochimilco. They held the rowing competitions here during the 1968 Olympics." Rodriguez glanced around. "Kind of like the canals in San Antonio. That boat is called a *trajinera*. My parents took me to a great restaurant here once. Best taco I ever had in my life."

The boat pulled up alongside them, and the gondolier yelled something. Rodriguez replied, and an oar was extended. He shoved his dry bag over the side, then awkwardly climbed on board.

"What are you doing?" Kelly asked.

"We can rent a boat. I'm done nearly drowning today." Rodriguez shook his head like a dog, spraying the nearby tourists with droplets.

Kelly let herself be hauled aboard. She dripped muddy water on the deck as a dozen passengers gaped openly at her.

"What the hell happened to you, sweetie?" asked a woman with a strong Texas drawl. She was dressed in a green fleece jacket and cowboy hat.

"Long story," Kelly grumbled.

"Here. Take my jacket." She stripped it off, handing it to Kelly.

"I can't—"

"Sure you can. Ugliest thing I own, but it's warm. I was gonna leave it here anyway."

"Thanks. I really appreciate it." Kelly took the jacket and slipped it on. Even over her wet clothes, it helped.

Rodriguez was conferring with the gondolier. Kelly saw him surreptitiously flash his creds. After a minute, he came over to where she and Jake shivered in silence.

"He's going to have a friend bring around a *trajinera* for us."

"Did he see anyone matching Stefan's description?"

Rodriguez shook his head. "This is his first trip of the day. He said he'd ask around, though. Any idea where Stefan was headed?"

"He said something about the time and date of the ritual being important."

"So you're thinking he won't wait until next month."

"I don't think so." Kelly shook her head. "We should

check that calendar again, see if there are any Aztec rituals associated with today."

"I'll call McLarty, see if he can get someone on that. Maybe he can convince the locals to put out a BOLO, too." Rodriguez dug a cell phone out of his dry bag.

The tourists shifted restlessly in their seats.

"I hope they'll give some of our money back," one woman complained, glaring at Kelly accusingly. "You know, we paid for a full hour."

"Hell, this is a lot more interesting than I thought it'd be," the Texan drawled, winking at Kelly. "I was half asleep before this."

The other woman grumbled but looked away.

Kelly took in the surrounding area. The canal was narrow, no more than twenty feet across, dotted with more of the brightly painted skiffs. On the shoreline rows of tropical trees swayed in the breeze. Just past them she could see small fields. An elderly woman in a straw hat rowed over, her canoe laden with bunches of flowers. A few of the tourists passed money over the side and came back with armfuls of garlands.

"This is bizarre," Jake said in a low voice.

Kelly nodded, suddenly exhausted. The adrenaline drained from her body and she staggered. Jake grabbed her elbow to keep her from falling.

"You should sit." He helped her down on a bench seat.

"Thanks." She started to lean her head against his shoulder, then caught herself.

He noticed, and drew her head down next to his anyway. She relaxed, inhaling his scent. The banks of the river climbed on either side, until all Kelly could see were mossy walls ascending toward the sky. Trees waved slightly in the breeze, lining the canal like sentinels. It was beautiful, a dramatic change from the noise and pollution of Mexico City. There was still a haze in the sky, but the sun was gaining strength, warming her. "I'm glad you're okay. And I'm really sorry," she said after a minute.

"Yeah. So am I." His voice was thick with emotion.

Kelly tilted her head to look up at him. "What is it?"

"I thought I'd lost you," he said without looking at her. "Why didn't you tell me you were going after him? I could have helped."

"Mark needed you. Besides, I was only checking out a lead that he was still alive. The rest of it…well, I didn't plan that part."

"God, Kelly." He shook his head. "The whole point is that we should be able to tell each other anything."

"I know, you're right." After a pause, she continued, "The funny thing is, running into Stefan actually put things in perspective."

"That is funny." Jake's voice was flat.

"You have every right to be angry." Kelly lifted her head. He was still avoiding her eyes. She sighed. "We should talk when we get back. I just wanted to say everything is clearer for me now. If you still want to get married, I think we should."

"What?" He finally looked at her. She managed a smile. "You're serious."

"I am. Before, I just…I was an idiot."

He looked away again. Kelly examined him, surprised. She could have sworn he had tears in his eyes. "Jake?"

"Let's talk about it later," he said thickly.

"Okay." She sat back up, wounded.

An empty boat pulled up alongside them. The gondoliers exchanged ropes, binding the *trajineras* together. Kelly let Rodriguez help her aboard.

After they were settled, he said, "So this guy will take

us back to the dock, we can try to find an internet place there. McLarty said he'd call back within the hour."

"Okay." Kelly nodded, but impatience gnawed at her. It was horrible to sit here, helpless, when Stefan might already be killing someone else.

Rodriguez's dry bag emitted a tinny ring. He dug through it and produced a cell phone. "It's yours," he said, tossing it to Jake.

When he saw the number, Jake's face clouded over. He clicked it open and asked, "How is he?"

Kelly and Rodriguez exchanged a puzzled look.

"Okay, I'm on my way." Jake snapped the phone shut and turned to Rodriguez. "I have to get to the hospital. Mark just got out of surgery."

"What? Why didn't you say anything?" Kelly asked, startled. "How bad is it?"

"Bad." Jake's head was bowed. "Chris is flying in, but I'm not sure he'll make it in time."

"Sorry, man," Rodriguez said consolingly. "He said it'll only take fifteen minutes or so to get back. The city isn't far away."

"I'm so sorry." Kelly wrapped an arm around his shoulder. "You shouldn't have come after me."

"What else was I supposed to do? You could have died down there." Jake dropped his head in his hands.

Kelly rubbed his shoulder. Mark's condition changed everything. She couldn't in good conscience go after Stefan now, leaving Jake to face this alone. "I'll go with you to the hospital."

"You don't have to."

"I want to."

"Fine."

They sat in silence. The gondolier's cell phone rang. After listening for a minute, he shouted into the receiver.

Slapping the phone shut, he dug the oar down hard. Their boat slowly pivoted.

"What's going on?" Kelly asked.

"Qué pasa?" Rodriguez called out to the gondolier. The man responded, gesticulating furiously as he jabbered. Rodriguez's brow darkened as he translated. "Someone grabbed a local kid, a young boy who helps his mom sell food from their boat. Yanked him right over the side. The mom tried to stop him, but the guy knocked her overboard. He's heading downriver to join the search for the kid."

"It's Stefan. Has to be," Kelly said.

"Yeah," Rodriguez agreed. "Bastard just won't give up."

"We can't let these people go after him alone. It's too dangerous."

Rodriguez's jaw worked as he looked downriver. "If he still has dynamite, he could really do some damage. No matter what we say, the driver is headed away from the dock."

"Have him drop me onshore, I'll get back on my own." Jake stood, grabbing hold of one of the support beams as he scanned the shoreline. The edge sloped up to a grassy field. "Has to be a road around here somewhere," he said.

"I'll ask," Rodriguez said. "I'm not sure how far away the docks are, though."

Jake didn't answer.

Kelly watched him, conflicted.

Jake looked down at her. "You want to go after him, don't you?"

Kelly hesitated before answering. "I'm going to the hospital with you."

"That's not what I asked."

"Of course I want to go after him," she said. "Stefan nearly killed me again. He's got a kid." With a shudder she remembered the corpse in the dump. "He skinned his last victim. It was one of the worst things I've ever seen, Jake. I don't want him hurting anyone else."

Jake knelt beside her and looked in her eyes. "Then you should go."

Kelly shook her head. "No. I'm going with you."

Jake cupped her face in his hand and ran a thumb along her cheek. "I haven't seen you like this in a long time."

"All beat up?" Kelly managed a weak smile.

"Like yourself again. That's the woman I want to marry." He looked up. They were nearly at the embankment. "I don't feel right leaving you here. Maybe I should stay and help."

"Absolutely not," Kelly said firmly. "Mark needs you. I've got Danny backing me up, we'll be fine."

"I guess." Jake eyed the shore uncertainly. "I've got a bad feeling about this, though. You're not on a good streak down here."

"When am I ever on a good streak?" Kelly said ruefully.

Jake laughed. "Not since we met, that's for sure."

"I feel awful about letting you go through this alone," Kelly said. Jake had left his wounded brother's side to come save her. Sending him to maintain a solitary vigil didn't feel right. "Are you sure?"

"Yeah, I'm sure. But don't get killed."

"I won't. Promise." Kelly wrapped her arms around him. He hugged her back, hard.

A few feet away from shore, the gondolier called something out.

"This is as close as he can get without beaching the boat," Rodriguez explained.

"Guess that's my cue." Jake kissed Kelly on the forehead, then on her nose, then on her mouth. "I love you," he said, holding her chin.

"I love you, too."

"Hospital Ingles. Call me when you get him." Jake handed his backpack to Kelly. "There's an H&K in there, won't need it where I'm headed."

"Okay." Kelly swallowed hard, trying to get rid of the lump in her throat. "Thanks."

Rodriguez shook Jake's hand. "Good luck getting back to the city."

Jake nodded. With one final glance back at Kelly, he set a foot on the gunwale and leaped to shore.

The gondolier dug his pole back into the shallow bottom of the canal and steered them forward. The sun was climbing in the sky and blue patches broke through the haze. As soon as Jake vanished over the lip of the bank, Kelly turned to Rodriguez. "Can you think of any temples around here where the Aztecs performed sacrifices? Stefan must have a specific destination in mind."

Rodriguez shrugged. "There are tons of them, depending on how far away he's willing to go. Pyramid of the Sun, Pyramid of the Moon…the Aztecs liked killing people, they did it pretty much everywhere."

"The closer, the better. He's not going to be able to travel far carrying a victim."

Rodriguez turned to the gondolier, who was back on his phone. He held up a finger for them to wait, then hung up. He said something in Spanish, jaw set as he paddled harder.

"His friend found a rubber raft beached about a mile downriver. They're all headed there now," Rodriguez translated.

"How many of them?"

"At least a dozen men. They're trying to raise some of the guys on shore to help out, form a net so he can't get away."

"He'll be dangerous cornered."

"We've got strength in numbers on our side, though. Better than when it was just us."

"I suppose," Kelly said uncertainly. The gondolier appeared enraged. She wasn't about to let a bloodthirsty mob kill Stefan, no matter how much he deserved it. The question was, would she and Danny be able to stop them?

Kelly leaned forward on the bench, shielding her eyes with one hand. "There it is—" She pointed. About twenty feet off the bow, a cluster of boats was strung together. They appeared hastily abandoned, no passengers in sight. Stefan's rubber raft was beached on shore, a rope securing it to the trunk of a tree. The bank surrounding it was steep.

The gondolier steered them over. When the boat got close enough, he tossed a bumper over the side and looped a bowline around the beam of the nearest boat.

"This is too easy," Kelly said to herself.

"What?" Rodriguez asked.

"Stefan's crazy, but he's not an idiot." She turned and scanned the opposite bank. "We should split up and check both sides, just in case."

The gondolier had already charged off, clambering from one boat to another.

Rodriguez called after him, *"Amigo! Espere!"*

Without responding the gondolier jumped into the water, sloshing the last few feet to shore. He scrambled up the bank, vanishing on the other side.

"So much for strength in numbers," Rodriguez sighed.

"So what do you think? Check the other side on our own?"

Kelly pursed her lips, debating. "I hate to think what'll happen if they catch him and we're not there."

"It'll be even worse if they don't find him," Rodriguez pointed out.

"Okay. Let's start on the other side." Kelly helped Danny untie the boat and push off. It was maddening how Stefan always seemed to stay one step ahead of them.

Rodriguez struggled with the oar, fighting the current trying to sweep them downstream. After ten minutes, he managed to steer them across to the other side.

"That was a hell of a lot harder than it looked," he said, wiping sweat from his brow.

Kelly swung her legs over the side and landed hip deep in the water, keeping a tight grip on the bowline. She awkwardly waded forward, towing the boat behind her. A few feet from shore, she looped the line around a tree stump and triple-knotted it.

Rodriguez landed beside her. "You'd think the water would be warmer out here," he grumbled as he passed her Jake's pack.

"At least we didn't have to swim." Kelly dug out the H & K and checked it quickly before tucking it in her waistband. She slung on the backpack as she eyed the steep riverbank. "Mind helping me up?"

Rodriguez clambered up first, cursing under his breath as his feet slid in the mud. At the top, he reached down to help her.

After a few minutes of struggling, she made it up. "Thanks." She wiped muddy palms on her sodden pants as she scanned the landscape. They were in some sort of field.

"They call these *chinampas*. They're kind of like rice paddies," Rodriguez said. "It's going to be swampy."

"I can tell," Kelly said. Her boots had sunk into the mud and water pooled around them.

There was a single shack at the far edge of the field, roof caved in. The rest of the terrain was barren, no houses, just a dirt road lined with telephone poles.

"I don't see any temples," Kelly said.

"I haven't been here since I was a kid, but I don't remember any," Rodriguez said. "And trust me, if there had been, we would have gone to see them. My dad never met a ruin he didn't love."

"I guess we should check the shack," Kelly said doubtfully. Everything about this felt wrong. Performing a ritual during broad daylight, in a field in the middle of nowhere, didn't mesh with Stefan's flair for the dramatic. But if he was planning on conducting the sacrifice somewhere else, he could have waited to grab a victim. Maybe snatching the boy had just been a diversion. But for all Stefan knew, she was dead and he was scot-free, so why bother?

Rodriguez shrugged. "We're here. Looks like a long shot, though. We could always get back in the boat, see if we can spot him downriver."

Kelly hesitated. "Let's check this out first," she finally said. "Maybe he's lying low until things calm down."

They crossed the field carefully, sticking to dry ground as much as possible. It was slow going, and Kelly was painfully aware of time slipping away from them. She couldn't stop picturing Stefan's look of triumph when he left her in the cave.

Ten feet from the shack, she turned to tell Rodriguez they should head back. As she opened her mouth to speak, there was a loud moan from inside.

Forty-Four

Kelly motioned for Rodriguez to circle around to the left.
She skirted the other side, trying not to make too much
noise as she squelched through the mud. The shack was a
mass of crumbling, rotted wood. A few strips of red paint
clung to the weathered boards.

Kelly strained her ears. Aside from a distant birdcall,
there was only silence.

She turned the corner. The front of the building was
gone, leaving it exposed on this side. From her vantage
point, it appeared empty save for a pile of accumulated
trash and debris.

Rodriguez's head poked out. He nodded at her, then
mouthed the words *one…two…*

On *three,* they swept into the shack, guns panning
along the inside.

"Nothing," Kelly said, puzzled.

Another small moan.

She whipped around. Tucked in the corner behind her,
a pair of scrawny legs jutted out from under the fallen
roof.

Kelly moved cautiously, keeping her gun up. She lifted

a corner of the wood. An enormous pair of eyes gazed up at her.

"No me moleste," he whispered faintly.

"It's the kid." Rodriguez tucked his gun away.

"Help me get this off him. I think he's hurt."

Together they lifted the junk off. The boy was no more than five or six years old, wearing a light blue T-shirt and a pair of ragged jean shorts. Both were soaked in blood.

Rodriguez murmured to him quietly in Spanish.

"What happened?"

The boy's voice quavered. As he spoke, Rodriguez checked him for injuries. Carefully lifting up a corner of his shirt, he exposed a deep gash across the boy's abdomen.

"He says the bad man brought him here and cut him. Then he left."

"He just left?" Kelly asked, puzzled.

Rodriguez was still listening. The boy's voice was weak. "He even told him to call for help once he was gone, but the kid was too scared. He's just been waiting here, terrified that the guy was going to come back." As the boy fell silent, Rodriguez met Kelly's eyes. "He wants his mother, he's begging us to take him to her."

"I'm not sure we should move him," Kelly said uncertainly. "Give me your phone, I'll call for help."

Rodriguez dug out his cell phone while maintaining a reassuring chatter. The boy's eyes followed his hands. His lids started to drift closed.

"Crap, I think we're losing him." Rodriguez tossed her his phone. "Dial 066."

"There's no signal," Kelly said, frustrated, as she examined the screen. "Try to stop the bleeding. I'll go back to the boats for help."

"Be careful. Stefan might still be out there."

"If he's smart, he bolted."

"Why does something make me doubt that?" Rodriguez grunted. The boy whimpered in pain and his eyes rolled back in his head. Rodriguez stripped off his dress shirt and pressed it to the wound. "Hurry, Jones. We're running out of time."

Jake stuck close to the river, following its twists and turns as he trotted upstream. As he went, he brooded over what Kelly had said. The irony of it was almost overwhelming. After all this time, she was herself again. She'd regained that glint in her eye, the passion that had drawn him to her in the first place. And on top of everything else, she was suddenly ready to get married.

Meanwhile, he'd just betrayed her in the worst way imaginable. He flashed back on the motel room, Syd's legs wrapped around him. He felt a pit in his gut. But if he was honest, it had been a long time coming. He had feelings for Syd, whether he wanted to admit it or not.

But he loved Kelly. On the boat, he'd realized that more than anything, he wanted to spend the rest of his life with her. He'd just have to see if she felt the same way once he came clean about what happened.

The riverbanks had flattened out. Tall reeds clustered in clumps along the shoreline. Jake heard voices upriver, a distant stream of chatter. He must be getting close to the main docks, where the restaurants and cafés were located. Most of the gondoliers were probably downstream searching for the missing boy, because the canal remained empty.

A roar off to his left. A police boat appeared, jets kicking up a two-foot wake, three armed cops on deck. Jake dived to the ground and pressed his body flat, hoping the reeds concealed him. The cops probably only had a vague description of the perpetrator, and any big white guy walking along the canal would have some explaining to do.

The engine roar receded. Good, he hadn't been spotted. Maybe Stefan had been found, and they were on their way to assist. His mind flashed to Kelly. He hadn't heard any gunshots yet. Part of him hoped Stefan was stupid enough to resist arrest. The bastard had tried to kill Kelly twice. Jake would put a bullet in his head if he could. At the thought, he felt a twinge of guilt for leaving her. He hated when she put herself in danger, but she was right, that was the life they'd both signed up for. And she was probably a lot safer out here, backed up by a partner and an angry horde of locals, than she had been driving through the streets of Mexico City with him and Syd.

Jake glanced at his watch: nearly 9:00 a.m. He got back to his feet and broke into a jog. From Syd's tone, Mark probably didn't have much time left. If his brother died alone, Jake wouldn't be able to forgive himself.

Around the next bend he caught sight of a cluster of buildings balanced above the canal on stilts. Jake picked up the pace. Every muscle ached, and his head throbbed. He pushed through the pain, spurred by the thought that he was only a few minutes away.

A series of connected docks formed a boardwalk. It resembled a kind of poor-man's Venice. The first few piers were empty, then he hit one thronged with people in front of a rickety ticket booth. Jake was forced to slow his pace as he made his way through the crowd. The vast majority of them appeared irritated.

As he pushed past, he overheard one woman complaining, "This is just so typical. Does it mean they're canceling the reenactment, too?"

Jake kept moving. The next dock had café tables set

inches apart, each packed with tourists examining maps and loudly discussing alternate plans for the day. Forced to weave between them, he stopped a harried waitress. "Taxi?"

She pointed farther up the dock.

"Gracias." Jake forged through to the next pier. Up ahead, he spotted a break between the buildings. The street was probably on the other side, he thought with relief. He skirted a large crowd that had formed outside the next building. He was almost at the alleyway when a voice intruded on his consciousness. It was a man, calling out as though preaching. And unless he was mistaken, the guy was speaking Danish.

Jake stopped and pivoted in the direction of the voice.

He'd lost the beard and long hair, but Jake still recognized him immediately. Stefan stood on the deck of a *trajinera* tied to the closest dock. He was wearing a soiled white robe and his arms were spread wide.

A young guy in a baseball cap held up his phone, taping it. "Man, this guy is great!" He nudged Jake with his elbow.

"What's he saying?" Jake asked.

"No clue. But it must be part of the show."

"What show?" Jake scanned the scene. Not a cop in sight. They were probably all downriver.

"This is like Aztec New Year," the kid said. "They're supposed to do a big show, fake a sacrifice, that sort of thing. You hear they're not taking anyone on the boats?" The kid shook his head. "Total bullshit, man. I took three buses to get here."

Stefan's head was tilted back, face to the sun as he spoke in a booming voice. Suddenly, as if sensing Jake, he lowered his head. Their eyes met. Stefan's face slowly split in a leer.

"Crap," Jake muttered. It had been years since they'd seen each other, but apparently he'd been recognized, too. And he'd given his gun to Kelly. All he had was a butterfly knife clipped to his belt.

"You know him, man?" the kid asked. "He's looking right at you."

"What kind of sacrifice?"

"What?"

"The sacrifice," Jake said impatiently. "What is it?"

The boy shrugged. "I dunno, something about drowning people."

Jake took in the scene. There had to be a few hundred tourists clustered on the docks, more in the surrounding buildings. Stefan had had months to plan whatever he had in mind. And he'd used dynamite to cause the cave-in that trapped Kelly.

"He's going to blow the docks," he said, realization dawning.

Kelly raced back to the river. Approaching the shore, she saw their gondolier on the opposite bank, arms crossed over his chest. When he spotted her, he waved a fist angrily and yelled, apparently unhappy about the fact that his boat was now across the river.

"We found him!" she cried, frantically searching her mind for the right words. *"El niño!"* she shouted, pointing behind her.

They seemed to understand. The gondoliers scrambled down to the boats en masse. Within minutes they were across the canal.

"This way," she said. "Come with me."

As she was about to lead them away, a police boat

roared around the bend. The three officers on deck spotted them and tore to the shoreline. One jumped onto the cluster of *trajineras*. He engaged in a brief conversation with the nearest gondolier, then made his way up to Kelly.

"Where is the boy?" he asked in a thick accent. A patch on his bulletproof vest read *Landa*.

"There's a shack across the field," Kelly said. "He's cut, do you have a medical kit? He'll need a doctor soon, he's lost a lot of blood."

Landa called out instructions to his men. One pulled a medical kit from below deck. He jumped off the boat and climbed the steep embankment, vanishing after the gondoliers. Landa stayed where he was, examining her. "Who are you?"

"Special Agent Kelly Jones with the FBI," she said. "The boy was stabbed by Stefan Gundarsson. He's wanted for murder in my country."

He eyed her uncertainly, taking in the gun tucked in her waistband. "Identification?"

"I lost it in the water," Kelly lied, hoping he'd wait to call and check on her. "I've been pursuing Gundarsson for a few days now."

"Did the boy say where he went?"

"No," Kelly said. "He just left him there."

The police boat's radio suddenly crackled. The cop at the wheel answered, then exchanged a few terse sentences with Landa.

"What's going on?" Kelly asked.

"We're needed at the docks," Landa said, climbing back on board his skiff.

"It's him, isn't it?" Kelly said, mentally kicking herself. She'd fallen for the bait as surely as everyone else. He'd deliberately taken the boy and injured him, knowing that would draw any authorities downriver. Then he'd be free to carry out whatever he had planned at the docks.

Aztecs murdered thousands a day, she remembered. It wasn't about one victim.

Stefan was planning to kill many, many more.

Forty-Five

Stefan stepped off the gunwale and into the boat. Keeping an eye on Jake, he untied the bowline, casting off. The boat drifted away from the dock.

"Stop him!" Jake called out. A few curious tourists looked his way, probably thinking this was part of the show.

"Dude," the kid said. "What's the issue?"

"Get out of here," Jake said roughly, shoving him back. "Get clear of the docks. Go!"

"Chill, man." Shaking his head, the kid tucked his phone away and moved off, muttering under his breath.

The crowd was dispersing; still, Jake found his way blocked. His attempts to push through were met with nasty looks and curses in several languages. Entire families grinned wide as they posed for pictures in front of the docked *trajineras*.

Jake watched helplessly as Stefan drifted down the canal.

"Hey, he's stealing a boat!" someone yelled. A cheer went up.

By the time Jake arrived at the edge of the dock, the boat had drifted too far away for him to reach. Stefan cocked a hand in a little wave, then crossed his arms over his chest as he floated downstream.

"Crap," Jake muttered. He got on his belly and peered beneath the dock. Nothing but boards. He braced his hands along the edge and scooted forward until his upper torso hung all the way off.

"Cuidado!" a voice cautioned from behind him.

Craning his head from side to side, he spotted cord wrapped around a bundle on the pier's concrete piling. It extended away to the next dock support, then the next. Jake looked in the other direction and saw the same thing. Probably Primacord, a type of fuse that detonated explosives in sequence. Used in mining, it was easy to get hold of and worked even when wet. The closest length of cord was set too far back for him to reach.

He had to get the docks clear before they blew. Jake waved his arms and yelled, "Bomb! *Bomba!"*

A few tourists examined him curiously, but no one moved. Either the bulk of the crowd didn't speak English, or they thought he was just another nut trying to get attention.

"Get off the docks, there's a bomb!" he yelled again.

Stefan's boat had come to rest in the middle of the canal, about twenty yards downriver. Looking back at Jake, he raised both hands toward the sky as if in supplication.

Jake jumped into the water. He broke the surface and swam to the nearest piling.

It took a minute for his eyes to adjust to the gloom. Once they did, he saw a bundle of dynamite bound to the piling with Primacord. If he cut the wire, it should stop the sequence. He'd slice each one, trying to make it back to the source before they ignited. Primacord burned fast, the detonations would only be seconds apart. And if he was close to one when it blew…

There was no other option. The detonating cord stretched away from him, extending into the shadows beneath the dock like a grim clothesline.

Unfortunately it was just out of reach overhead. Jake scissored his legs together, propelling himself out of the water as he grabbed for the cord. He missed, and fell back in with a splash. Grunting, he tried again. This time his fingers latched on. He pulled the line down to the surface of the water as he fell. It cut into his hands, and he swore.

Suddenly a bright flash to his right drove away the shadows. Jake's retinas burned from the glare. An explosion, then the sound of something large hitting the water. Screams and panicked feet running above him. A spark danced along the fuse a dozen yards away, approaching as fast as a train.

Jake frantically sawed at the cord. Another explosion to his right. More screams, followed by another crash. He didn't dare look at the swath of destruction racing toward him. In his panic, the knife kept slipping. He slashed his thumb, winced, but kept going. The final strands were separating.

Just then, fire darted into his line of vision and the cord suddenly burned hot. His fingers reacted, dropping it in the water.

The piling ten feet away exploded. Jake was momentarily stunned by the blast. The boards above him rolled and split. An instant later an enormous wave lifted him up, slamming him hard against the underside of the dock before sweeping him away.

Upriver there was a boom, followed by a series of similar percussions. It sounded like firecrackers. Kelly froze.

"*Mierda*," Landa spat.

A wave appeared around the bend.

Landa issued orders to his men, then turned to Kelly and yelled, "Hold on."

The wake lifted the boat up, the propellers churned air. Kelly clutched the siderails, fighting to keep her balance. As the skiff slammed back down in the water, the propellers caught. The boat bucked wildly from side to side, nearly capsizing. The cop at the wheel powered down the throttle, shouting as he tried to keep them afloat.

The waters surrounding them stilled.

"What happened?" Kelly asked.

Landa ignored her, calling out another command. The boat accelerated again, jetting upstream.

The canal ahead was clotted with debris. The driver slowed the boat as they approached it. Kelly recognized brightly painted wood from *trajineras,* now in jagged pieces. More boards, plain this time. A shoe. As they passed it, Kelly was horrified to see a leg, but no body.

"Oh my God," she said. "We're too late."

Forty-Six

Jake came to with a jolt. Disoriented, it took a second to remember where he was, what had happened. Something hot ran down his face. Swiping at it, his hand came away red: blood. He craned his head. He was floating in the canal—thank God he'd landed faceup. The water surrounding him was filled with chunks of concrete, plastic chairs, brightly colored logs.

A massive cloud of smoke shrouded everything. Through it he could see the boardwalk. It looked like a giant had punched holes through it. Burning boards canted up at all angles. Some sections had collapsed completely into the canal. The remaining docks were filled with hordes of panicked people running in every direction.

But that was only the right half. The rest of the piers were unscathed. He'd been able to stop the chain reaction before it progressed too far. Jake blew out a sigh of relief.

The sound of a baby crying. Jake spun himself around. It was hard to see over the junk floating around him, he was almost completely penned in by it. He crawled on top of one of the thicker logs nearby, then carefully sat up to look around.

Jake spotted a woman treading water with one hand, her other arm wrapped around a baby. She was frantically fighting to keep the child's head above water. Just past them another body floated facedown. The canal churned with people, some swimming for shore, others motionless.

Fighting through the debris, Jake made his way over to the woman. As she slipped beneath the water's surface, he managed to grab hold of her collar. He towed her to a large hunk of floating wood.

"Grab hold," he said.

She didn't appear to speak English, but tucked the wood under her arm and leaned on it, raising the squalling baby farther out of the water. Jake pushed on the log, slowly guiding them through the glut toward a flight of stone stairs that had probably served as a launch before the docks were built.

As soon as her feet hit the steps she was out of the water. She dashed up the stairs, clutching the child to her. Jake turned back. An elderly man ten feet away clumsily paddled toward him. Jake swam over and assisted him to the stairs. Other people descended the staircase and helped him to the top.

Many of the victims had struck out for the opposite shore. Most appeared to be all right.

The sound of sirens approaching. *Good,* he thought. Help was on the way. He dug out his cell phone to call Kelly and tapped the first few keys before noticing the blank screen. Submersion in the water had destroyed it. He could wait around for the authorities to arrive, try to convince them in broken Spanish to help him pursue Stefan. He dismissed the thought. The scene was too chaotic, no one would bother with a crazy American.

Jake's view was obstructed, he needed to find a better

vantage point. He fought a wave of exhaustion as the adrenaline rush abated. His feet seemed to weigh a hundred pounds each as he staggered up the stairs. The flight ended at an alley that sloped slightly up. The buildings on either side were undamaged. An ambulance skidded to a stop at the far end of the alley. Jake turned and scanned the scene behind him.

Paramedics had arrived and were bent over the most severely injured. Across the canal, Jake spotted the boat Stefan had been on. Now empty, it bobbed against the opposite shore.

In the confusion, it would be easy for Stefan to slip away. Jake couldn't allow that to happen. This act of madness probably only marked the beginning of what he had planned.

The canal and surviving docks were a mess, but maybe he could cut through the surrounding streets to reach the opposite shoreline. Deciding, Jake headed up the alley. He emerged on a narrow street clogged with emergency vehicles. He dodged and clambered over them. The road arced right. Jake peered into each alleyway as he passed, trying to find one that was clear. Five minutes in, he spotted one and turned down it, passing two men bearing a teenage girl on a stretcher. She wailed while clutching a broken arm, her face covered in burns. Jake kept going.

At the end, he took a second to get his bearings. The collapsed docks were to his right now. It looked like Stefan hadn't bothered with this section, probably because it appeared residential, mostly rickety apartment buildings. Farther down the buildings that had been perched on stilts weren't as fortunate. The roofs of a few poked above water, while others tilted down as if they'd dropped to their knees in submission.

A small footbridge led to the spot where Stefan's boat

had been beached. A group of survivors were using the *trajinera* to fish casualties out of the canal. Jake raced across the bridge.

It terminated in marshy grass. There was a smaller channel here that hadn't been visible from the other side. Jake followed it, ducking through a copse of trees. He emerged on the edge of a boggy field. Tufts of grass sprouted plastic bags, cans, other signs that life on the canal had spilled over here. Incongruously a cow grazed in the center of it. It turned its head to regard him, then lowered back down and grabbed another mouthful of grass. The idyllic scene stood in stark contrast to the chaos and destruction less than a hundred feet away.

The canal branched off into two channels: one ran north, the other east. Stefan could have stashed a boat and headed down either of them. Or he could have taken the land route across the fields.

Jake debated. It had been at least fifteen minutes since the docks blew. Stefan had a hell of a head start. He scanned the ground for footprints, anything to suggest which way Stefan had gone.

He had a clear line of sight across the field for about a half-mile in either direction. The field was muddy, more bog than anything else. It would have taken Stefan time to traverse it, probably long enough that he'd still be visible.

So Jake struck a course parallel to the larger canal headed north. A few hundred yards in, he was ready to give up. There was no sign that a boat had been left here, no fresh footprints or other indication that someone had recently passed through. If Stefan had stashed a motorized boat, he could be a mile away by now.

But before he headed back to the docks, Jake figured he had nothing to lose by venturing a short distance down the other canal. As he approached the first turn, a bright red bird flitted out of the sky, landing at the base of a tree twenty feet away. It appeared to be bathing, ducking its head and shaking off droplets. After a minute, it flew away with something bright clutched in its beak.

Curious, Jake went to check it out. When he got closer, he saw a small bowl tucked among the protruding roots. A tiny set of blue-green paper wings floated on top. It looked like some kind of offering, different from those he'd seen back in Mexico City. The water was clear. Someone had set it there recently.

Jake straightened and scanned the surrounding area. Maybe Stefan hadn't been able to resist witnessing his handiwork before taking off. There might still be time. It was a long shot, but if he headed back for reinforcements, chances were they'd never catch up.

Jake moved as quickly and stealthily as possible, sticking close to the river's edge. His eyes panned back and forth between the still waters of the canal and the fields alongside it. The foliage grew thicker, palm trees ceding way to others he didn't recognize. The canal sank away beneath him, banks steepening. Tree branches arched over it as if reaching for their brethren on the other side.

Jake was about to give up when he spotted a footprint in the mud beside the canal. He slid down the embankment for a closer look. He was no expert, but it appeared fresh, water was still pooling inside it.

Jake frowned. The canal was empty, not even a ripple marred the surface. It was wider here, easily thirty feet across. He tried to peer into the depths, but the water was brackish and murky, the surface slick with patches of oil casting iridescent rainbows. He wondered if this canal led to a road.

There wasn't much more he could do—the trail seemed

394 *Kidnap & Ransom*

to have gone cold. Kelly might be back at the docks by now. He should go see if they could persuade the locals to join the search, maybe set up some roadblocks. It was frustrating. No matter what they did, Stefan always seemed to slip through their grasp.

Jake took hold of a tree root jutting out from the side of the embankment, preparing to haul himself back up.

When a hand reached out and grabbed his ankle, dragging him below the surface of the water, he was too surprised to cry out.

Kelly's chest clenched at the sight facing them. The police skiff slowed as they inched their way through a floating debris field. One of the cops stayed in the bow, using a pole to clear the larger items from their path.

Landa stood beside her, jaw tight as he surveyed the damage. "Do you see this man Stefan?"

Kelly shook her head, although Stefan wasn't who she'd been looking for. She scanned the water, the docks, then the shoreline. A few people still flailed in the canal, but most of the survivors had already made it to shore. Still, the water was littered with bodies surrounded by dissipating pools of red. She prayed that Jake wasn't one of them.

"We should help these people," she said.

"There are already men doing that." Landa gestured toward men in uniform maneuvering boats across the canal. "Do you know where he might have gone?"

"No," Kelly said, defeated. She sank down on the bench seat at the rear of the boat. "I have no idea."

They pulled up alongside a *trajinera* filled with shivering people dripping water. Survivors were still climbing on board and the sides had sunk dangerously low. Landa called out to the passengers. A few chattered over each other in response, excitedly pointing toward the deserted shoreline opposite the docks.

"Gracias!" Landa said. Without warning, the police skiff roared away.

"What did they say?" Kelly asked.

"A crazy man left the *trajinera* and got in a smaller boat. He went that way." Landa pointed to where a narrower channel snaked through the trees.

"He could be anywhere by now," Kelly said.

"He will head back to the city along the main canal. We will have another boat come from that end. He will be trapped."

"Okay." Kelly hesitated. "I should go back to the docks to look for my fiancé."

"We have no time. If he was hurt, they already are taking him to hospital. If not, he will wait for you." Landa turned away, cutting off any discussion.

The skiff swung around a corner into a narrower offshoot of the canal. As they rounded the bend, Kelly saw that it split farther: a wide channel headed north, the smaller one east.

"How can you be sure which way he went?" Kelly asked doubtfully.

"The main canal leads back to Mexico City. It is deeper. A boat would run aground on the other one," he said dismissively.

"Maybe someone should check it just in case," she suggested.

Landa shook his head. "I cannot spare men for that."

"I know this guy. I've dealt with him before," Kelly argued.

"The other canal ends in a marsh. No road, nothing. You want to go see, fine. But we are going north."

"Drop me off," Kelly said. It would be just like Stefan

to thwart authorities by taking an unexpected escape route. And if they were right, she'd double back to the docks to look for Jake. For some reason she couldn't quell an uneasy feeling in the pit of her stomach.

The driver throttled down, easing the boat into the shallows. Landa waved impatiently for Kelly to jump off. She did, landing in a few inches of water. Without pausing, the boat gunned back into the center of the canal and roared away, churning the water white-green in its wake.

Kelly awkwardly made her way to dry ground, her feet sinking in the boggy mud. A cow in the middle of the field gazed at her. "Did a big white guy come through here?" she asked.

The cow stopped chewing for a second, then lumbered away.

"I'll take that as a yes," Kelly said. With great care, she picked her way through the mud and headed east.

Forty-Seven

Jake's attacker dragged him backward underwater. Jake lashed out, kicking, but the vise grip around his throat was relentless.

His feet brushed the canal bottom. Jake drove his weight back and down, pinning Stefan. After a second, the pressure released. He pushed up and away, kicking hard. Stefan grabbed his leg again, but this time he was prepared. He landed a hard blow, felt something crunch under his heel. Paddled as hard as he could until his head broke the surface.

Jake gulped in air, swimming frantically until his knees hit solid ground and he stood. He eyed the water as he backed toward shore, braced for another attack. His hand went to his belt for his knife, only to realize he'd lost it in the explosion. He'd have to hope Stefan wasn't armed.

A bald head emerged from the water ten feet away. Jake tensed, arms by his sides, ready to fight. Then he saw the nasty-looking knife clenched in Stefan's hand.

Stefan didn't speak. He eyed Jake, sizing him up.

"What you tried back there—it didn't work," Jake said. "Most of those people survived."

Stefan approached slowly. He was talking under his

breath, a steady murmur of what sounded like Danish again.

Jake matched his pace, stepping back as he kept an eye on the blade, waiting for him to charge. If he did, Jake didn't have many options. He was exhausted. The likelihood that he'd be able to disarm Stefan was slim. If he could find a stick, something to fend him off with, he might have a shot. If not, he'd have to seize the first opportunity to turn and bolt. The riverbanks were steep. Climbing them would consume precious moments during which his back would be exposed.

Stefan's approach reminded him of a snake, head bobbing and weaving, waiting for the perfect moment to strike. One time, when they were kids, he and Mark had tried to shoot the rattle off a rattlesnake. Jake missed the shot, hitting the center of the reptile's body instead. Trying to finish it off, Mark got too close and the animal lashed out at him. Their mother hadn't spoken to them the entire drive to the hospital.

Stefan's eyes suddenly darted right. Jake lunged in the opposite direction, but it was a trick. The knife caught him under the ribs. Jake gasped as it slid in, felt it penetrate his back on the other side. Stefan pulled him close, bloodshot eyes huge, breath hot as he murmured, "We all must sacrifice."

Kelly picked her way along the embankment, careful not to get too close to the edge. She alternated between watching the ground in front of her for ruts and dips and scanning the canal. About a mile in, she stopped. Maybe Landa was right, and she was wasting her time. They might have caught Stefan already. She should head back, try to find Jake. Hopefully he hadn't been hurt in the blast, and was already at Mark's bedside.

Kelly turned around. The canal snaked along, trees clustered tightly on the banks. She slowly limped back. The physical toll of the past few days had caught up to her. Her whole body ached, her eyes smarted from fatigue. She felt like she'd just gone twelve rounds with a prizefighter, then run a marathon. She staggered a few steps, then sat. She needed to take a minute.

Kelly watched a dragonfly flit through a patch of reeds along the shoreline. He landed on one, sending it swaying before he darted off. Her head dropped to her chest, then she caught herself. She couldn't let her body shut down, not yet. She had to get back.

Movement out the corner of her eye. Kelly clumsily got to her feet and drew her gun. Something large was drifting downriver. It looked like a pile of clothes. It took a second to realize that the figure lying prone in the water wasn't Stefan.

Kelly went into autopilot. She jammed the H&K back into her waistband, skidded down the embankment and plunged headfirst into the water. Three strokes brought her up alongside Jake. She struggled with his weight, straining to flip him over. He felt like a sodden rag doll. It took all her remaining strength to turn him. She pressed her cheek to his, looking toward his chest. He wasn't breathing. There was a jagged hole in his shirt, and blood seeped out at an alarming rate.

Kelly flung her arm around his neck and dragged him toward shore. The current pulled them downriver as she swam. She kicked as hard as she could, stroking awkwardly with her free arm.

Jake's skin was waxy, with a bluish tinge. "Just a few more feet," she said, breathing hard.

She turned back to see how far they were from shore and nearly let go. Stefan had surfaced less than a foot away and was grinning at her, water running in rivulets down his face.

Kelly reflexively reached for her gun. Before she could free it, an enormous hand clamped down on her head, driving it underwater. Kelly didn't even have time to take a gulp of air.

She struggled against him, but the arm felt like iron. She fired off a few shots, but Stefan was like a ghost, none of them seemed to make contact. Her eyes popped, lungs straining. She had the overwhelming urge to breathe in, but knew that would kill her.

She only had one choice. If she was going to survive, she had to let go of Jake. Kelly hesitated, then released her arm and felt him drift away.

Rage sparked inside her. Kelly kicked forward with all the force she could muster. Her heels made contact, and the pressure on her head abated slightly. She jerked down, an unexpected move, and the grip released entirely. Kelly broke the surface and gulped in air, gasping.

Stefan was a few feet away, face tight with pain. He growled as he splashed forward. Kelly caught sight of Jake's body drifting downstream. Stefan lunged for her again, but this time she was ready. She squeezed off three rounds in quick succession, aiming for his chest. He grunted, face caving in. At least one had hit its mark.

Stefan gurgled something, then suddenly went still, face slack as he rolled onto his back.

For a second Kelly thought it was another of his tricks. She cautiously kicked out with her leg, tapping him as she kept the barrel aimed squarely at his chest. He didn't flinch. The water surrounding him turned crimson. His body slowly sank beneath the surface.

Kelly spun. Jake was twenty feet away, the distance between them increasing as the current swept him downriver.

In a moment he'd round the bend and vanish from sight entirely.

She plowed forward with strong strokes.

Just when she feared he'd drifted too far ahead, she caught a flash of white. With renewed vigor Kelly clawed her way through the water. It felt as if the current was deliberately keeping him just out of reach.

Her fingers suddenly closed on fabric. She grabbed a clump of it, using it to haul herself up to him.

Kelly wrapped her arm around Jake's neck and towed him to shore. The banks were less steep here, and she was able to drag him out among some reeds. She bent down, pressing her ear to his chest. She couldn't detect a heartbeat. Tried to take his pulse, but her hands were shaking too badly. She did a mouth sweep with two fingers, then started CPR.

Kelly blew air into his mouth, watching his chest rise and fall. She repeated the breath, then started compressions. Water and blood poured out of his wound with each pump of her hands. After the third cycle, water gushed from his mouth. Kelly caught her breath, waiting, but he remained still.

She kept going. Kelly tried not to calculate the minutes he had been unconscious and bleeding, or that it had taken her so long to reach him. Tried not to think about the fact that if it hadn't been for her, he would never have been there. He should have been maintaining a vigil at his brother's bedside, not trying to save her from a lunatic she insisted on pursuing.

Breath, breath.

Thirty compressions.

Breath, breath.

Every time Kelly bent down and locked her lips over his, her mind flashed to other kisses. This seemed like a mockery of those. These cold blue lips couldn't possibly belong to Jake. She remembered the last time they'd really been together, in that shabby motel room.

Breath, breath.

Thirty compressions.

A breeze stirred, raising the hairs on her arms. Kelly kept going. Help was coming. By now Landa would have realized that he'd been wrong, they'd check the other canal. She didn't let herself think about how far away that help might be, how long it might take. They would get here. They had to get here.

Kelly tasted salt and realized she was crying, shoulders heaving with sobs as she pressed on his chest cavity, elbows locked out. She'd lost her brother, she'd lost her parents. She couldn't lose Jake, too. She should have married him right away, as soon as he asked. She'd always held him at arm's length, never let him get close. He rarely complained, though she saw the hurt in his eyes. But she ignored it, protecting herself. Somehow he'd managed to infiltrate, regardless.

"He's dead."

Kelly started and looked up. Stefan was bent double twenty feet away, hands clutching his right side, blood running through his fingers. He had an odd expression on his face. If Kelly didn't know better, she'd swear it was remorse. Kelly ignored him, turning back to Jake. She tried to breathe into his mouth again, but couldn't seem to draw enough air into her own lungs to give him.

She tried again, then gave up and sat back. Jake's eyes were open, gazing blindly at the sky. Kelly followed them up. Tree branches reached out over the canal, tops dancing in the wind. The sun had finally broken through the polluted haze.

"Beautiful day," Stefan commented, following her eyes.

Kelly stood and turned away from the river. The bank sloped up at a slight angle. Her legs ached from the effort of even that small climb, but the pain felt far away, as if it belonged to someone else.

"I'm shocked that you shot an unarmed man, Agent Jones." Stefan sounded bemused as she approached. "Now I'll have to subject myself to third-world medical care."

Kelly drew the gun. Stefan's eyes widened. Without breaking stride she fired into his chest. His body convulsed with each impact. She kept pulling the trigger, emptying the clip, firing even after it only produced clicks.

Stefan's mouth opened and closed a few times as Kelly stood silent, watching. He dropped to his knees, then fell to one side. His body twitched and he moaned.

It took a long time for him to die.

When it was over, Kelly returned to Jake. She sat down beside him, gently drawing his head into her lap. She stroked his hair with one hand, the other cradling his cheek. She started by apologizing for everything she'd done wrong, all the things they'd never do together, the life they wouldn't share.

It was nearly dusk when Rodriguez found her there. He wrapped a blanket around her shoulders and together they watched the last rays of sunlight slide down the tree trunks, turning the surface of the canal into spun gold.

MARCH 15

Forty-Eight

Syd glanced up at the knock on her door. Mark Riley was propped on a crutch, looking uncomfortable in a wool suit.

"I'm heading out," he said. "Sure you can hold down the fort?"

Syd shuffled the pile of papers in front of her. Since the implosion of Tyr, their business had kicked up exponentially. She'd taken on a dozen new clients, hired more employees. Staying busy had helped her deal. Now, though, things were settling down. "Flores is running point on the Somalia situation. I think we're all set."

"Great."

"Anything else?" Syd said, looking up to find him still standing there.

"Just wanted to make sure you hadn't changed your mind about coming."

Syd avoided his eyes. "I already said goodbye. Besides, we're swamped right now."

"All right, then." He paused. "Thing is, I know what it's like not to get closure. Made that mistake once myself."

"It's just a memorial service," Syd said sharply. Jake's

body had been cremated weeks earlier. It had taken some time to arrange, but they were going to bury some of his ashes in a grave beside his mother's in Texas.

"I know, but it might help."

"I'm fine," she said. "Have a safe trip."

He left, easing the door shut. Syd sank back in her chair and gazed out the window. Spring was arriving in Central Park, through the window she could see smatterings of green among the gray. Early blooms were battling the resurgence of low temperatures. She got up after a minute and went to her office door. Opening it, she stared down the hall.

The door to Jake's office was closed. She hadn't been able to bring herself to reassign it yet. By all rights it should go to Maltz, since he'd assumed a larger role in the company. Kelly had come by a few weeks earlier and removed a box of personal items. Now all that remained was standard office equipment. Still, she couldn't bring herself to change the name on the door.

Syd hesitated a moment, then walked down the hall. She entered the office and shut the door behind her. Funny, she wasn't generally a sentimental person. And it wasn't as if Jake was ever really more than a friend anyway. Still, she could swear there was a trace of his scent in the air. She crossed the room and slowly sank into the chair behind his desk.

Syd rubbed an indentation in the oak with her thumb, the spot where he always rested his heels when he kicked back in his chair. She half smiled, remembering his grin, the laughter in his voice when he teased her.

After a moment she picked up the phone. "Call the engravers," she said, voice throatier than usual. "Have them make up a name plate for Maltz."

* * *

Kelly stood beside the freshly dug grave, gazing down without seeing it. Rodriguez had just left with his wife, after squeezing her elbow and offering the standard condolences. He was back on active duty after a brief suspension—somehow McLarty had managed to smooth things over with the Mexican Consulate. Apparently the U.S. government would provide a loan to assist with future excavations on the Templo Mayor site.

Stefan had been buried in a pauper's cemetery somewhere outside Mexico City. Kelly hadn't asked where, and Rodriguez hadn't offered the information. At night when she stared up at the ceiling, unable to sleep, she could still feel that gun in her hands.

A few other mourners shuffled around, shaking hands, conversing in low voices. Kelly felt a presence at her side but didn't look up.

"Should have been me," Mark said after a moment.

"That's what I keep thinking," Kelly said. "He wouldn't have been there if it wasn't for me."

"None of you would have been there if our mission hadn't been compromised. You can't blame yourself."

Kelly looked at him. Mark had lost weight during his hospital stay. Gaunt hollows carved out his cheeks. His suit hung loosely around his shoulders. In some ways it made the resemblance to Jake stronger.

"I heard you went to work for Longhorn."

"Yup. Should have been there all along, I was just too damn stubborn." He shook his head. "My mom always used to say that if you spend your life racing the devil, eventually he'll win. But she meant me, not Jake. Every time we got into trouble, it was my idea." He nudged a chunk of loose sod with the heel of his crutch. "I still can't believe he's gone."

Kelly couldn't answer. She stood rigid, staring down at the dusty mound of soil.

"I'm scattering some of his ashes in this gully we used to hang out in when we were kids, if you want to come along," he offered after a moment. "Chris and Susie are having people over, too."

"I know, they invited me. I just… I can't."

"Okay." He nodded, then reached over and awkwardly hugged her. "Hang in there, okay?"

"You, too."

He swung around on his crutches. Kelly heard an engine start, the sound of a car pulling away. She couldn't move. She kept waiting for tears to come, but since that first day none had. She was numb inside. Kelly had barely stopped moving since the plane landed in New York. Without allowing herself to think about it, she found a new apartment and moved overnight. Packed up all of Jake's things and shipped them off to Chris. All she had left was a stack of photos and a windbreaker she'd found on the final pass through their empty apartment, tucked away in the far corner of their bedroom closet. She'd pressed it to her face, remembering when Jake wrapped it around her shoulders on a blustery day, but still—nothing.

"What are you going to do now?" someone asked.

She turned to find Maltz gazing levelly at her. "I have no idea."

"Syd would be happy to take you on."

"No, she wouldn't." Kelly managed a tight smile.

"I could get her to do it anyway," Maltz offered.

"I'm not cut out for that." The clouds overhead parted, and the rays of a weak winter sun sifted through. "I'm talking to my boss back at the FBI on Monday. Maybe they'll put me on active duty."

"Good luck with that."

"Thanks," Kelly said.

They stood in silence for a few more minutes. Then Kelly forced herself to turn and walk back to her rental car, arms wrapped tight against the cold.

* * * * *

Author's Note

In December of 2008, I stumbled across a news report on the kidnapping of Felix Batista. Batista was an American security consultant for ASI Global. Over the course of his career, he had personally negotiated the release of more than a hundred hostages. He was in Saltillo, Mexico, to offer advice on handling the uptick in abductions for ransom. While dining with local businessmen one evening, he received a series of cell-phone calls and excused himself from the table. On his way out of the restaurant to get better reception, he handed his companions his laptop and a list of phone numbers in case he didn't return. Moments later an SUV pulled to the curb and Batista was forced inside. Since then, no one has had any communication with him, and no one has claimed responsibility for his kidnapping.

The irony of the story started the plot wheels spinning in my mind. I want to emphasize that the character of Cesar Calderon is not meant to represent Felix Batista in any way, shape, or form. I sincerely hope that Mr. Batista is returned to his family unharmed.

Kidnapping for ransom has been on an upswing worldwide. All of the facts and statistics cited in this book are true to the best of my knowledge. Iraq, Mexico and Colombia currently rank as the kidnapping capitals of the world, although the former Soviet bloc nations are not far behind. According to Insurance Carrier AIG's Crisis Management Division, over 20,000 kidnap-for-ransom incidents are reported annually, with forty-eight percent of them occurring in Latin America. Approximately eighty percent of kidnap-for-ransom cases go unreported, so that means an average of 100,000 people are snatched and held every year. The number of cases has increased exponentially in the past few decades as drug cartels and terror groups seized upon kidnappings as a relatively low-risk source of additional financing. Books such as *Ransom: the Untold Story of International Kidnapping,* by Ann Hagedorn Auerbach, and *Kidnap for Ransom,* by Richard P. Wright, were extremely informative on this subject and, at the same time, terrifying.

I relied on a number of first-person accounts to construct the story of what a hostage experiences after being taken. The most helpful (and heartbreaking, and harrowing) were *Out of Captivity,* by Gary Brozek, Marc Gonsalves, Tom Howes, and Keith Stansell, and *Deliver us from Evil,* by Ernestine Sodi. Many kidnapping victims are held for months, or years. Some continue to be held even though their ransom has been paid. Many never make it home again.

I dedicate this book to them, and to people like Felix Batista who devote their lives to freeing them.

As always, I have many people to thank. This book marked a particular challenge for me, since it's the first time I set a story in a place I've never had the opportunity to visit. I relied heavily on people far more familiar with the territory, particularly Mauricio Marban, who was also kind enough to correct my egregious Spanish errors—any remaining mistakes are mine, not his. Please forgive me for taking some liberties, particularly with the geography of Xochimilco.

On the recommendation of Patrick Millikin I delved into the work of Paco Ignacio Taibo II, Mexico's reigning noir king, to get a feel for day-to-day life in Mexico City. David Lida's book *First Stop in the New World* was also a great resource, as was Luis Urrea's, *By the Lake of Sleeping Children*.

Doug P. Lyle, M.D., answered medical questions including survival rates for gunshot wounds, states of unconsciousness and proper use of defibrillators, all for the bargain price of free future drinks. I doubt he'll ever be able to produce a bar tab adequate to the debt I owe him, however.

Steve Kurzman's blog mynewleg.net provided extremely helpful details about the trials and tribulations of adapting to a new below-knee prosthesis. Steve was also kind enough to answer questions about what Kelly's capabilities would be, thanks to her new condition.

Joe Collins, pyrotechnician, illuminated me (no pun intended) as to the best way to blow up a dock, and to the explosive potential and properties of Primacord.

And as always, thank God for Google Maps and the internet, I'd be lost without them. Literally.

My beta readers went above and beyond the call of duty this time. I'm particularly grateful to Kirk Rudell, who has a gift for pinpointing exactly where the plot went off the rails, and better yet provides helpful recommendations for getting it back on track. Jason Starr is always kind enough to listen to my rants and to help me brainstorm, plus he's a surefire title generator. My fellow bloggers on The Kill Zone: Clare Langley-Hawthorne, Kathryn Lilley, Joe Moore, John Ramsey Miller, John Gilstrap and James

Scott Bell are invaluable sounding boards, as well as a damn fine group of people to virtually hang out with every week. My Sanchez Grotto–mates Raj Patel (aka The Maitreya), Kemble Scott/Scott James, Diane Weipert, Joshua Citrak, Shana Mahaffey, Alison Bing, Ammi Emergency, and Paul Linde are always kind enough to come to my events, even the nuttier ones (although let's be honest, those tend to be the most fun) and to provide feedback, constructive criticism, and very welcome interruptions. Some of my Facebook and Twitter friends provided character names: a special thanks to Clifford Fryman, Penny Ash, Elizabeth Sneed White, Nick Daniels and Sean.

Thanks to David Fribush, Ty Jagerson, Dave Kane, and Michael Maltz for continuing to lend their names to the commando boys.

The folks at MIRA including Lara Hyde, Valerie Gray and Miranda Indrigo are a pleasure to work with.

My sister Kate has, as always, shepherded this book through from the first draft to the last, in exchange for occasional dinners and borrowed clothing. My parents correctly claim that when it comes down to it, every book should be dedicated to them (but they have graciously conceded that I may give other people a chance from time to time).

Last but never least my husband and daughter, for endless supplies of love and support.